THE SUNSHINE BOY

K. L. MINIER

Note for Librarians: a cataloguing record for this book that includes Dewey Decimal Classification and US Library of Congress numbers is available from the Library and Archives of Canada. The complete cataloguing record can be obtained from their online database at: www.collectionscanada.ca/amicus/index-e.html
ISBN 1-4120-6550-x
Printed in Victoria, BC, Canada

All events and characters depicted in this book are fictional.

Printed on paper with minimum 30% recycled fibre.

Trafford's print shop runs on "green energy" from solar, wind and other environmentally-friendly power sources.

TRAFFORD

Offices in Canada, USA, Ireland and UK

This book was published *on-demand* in cooperation with Trafford Publishing. On-demand publishing is a unique process and service of making a book available for retail sale to the public taking advantage of on-demand manufacturing and Internet marketing. On-demand publishing includes promotions, retail sales, manufacturing, order fulfilment, accounting and collecting royalties on behalf of the author.

Book sales for North America and international:
Trafford Publishing, 6E–2333 Government St.,
Victoria, BC v8t 4p4 CANADA
phone 250 383 6864 (toll-free 1 888 232 4444)
fax 250 383 6804; email to orders@trafford.com
Book sales in Europe:
Trafford Publishing (uk) Ltd., Enterprise House, Wistaston Road Business Centre,
Wistaston Road, Crewe, Cheshire cw2 7rp UNITED KINGDOM
phone 01270 251 396 (local rate 0845 230 9601)
facsimile 01270 254 983; orders.uk@trafford.com
Order online at:
trafford.com/05-1461

10 9 8 7 6 5 4 3 2 1

With love and thanks to
Jake, who always listens

PROLOGUE

HE WROTE A PERSONAL check for one hundred and twenty-nine thousand, eight hundred and seventy-nine dollars and forty-two cents using his own fountain pen and the sales rep's clipboard. Since he was trading in his Cadillac, he methodically went through it, removing his things. Once in the leather wraparound seat of the new car, he dropped the CD into the disc player and pushed the start button before adjusting mirrors, seat belt, or even seat position. He had to; the transaction had taken over two hours and he was sweating profusely in the effort not to black out.

He wasn't feeling faint – oh no; it wasn't that simple. If the gray fog turned to black he literally winked out of his own reality. It had happened to him eight times in the last year – each of the eight times, in fact, that he had attempted suicide had ended in complete failure because of it. And to make things worse, he never had any memory of where he had been or what he had done, when he came back. That blankness was horrifying.

He was failing on all levels now, and he had to find a way to make it stop. Until then, for some reason, Vivaldi seemed to anchor him a little, so these days he never left home without it. The CD sounded good filtered through the ten-speaker sound system. But even after finally escaping the showroom and reaching the interchange from Interstate 35 South, the weird gray fog of warning still eddied through his mind. He was forced to pull into the weedy parking lot of a bankrupt strip mall. There, he grimly smoked one Marlboro after another while he waited for his new toy to stop representing death. It did, but he couldn't think about it like that. He didn't want to die the death the brand new Porsche 911 Carrera offered. And, if he anticipated any kind of death at all, the car wouldn't even be able to offer that. No, the whopping impulse buy was nothing more than a rare gift to himself, and he had to be determined to enjoy it.

It was, after all, just a car.

Eventually, he was reconciled enough to take the road again without the risk of killing anybody else. He had stopped breathing in erratic chunks. Hawkish anticipation had settled back down into the nauseating ooze in his belly, ooze that was annoying, but familiar. He swallowed mouthfuls of antacid to compensate for the nausea, and mopped the sweat from his face. Then he dumped the ashtray and the empty bottle into a roadside bin with hands that barely trembled. He rolled up his window and restarted the engine. Before setting off, he tapped the repeat button on the CD player and balanced the levels and volume until his head was filled with Perlman's consummate interpretation of "Spring". He turned west, onto Interstate 90.

Southwestern South Dakota was wide open and moon-sterile—ideal for his elemental lust for anything that hustled him to the howling edge. He cruised at 135 mph, racing the stereo's violins. Spending large amounts of money on a whim was something he *never* did, not even these days when he finally had it to spend. But he smiled at the power surging from the new engine to his gratified soul.

This was fun.

Was he becoming impulsive as well as unhinged? Or was one merely a symptom of the other? They were interesting questions in an intellectual way, but at this precise moment he didn't give a damn about answers he didn't have. It was enough to be free of the deterioration that had razored him so closely in that deserted parking lot. Who cared if he was shredding like cheap wrapping paper?

For that matter, who cared if he had turned into a complete and utter failure? What did it matter, really, that he had been forced to abandon the only meaningful thing in his life – his job – or that he was only alive because of the ruthless blackness he couldn't avoid? In fact, right now who the hell cared that he had failed even to understand what had dropped him over the edge of insanity? Everywhere he looked inside was failure, but it didn't take sanity or success to drive like this. It took skill, practice, and talent. He still had those things, and it felt damned good to use them again.

The faultless car sped for hours under the July-scorched sky.

CHAPTER

1

JARED MCCORMICK HATED GIVING up the freedom of the Interstate, but the Porsche obediently hugged the narrow highway he put before it. Bothered by their chronic fatigue, he took off his dark glasses to massage his eyes. Quaint local advertising sprouted out of cattail ditches, giving him something to squint at besides faded yellow lines. He turned down the music and checked his watch. It was exactly 2:20 p.m. when he rolled the Porsche into Shady Rock, South Dakota, pop. 4,678.

He lowered the windows. The pervasive dustiness of the summer air instantly rushed him backward in time, sparking memories of barefoot-scorching, acrid asphalt, and the weekend perfume of newly cut grass. Ah, yes, Home Sweet Home.

The clawed things inhabiting the sludge in his gut snarled at the stupid sentiment. Who was he trying to kid? Home had never been sweet. And being here after all these years meant something much too significant to call a whim.

His end was a foregone conclusion, but how to achieve it with meaning—even if that meaning only meant something to him—was something else again. Since all else had failed, he had finally come up with a death plan he could live with, so to speak. His goal was to go out remembered with respect by the town that had spawned and hated him. A selfish goal maybe, but in the light of his ultimate acceptance—that he had become a mad dog and had to be put down—what did he have left but selfishness?

Too bad straightforward suicide hadn't worked. Over the last year he had attempted several quick and simple methods, but had at last concluded that for him there could be no such thing. As much as he wanted to – no matter how hard he tried – he physically could not take his own life. Obviously. Here he was, still coddling his weaknesses and ducking the net he knew should have been thrown over him long ago. He was dangerous now, barely maintaining. He was desperately tired of maintaining—ergo, he had to die. If he couldn't die with the respect he wanted in this, his hometown, he would just have to go out a coward in his deadly new car.

Which was unthinkable, of course. He had been many things in his life, but never a coward.

A much more tolerable plan hinged on his hope that there would be something going on in Shady Rock, something dirty enough to let him shine, yet not compromise the uneasy truce between his gastric demons and his multiplying phobias. An event he could manipulate to a satisfactory ending for all concerned—in other words, his death on a happily resolved or resolvable footing. Small-time, small-town crime with an opportunity toward a fatal accident: that's what he was looking for. Well, Shady Rock was indubitably small, and in it – hopefully – he could die with dignity.

He liked the efficiency of the plan, too; nothing like killing two birds: himself and his misbegotten and never forgotten teenage reputation, with one stone.

On Main Street, he eased the lethal black Porsche past old women in print dresses and sensible shoes. He geared down to turn left at the junction of Main and Sadler, looking for the police station. It was still there, a one-story tan brick building facing Sadler, just down from an optometrist office on the corner. As soon as his skin stopped crawling at the sight of it, he would check in. It was the civil thing to do. Just because he was psychologically challenged didn't mean that he couldn't still be polite. Besides, he didn't have much time; he needed a cop to point out the nearest crime.

He parallel parked at the empty curb out front, flagrantly disregarding the diagonal white lines painted on the street. After rolling up the windows, he got out and locked the car doors. Scratching his jaw, he habitually glanced up and down the sun-beaten sidewalk. He checked out rooftops, doorways, and a beat-up, elderly Chevy slowing for the corner, puffing oil. He turned his back on it all and angrily mounted the two wide steps. What the hell had he sunk to?

The air wasn't any cooler inside the police station, but the contrasting dimness of the small lobby furnished an illusion. He paused, slipping and sliding on patches of growing fury. Fifteen years ago he had been dragged past that very same plastic-covered courtesy table, in handcuffs. He distinctly remembered sending one of the patrolmen crashing into it. Funny, though, he had grown up with the kid, but now he couldn't recall his name. He stood for a moment studying the table, actually feeling old Neugebauer shoving and punching him into a cell in back.

Shady Rock had always labeled him as a pain-in-the-ass troublemaker, but before he was through with it this time it would, by God, remember him for something better than that.

The lobby was unmanned, but a chime over the door had sounded at his entrance. He stalked under the high ceiling fan to the table. After pouring a cup of coffee from the steaming pot, he added sugar in an attempt to mollify the vigilant devils in his gut. He was leaning against the wall next to the table—at least the picture of relaxed nonchalance—when he heard footsteps.

A very young uniformed officer poked his head around a doorway. The kid did a double take, gawked, then scuttled into the lobby to stand behind the control desk.

"Uh, can I help you?" The question was polite, the tone, not so much.

Jared smiled inwardly, suddenly as contemptuous as he was furious. Apparently, to this rural, righteous mid-western boy, ass length hair was grounds for rudeness. Pricey charcoal pleated pants and unstructured silk jackets were too, despite their tailored fit. Black Italian loafers with tassels seemed to bother the farm boy the most, as his stare lingered there the longest. No, the kid actually scowled when Jared tossed the mane back, exposing his single silver earring.

The Ray-Bans were in the car, but even without them, to the hick kid he probably resembled an upscale drug baron from Miami, or perhaps a wealthy, spoiled promoter of some sort—certainly nothing normally seen around here. Nor welcome. Suddenly hoping that Neugebauer was retired—or better yet fucking dead—Jared pushed away from the wall.

He'd kill the fat bastard if he came around that corner next. Which would be too bad, because the farm boy wouldn't have either the balls or the speed to put him down afterwards, and the rude little son of a bitch would be dead, too.

No, no—he had to maintain his cool.

"I'd like to see your chief, please," Jared said nicely. "Is he or she in?"

"What's it in regard to?"

Jared maintained for a minute, then moved a shoulder. "If he wants you to know, sport, he'll tell you. Is he available or not?"

The kid picked up a phone. Punching a button, he turned away before saying a few inaudible words. His jaw sagged when he saw the black Porsche illegally dozing broadside at the curb. In a community this small and behind the times, the imported car was probably as extraordinary as tattoos on a nun. Or else it was about to get a ticket.

With another fast sidelong glance at the car's equally outlandish driver, the kid spoke a few more terse words, then hung up. "Chief Griffin will be right with you," he said, his eyes hungrily fastened to the Porsche.

Jared turned back to the table and grimly added another packet of sugar to the bitter, over-cooked coffee. He didn't recall a Griffin, but at least he wouldn't go ballistic on goddamned Neugebauer, ruining everything in the first five minutes.

He looked out the window, too. Across the street, at a corner gas station/convenience store, a harassed-looking woman in shorts was pumping gas. The green and white canopy shaded her while she yelled at some kids through the rear window of her late model station wagon. The battered Chevy had pulled up to the curb at the side of the building. Two men in white tee shirts and blue jeans were arguing beside it, gesturing with cans of Coke. A scruffy brown and white dog loped by on the sidewalk below the window, its tongue lolling. Traffic was based on the predominant local ranch economy; Jared had counted four passing pick-up trucks for diversion before he heard another set of footsteps coming down the hall. He turned when they stopped.

Shady Rock's current chief of police appeared to be on the verge of folding into a nondescript, mid-fortyish heap. Lined and haggard, he was four inches taller than Jared's five-ten, and rangily built. Fatigued defeat emanated from every ropy muscle. Even his thinning hair was a tired color of dusty brown, going neutral.

His examination of Jared, however, was direct and swift, head to toe, with no change in his professional blandness. "Yes? I'm Howard Griffin. What can I help you with?"

Jared reached into his jacket. The punk at the desk reacted audibly. At the smothered yelp, Jared made himself freeze.

Griffin froze too. He frowned, first at Jared, then over at his man. His broad shoulders slumped. "Jeez, Randy!" he said with some amazed anger. "What's the matter with you? I'm sorry, sir," he apologized gruffly to Jared. "I'm just breaking him in. He's nervous; takes himself a little too seriously."

While keeping an eye on the twitchy kid, Jared finished bringing out a business card.

Griffin crossed the six steps between them to take it. His eyebrows shot up. "Huh," he grunted, trying too late for non-committal. "Interesting. What can I do for you, Mr. McCormick?"

"I'm in the area—thought I'd pay my respects."

"I see. Any special reason that you're in the area?"

It was a reasonable question, but combined with the older man's startled reaction to his card, it raised a few hairs on the back of Jared's neck. There was more here than met the eye. Or else paranoia was creeping into him, as well as impetuosity.

"No special reason," Jared lied coolly. "Just some personal business. But I've found it saves aggravation to stand up and be counted by those who might care when I'm around. To avoid unfortunate misunderstandings," he added, punching the sarcasm.

The young patrolman behind the desk stopped eaves-dropping and became red-faced, and very busy.

"I see," Griffin said. "Well, if you have a minute, bring your coffee and come on back. I'm waiting on a phone call."

"Keep an eye on the car?" Jared asked with some irony of the kid, who was again doing just that.

Griffin led the way to an office stuffed with a desk, three chairs, file cabinets, and shelving. Messy stacks of files leaned everywhere. Folds of printouts cascaded onto the tile floor. Oily-skinned coffee in abandoned cups dotted the room. The over-all effect was one of sheer pandemonium, but at least it looked more functional than the last time Jared had been in here. The rack of longhorns with the sweat-stained Stetson impaled on one horn was no longer crookedly nailed to the wall above the desk, and the over-sized feed-and-tit calendar had been replaced by a large utilitarian bulletin board. The computer taking up half of the desk was also new to Jared, as were three framed documents proudly forming a less than overwhelming trophy wall.

"Have I caught you at a bad time, sir?" Jared asked as he picked up a pile of manila folders from one of the chairs and set it on the floor. He placed the chair squarely in front of the desk before sitting. "Or did the maid quit?"

Oblivious, Griffin sat forward, his elbows on the blotter, his chin on his hands as he studied Jared's cream-colored business card. It contained four embossed words: International Security Company, Inc., a phone number, and Jared's name in tiny script letters in a bottom corner—Griffin read it like it was pages long. He finally poked it a little away from him, after clearing a space among reams of paper, boxes of stickpins, and a stapler.

"I've heard of ISC, of course," he announced, finally looking up. "It's been making some headlines—out of Chicago and London, right? You work for it?"

"Harder than anybody. I own it."

Griffin's eyebrows misbehaved again. This time, he didn't seem to mind that Jared saw his reaction. "Really? From what I've heard, the CEO is a retired government agent."

Since establishing of his credentials was a significant part of the plan, Jared leaned forward and pulled his Glock from the Sport Combat holster at the small of his back. He released the magazine and placed the unloaded weapon on top of his business card. "That's correct information, Chief," he said with his own version of blandness. "It's a catchy selling point, don't you think? I retired from the Bureau a few years back, but once upon a time I worked deep undercover for those boys. They're nice enough to let me carry that for my own protection." He held up his wallet, exposing a colorful government seal behind a plastic window.

Griffin studied it, then him—his face, his hair, his thousand-dollar jacket. "You worked undercover?" he asked, dubious.

"I scuff up as well as I clean up," Jared murmured modestly.

"But you're a little young to be retired, aren't you?"

"Implying what?" Jared asked, eyeing the ceiling instead of leaping the desk in furious reply to the impertinent question. "I retired to open shop, but I left behind a sterling record, or I wouldn't have been issued that particular permit."

Griffin nodded, waving an apologetic hand. "I don't doubt you did. You say you're here on personal business? What might that be?"

But before Jared had time to trot out his pre-scripted reply, the phone on the desk rang. At the same time, the fax machine in the corner chimed and began to drone. Griffin snatched up the receiver. He swiveled his chair and hunched over the fax. He muttered for several minutes, giving Jared time to retrieve and reload the automatic as well as finish the too-sweet, terrible coffee.

Griffin hung up at last and turned back, looking even more defeated. "Listen," he said sternly. "I don't have time to fence with you. I don't know why it would be, but is International Security interested in these murders too? I mean, I don't care; I just wish whoever called you in would have informed me."

"Murders?" Jared repeated, vigorously keeping his face still.

"I appreciate the tremendous help we're getting, I really do, but I'm losing track of the participants. So just tell me if you're working, okay?"

Jared shook his head. "No, sir; I don't know what you're talking about."

"You don't?"

"No, sir."

"Weren't you once married to Leslie Ann Doherty? Aren't you that Jared McCormick?"

Jared started to speak, then didn't. He couldn't; he was too appalled to form thoughts, much less words. He had completely forgotten that he had an ex-wife from here.

Griffin sighed in his blank silence. "Any time now, Retired Agent McCormick," he said wearily. "I recognized your name."

"Yes, I saw that," Jared replied. Still stuck in the incredibly huge glitch in his processes, he wondered how did you forget something like a wife? "The question is, in what context?"

"How about this context," Griffin said. "Miss Doherty was murdered a month ago."

"She was?" Jared frowned. "That's too bad."

"Yes, it is," Griffin agreed dryly. "I'm sure you remember Bud Doherty? He brought up your name when it happened. I had no reason to consider you a suspect, though, and I told him that. So, tell me why you're here?"

Still appalled at the frightening glitch, Jared said, "I'm on vacation."

That was the story he had come up with, and he would stick to it.

"Sure you are," Griffin said sourly. "Listen, your history with Bud is legendary in Shady Rock. Is he your personal business?"

Jared found himself out of the chair and at the bulletin board where a map of the state was pinned. Dragging his hair into a thick, loose ponytail, he stretched widely with it in his hand until his spine cracked. He darkly contemplated the blunder he had made by taking Shady Rock's placidity for granted. But how could he have known Leslie had gotten herself murdered when he hadn't thought about her at all?

"That son of a bitch tried to implicate me in Les's death?" he gritted at last. "Why am I not surprised?"

"Bud's well thought of around here," Griffin warned. "Even more so than when you were growing up."

"Of course he is," Jared sneered at the map. "Keeping his ass kissed was a community project. Why would I expect it to be any different now?"

"As I recall, McCormick," Griffin said grimly, "and I do vaguely remember you, you had a pretty big chip on your shoulder as a kid. It doesn't seem to have gotten any smaller."

Jared swung around. "Well, see, it's like my dick, Chief," he returned. "It gets bigger with stimulation."

"Are you going to see Bud?"

"Depends on how stimulated I get."

Griffin stood up. The gray pallor behind his tan had taken on a tinge of red. "Look, Retired Agent McCormick," he gritted, "I already have a multiple murderer laughing behind my back and a string of burglaries hanging around my neck. I don't need an FBI graduate waltzing in here and pitching a fit in my face. I only asked a question!"

Jared registered raw information and its use thereof at top speed. Burglaries? And bodies—for Christ's sake, more than one? "Forget the title, please," he said coldly. "I have. And I assure you; I'm not here to see Bud."

"Uh-huh. I want you to know," Griffin sighed as he sank back into his chair, "that if I had my way I'd tell you to get on your horse and ride. I don't have to cooperate with private agencies. But my wife would kill me if I did."

"Your wife?"

"Yeah," Griffin said, rubbing his eyes. "I married your sister."

Jared couldn't help a curt laugh of incredulity. Maggie was married to the top authority figure in Shady Rock? Well, well, it seemed he hadn't been the only one looking for a daddy all those years ago. "No wonder you recognized my name," he warily conceded. "So how is she?"

"I don't remember getting your last fourteen Christmas cards. Do you really care?"

Jared flinched, ungraciously giving the asshole the point. "Keep in mind, sir, that I left Shady Rock with Bud's underage daughter. I lost a lot of sleep waiting for him to drop an ax on me, and when it finally happened, there didn't seem much point in trying to pick up old ties. In fact," he lied more expansively, "at the time I believed it was better for Maggie that I stay away. How did I know what Bud would do to her, to get to me?"

Griffin didn't look remotely satisfied, but he obviously

knew the stories. He grudgingly volunteered, "Maggie and I have been married almost fourteen years. Five kids."

"Good God."

Griffin's choice of profession certainly made sense, Jared caustically thought. Since profiling was second nature, he stared at Griffin, reaching for the man's soul. With a paternal streak that wide, Superstud would see the town as one big happy family. No wonder he appeared to be on the verge of collapse; the idiot would be taking murder personally, as if he had failed his townspeople children somehow.

And, Jared also saw in a flash, on top of that personality flaw Griffin would also be harboring a natural resentment toward higher authority. Multiple murders (had he heard that right?) meant that a long chain of command would inevitably be in place by now, effectively forcing Griffin to step aside and watch a bigger stick take over his turf. That bastard Neugebauer would have handed over the town on a platter and gone fishing; Griffin was giving himself no choice but to tough out the firestorm from the bottom of the heap.

And now along comes the town's former whipping boy—a murder victim's ex-husband, a professional predator, and a lousy brother-in-law, all rolled into one. No wonder the man was a little sensitive at the moment.

"I dropped in out of the blue," Jared reiterated calmly into the silence Griffin was leaving him. "If you think it's okay for me to see Maggie, I will. Otherwise…"

He let the sentence trail off, counting heavily on Griffin to pick it up. Burglaries sounded promising—they could go sour fast, if the right pressure could be applied at the right time.

Griffin laughed harshly. "If she found out you've been here without seeing her, she'd kill me! Where you staying?"

"I saw a Best Western over by the Interstate."

"No," Griffin disagreed. "We still have your mother's motel; you can bunk in one of the cabins if you don't mind roughing it a little. Never did get around to putting in a pool."

His crow's feet deepened a little. "In fact, you'll be lucky to have a TV that works."

"I wouldn't want to impose," Jared said politely.

"Too late, huh?" Griffin shook his head, blurting, "Man, Maggie is going to flip right out when she sees you!" Then he collected himself. "But do us both a favor and don't go there until I've had time to let her know, okay? She hates surprises. She's not home yet anyway; she helps out with the school's summer program. And, look," he added reluctantly, "if you are interested, Bud's in the new nursing home out on County 3, north of town. It's part of the hospital. He's been there about a month now, recovering from diabetes-related surgery. But take it easy on him, will you? He's an old, sick man."

Jared stood up, shaking the wrinkles out of his pants and letting in some relief. How fortuitous that his sister was a direct link to his main requirement—a cop with troubles. "Don't traumatize Maggie, and don't shit on Bud's bed," he itemized, hiding his hostility at being dictated to by this small town masochist. "You got it, Chief." Then he smiled with a dash of disdain. "You're lucky—I only turn berserker on alternate Tuesdays."

CHAPTER

2

In the stifling lobby, the kid named Randy tried to recapture his rookie cool as Jared walked by. It only made him look younger and dumber.

"There were a few lookers, sir," he told Jared with an air of importance, indicating the car on the street, "but nobody touched it."

"No, you misunderstood," Jared tossed over his shoulder as he went through the front door. "You were supposed to protect the folks from it."

As the door swung closed behind him, he heard gunshots. His automatic was in his hand before he knew where the sound had come from; he stupidly focused on echoes. What finally kicked his mind into catching up with his hand was sight of the beat-up Chevy, still parked across the street at the gas station. Two Coke cans lay crumpled on the concrete beside the back tire, and an empty whiskey bottle stood close by. Jared's eyes naturally went from them to the building. The convenience store faced Main, but he could dimly see figures moving through the advertising-plastered glass of the smaller side window.

Randy ran out of the police station behind him, asking what was wrong.

Jared reached out with his left hand and pulled the dipshit against the Porsche. "Go run that plate," he ordered, indicating the Chevy with a jerk of his chin. "Have an ambulance on stand-by a block away, no sirens, and get Griffin out here."

He spun the kid around and pushed him toward the steps. The patrolman stumbled, but Jared ignored him. He braced the automatic on top of the Porsche, both hands around the butt. His eyes quartered the area, dividing, scanning, interpreting...how was this for fucking luck? All he had to do was leave the cover of the low black car and trot into the street throwing a few slugs. Then he would be dead, with Griffin and his boy as witnesses to his misguided heroics. It was that simple.

Or was it?

Could he be irresponsible, as well as impulsive and forgetful? No, he couldn't. A man was ignorantly feeding a Taurus at the pumps under the wide canopy, and Jared had no way of guessing how many people might be inside, with the gunmen. Goddamned complications everywhere.

Jared whistled, catching the customer's attention. He motioned him down, and the man uncomprehendingly obeyed. Jared saw his puzzled expression turn to fear at the sight of the automatic pointed in what must have looked like his general direction.

Griffin banged into Jared's shoulder, his .38 in his fist.

"Running the plates?" Jared asked conversationally, his eyes glued to the windows across the street.

"Randy's on it," Griffin growled, his glance darting over the street. "What the heck is going on? Wasn't it a backfire?"

"Nobody's firing back," Jared turned it around with a quick, meaningless smile. "I've heard only one weapon so far. Who's supposed to be in there?"

"You mean somebody's robbing the gas station?" Griffin scowled at it in disbelief. "Just Tom, the owner, as far as I know. His mechanic knocks off at noon. I wonder if I can get around back? I—" He tensed as the front door of the gas station opened.

No one came out. The door reflected the sun for a few seconds, then closed again, seemingly of its own accord.

"How's this for utterly moronic?" Jared snorted. "Fifty feet from the police station? We're looking at two white males with one brain cell between them, white over blue. I saw them when I pulled into town. Looks like they sat over there diving into that bottle for some balls. I'll bet mine that they're on the run and out of gas – ah, yes; hello, here we go," he purred gently to a hesitant figure, indistinct in the doorway. "Come on, come on."

The customer on the ground had reached up and turned off the pump, and was now peering around the tire toward the front of the store. He looked across at Jared and Griffin, nodding wildly. A man in a dirty white tee shirt stepped out into the sunshine, pistol in hand. Jared felt Griffin go rigid.

"You want them down or dead?" Jared asked, being only semi-facetious. The second idiot poked his head out and said something to the first, who looked around at the customer on the ground behind the silver car. "I'm taking requests," Jared prodded, "because this waltz is going to go to cut time in about two measures."

"Don't kill them!" Griffin snapped, sounding scandalized. "Don't shoot at all unless—shit!"

The outside idiot waved his pistol toward the Taurus. Jared watched that weapon with one eye and the still-empty door with the other while he laid the Glock on the top of the Porsche. He plucked the .38 from Griffin's hands. The second white tee shirt appeared behind the glass as the door swung wide. A shotgun barrel nosed out as Jared leaned on the Porsche and squeezed the trigger twice in rapid succession. The glass door exploded, but before the tinkles stopped, he had twitched the .38 to the left and squeezed twice more. The outside idiot's tee shirt blossomed red. The pistol flew into the air as the man dropped to the pavement between the pumps.

The third slug had missed, Jared was pretty sure, but the

fourth had taken out a collarbone, nicely doing the trick. He peered over the Porsche, watching the man flop as he scrubbed Griffin's .38 thoroughly with the bottom part of his jacket. Then, he held out the weapon butt first, still wrapped in cloth.

"Merry Christmas," he said without expression.

Griffin stopped gaping and howled something in outrage as he bolted around the front of the Porsche.

Thinking uncharitable thoughts about his lack of gratitude, Jared slipped his automatic back in its holster. Then, out of the corner of his eye he saw a cherry red pick-up truck burst from the alley and swerve onto Sadler. Without taking the time to think oh shit, he vaulted onto the hood of the Porsche and, with enormous effort, threw himself as far into the street as he could.

He hit running, then launched into Griffin, grabbing him with both arms and slamming him forward. Jared turned out of the tackle, yanking them away from the speeding front bumper. Tires squealed as he and Griffin landed sloppily in the far gutter. Jared heard the truck meet something solid, then he opened his eyes to look into Griffin's face, only inches above his. The larger man sprawled full length on top, crushing him into the sticks and gravel that lined the street.

Griffin was utterly immobile, his eyes blank as he stared down at Jared.

"And Happy New Year." Jared frowned. "But if I scratched my new car, goddammit, I'm going to shoot you, too."

He unlocked his hands from the small of Griffin's back and poked him hard in the ribs. It worked; Griffin blinked, finally focusing. With a gasp, he rolled off and staggered to his feet.

Jared stood too, slapping dust and debris from his pants as he surveyed the scene. He paused with a sinking feeling; there was something very wrong with this picture. A body propped the shattered door open, a groaning body lay in the middle of the pumps under the canopy, and a body slumped in the front seat of the pick-up truck, which had stopped head-on against the light pole on the corner. But there wasn't a body in the middle of the street – his.

People were beginning to emerge and gather. With a last wild look at Jared, Griffin turned and ran.

Jared sadly shook dried leaves out of his hair. What the hell was the matter with him? It would have been so easy. For Christ's sake, he could have pushed instead of danced, in front of that damned truck. That's all he would have had to do. Griffin would have been safe, and everybody would have stood around saying what a brave thing he had attempted. Goddammit, an ideal scenario—made to fucking order—but he had screwed it up.

Out of long habit, he walked toward the crunched truck. A man and a woman stood by the sprung passenger door, their faces green. He suddenly realized what he was doing. One more step, and he would be knee-deep in blood.

"He dead?" he asked, abruptly backing off.

They jerked their heads in a sickened negative. The ambulance nosed around the corner and Jared impatiently waved it over. Griffin trotted past to give the contents of the truck the look he hadn't. Couldn't. Thoroughly disappointed at being so useless, so deranged, and so alive, Jared returned to the police station.

Randy leaped up from behind the desk, mike in one hand, telephone in the other. He stared at Jared as if he was a seasoned star traveler from Gamma Hydra 6.

Jared poured and sweetened the last of the muck that came out of the pot, then stood watching the rapidly crowding scene through the windows. "The man inside?" he said indifferently. "Tom?"

"In the cooler!" Randy gulped. "Sir! Um, Chief says not dead—just knocked out."

Jared squinted at the sun glare from the magnificent black Porsche. "Wants or warrants?" he prodded.

"They're escaped prisoners, sir," Randy managed in a more grown-up tone. "From Texas. They're brothers, considered armed and dangerous. One's supposed to be serving time for armed robbery, and the other, murder." Jared heard him swallow hard again. "I saw what you did, sir. Getting the chief out of the way like that…I never saw anybody move so fast!"

If he could go by the quaver of adoration in the kid's voice, his goal was off to a good start. But it could have been all over. "Driver of the truck? Blond teenager."

"Tad Kelly, sir. He lost his license a few weeks ago for drunk driving. He's still alive—um, so far, anyway. They'll ambulance him to Rapid City."

The radio crackled and Jared heard Griffin's voice. "Randy, is McCormick there with you?"

"Yes, sir!" Randy squeaked excitedly. "He's right here!"

"Tell him to meet me at the hospital. We're transporting the prisoners for treatment. Let the sheriff know we have them, and don't want 'em."

Jared didn't want to meet anybody at a hospital. He wanted a ten-course meal and about a month's worth of sleep. Since those things weren't possible, he wanted to be dead. He set his cup on the table and went back outside.

Barricades were going up around the filling station and crime scene tape flapped in the hot breeze. He walked around the Porsche and got into the driver's seat. Smoking a cigarette, he glumly pondered his abysmal behavior as he drove; he hadn't even tried.

He got hung up behind a little old lady in an antique Buick. All he could see were the flowers on her hat, nodding over the potholes. She lumbered around a corner a block further down. When Jared got to the arterial highway, he encouraged the Porsche to seventy for the quarter-mile trip. He hated dawdlers. At the hospital parking lot, he was forced to dawdle through another cigarette, waiting.

A city car pulled up, and Griffin jumped out of the passenger door. "I don't care what it takes, Gus!" he strenuously addressed his driver. "On top of all this other crap, we need to know where that stolen truck went! It probably hauled off half of the Coast to Coast." He turned his black scowl on Jared. "Give us a hand," he ordered as he opened the rear door. He extracted a leg-and-wrist manacled Texan with wads of gauze taped to his bloody, shirtless side.

Jared quickly looked down to step on his cigarette butt. The fat patrolman opened the other car door, and Jared turned away from that gory sight, too. "What, you want me to carry him?" he demanded peevishly across the trunk of the car.

"Wait for a wheelchair!" Griffin threw over his shoulder as he hustled his prisoner toward the door.

"Do I look like goddamned Florence Nightingale?" Griffin didn't answer, so Jared set off after him. "Be sure you wear gloves, Gus," Jared primly advised the fat patrolman as he passed the open car door. "That's messy."

Inside the small emergency bay, Griffin hovered beside a gurney containing his prisoner. "What are you doing?" he frowned when he saw Jared. "Help with the other man."

"I'm on vacation," Jared said disagreeably, "not your mop-up detail."

"All right, but we need to talk, so don't go anywhere!"

Where was he going to go? The problem with needing a cop was in the word need. With the fizzing contrariness still firmly in charge, Jared looked for someone less necessary to vent his irritation upon. Two efficient nurses trotted around the large, open room. They didn't cause any particular thrill, but the little guy who came in next gave Jared back his hostile sense of humor.

The little squirt begged to be bothered, with his neat sandy hair, his sensitive hands, and his melting, winsome brown eyes. The precious-looking princess was so engrossed in what Griffin was telling him, it wasn't any trick to get in his way.

Jared timed his move, and was rewarded with an astonished gape as they collided.

"Excuse me," Jared drawled. Leaning against a cabinet with folded arms, he put a challenging smile on his target.

The pretty little beggar melted before him with a stinging blush.

"What are you doing, McCormick?" Griffin demanded from across the room. "Are you watching the other prisoner?"

"Does a doctor have a stethoscope?" Jared laughingly taunted the staring cutie. "A real doctor, I mean. Not somebody who got into the wrong closet."

Before Griffin could say anything, the cutie in the white lab coat gamely stuck out his hand. "I'm Rick Lightner," he said with an excruciatingly shy smile. "The coat fits, so it must have been my closet after all, huh?"

"This is my brother-in-law, Doc," Griffin said stiffly. "Jared McCormick. He, uh, helped me apprehend the suspects."

"Your brother-in-law?" Lightner repeated, even more wide-eyed.

Griffin added, "He's a former FBI agent."

"Then his help must have been invaluable," Lightner said warmly. "How do you do, Mr. McCormick?"

"Depends on what needs doing," Jared purred at him, "and how you like it done."

Lightner's blush intensified, but his attention was too quickly distracted to suit Jared's billowing exasperation. As he shook Jared's hand, Lightner nodded to one of the nurses. She began setting up a tray of instruments near the other prisoner.

Lightner let go of Jared's hand, saying, "I guess it does. Will you excuse me? I need to get these wounds under control." He went to the first gurney. "Thank you, Alice. And hand out the joy-juice, will you? No sense in making these men suffer any more than they already have. Howard, it looks like the bullet went straight through here, and took the clavicle with it. Hmm, yes; a nice, clean break. I'll just get a few pictures of—"

"I suppose everybody needs a purpose," Jared rudely interrupted. "Even if it is just patching up a pair of loser rip-off artists."

"We gravitate toward what we're suited to do," Lightner replied absently, unshakable in his duty. "Don't we?"

Jared snorted, "Somebody better mention that to these dimwits."

The little prick didn't look up or even smile. "Judging by their condition, I'd guess somebody has," he said. "But except for the clavicle, they're all minor flesh wounds." Lightner patted a sterile draped leg, and moved on to the next gurney. "They'll probably learn something from this failure."

"Learn?" Jared scoffed. "Them? You've been popping too many of your own pills, sport. This kind never learns."

Lightner took the jibe with another painfully shy smile, but he had lost his blush. "How about you, Mr. McCormick? Do you learn from your failures?"

"There's no such thing as failure," Jared stated. "Only giving up."

"Or being aware of and accepting fundamental limitations," Lightner offered thoughtfully.

"That's called giving up," Jared laughed.

"No, it's probably called growing from our experiences," Lightner returned, looking him in the eye. "One who never fails, never grows, do they? May I?"

Without waiting for a reply, Lightner stepped away from the gurney and reached for Jared's hand again. Surprised by both the cutie's tone and his unexpected boldness, Jared let him study his fingernails. Then Lightner lightly prodded and pinched the skin under his jaw. He started to take Jared's pulse. Something odd was creeping into those pretty brown eyes, something puzzled enough to send a crawly sensation up Jared's spine.

Griffin was frowning over at them both, and even the nurses had paused in an expectant silence.

Jared shook Lightner off. "You aren't going to get me to cough," he said coldly. "One of us might like it too much."

While slowly rubbing the palms of his small hands together, Lightner cocked his head, like he was listening to something elsewhere.

"What?" Jared said.

"Do you suffer from nightmares, Mr. McCormick?" Lightner asked very quietly.

"No, did you want to borrow my night light?" Jared whispered back.

"Night sweats? Insomnia? Nausea? Have you been losing weight? Are you presently taking any medications?" Jared kept shaking his head. Lightner stopped with a mild frown. "No? Hmm—well, let me know if I can ever be of any help." He turned away again, saying briskly for the room to hear, "Let's get those x-rays, Marie."

Jared tried not to stare after him. He had heard it all before, but Jesus, never that fast, and not without his direct input.

This wasn't good.

"McCormick was married to Leslie Doherty, Rick," Griffin stated unhappily, breaking into Jared's silent, suspicious certainty. "Years ago. He's in town to visit Maggie, but he'll want to say a few words to Bud. Is that all right?"

"I don't see why not. If you light that in here, Mr. McCormick, I'll just have to ask you to put it out."

"Let's go!" Griffin barked, herding Jared past the beefy patrolman, toward the hall.

Holding the cigarette he didn't remember taking from his pocket, Jared went. He paused at the propped-open ambulance bay doors to light up, though—as if he had meant to all along. Then he stepped into the dry sunshine. He leaned against rough, hot brick, hoping he wasn't sweating too visibly. Yeah, Lightner could help him, all right…he could crawl back into whatever psychic closet he had come from, and close the door.

"Odd little shit," he grumbled on an exhale, to detract from whatever else he might have done wrong back there. "I wouldn't trust him to treat a hangnail. You want one of these?" When Griffin only continued to glower severely at him, Jared put the pack away. "You got a lead on your heists, huh?" he asked. "Something about a stolen truck? Your lucky day."

"Right," Griffin clipped. "I have five unsolved murders, a bunch of burglaries, a citizen with a cracked skull, a spoiled teen-ager crippled for life, and an ex-government sharp-shooter who put holes into two escaped felons with my gun. It's my lucky day, all right."

Jared stuck to the point, but he was thinking *five*? "So how good a lead is it?" he asked hopefully. "The truck, I mean."

Griffin gritted his teeth while Jared floundered over the sheer numbers and continued to sink into an ocean of cold realization. He had instinctively pegged Lightner as gay, but had the pretty little man pegged him, too, with that same quick look?

This was very bad.

"Okay," Griffin said over-patiently, "I also have a stolen truck that I would love to tie to the burglaries, which have been nothing but weird. The old man at the Coast to Coast Hardware Store has forgotten to lock his doors three times in the last month and he was robbed last night. I usually check the doors myself when I go home, but with all the other crap going on, I forgot, too."

"No forcible entry on the others, either?" Jared guessed. That would be weird.

"None." Griffin abruptly rubbed his face with both hands. "Maybe someone hid in the clothing store dressing rooms, and another place has a small window on the alley that hadn't been locked for years. I don't think they went in that way, but I can't prove otherwise. Then there was a lost set of keys and a lock that was never changed…anyway, we've had about fifteen thousand dollars-worth of merchandise boosted in the last two months. The truck turned up missing this morning—I doubt it has anything to do with anything." He stopped. "Why are we talking about this?" he asked a little helplessly. "Why did you take my gun?"

"Are you asking for my statement?" Jared asked. "I did it by the book. I heard gunshots and waited for backup, and—"

"Whose book?" Griffin suddenly yelled. "You took my .38! Why did you do that?"

"Simplicity. Your town, your hardware, your collar."

"But you shot them!"

"Prove it. That .38 pulls to the right, by the way."

"Prove it?" Griffin squawked, his face mottled red. "I—you can't do this! I didn't—"

"Sure you did," Jared said smoothly. "And won't it look good on your resume?"

Griffin struggled to get a grip. "What about the eye-witness accounts of you leaping your car like Superman and putting yourself in mortal danger in front of that truck? How are you going to deny that?"

He wasn't dead; for now he would settle for looking like Superman. "I won't," Jared said. "That'll look good on my resume."

"Are you crazy?" Griffin sputtered. "We both might have been killed!"

"Oh, as opposed to just one of us?" Jared laughed, pissed. "I was supposed to just let you get squashed like a bug? That punk was on top of you, and you didn't even see him coming! Was I going to yell 'yoo-hoo!', and hope you got the fucking picture?"

Griffin turned away in frustration. Jared eyed him angrily. That truck should have been his, goddammit. Heroic or not, he had to figure out how to put a goddamned lid on Superman or he'd continue to get nowhere. If Griffin didn't arrest him first.

"May we please drop the subject?" he suggested. "When I get a minute, I'll write up my eye witness account of how you compacted the Texas garbage, and give it to your secretary."

Griffin checked his watch, looking even more exhausted. "You do that. I need to call Maggie."

"I'd be glad to take Mr. McCormick to see Bud," Lightner offered from the open bay doors. "You can meet us, Howard."

How long had he been standing there? Suddenly beyond angry, Jared stepped on his cigarette. "Am I going to get lost?" he snapped at him. "The place consists of six rooms and hall—I don't need a guide dog. I don't even want to see the son of a bitch!"

"That's fine with me," Griffin said quickly, but Lightner interrupted with, "Oh, but it would probably do Bud some good to see a new face, Mr. McCormick, and I need to make my rounds anyway. Your ex-father-in-law is my star patient."

"They didn't part on good terms, Rick," Griffin told him uneasily. "They aren't exactly friends. If McCormick doesn't want to—"

"But they share a common loss in Miss Doherty. It might mean some kind of closure for them."

"He's right, McCormick," Griffin sighed. "You're here, you might as well see him now instead of later." He added with a wryly-hopeless shrug, "If you give him apoplexy, Rick can handle it. I'll be with you guys in a minute."

CHAPTER

3

JARED HAD SPENT HIS entire lifetime allotment of sympathy years ago, hanging around Chicago emergency rooms with gut-shot junkies and whores who hadn't come across. The harsh white lights and plastic hospital decor didn't bother him; he didn't even see them. Besides, he was too intent on not letting Lightner near him again. He stayed three aggressive steps ahead, following the signs to the new wing.

A woman in a high-necked blouse with a purple brooch at the neckline served as a buffer between the public and the elderly inmates. "Can I help you?" she asked, barely looking up.

He wasn't a relative or a friend, and she wasn't prepared to be concerned with anyone so obviously out of place. Bitch. The smile Jared dropped on her in passing wasn't the playful one he had stupidly used on Lightner, the one that caused his dimples to dig in and work for him. During the dirty, gritty years, his use of that seductive tool had been off-hand, but it had generally retired when he had. Still reeling from Lightner's dangerous shrewdness, he wished it had stayed retired.

The woman straightened anyway, doing a double take as he went by.

"Janine, I wonder if you...hello? Earth to Janine?"

Lightner had stopped at the desk, but Jared didn't pause

until he came to a door that had Bud's name on it. A TV muttered to itself from within. What the hell was he doing this for? To placate Griffin, that's what. They weren't even close to connecting yet, despite all Jared had done for him. Jared nodded to a turtle-paced old man inching a walker his way, and pushed the door open.

Bud Doherty was propped up and snoring in the hospital bed, his head drooped sideways. The thin drapes in the little room were drawn, but even in the gloom Jared could see that the fucker had aged a century since he had last seen him, almost ten years ago. His barrel chest had collapsed. His thick hair had thinned to white fright-mask wisps, and the craggy, stern face had eroded from granite to gravel. He was covered to the waist by a sheet and blanket, but the space where his legs from the knees down should have been was flat.

Some surgery. Staring at the ominous space, Jared shriveled inside. Breathing the same air Bud did sucked; what the hell could they possibly have to say to each other? Grinding his teeth at the erratic snores, Jared impatiently ran a hand through his hair. He tossed it off his lapels, then automatically glanced into the small closet and the lavatory. The muted audience whooped uproariously on the wall above his head. Then Lightner came into the room, further setting Jared's teeth on edge.

The little guy set a chart on the bed and rested a hand on the old man's shoulder. "Rise and shine, Bud," he said softly. "You have a visitor." Amidst the resulting coughs, wheezes, and grunts Lightner stepped back. "You have a visitor, Bud," he repeated, smiling at Jared. "I'll be right outside."

Jared stared at the wreck on the bed, flashes of loathing hurting his chest. He wondered how many actual, coherent words would pass between them before they were reduced to animal snarls.

Bud peered through the semi-darkness. "Who's there?" he croaked. "I don't have my glasses on; I can't see a damned thing! Is that you, Abe?"

Jared stalked to the low cabinet where the glasses lay. He dropped them onto the old man's covered stomach and turned to draw the drapes, letting in a bright shaft of sunlight. He squinted at the view of the empty brown field across the gravel road.

Bud growled, "Who the hell are you? What are you doing in my room? Speak up, or I'll have you tossed out on your butt!"

"You did that so many times my butt still has calluses," Jared grated as he faced the bed.

Bud started as if he had suddenly encountered a spider in his sheets. He swallowed hard, trembling his old-man wattles. "It's you," he accused, recovering somewhat. "Huh. Did you hear? Leslie's dead!"

"I heard."

"So what are you going to do about it?"

"Me? Not a damned thing."

"Figures," Bud sneered back, looking him up and down with growing contempt. "Pretty clothes, too much hair; you look like a goddamned gelding, all show and no go. You got no use for women anymore?"

"Not bad," Jared complimented tightly. "From eunuch to fairy in two sentences. Who have you been practicing on since I've been gone?"

"It don't take practice to call a whore a whore and that's all you ever were, McCormick!" Bud spat, his sunken chest suddenly heaving. "Falling on your back every time I walked by, hoping for a shot at the Flying D!"

"I did not!" Jared disagreed in amazement. "You had work for me to do, and I did it! I can't count the number of times I'd work half the goddamned night for you, just to get the job done. You hired me, Bud—you practically begged me to hang around out there!"

"I didn't pay you to grunt over my little girl every chance you got, you pig! How many times did I pull you off her—catch you like the rutting—"

"Shut up," Jared hissed, advancing a step.

"That's enough!" Griffin barked over Lightner's shoulder at the door. "Both of you!"

Jared put his back to all three, furiously retreating to the window.

"It's about time you showed up, Griffin!" Bud hollered without missing a beat. "I been calling you all damn' day!"

"I've been a little busy, Bud. What did you want?"

"I want you to find out who killed Leslie! That murdering freak didn't do it. Damn it, nobody around here seems to care about the truth!"

Jabbed by a new dart of pure hate, Jared spun around. "What you know about truth would fit loosely in a teaspoon!" he jeered. "How dare you use the word without a snicker?"

Lightner put a restraining hand on Griffin, who was still ready to step in. The witchdoctor was looking puzzled again, so Jared ground his teeth and maintained.

Bud muttered under his breath, glaring up at the TV. "Somebody's been breaking into houses," he growled to nobody in particular, "killing women. But Leslie wasn't one of them, and that's the truth!"

"It's being investigated, Bud," Griffin said heavily. "By a lot of people."

"I want him to do it."

Bud poked a gnarled thumb toward Jared, but didn't look at him. Griffin and Lightner did.

"He's not authorized—" Griffin started to say.

"He don't need to be!" Bud shouted at him. "Didn't you bother to look at him when I asked you? You useless son of a bitch, I had Abe poke around a little—somehow McCormick's got himself up to be some kind of a joker who don't need no authority! He sells himself to the highest bidder—big surprise! I'll give you ten thousand dollars," he snarled at Jared. "You just look into it!"

Jared tugged his cuffs straight instead of spitting on the old man. A dull headache buzzed somewhere nearby. He had been lucky to get three hours of sleep last night before the nightmares had jolted him awake—lucky, because more often than not he didn't sleep at all.

"I'm on vacation," he said coldly.

"Vacation?" Bud howled. "You never did an honest day's work in your life, you lazy bastard! What are you vacationin' from? I'm offerin' you some walkin' around money—you find out who killed my daughter. Your wife!"

"She wasn't my wife; you saw to that!"

"Fifty thousand!" Bud yelled.

Griffin blinked, and Lightner's eyebrows shot up.

"Fuck you," Jared said tersely, turning for the door.

Claustrophobia settled over him like a sodden quilt—he had to get out. Now. Shouldering Griffin aside, he was stopped by a petite nurse who bounced off him in the doorway.

"Oh, excuse me!" she laughed gaily.

She didn't get out of his way, though. He could read her mind, and it certainly wasn't on her job. He almost couldn't conquer his next fractious urge, the one that wanted to slap her into some sense of reality, to remind her of who and where she was.

He didn't want her looking at him like that. He had nothing to offer—anymore, dammit, he was all show and no go. Too, too, aware of Lightner, he stared back at her with suppressed fury. She seemed to find that as fascinating as his earring.

"Better run, honey," he heard Bud warn from the bed. "I know that look—he'd screw a garden slug if he could figure out which end was which!"

"Jeez, Bud," Griffin groaned.

The worried cop interrupted a serious case of the sulks when he slid into the Porsche's passenger seat a few minutes later. Jared mutely refused to participate in his explanatory chit-chat over Bud's triple plights of grief, crippledom, and advanced age. He had run out of excuses, but he didn't see why he had to choke down Bud's, too. He stabbed out his cigarette and started the Porsche. Griffin took the hint and fell silent.

The hospital and nursing home were a half-mile from the railroad tracks on the northeast edge of the city limits, with mostly open prairie in between. Jared geared the Porsche to a disappointing 25 mph and passed the first of the houses that lined the streets. This was the 'good' end of town. He hadn't spent any time here as a kid, except to pass through on his way to more important places. The tiny business district began immediately after the fifth block. He found himself looking more closely at that.

The First National Bank was on the corner, still in the vintage four-storied sandstone block building that was the cornerstone of the district. It had been an accomplice in his father's death three decades ago; Jared didn't do more than give it a glance. Sears was gone, but a discount store of some kind occupied the building now. Coast to Coast Hardware, Ben Franklin—the dime store where he'd committed his first crime by shoplifting a pack of baseball cards—a dress store, a jeweler's, the Shady Leaf Tobacco Shop that also sold penny candy and comic books, the post office…tiny, two-front-windows-and-a-door places that had been the backdrop for the war-zone he called childhood.

"Stop at the station, will you?" Griffin said despondently.

Jared turned off Main onto Sadler Avenue and parked across the lines.

Inside, Randy was still behind the desk. "I just made coffee, sir," he offered meekly as Griffin disappeared down the hall.

Coffee was the last thing Jared needed in this mood, but he took some anyway, carrying it back to the office. He heard Griffin's voice from the cells to his left, and other voices from the office. Gloomily weighing his inflamed impatience against the promise of burglaries, he leaned against the wall, forcing himself to dawdle once more.

Griffin stalked by, closing the office door on him. It

opened a few minutes later and two uniformed patrolmen came out, Griffin telling their backs that he wanted it Found Now. The door stayed open.

Jared pushed off the wall and went in. He lowered himself into one of the chairs in front of the desk. "Good thing Bud wasn't packing his shotgun," he commented as he lit a cigarette. "That might have pissed me off."

"He really hates you," Griffin said unhappily.

"Oh, yeah," Jared agreed with a forced chuckle. "Yes, indeed. But I bet I can still outrun the prick."

"His feet had to be amputated, damn it! If you're trying to be funny, McCormick, it isn't working. I have no sense of humor when it comes to Bud Doherty!"

Suddenly feeling more sick than usual, Jared said lightly, "Neither do I, Chief. It would take ten shrinks a full year to pick apart all the nasty threads running from him to me and back again."

"Then why does he want to give you fifty thousand dollars?"

"Beats me."

"You don't care that Leslie was murdered?"

"I'm on vacation." Jared yawned. "Listen, since you don't want me calling the lying, manipulative, bastard son of a bitch names, how about giving me a rundown on—"

The telephone rang.

Griffin shoved an ashtray at him, then got entangled with the Texas authorities.

After a minute, Jared irritably went to reheat his coffee. He spotted Randy out on the sidewalk, crouching beside the Porsche. The farm boy peered worshipfully at the fixed rear spoiler. Jared took his cup outside.

"Oh, hi!" The kid jumped up guiltily. "I'm sorry. I was just looking."

Jared grunted, glancing at the alley. No, another drunk in a truck would be too much to hope for. Aside from a few late rubberneckers, the scene across the street was deserted, too.

Griffin came out into the sunshine a few minutes later and stood next to Jared. Randy didn't see him; he was at the driver's window, devouring the dash in large gulps with his eyes.

"Please don't ever give him those," Griffin said, indicating the key ring in Jared's hand. "That piece of machinery would eat him alive. Randy? I'm going home. John's coming in; he'll take over until I get back. There'll probably be more calls about what happened across the street, so I left my statement to the media on my desk. Stick to what I've written, understand? Don't start adding adjectives, especially about my near-miss with the Kelly boy."

Randy's blatant idolatry of the car spread to Jared. "Sure, Chief!" He took the empty cup Jared held out. "Thanks for letting me look at the car, sir."

As they watched him hop up the steps and trot through the door, Jared shook his head in disbelief. "Is he even potty-trained?"

Griffin surprised him with a real smile, the first since they'd met. Not a laugh or a grin, but maybe it was progress. "We all had to start somewhere. Even you, McCormick. I walked to work this morning; you mind giving me a ride home?"

Once in the car and rolling again, Jared lit a Marlboro and offered the pack.

Griffin took one this time—definitely progress—and used Jared's solid gold lighter. "This does run nice, for a deadly weapon," he allowed as he exhaled. His fatigue spoke of other things on his mind, but he looked at the dashboard with almost as much passion as Randy had. "What'll it do?" he asked.

"Street start, five to sixty in about three and a half seconds," Jared replied. "Wrap it up, drop the clutch, and you're there. There's no boost lag between gears, so if you aren't mindful of the tach, you'll kick in the rev limiter every time. I understand it'll top 180-plus—but of course I wouldn't know that from personal experience."

This time it was almost a grin. "Of course you wouldn't," Griffin said.

"Shall we check it out?" Jared dared.

He chuckled evilly at the doubt he saw land squarely on Griffin's face.

CHAPTER
4

HE PARKED TO THE right of the door marked Office, under the neon SunSet Motel sign. Griffin got out and waited at the step to the motel residence, but after closing the driver's door, Jared was suddenly plunged into a deep vat of ice cold certainty. Did he really want to be here? Absolutely not. The dousing staggered him, but he covered by looking around. Other than some new paint, a new roof on one or two of the ten cracker-box units, and a few oaks missing from the grove that clothed most of the area, the place looked about the same. The blacktop was pitted, but when he had lived here a lifetime ago the driveway had been nothing more than dirt. He guessed that the potholes were an improvement. There were bright flowers in cast-iron pots beside each door, down the sidewalk.

By the time of their mother's early death, he had had no interest in the world but Leslie Doherty. He clearly remembered telling his older sister Maggie to sell the dump and get away from Shady Rock. Maggie had been woefully undecided on the subject of the old motel, and he had run away with Leslie without knowing what she had done about it. With a rumble of premonition, he now wished Maggie had left, too. He really had no desire to see her.

The front door of the office flew open and Maggie burst onto the porch amidst a noisy tumble of kids. She ran down the steps and threw herself at him. Inwardly cringing, he looked over her artificially curly red head at Griffin, who had picked up the smallest child. Griffin watched his wife indulgently while being attacked by his other children. Jared smelled fried chicken and perfume before Maggie stepped back to gulp tears at him. Clenching his teeth, he pulled out his handkerchief and gave it to her.

She clutched it, and him, with both hands. "Where on earth have you been, Jared Jordan McCormick?" she wailed. "Why didn't you ever write or call? Do you know how long it's been? I was afraid you were dead! Oh, just let me look at you!"

She held him at arm's length, eating him raw with her streaming eyes. He prickled at the sentimental depths of her emotions, and ignored the questions altogether. He had never been required to account for himself here, and he wasn't about to let it start now.

"Hello, Mags." Remembering Griffin, he leaned to peck her on the cheek. "You're looking good."

"No, *you* look good!" Maggie exclaimed in wonder, still gripping his arm. "Doesn't he look good, Howard? I mean— just look at you! I can't believe how you've grown up! But what's all this?" Still sniffling noisily, she grabbed a handful of his hair and gave it a tug. "Good grief; what would Mother say?"

Jared was thinking she would say exactly what you are, Mags; you even sound like her. He felt sick. Sicker.

After more weepy scolding, Maggie finally turned him toward the kids gathered around their father. She proudly named them off as they milled. Fighting the trap he had dropped himself into by agreeing to stay at the motel, Jared barely noted that the boys were blond and blue-eyed like their father. The eldest child, however – the only girl—had inherited his own Irish-Scot coloring: dark hair and eyes over very fair skin. A developing thirteen-year old, she stared at him with her mouth open.

Maggie tugged her forward, giggling tearfully, "And this is Molly, our first effort. Howard hadn't hit his stride yet, as you can see. I've been accused of awful things because of her!"

Molly flashed anguished eyes at her mother.

"Let's go in, Maggie," Griffin yawned. "I'm beat. And hungry. I have to go back later, but I'll help you get the brats to bed."

Bouncing the littlest brat on his hip, he turned to go up the steps. Maggie hugged Jared's arm, but he shook his head. No. No way was he going to do this. He couldn't. The fried chicken smell made him queasier by the second.

"If you'll excuse me, Chief," he said to Griffin's back, disentangling himself from Maggie, "I'm tired, too. I wouldn't be very good company."

"But I made a big dinner for you!" Maggie burst out, vastly hurt. "And Molly's baking you a chocolate cake! Come on in here and eat with us, Jared McCormick. I want to hear all about what you've been doing. My God, we have fifteen years to catch up on!"

"Not tonight, Mags." Jared avoided Maggie's stricken look and added, "I'll come by your office in the morning to make that statement, Chief."

Griffin handed the baby to little Molly. "Maggie, take the kids in the house and get supper started. I need to talk to your brother for a minute."

Maggie was crying silently again and Jared felt his shoulders cramp. What had he been thinking? He needed anonymous and sterile, not this cozy universe of saccharine domesticity. He mentally shook his head at the tentacles of claustrophobia he felt rewinding through him, and turned to the Porsche.

"Hey, wait a minute!" Griffin half-laughed behind him. "You agreed to stay, remember? I'll put you down there at the end of the row for some privacy, but I would like it very much if you would come in for supper. It's the least I can do, after what you did for me this afternoon. Tad's truck, I mean," he ended with a confused frown. "I'm still not sure what to do about you taking my .38."

"You don't have to do anything about it," Jared said impatiently. "Nobody saw me. Listen, I'm not trying to be rude, but—"

"Is it the kids?" Griffin interrupted as a sudden thought. "It's the kids, isn't it? I forget that not everybody likes them. We'll put them in the kitchen if they make you nervous."

"I'm not nervous," Jared heard himself bristle.

"Good." Griffin put his arm around Jared's shoulders and drew him to the steps. "The baby isn't happy without one of us around. A quick bite, okay? Then we'll let you go."

Jared somehow found himself seated on the left side of the old oak dining table between two small boys—just one of the kids. Young Molly was across from him, her eyes fastened to him like lampreys over the mashed potatoes. Maggie, much happier now that things seemed more small-town normal, ran around the table setting out platters and bowls. Griffin passed Jared the chicken.

To add to his acute discomfort, Maggie wasted no time in pulling out dusty Jared-stories. She prattled on and on about classmates that he didn't recall and teachers at the high school who, he was sure, had done their best to forget him. He felt his shoulder muscles constricting further under the weight of the old trash that she heaped on him.

"And do you remember Alice Harvey, the high school science teacher?" Maggie chatted brightly as she spooned mush into the baby. "I think she got married when you were a junior? Anyway, she still talks about the time you and Terry Anders turned all of her white mice loose on the football field!" For a moment, she actually sounded angry with him for something that had happened twenty years ago. And then she sounded proud, as if the prank, being his, had been something truly grand. "You two were always getting into trouble!" she laughed gaily. Jared studied her with angry fascination as she went on. "She keeps the mice locked up in the janitor's room now; doesn't she, Molly?"

Jared saw Molly's tiny nod, but put down his fork. He was going to get sucked in here, too; he could feel it coming. As with Bud, he found himself defending things that shouldn't matter anymore but apparently did, because he suddenly couldn't keep his mouth shut.

"Oh, is she still poisoning them?" he asked coolly. "What a shame. She may call it research, but it's torture, pure and simple."

Griffin, he knew, was looking from him to his wife, but Maggie merely laughed again and reached for the bread.

"Oh, you always were such a softy, Jared! Remember that old dog you brought home from the Flying D? The one that was all dirty and blind? I thought Mom was going to faint when you let it into the house. The smell, and the fleas! What ever happened to it?"

Jared willed himself to look down at the paper napkin in his lap, instead of bolting from the shrinking walls. He was folding it smaller and smaller, paying close attention to getting the corners just right.

"It died," he said distantly.

"No, there was more to it than that, wasn't there? I'm sure there was. Didn't you take it out to old Doc Evans at the hospital?"

Jared realized he was obsessing over the diminishing square of paper, and dropped it as if it had bitten him. This had been a very big mistake.

"I did, yes," he replied with some venom. "I thought he would put it down. But I was informed in no uncertain terms that he couldn't be bothered." He looked at Maggie, imperviously selfish, busy with her dinner. "So I carried it all the way home again, and killed it with a fucking shovel."

The rude word served its purpose. Maggie looked up, blessedly quiet. Her face was a mask of innocent surprise.

Cringing excitedly, the kids gaped at each other. Griffin cleared his throat and reached for the butter.

"You've embarrassed your brother long enough, honey," he said with a quick smile at her. "Change the subject."

"Oh, no!" Maggie giggled at him. "I'm just getting started! Jared, what about that time I had to—"

"Maggie," Griffin interrupted. She looked at him as if he had pinched her. "That's enough," he said more gently.

Jared tossed the napkin on the table beside his plate, and stood. "You'll excuse me now," he ordered Griffin.

"But you didn't touch the chicken!" Maggie gasped, half-rising. Fear and disappointment lurked in her face—she had failed to please him with the table-full of food. "And what about the cake?" she asked wretchedly.

"Maggie!" Griffin snapped.

Jared didn't wait to hear the rest; he left. Outside, he thought about leaping into the athletic Porsche and blowing the place completely. Not only had he not connected to Griffin, he had caused a domestic dispute. He didn't need this kind of aggravation at all. Not on top of his own. He was pissed at himself for over-reacting to Maggie's blasts from the past, but he was more pissed at his dependency upon Griffin and his two-bit burglaries. Nobody knew better than he that when others had to be brought onto the playing field, autonomy was lost.

Christ, what *had* he sunk to?

The motel units were one room with a tiny bath in the corner. In the Seventies, the decorating style had been green and gold with a lot of shag. Maggie had brought this room into the numbing Eighties and had left it there, he saw as he turned on the table lamp. Everything was blue and mauve with a lot of country cute. He winced as he took it in. There were dried flowers on the desk, smiling wooden teddy bears above the door, and a seed packet calendar on the wall. Instead of a trivial seascape above the bed, there was a large framed picture of a shelf laden with rag dolls, more teddy bears, and a stack of wooden blocks spelling out "Welcome Friends".

Thoroughly depressed, Jared locked the door behind him and put the suit bag on the low double bed. He took his portable CD player from his briefcase and plugged it in, on the desk. The opening concerto swelled into the room, instantly throwing water on the remaining sparks of his idiotic mouse-dog defensiveness. What the hell did any of it matter?

He went to the tiny closet area beside the bathroom. The lilting melody of "Spring" wrapped him in a removed peace as he emptied the garment bag and filled the rod. He took his shaving gear into the bathroom, noting the teddy bear shower curtain with an inward sigh. He felt like he had been put into a nursery, and, judging from his actions, it was exactly where he belonged. He had to do better or prepare to accept the consequences.

No, he inwardly seethed. He would *not* die a coward's death in the Porsche. He didn't remember the drunken, abusive father who had attempted to rob the bank uptown, but he knew damn well that he didn't want to follow in his fucking footsteps. The asshole had died at the end of a high-speed chase spanning half the state, after deliberately rolling the truck he was driving…one coward in the family was quite enough.

Following his shower, Jared toweled off, avoiding the raised scar that puckered the skin under his left arm and slid on down to his hip. The rough, skimpy towel felt good on the ones on his back. All of his wounds were old, but they were something he lived with—just like he was going to have to live with this town. For a while. He could do it.

He thought about shaving—his five o'clock shadow couldn't tell time—but decided he couldn't be bothered. While the violins lit up his soul, he debated the idea of going out to find something stronger than the soda Maggie sold in the lobby. The tomato slice that had comprised his meal sizzled in his stomach, competing with the unending nausea. It made up his mind about that drink, but it was early yet, and he wouldn't be able to sleep anyway. He had to find something to do. He buttoned the clean, gauzy cotton shirt, precisely rolling back the cuffs twice.

Someone knocked. The sound was jarring over the soothing strains of the violin.

Griffin stood outside, looking like he had returned to his first instincts, and was about throw him out of town. Dandy. Wordlessly, Jared went to reduce the CD volume by several notches. Waiting for the worst, he shook out his hair, then quickly ran his fingers through it. The damp heaviness cooled his back, but the stifling breeze hurrying through the open door would speed its drying. He put on his socks, then lit a cigarette. After half-reclining against the pillows with one foot on the floor, he looked at Griffin, who was still planted on the stoop. Maybe tar and feathering wasn't on his agenda after all.

"Well, come in," Jared shrugged on an exhale of smoke. "Pull up a chair or something." He added grudgingly, "I'm sorry I said fuck in front of your kids."

"No, I'm sorry," Griffin said stiffly. "Maybe I shouldn't have insisted you come in. I didn't realize what kind of…I didn't know—" He stopped. "I don't know what I don't know, but I really don't know what got into Maggie! It hurt to see her being so insensitive."

"Outstanding," Jared exhaled grumpily. "Now we're all fucked, and none of us enjoyed it. What else was Maggie going to talk about, Chief? Her idea of me is frozen to the year I left. I just wasn't ready for it."

Griffin stepped into the room. He pulled out the desk chair and sat. "Why didn't you keep in touch, McCormick?"

The question didn't even compute. Stay in touch with what?

"Other than to say that my life took off in a direction that didn't allow time for anything but work," Jared replied, "I have no excuse whatsoever. And you know what?" he complained. "Now that I'm here, I feel like I'm in a time warp without a force field. Jesus, my sister has turned into my mother, and this entire homespun event has me in bunches. I hate being bunched! It's humiliating the hell out of me, in fact. Give me a minute to grow up again, will you?"

Griffin smiled a little. "Nah, let's just drop it."

"Fine with me," Jared muttered, watching him.

The transparent cop went from worriedly miffed straight into a poor imitation of cunning. "So...what did you pay for that car?"

"Enough that my accountants and financial advisor will have collective heart attacks when they hear about it." Jared flicked his ash, re-masking his impatience. Why couldn't the man just get to the point? "A hundred and thirty grand, give or take the odd nickel. Are you fishing?" he couldn't help prodding. "Set the hook; yank me in."

"Okay," Griffin said slowly. "I admit I'm curious about you – your apparent successfulness. I called your business card number."

"Of course. Was anybody home?"

"I was transferred to someone named Emilio?"

"Ah." Jared contemplated the ceiling. "Emilio Rivera is my legal ward. I tripped over the little rascal in a slum in Bogota three years ago, where he was peddling his only marketable asset on the street corner. He helped me with some things there, and did it very well. I brought him home so he could help me with some other things." Jared smiled at the dingy corner where wall met ceiling. "Even for a street rat he has an amazingly corrupt and devious mind. Maybe we should put Emilio and Randy together, huh? Something of one is bound to rub off on the other." His attempt to joke fell flat.

"I got the feeling Emilio likes you, too," Griffin said.

"Well, he'd better!" Jared found a wry laugh in the impersonal subject. "The little Spic bastard is costing me a fortune in education, wages, and perks. But more to the point, did he say anything *you* liked?"

"Well, he told me to thank God that I had you in my town, and to watch my back if you ever got behind it. Oh, yeah, and he said that if I didn't take good care of you, he would send his six big brothers here to exact retribution upon me and mine—something like that." Griffin's questioning glance was brief. "It was quite a conversation…what I understood of it. Most of it was in Spanish."

Jared sagged, suddenly wishing he was home. "I keep telling the little pecker if he's going to answer the phone, he has to speak English, goddammit. He thinks it's funny to play the dumb greaser—I can't take him anywhere without ending up looking like a fool. And he doesn't have six brothers; he has a gorgeous younger sister. He keeps her stashed in a convent, now that he's found a gullible gringo patron." He shook his head in amused exasperation. "Shit, I'm surprised you let me anywhere near your nest, after talking to him!"

Griffin said, "I know loyalty and respect when I hear it. Or is he more than a friend?"

Since Griffin was obviously leading up to something, Jared decided to field the question instead of hammering its political incorrectness. But what part of ward didn't he understand? "I've tested my own authenticity," he said calmly, "and personal actualities long enough to know by now that I'm basically heterosexual." Then he frowned. "Who knows what Emilio is?"

"I did more than call the number on your card," Griffin announced, again refusing to acknowledge Jared's attempt at humor. "I didn't have time to do a full background check, but I talked to a couple of agencies and one of your competitors. I heard a lot about International Security's phenomenal track record. It's a lot bigger than I thought, too, and getting bigger all the time."

"But it doesn't pretend to be a police department, Chief." Jared remained as unruffled as he could. "International Security, not International Enforcement. For the last time, I'm not here for anything but a vacation. Really."

"Okay," Griffin said, nodding. "I believe you."

"Good. I get bored easily, though," Jared added strategically. "I might do a freebie burglary while I veg out for a week or so. If you ask nicely enough."

Griffin looked at him for a minute longer, then said, "You'd take burglary over serial strangulation and necrophilia?"

Jared felt his jaw drop. "Well, wouldn't you?" he demanded. "Good God, what the hell is going on—?" His mind was suddenly racing down roads he didn't dare take. "No," he said firmly. "Never mind; I already get it. The murders were obviously nothing but a blind. See, Bud screws me every chance he gets, so it follows that he's your body-humping froot loop. He's been working up to killing me, and then he'll fuck me again. Bud's your man."

"Can we leave Bud out of it?" Griffin growled. "He tried to hire you, and you said no. That's why I believe you aren't here in a work capacity. Besides, nobody could seriously expect you to be able to conduct an unbiased investigation into the death of your own ex-wife."

"Wait, wait," Jared cringed, putting a hand to his cheek. "Damn, I hate being slapped like that!" Griffin raised his eyebrows; Jared lowered his. He sat forward, resting his forearm on his thigh. "I *am* International Security, Chief Griffin," he said grimly. "Phenomenal is my middle name. Aside from the heights I've scaled in both government and private sectors over the last fifteen years, I've collected four major and several minor academic and criminology degrees. I'm playing with the idea of finishing up two more when I get a minute. Not to brag, but I'm a PhD in deduction. A master of mayhem. A goddamned Sherlock Holmes in Italian threads—are you catching my drift? And I'll tell you this just once: there isn't a thing in this world that I haven't done. Not one single thing. The combination of Grade A testosterone and world class intelligence has made me—I don't think like you, and I don't feel like you. I don't even exist on the same plane you do. While you're spouting words like 'unbiased' and 'investigate', I'm somewhere else entirely, writing new definitions for them!"

He sat back, inexplicably furious. No, not inexplicably. He might be crumbling like a bad batch of cheese, but he still had his pride, goddammit. Nobody was going to take that from him, especially not an over aged boy scout living in a dumpy motel in the middle of nowhere.

Griffin eyed him for a minute, evidently lost in uneasy thought. Jared violently lost himself too, in the music that suddenly wasn't nearly loud enough.

"What are you really doing here?" Griffin asked at last, bluntly.

Jared opened his eyes to grinning teddy bears and scratched his stubble. He wasn't doing a goddamned thing. Until events unfolded in exactly the right sequence, he was stopped cold. And making Griffin fidgety wasn't helping.

"You keep asking that, but what am I doing?" Jared groused. "I'm sitting here playing show and tell with you, but I can't for the life of me figure out what I've done to cause all this insecurity!"

Griffin laughed, still not happy. "I saw you shoot down two men in the space of a half a second, and then go for coffee, McCormick. You scare the hell out of me!"

"But I'm not the barbarian screwing your dead people," Jared snorted. "I only get into that kind of thing in odd months."

Griffin's next nod was stronger. "Yeah, okay," he said with an air of making up his mind. Finally. "Look, I'm not happy with where your ethics are leading me, but you already know that. And I'd never even consider this under normal circumstances, but nothing has been normal here for months—I'm losing my town, and I'm losing my perspective. So I'm asking, if you're really bored, how about taking a look at our killer? I can't bring you in officially, but I'd share the files to get your opinion."

Startled, Jared stared at him. Sure, that's all he needed, to be exposed to the very thing that had driven him out of the Bureau in the first place. He wanted the burglaries, for Christ's sake. How many ways could he say it? Ready to decline in no uncertain terms, he stopped to think. His own big mouth had gotten him into this, but what would it hurt? It was only paper, and it was a perfect splice point.

He shrugged coyly. "Sure, I could look, if you think I might help."

CHAPTER

5

THEY TOOK GRIFFIN'S AGING black Tempo back uptown.
Jared rode shotgun, and used the time to deal with his still-
damp hair. It was no small task, in the small confines of the
front seat. Griffin stopped to check the door of the darkened
hardware store before he said anything about it.

"You've been growing that a while," he commented with
some gruff reproach. "A diversion, like the fancy clothes?"

"Isn't that taking a huge leap from pure ignorance?" Jared
asked, jabbing the comb in his direction. "I'm not undercover
anymore. I'm retired, right? I always dress nice these days;
I like the feel, and I can afford it. As a kid, I got two pair of
blue jeans and one pair of ugly brown corduroys a year. Ma
always bought them too large so I could grow into them, and
that meant the damned things fit right for about two months
out of twelve. Then I got into uniforms and plain blue suits,
more sartorial gag-me's. Psychologically speaking, I imagine
it's a regression thing with me at this age, thumbing my nose
at years of acute embarrassment. Emilio tells me that I'm into
narcissism as well, taking myself like a drug. All I can say to
that is who am I to deny perfection?" Griffin was amused at
last. He smiled. "The hair, on the other hand, is purely sexual
advertising," Jared ended complacently. "The longer it gets,
the more I get. Somebody ought to do a study—I'd volunteer."

Still smiling, Griffin turned into the shadowy alley and parked behind the police station. After unlocking the back door, he led the way through a small storeroom and then through the dimly lighted cellblock. It contained side-by-side cells, holding a bandaged, cranky Texan each. Jared paused in front of them, abruptly enough that Griffin stopped too, and looked back at him. The prisoners glared, silently malevolent, but Jared didn't see them.

"What happened to Neugebauer?" he demanded, staring at the lidless toilet in the corner of the cell on the left.

"He retired to Florida a few years ago, when the county consolidated us with Whitewater and Yellow Springs. I took over for him. Why?"

"No reason," Jared said, riding the ugly loop. "I just wondered." He moved away almost reluctantly.

They came to the hallway and Griffin turned left, entering the dark office. He flipped on the lights and pointed to one of the two visitor chairs. Jared sat, uselessly lacing his fingers over stirring demons, while Griffin checked his messages. They were tossed aside in disgust.

Then, Griffin leaned forward and clicked the mouse on the pad. "It's all on the computer here. You know computers?"

Jared looked up, at the really stupid question. Back in the saddle, Griffin was distanced again. And, apparently, brain-dead. Jared cracked his knuckles, flexed his fingers and winked. A tinge of red crept up past Griffin's starched collar.

"Yeah, okay," he muttered. "Sorry, I forgot who I was talking to. Anyway, I save all the paper as backup, so it's here in either form. Which do you want?"

"Computer, thank you. I forgot my reading glasses."

They stood to trade places but in passing Griffin dubiously asked, "You really need them?"

"Need what?"

"Reading glasses?"

Ah, a reality check; since when did supermen have poor vision?

"Don't worry about it," Jared purred, taking the CD player from his briefcase. "They're tasteful in tortoise shell, a worthy accessory to the Italian threads—when I remember to put them in my fucking pocket." He set the player on one of the overflowing shelves. After detaching the speakers, he spread them as wide as the wires would allow. "Do you mind?" he asked, reaching for the CD. "I have headphones, but they suck."

"What is it?"

"Vivaldi."

Was there anything else? Not lately; not for him.

Griffin cleared an outlet and plugged in the player for him. Jared pushed the start button and set the volume as high as he dared in the presence of the un-obsessed. Then he settled into the swivel chair and lost himself in the enticing interplay between information, imagination, and intellect.

He went through the essential data in fast-forward, picking up just the bare bones. Technicalities too soon, he had always found, only clogged insight. He came away with a fairly complete skeleton of the crimes within thirty minutes. Yup, five women were violently dead at the hands of person or persons unknown.

Irene Madden had died in her home February seventh. A widow of fifty, she had been popular in her church, and in the town. There had been clear evidence of a forcible entry; her body had been found in the kitchen by her sister. She had been sexually molested, an event proven to have taken place after death.

Jennifer Lacey had been considerably younger, 27—a secretary in one of the two law offices in town, and a Sunday school teacher. Although engaged to be married at the time of her death March tenth, she had lived by herself. The break-in at her house had occurred in an attic window beside a large tree. No discernable footprints had been found in the carefully turned flowerbeds below, but the evidence at the window was straightforward. She had been assaulted after death as well.

Adele Forester, age 30, had died on her acreage April fifteenth. Married, but her husband had been out of town for the week. Considered something of a snob by her neighbors, she tended her prize roses and lawn. It had taken careful searching to find the basement window that the murderer had used to gain access. Her death had been more violent, and her body had been trashed extensively.

Marcie Johns had been 30 also, and a quiet, retiring person who lived for her five cats and her prize vegetables. She had died May first, after an intense struggle. The terse description Jared read betrayed the shock the writer had felt upon viewing her body.

Leslie Doherty had died in her dining room June twenty-eighth, three weeks ago. Evidence of post-mortem molestation was present. Jared was a little surprised to learn that two small children survived her. She had obviously forgotten all about him, too. She had owned a pet shop on Main Street.

After turning over the computer to Jared, Griffin sat in the visitor's chair and paged through the hard copies. He sometimes tapped a pencil in time with the music. That irritated the hell out of Jared, but eventually Griffin stood, saying something about coffee. By the time he returned Jared had stretched himself out in the chair, his feet up on a drawer opened for that purpose. His left hand was twined in the hair that hung over the chair back; he was comfortable, computing, and a million miles away. The sweetie in the white coat was absolutely right; you did gravitate to what you're suited to do, and it felt so good when you got there.

"Nice music," Griffin grunted as he set down the cups. "Classical, right? The only violins I know are bluegrass."

Jared, cruising at a trillion knots, shortened his gaze in annoyance at the hick remark, but let it go. "Photos?" he asked. "The real thing, please; I'm going blind here."

Griffin handed him four large envelopes. Jared shoved the

drawer shut with a foot and sat forward, all business. Elbows on the cluttered desk, he shuffled through the first set of black and whites, preferring the neutrality forced on him by the lack of color. When he finished examining those, he dealt out the second and third sets, sometimes holding the stark glossies at arms' length for closer scrutiny. The fourth envelope he barely looked into before laying it with the others. He held out his hand for the file Griffin had omitted – Leslie's.

"It's all the same, McCormick," Griffin began. "The MO is exactly the same – you don't have to look at them."

"I'm here at your request," Jared reminded him. "If you want my opinion, cough up the prints. I'm not going to wrestle you for them, but I promise I won't burst into tears."

Griffin mumbled something uneasy as he pulled out the last file. Disregarding him, Jared sorted those black and whites by subject. He absorbed the body shots of his dead wife one by one, easily staying in the place years of experience had built for him. It was a case, not a peepshow. After a minute, he flipped one of the body shots aside facedown and returned the others to the sleeve. He riffled through the ones of the crime scene, then put them away. Finally, he reached for his cigarettes. He took one out, looked at it, and put it back.

"Psych work-ups?" he asked with closed eyes, allowing the precision of the music to line him up and take the lead. "I'm too lazy to read everything, so give me a gist."

"The behavioral experts with the FBI have it, but I haven't seen much from them yet," Griffin said heavily. "With all the organizations involved now, I'm not at the top of the priority list." Jared heard Griffin's trademark sigh of helpless defeat. "It's turned into a circus, of course. I don't understand why this guy is still out there!"

"You're the man on the scene; do you have any personal theories?" Jared opened his eyes and patted the desk. "Put 'em out here."

"I have a few ideas," Griffin admitted with reluctance. "Nothing very helpful, really. I figure he's under fifty, in good shape. Some of these women fought back hard, but lost badly. I'm pretty sure he must live in the area, not just be traveling through. We would have seen cases statewide by now, if he was moving around. Besides semen, we have some possible fingerprint and hair evidence, but nobody to match it to, of course…I don't know, he gets his kicks in having violent sex with the dead—a real nut, I guess."

Jared nodded, expressionlessly looking through him. Then he broke down and took a cigarette. He tossed the box over. He lit his, and then slid the lighter to the box.

Griffin lit up too, frowning over the deep engraving in the gold. "What's it mean?" he asked curiously.

"It's Basque," Jared replied from a great distance. "Says 'Death is absurd also.'"

"Oh."

"It was a gift from a man named Lackore, who owns a castle not far from here. Do you know it? It's an amazing place. Anyway, Lackore and I swore one time that we were going to quit smoking. I never did. The self-righteous prick sent it just to aggravate me."

"I quit a few years back," Griffin said sadly. "Until today."

"Oh, I'm sorry." Jared mocked him with a solicitous look. "I've demoralized you that much already? Good, then you won't be surprised when I tell you something that you aren't going to like. But before we get into that, I'll say I see one itty-bitty flaw in your take on this shitbird."

"What's that?"

"I look at these bodies and I don't see rape; I see inability."

Griffin blinked, then frowned. "Inability? What kind of inability?"

Jared narrowed his eyes at nothing, still sorting and filing. "The gentleman who perpetrated these crimes might be a true misogynist," he expounded matter-of-factly, "in which case he'd be unable to perform, but why would he want to? Or possibly he's homosexual, and for some odd reason is trying to score with women. Whatever his psychological footprint is, he's looking for love in all the wrong places. When she asks for it, his dick doesn't work and he gets mad. Once she's dead and through nagging, though, his snit passes and he's able to reach ejaculation."

"You don't think necrophilia is the issue?" Griffin asked sharply. "That's the unanimous consensus, McCormick. The sexual attacks were perpetrated after death, after all."

"It's happening," Jared agreed with a smothered yawn. "No question about that, but it's definitely not the perp's burning issue." He nudged the stack of files closer to Griffin, spilling a box of paper clips. "Look at the pictures again; these women were each strangled from the front, right? So let's be real. If he'd just wanted to screw a body, he wouldn't have risked the struggle. Believe me, it's much easier to garrote from behind. Since the attack is frontal and barehanded, I can easily picture them sitting in front of the fire all kissy-huggy—her looking forward to bigger and better things and him shrinking away to nothing. His anger is instantaneous and supreme, and he's on them like Godzilla. This is a frantic man."

"Hmm," Griffin said, raising his eyebrows in doubtful possibility. "But then why the rape? They're not fighting him anymore, why does he mutilate them?"

"Now, see?" Jared warned with a chilly flinch. "There you go again, leaping from that platform of sheer ignorance. You weren't there, were you? Why do you categorically call it rape?"

"Well, shoot!" Griffin sat back with a short, disbelieving laugh. "Maybe you didn't notice without your reading glasses, but at least three of these women were really torn up, both vaginally and anally. And being dead, I don't think they were begging for it! How can you not call it a violently aggressive act—in other words, rape?"

Jared shifted his gaze from Griffin's face to a blank spot on the wall over the man's shoulder, concentrating.

"Can you actually rape the dead?" he asked thoughtfully.

"By definition, necrophilia is an erotic fascination with a corpse, sometimes accompanied by the performance of gross indecencies upon it. Right? But this guy is neither fascinated by dead bodies, nor by the grossness of his indecencies." Griffin continued to look muddled, so Jared added impatiently. "Stop trying to add hands and numbers to equal clocks, Griffin. Pillows plus mattresses do not equal sleep. You see blood and private parts and are concluding a violent act of intimidation or coercion, but these women were killed before the act, not during, not after. Get it?"

"No."

"Okay, here's this schmuck living some kind of a sexual crisis—take that as established for a minute. For whatever reason, he can't successfully get it up in female company. Proof of theory? Starting in February, he comes down a crashing failure with Miss Madden. He gets pissy when she laughs or nags, and he chokes her. Now he's alone just like every other time he's jerked off, but this time he doesn't need the sock on his hand, or the butter or the vacuum cleaner, or whatever he's normally in love with. He's got the real thing right in front of him. It's what he wanted in the first place, or he wouldn't be there, no doubt about it—and she isn't laughing at him anymore, is she? She's done making him feel stupid and inadequate. So, what the hell? He tries it and, by God, it feels good. It feels real good. You getting this now?"

Griffin nodded, staring at him.

Jared listened briefly to the music soaring from the walls, and then nodded in return. "Good. So, he's down to business and tickled pink. He's finally doing what real men do, huh?" Jared laughed, "Chief, it's plain old sex he's after, not a thrilling hit of the abnormal. And if you were taking notes here, you'll have an appreciation for why bodies three and four were in the condition they were."

Jared smiled at the images in his head. This wretch was so clear to him for the moment, he might have just finished an intensive interrogation with him. He could see everything but his fucking face, and he briefly lusted to bring him down.

Griffin cleared his throat. He looked away uncomfortably, shaking his head before he spoke. "I don't know," he said somewhat weakly. "And you don't know, not for sure. You weren't there, either."

"I'm hurt," Jared said, keeping his smile. "After all we've been to each other, you still don't find me phenomenal? But I'll finish it for you anyway—what those snaps are showing you is that it's a question of being polite, that's all."

"Polite?" Griffin parroted, frowning harder at his hands in his lap.

"Absolutely. Say you're romping around the bedroom with my sister—which is an image, by the way, I'll try not to dwell on—and you're feeling adventurous. Maybe extremely kinky adventurous. If Mags didn't like what you had in mind, you'd do the polite thing and stop. You're experienced, she's experienced, and you're both operating on a thing called love."

"They couldn't tell him," Griffin breathed, his eyes sharpening, his shoulders tensing. "And if he'd never done it before, he wouldn't know what would hurt them."

"Crude and rude inability," Jared re-identified succinctly. "It explains why bodies one and two were merely battered. As a social virgin, he was fairly timid. Bodies three and four ended up looking like ground beef because—"

"Because he was getting more confident with the sex act itself!"

"Sure." Jared served the word with a shrug. "Quote normal people learn what is and isn't acceptable to their partners, from their partners. Your yo-yo probably knows this gore can't be right, but who cares? Nobody is asking him to stop and be polite, now are they? He's having a time, that's a given. I'll also go out on a skinny limb and say that he's younger than fifty; it looks to me like this horny incompetent is just getting started."

Griffin frowned, his growing excitement abruptly dashed.

"No—but wait! Wait. What about Leslie Doherty? She was barely bruised at all, and she was the fifth one. If you're right, then she should…?" Griffin let the question trail off, obviously hoping for another fast answer.

Jared mentally gave him marks for quick perception under extreme fire, but he was pretty sure that the miraculous answer would plunge the man into an even deeper despair. Oh, well; he had asked for it. Jared flipped over the photo he had saved out, a graphic, full body shot of his ex-wife spread obscenely on the floor—naked, strangled; dead. Something shiny and wet puddled between her tidy breasts and spattered her blue-swollen face. But there was no blood at all. Jared casually sailed the photo over the desk to Griffin, who grabbed and caught it.

"If I'm correct," Jared supplied without a wince, "and I assure you I am, Les should have been trashed at least as badly as the last victim. Does my grand theory fall apart here? Not at all. Check the DNA profile against the others, but that crippled old dirt farmer is right; you've got two crimes, two programs—a copycat as well as a froot loop. So," he ended brightly. "Did I make your day or what?"

"Oh, shit." Griffin wilted forward and thumped his head on the desk. "Shit, shit!"

He dropped Jared in front of number ten without even standard parting pleasantries. In fact, he hadn't said another word, proving how committed he was to believing the terrible revelation. Jared stood beside the Porsche with keys in hand and watched him park beside Maggie's Toyota wagon. The devastated cop crept inside the darkened motel office like it was the mouth of hell.

Welcome to the neighborhood, Jared thought with bitterness. Then he decided that he didn't just want a drink, he had earned one.

6

THE STONY CREEK BAR and Grill was still in operation. Located on the eastern outskirts of town, its low cinderblock walls couldn't contain the lights and laughter and music that spilled from them, this hot summer night. Jared parked the Porsche as far away as he could from the other vehicles scattered haphazardly in the gravel lot. Inside, he disregarded the good smells coming from the grill-half of the building. Just because he had worked up an appetite now didn't mean that he should do anything about it. Sometimes that was the worst time to eat, when he was hungry. It didn't take a rocket scientist to understand why he had dropped so many pounds lately, but he still couldn't see how it showed enough for a complete stranger to pick up on it as fast as Lightner had.

It was nearing ten. Jared followed the teeth-aching strains of country music belting from a flashing jukebox to the bar in the back. The open room was dim, and overly rustic for his taste. Several mixed couples cuddled in dark booths and lounged around the tables, and five, two male and three female, bellied up to the bar. The three females were noisily together. The bartender stood back with a towel in his hands, listening to their whoops and hollers with a tolerant smile. He was big and clean-shaven, as Jared thought all bartenders should be. He was also attentive, coming to the end of the bar to greet Jared.

Jared ordered Jack Daniels, neat. Before his change could be counted, he tossed the whiskey down and asked for another. The friendly sting it left in his throat couldn't begin to compete with the conflagration it was going to light later, but he drank down the second without pause. Five dead, and he couldn't do a damned thing about it. Except heap more shit onto an already overburdened cop, of course.

The accommodating bartender poured him a third shot without being asked. Jared left the change as a tip, and carried his glass to an empty table beside the door. He studied the drink for a while before swallowing half of it. The impulse he'd had in the motel driveway to get pleasantly high as a reward for good work, and maybe as a prospect for sleep, was evolving.

It didn't seem to matter that he knew better. Over the dire warnings of the third gastric specialist he had consulted in Chicago, he was hearing a fierce, urgent voice in his head cheering him on; the investigative framework was up and solid—the direction clear. The voice was asking what earthly difference it would make if he took on one or both of Griffin's killers? He was going to die anyway; why not use one of them to achieve it?

But his only argument still held—he wanted to go out with dignity, not as a spectacle. If he went anywhere near the next bloodbath—and he was as sure as could be that there would be a next—he would expose himself as the sideshow he had become. That wasn't going to happen.

He seriously contemplated before making the last of the third shot vanish. Useless crap. Booze hadn't worked the last time he had tried it, in combination with the Glock. Obviously. And he was going to pay for this foolishness. But he emptied the glass anyway, painfully tangled up in the scattered, untidy chords and sappy lyrics howling from the jukebox. This was not at all where he wanted to be, but where was he going to go, back to the teddy bears? He was thinking about just curling up in the Porsche's leather seat in the comforting dark when the bartender came up with a tray containing three more shots and a new napkin.

"From the gals at the bar," he explained with a friendly leer, setting the shots in a line in front of Jared. "Get your lasso ready, pal."

Jared lifted one of the drinks toward the bar in polite acknowledgment. It was a diversion, of sorts. Amid their delighted nods, he quickly decided that it would be the blonde who would hit on him; blondes always had more balls. She followed the other two into the restroom, but came out first and walked across the small dance floor to his table. She was about his age, and fashionably emaciated underneath the inevitable cowboy gear of pearl-buttoned checked shirt, jeans, and boots. She had the disillusioned aura of a divorcee, and the eyes of a starving child. Nice legs, no tits. Jared got to his feet at her approach.

"Can I join you, honey?" she asked, putting a long cigarette between crimson lips.

Jared impassively lit it with his lighter and pulled a chair out for her beside his. He signaled the watching bartender, then sat down.

"You looked awfully lonely over here all by yourself," she crooned with a sympathetic smile. "You aren't from around here, are you? Just passing through?"

"Close enough," he agreed.

Her beer was brought. The other two women came out of the restroom, giving them sidelong looks. The cowgirl moved her chair and reached to finger Jared's hair. Without looking, he took her hand in his and held it loosely on the table between them. Did he really need probable disgrace on top of actual depression?

"I'm not in the mood," he said. "But thanks for the gesture."

She smiled closer, trying to interpret what mood he was in. Then he felt wiry fingers crawling across his thigh under the table. They became shamelessly personal.

"Are you sure, baby?" she teased.

Well, maybe he wasn't sure. Whether it worked out for him or not, it would kill some time.

She said something else, but just then Jared caught a resigned, semi-fearful expression spreading across the bartender's moon-shaped face. Jared automatically traced its trajectory to the door beside his table, where a blockade had gone up. Four men and one possible woman had just rolled in, dripping chains, fixed blade knives, and intimidation. Jared glared at them, affronted by their mere proximity. Then, he had a flash of inspiration. Hardcore bikers? Why not? His heart abruptly pounding, he watched as salvation lurched right for him. He barely noticed the cowgirl flee.

"Hey, man—gimme a light," the lead bull rumbled at him from deep in a leather-vested, mossy chest.

The degenerate didn't have anything to smoke. He also had trouble focusing as he loomed over Jared. Jared stared up at him, fighting the instantaneous effects of his inspiration. At his hesitation, the biker used his massive, tattooed forearm to sweep the glasses and ashtray from the table.

"Light me!"

In the fog spreading through his head, Jared teetered between the instinct to righteously drop the ugly fuck, and the desire to give himself to it. One dumb move and the herd would tear him apart. They were wasted enough not to care about consequences, and he was desperate enough to take a little pain along with his final reward. It would happen fast. But was it too late? He had thought about it too long—he was only a few heartbeats from blacking out. All that remained clear in his head was the ultimate, burning, question: how many would die with him, when it happened? How many would he inadvertently kill, trying to defend himself without knowing he was?

The bartender was reaching for his bat. The couples at nearby tables had shrunk to half their size, too afraid to make a run for the door, while the single drinkers, including the three women, cowered at the bar. No, there was no clean way out. Jared stepped on his short circuiting mind with sheer attitude.

The asshole still didn't have anything to smoke.

"Shall I begin with your hair, or your clothing?" Jared snapped in agonized frustration. He flicked his lighter and held it up.

The biker snorted and snuffled something rude, ready to charge.

Jared dropped the lighter, leaning forward as if he couldn't hear. "Excuse me?" he sneered, battling the fog, reaching for the Glock.

Bringing out the automatic, he erupted to his feet, jamming the barrel to the broad forehead with an audible thump. In the same move, his shoulder caught the drunken shit under the chins, tipping him full length to the floor. While pointing the weapon at the center of the milling herd, Jared kicked him in the head to end the incomprehensible roar at his feet. The jukebox chose that moment to stop.

"These beings are none of my concern!" Jared barked at the bartender in the aghast silence. "You call it."

The bartender cleared his throat. "Well, uh, sir, uh—maybe you could just ask them to leave?"

"Maybe I could." Almost fully recovered, Jared lifted his chin at the top-heavy, sweating female. "Hit the door, babe." He didn't watch her; he had the rest of the bar to do that for him. When he was sure she was out, he signaled to a green, ragged, Mohawk. "You next, Tonto."

Breathing hard and uttering mumbled rancid threats, the herd filed out under the motionless eye of the automatic. The beast on the floor under Jared's shoe had to be dragged by the last. Jared replaced the Glock and dropped back into his chair, breathing too hard. Space was closing in on him now, but he was okay. Disappointed, but as long as he didn't try to follow the bikers he could keep the black chaos from overtaking him.

External awareness was seeping back in—he heard the titless cowgirl talking to her friends, her nasal tones screechy over the rest of the excited bar-buzz. The jukebox blared again, and the burly bartender approached with a sealed fifth, a glass and a napkin.

"On the house," he crowed, setting it down with a grateful clunk. "They'll be back, but maybe we'll have one night without their company, anyway! Thanks, mister. You a cop?"

"Not anymore," Jared said, wiping his face with his handkerchief. "Keep it; I've exceeded my limit."

"No way, man; you were icy! Then take it along—on the house!"

"No thank you."

"All right, I'll save it for you," the bartender said cheerfully. "What name should I put on it?"

Just to get rid of him, Jared gritted, "McCormick."

He restlessly ran his hand through his hair, lifting it from his neck. Whisky fire licked his stomach. He had to get out.

"Jared McCormick? No way!"

Jared unwillingly looked up, slowly dropping his hair.

"No way!" the bartender gaped. "Is that you? Don't you remember me? Mike Butcher?"

Jared stared at him. What was with this town? Goddammit, he had been here for more than eight hours now and had done nothing but socialize with negatives. Griffin had no life, Bud had no fucking legs, Maggie had no clue, and the bartender evidently had nothing to do. What the hell was he supposed to make out of this?

"Sure, Mike," he shrugged. "How's it going?"

"Well, for Christ's own sake!" Butcher raved, grabbing his hand and pumping it vigorously. "You're the last person I expected to see in the place tonight, that's for sure! Where the hell have you been all these years?"

"Somewhere else?"

"Well, it's great to see you! Have you run into any of the other guys yet? Let me call 'em!"

Jared stood, wondering what other guys. His childhood had not been fraught with hordes of pals. "Another time. It's been a day, Mike."

"Well, Jeez, stop in tomorrow!" Butcher jabbered at his back. "I'll have your bottle, and maybe Terry or Rick will be in. Man, they aren't going to believe you're back!"

In the Porsche, Jared gripped the wheel and squeezed his eyes shut. Spark after leaping spark raced up his back, fed by the goddamned booze. Hunching in pain, he rummaged in the glove box. Of course he had forgotten to re-stock it with antacid. He closed the compartment with a nasty word, and tried to think. Would there be anything as civilized as an all night grocery in this burgh? The convenience store. He remembered the colorful advertising he had seen in the window while waiting to neuter the Texas deadheads. It was an all-nighter, but would it be open after the attempted robbery? Well, maybe he'd have to open it. He turned the engine over and spun out of the lot. He had to do something.

He had the streets to himself, but he dutifully braked at the light at Sadler and Main. While he scowled at the boarded-up, dark, building to his left, he tried to re-swallow the burning things crawling up his throat. Then, he saw something that took precedent over his desperation. He threw the Porsche into reverse and darted back twenty feet to look more closely…scarcely hoping.

Yes. The convenience store was on fire. Large, beautiful, black skeins of smoke seeped out of a vent near the back of the building—but he couldn't think about it. He abandoned the Porsche on the concrete apron, under the canopy. A sheet of plywood had been screwed to the door he had shot out, but through the other one, he could see that the fire hadn't yet spread to the front. He had to get inside.

Without hesitation, he snatched up a large ceramic pot filled with pink petunias and hurled it two-handedly through the nearest plate glass window. He ducked, covering his head from the flying glass, deafened by the clamor of a burglar alarm. Now he really had to hurry. He jumped through the jagged hole, knocking over low shelves.

In the acrid gloom, he scattered fallen merchandise as he skidded to the first door he saw. Closet. He tried the next. Jesus Christ, the damned cooler. The third door opened onto an atrocious-smelling wall of smog. Gagging instantly, Jared dragged his jacket around his face and dove into it.

Something brushed against his ankle, going the other way. He plunged on, once again fighting the peculiar blotching in his head that told him he had only seconds before he would cease to have choices. Tripping over something metallic, he sent it clanging to one side as he neared the flames. He had to be close to the source to make it look good, but nobody said he had to roast like a pig. The smoke would kill him faster, anyway. His final conscious effort was to yank his jacket off and throw it toward the hellish glow, either as fuel or as evidence of his heroism; he didn't care which. He fell to his face, breathing as deeply as he possibly could...finally successful.

...somebody out of the oblivion roused him into a murky consciousness. He was being half-carried, half-dragged— then was roughly handed to someone who unceremoniously threw him over a shoulder. He struggled, but dimly came to his senses. No; no good—it hadn't worked. Groaning, he gave up...was put flat on his back in a dropped-elevator sensation of disappointment. Feebly digging at his eyes, he was suddenly terrified that all he had succeeded in doing was blinding himself. Two strong hands stopped his.

"Just wait, Mr. McCormick," he heard in a soft voice that made his blood freeze. "That'll make it worse. Let me flush them. Are you burned anywhere?"

Too smoke-choked to speak, Jared forced himself to hold still while something cold was poured over his face. When he tried to breathe, he started hacking. An oxygen mask was snapped over his nose and mouth. After a lot of blinking and gasping, Lightner's good-looking but sober face swam into view. He dabbed at Jared's eyes with wet paper towels, then unbuttoned his shirt and pulled it off. Jared's undershirt was laid open just as quickly, with a few snips of a scissors. The cold, wet towels on his neck and chest felt good, but Jared attempted to watch the little bastard's hands. Tears and grit and wracking coughs made that difficult. The strobe effect of the ambulance lights didn't help, either. He was beside the vehicle, the gurney on the sidewalk, under a flickering streetlight.

"Just making sure we don't have anything here that needs treating, Mr. McCormick," Lightner murmured busily. "I don't think there is, but we'll just check."

Taking scant sips of air through the mask to avoid heaving up his lungs, Jared mentally swore as another blinding stream of water hit his eyes. A dry paper towel was placed in his hand, and he weakly scrubbed them. But nimble fingers on his belt pissed him off enough to grab. The fingers evaded his, and re-adjusted the mask. Jared clung to the sides of the gurney; a wave of vertigo had slapped him sideways.

"Your pants are smoldering," Lightner explained, sounding surprised at being hindered. "They have to come off." Before Jared could assure him in no uncertain terms that they didn't, Lightner said, "Oh, hello, Howard. Give me a hand?"

"Jesus Christ!" Griffin howled as he ran up, a blurry shape under the faulty streetlight. "McCormick! Are you all right? Is he all right, Doc?"

"Looks like smoke damage for the most part," Lightner replied, busy again. "How did the fire start; do you know yet?"

"I just heard about it; I don't know what's going on! How did you get here so fast?"

"I was at the hospital when the 911 came in, and decided to ride along. Was it set?"

"Set?" Griffin gaped at the question. "You mean arson? What makes you ask that?"

Lightner looked down at Jared, whose breathing had gotten even shallower—not a boon to his smoke-damaged cognitive abilities. What was the witchdoctor saying?

"Just call it an exercise in probability," Lightner hedged shyly. "I need permission to transport you to the hospital for a more thorough examination, Mr. McCormick."

Jared shook his head, sending his horizon spinning again.

"But if he needs to go, Doc—?" Griffin started to say.

"I can't make him," Lightner said reasonably, "if he refuses. I'm going to get the rest of your things off and look under the soot for burns, Mr. McCormick. Use the mask as much as you can, while you have it." He recoiled at Jared's second, fast preventive reaction at his belt. "Relax," he counseled while loosening his vised fingers along with Jared's buckle. "Your clothes are ruined anyway. And I'm just going to look."

But there were things Jared didn't necessarily want Lightner to see. A back full of scars, for example. Why give him more to work with?

"—don't doubt that!" Jared gagged with as much outrage as he could. "—not the time or the place, honey!"

With a startled expression, Lightner hastily qualified his statement. "For burns," he explained with a neon blush in the streetlight. "That's all I meant."

The tech arrived to help, and, still struggling to breathe, Jared found he was in no shape to stop himself from being clinically stripped. But Lightner avoided his eyes while he experimentally rubbed a wet towel over a spot on his forearm, one on his ribs, then on his left shin. Jared, feigning impatience, batted him away when the little beggar tried to roll him over.

The tech replaced the thin cotton sheet with a pair of loose scrubs with a drawstring waist. Jared helped fight them on, but the effort was almost too much. Then he felt a tug, and raised his pounding head to look. Lightner had tied a lavish, quirky, bow at his waist with the cotton strings.

Griffin paced only yards away, trying to keep an eye on everything. He was too close for comfort, but boundaries were being grossly overstepped here. Familiarity was a well known door to treachery.

Jared fumbled the mask off and heaved himself upright. He snatched the scrub shirt from Lightner's hands and yanked it over his head, hiding the scars. "Cute," he hissed at Lightner as he wrenched at the offensive bow. "Since when did Martha Stewart start teaching at quack school?"

Most of it came out in a hacking cough though, which spoiled the effect Jared was aiming for. Renewed giddiness nearly sent him face first to the concrete. Lightner quickly crouched beside the gurney, giving him access to his stationary support. The tech handed Lightner a packaged bottle while Jared clung to him with as much threat as he could muster. After snapping the seal, Lightner pressed the bottle into Jared's sooty, shaking hand. Jared squinted down at it.

"Go ahead," Lightner urged at his ear. "It has sugar and things in it that will help the dizziness."

"Things?" Jared rasped back nastily. "What kind of fucking medical term is 'things'?"

"Just drink it," Lightner urged again. "It's nothing—firemen use it all the time for dehydration. Think of it as Gatorade plus Alka-Seltzer."

Since it had been sealed—and opened under his nose— Jared figured it was safe, as in dope-free. Besides, if Lightner had plans to net him, he could have done it a hundred times by now, with the help of the Shady Rock Volunteer Fire Department and Howard Griffin. Jared chugged the tepid liquid down.

Lightner stood and tossed the empty into the back of the ambulance. He put his hand over Jared's, still clamped to his arm for stability. "How do your eyes feel?" he asked, looking down into them. "You must have kept them closed; they look amazingly good. You stayed on the floor, didn't you?"

"What the hell are you implying?" Jared demanded as

viciously as he could under his ludicrous circumstances—croaky rasp, bare feet, and bedraggled but jaunty bow. "I did not set that fucking fire!"

Lightner shrank deeper into his nylon ambulance jacket. His pretty eyes were strangely opaque under the streetlight. The asshole was scared shitless; Jared could feel it.

"Then isn't it fortunate for us that you were here to take a hand?" Lightner managed with a crooked smile. "Again?"

" – you don't seem to think so!" Jared hacked.

Scared or not, Lightner had the audacity to nod in agreement. He suddenly radiated an understanding he shouldn't possess. "Coincidences make me uncomfortable," he said. "You didn't instigate this afternoon's trouble at the gas station, but you were in the middle of it. And here you are again, already in another life and death situation. That seems peculiar to me."

"Oh, does it?" Jared shot back. "You should get out more; it's just another day at the office to me."

"You don't have to do this," Lightner said softly. "There are other ways."

But none of them workable. And this had gone far enough, but before Jared could rip out Lightner's tongue, snap his neck, or even tell him to fuck off, Griffin broke loose from a conference of cops, firefighters, and bystanders.

He stormed up, shoved Jared flat to the gurney, and loomed over him. "Okay," he growled. "It's almost out. Now, tell me what the heck you were doing in there!"

Lightner faded into the darker, bustling, background, leaving Jared free to deal with this fiasco. No, fiasco didn't describe it; he was down, dirty, and, once again, defensive. Somehow, his life had taken on the flavor of a slapstick comedy routine.

"Well, see," he coughed, "it's no big deal. I felt like a cup of coffee and a plastic doughnut, and—"

Up to his ears in guilt over his ongoing failure to the town, Griffin once again had no sense of humor. He jabbed a finger down at Jared. "No, start at the beginning. I want to know exactly what happened!"

"I left the bar at eleven ten," Jared reported, wheezily instead of coldly. "I drove through town, stopped at the light, and saw smoke. I broke the window and entered the burning premises to—"

"But why did you enter the burning premises?" Griffin pounced. "Why didn't you just go across the street and report the fire to John?"

"I set off the alarm," Jared croaked with a shrug. "Why waste time by going across the street?"

"Are you saying," Griffin challenged, "that going into the building was a foregone conclusion with you? Is that what you're telling me?"

Jared looked for Lightner, who stood back—meekly, foxily unobtrusive—then back at Griffin, who wasn't. "Sure," he hacked. "Was I going to hang around and shoot the shit with John while we waited for the fire trucks? Why are you jumping ugly at me? I thought I could put it out, okay?"

Griffin straightened, still bulging with worry. "And you almost died! Again! I can't for the life of me decide whether you are stupid, or just plain crazy!"

"Stupid?" Jared gagged, insulted on top of frustrated. He lurched to his feet, forcing Griffin back two steps. "Look, I broke the window knowing the alarm would go off," he lied on the fly, dragging his smoky hair into submission. "I went in there to see how bad it was," he coughed, "and when I saw I might be able to put it out, or at least keep it from spreading, I did what I could!" And he would have, too, under normal circumstances. He perversely smiled—hating everybody in sight. Especially Griffin, who just wouldn't lighten up. "I'm trained to go balls first into a situation and take care of it. What is your problem with that, Chief?"

His little speech would have been more effective if he hadn't staggered at the end of it.

Griffin grabbed his elbow. "Here, you better sit down," he said gruffly. "Doc?"

"I'm not going to sit down," Jared growled, shoving him away and glaring Lightner farther into the shadows. "I'm going to go take a goddamned shower! Where's my goddamned car?"

"Okay, okay," Griffin gave in, "but take it easy! Rick, where are his things? Just wait a minute—wait, McCormick! I'll follow you, make sure you get to the motel all right."

An hour later, scrubbed and exhausted but sweating, Jared lay in bed cursing Lightner's super-juice. It had somehow jump-started the bonfires that had gone out while he was trying to die. He still didn't have any antacid.

As the first birds heralded the new dawn, he couldn't stand it anymore. He got up, yanked on a pair of pants, grabbed his wallet, and crossed the lot to the front door of the motel office. It was locked. Jesus, was that any way to run a business that counted on nocturnal customers? He popped the cheap lock with a twist and a lift, and went in. The check-in counter was dim under a nightlight. He zeroed in on the kitchen of the residence completely from memory, in the darkness. He opened the refrigerator and reached for a gallon jug of milk.

Whole milk, he saw with a pang of hope that competed with the pain that kept him dripping sweat. He uncapped the jug and started swallowing. When he couldn't choke down any more, he dropped a five on the shadowy countertop along with the blue cap from the jug. He re-locked the door, and went back out into the breaking morning.

7

THE BLACK COMEDY WASN'T over. Griffin woke him at eight a.m., less than two hours after he had at last edged into sleep. The steady pounding on the door vaulted Jared from a hideous place, and its clamor didn't warrant time to even put on his pants. When he got the door open, Griffin also didn't give him a chance to speak; he crumpled the five dollar bill forcefully into Jared's surprised hand and yelled at him for breaking in. He yelled some more about an incident involving some long haired hero with a big gun at the bar last night that he'd only just heard about, and then he briefly, rabidly, rehashed the fire and Jared's idiotic role in that.

Once he got those things off his chest, Griffin geared into overdrive. He informed Jared with deafening vehemence that Bud Doherty had spent yesterday and last night bragging to everyone within earshot that his son-in-law had come home to show the town what nincompoops the local cops were. Griffin had personally heard all about it from the mayor at five-thirty this morning. And the sheriff was out for blood, thank you very much.

Griffin thrust a business-sized envelope against Jared's chest, shoving him back, and slammed the door hard enough to dislodge a teddy bear.

Emilio would have labeled Griffin's semi-hysterical outburst as a serious short in their tenuous connection—and

Jared fuzzily had to agree. Terrific. He wearily stumbled back to bed with the envelope. It had his name on it, and the name of the motel, but no postage. Hand delivered? On his back again, he ripped it open. A minute later, he sat up and groped for the lamp. He squinted quizzically at the birth certificate he had fished from the envelope until another knock wobbled the door. He yanked the door open once more, cringing at the flashes of sunlight now filtering through the trees. They threatened to explode his insomnia and smoke scratched eyes. Before he could stop her, Maggie edged past him with a tray.

"Room Serv—oh, sorry!" she squeaked, hastily averting her glance from his black boxers. "I didn't mean to wake you, Jared, but I wanted to catch you before you went out. I was hoping we could talk a little."

"What's that?" He coughed on leftover smoke, looking with suspect at the bowl of Alpha-Bits.

"I'm sorry for supper last night!" she answered in an embarrassed rush. "Well, not for the supper, but for making you so angry! I'm really, really sorry."

Jared unwillingly closed the ineffectual door.

Maggie set the tray on the desk and pulled the chair out for him. She admitted with a small, anxious laugh, "Ever since Howard called yesterday and told me you were in town, I've been so nervous! But happy, don't get me wrong—I was always afraid that something terrible had happened to you, honey. When Leslie came back to town, she told me that you were a policeman in Chicago. I thought, Chicago, my God; why would anybody want to be a policeman there? And you a policeman? After all the trouble you got into with Rex Neugebauer? Anyway, when Howard said guess who had walked into his office, I nearly died!" She frantically twisted her wedding band while blurting, "I always felt I let you down after Mother passed away. I couldn't be her, you know? And when you never wrote or called, I thought you hated me because I couldn't. That's why I've been so nervous, I guess. I feel so bad…you don't hate me, do you?"

Jared sank into the chair, achy and exhausted. "Nothing like that," he yawned. "I got busy and the next thing I knew, it had been fifteen years."

Maggie gingerly perched on the foot of the bed, facing him. A smile played over her face. "I can't get over how wonderful you look!" she breathed. "Sort of exotic and wild…and just look at all of those muscles! I swear the phone hasn't stopped ringing since yesterday—everybody in town called me about you saving Howard from the Kelly boy, and then the fire? And Howard said you were a big help to him last night at the office." She laughed, coloring prettily. "I know he seems like a big friendly guy, but he's careful about who he likes, Jared. I can tell he really likes you!"

Big friendly Howard hadn't liked him much this morning.

"He told me to ask you if you're a vegetarian, Jared," Maggie babbled on. "It's okay; I do a great vegetable pie! You never used to be one, but Howard reminded me that you're not the same person who left here, all those years ago. Well, I said that was silly; I know that! And I can tell that you haven't been very happy."

Jared frowned, his temples throbbing. "I'm happy."

"Ha ha," she sniffed archly. "You left here a skinny, mad kid, determined to have Leslie forever—something sure changed! Just—well, just tell me you didn't beat her."

Like dear old Dad, she didn't have to add; Maggie had been old enough to remember him.

Jared rubbed his face, hating the numbness he was feeling there. "Jesus," he growled. "Is that what Leslie said?"

"I didn't ask," Maggie sighed apologetically. "I didn't really want to know."

"Maggie, Les left me because Bud finally found us in Chicago, and wouldn't leave her alone. I was working an extra shift and going to school…that son of a bitch showed up and in the space of a week, she was packed and gone!"

"You be careful around that old man, you hear?" Maggie chided worriedly as she got up and opened the curtains. "I don't want any trouble with him, like in the old days! Now eat the nice breakfast I fixed you."

Jared frowned at the cereal, but reached for the small bunch of grapes. While he chewed one, he stretched, trying to dispel some of the leaden sensation caused by lack of sleep. His attention kept going back to that envelope.

"Mags, what do you know about Leslie's kids?" he grumbled.

"Jordan and little Tommy?" Maggie asked brightly from the wastebasket, where she was emptying the ashtray. She didn't question the question; she would have talked about aircraft carriers, to preserve her cozy moment. "You know, I always thought it was sweet that Leslie gave her girl your middle name. She still must have cared for you a little, even if she did marry that guy in France right after your divorce."

That hadn't been in Griffin's files.

"She did what?"

"He died in an accident over there," Maggie said sadly. "Isn't that awful? She came home to have Jordan. That was almost nine years ago, now. The new baby's only six weeks old." Maggie blew her nose on a Kleenex she fished from her apron pocket. "I'm sorry. It just makes me so sad to think of the poor little things without their mother!"

Anything to do with France was patently absurd, if the date was right on the birth certificate he had just been gawking at.

"Who does the baby belong to?" Jared asked unwillingly.

"Well, Steve Reynolds is his father, but the skunk didn't want him! Bud has custody of the kids now. They say that he has all kinds of trust funds set up for them, so I guess they'll be all right."

As Maggie spoke, she pulled the covers up on the bed

without finding the envelope under the pillows. She began to run a rag over the furniture. Jared went into the bathroom to pull his pants on, thinking darker and darker thoughts. What the hell was going on here? Bud's bitching and bluster hadn't meant anything but a headache yesterday, but now what did it mean? As he reached for a shirt at the clothes pole, Maggie started past him to collect yesterday's towels. He heard her make an odd sound. He looked over his shoulder. She was staring at his waffle-scarred back, her hand pressed to her mouth. He mentally cursed his abysmal carelessness.

"It's nothing, Maggie," he said curtly. "No big deal."

"But—what happened?"

Reminded of Lightner's pithy little comeback about growing from failure, he said, "A learning experience."

"Oh, and this!" she squealed in fresh alarm.

She reached out to the long, raised knife scar down his side. He evaded her touch, and her eyes. His scars were nobody's damned business, not hers, not Lightner's, not anyone's.

Maggie burst into tears, sinking onto the bed. "I just don't understand anything anymore!" she sobbed. "Shady Rock can't have a murderer in it! It's my children's home, not a big city! And why did you end up in a job that could hurt you like that?"

"These days," he grunted, buttoning his shirt, "I'm not doing anything more dangerous than riding the Internet."

"But what happened to Mama's sunshine boy?" she wailed, pulling him around by the arm. "Where are those gorgeous dimples? That's another reason I was so rattled last night—Jared, the smile I saw on you would have scared the socks right off of Mom! I know you aren't the same person you were fifteen years ago, but what have you become?"

The single grape was suddenly cutting into his stomach like a piece of broken glass. If she only knew. She didn't really expect an answer, though; his sister was too rooted into her own backyard to be sincerely interested in his. But Jared found himself unsuccessful in denying the powerful urge to tell her at least the good part of the story. Lightner wanted him to talk himself into a straitjacket—all he could do about that was keep the scary little shit at bay, but with time coming to a rapid close, Jared understood that he suddenly wanted someone to know what he had achieved—who he had been.

"I became a success, Maggie," he told her. "Shady Rock looked down on us because of Dad, but it can't—"

"What do you mean, looked down on us?" Maggie broke in incredulously. "It did not! Everyone here is wonderful—I love them all! There were some bad times, yes, but we got through them just fine!"

He shook his head, cut off and shut down by her staunch denial. She couldn't possibly understand his accomplishments, or his now shattered life, in her cocoon-like blindness.

She sat up straighter. "And we're going to get through all this just fine, too!" she insisted. "It'll all just go away. Bad things always do." Her smile was as alien to him as her concept of reality. She jumped up to hug him. "Oh, Jared, it means so much to me, just to know that you're here. I can't wait to get to know you all over again!"

Again? he was thinking as she left. The only person who had ever bothered to get to know him in Shady Rock was Leslie, and in the end she had dumped him like a bag of trash. But what else had she done?

8

THE SMALL NURSING HOME bustled at this early hour. Inmates were herded here and there, and cleaning people mopped and vacuumed around their feet and wheels. Jared strode through the lobby oblivious to everything but his state of mind, which was lousy. Among several other things that were entirely Bud's fault, Griffin's chewing out still grated on his nerves. He and the disgruntled cop were supposed to be splicing, not warring. And now Jared had questions that only Bud could answer. He wasn't entirely sure he wanted them answered, but here he was, still killing time.

He tapped once on Bud's door and went in. The shrunken husk of a man was upright on the pristine bed, doing a number on his breakfast tray. He had dumped his coffee into the cooked cereal and the juice over the Jell-O. He was in the process of shredding the toast into tiny pieces and flicking them toward the windows. Crumbs dotted the carpet.

"Who's the pig?" Jared snorted as he grabbed up the chair and stepped over the bread balls.

"Goddamned lousy food," Bud grumped. "I tell everybody I can't eat it, and what do they do, they just keep hauling it in here like they don't even hear! They want me to get my strength back, they better stop bringing me this crap. What the hell do you want?"

Jared pulled the envelope out of his breast pocket and

held it up. "This has your stink all over it. Why did you send it around to me?"

"'Cause you weren't listenin' to me yesterday, that's why! 'Cause I don't want those goddamned vultures to get the Flying D when I'm dead and gone!"

"I'm going to regret asking, but which vultures would those be?"

"Those two no good sons of mine! Lousy, lazy pickpockets—I spent more cash money on those two in the last year than I ever did on myself. I sure as hell don't want them to get their hands on what's left!" Bud gave Jared a sly sidelong look. "Help me out. I'll make it worth your while."

"What part of fuck you didn't sink in?"

"Oh, you don't want your daughter?" Bud returned testily. "Fine, then get the hell out of here!"

"My name isn't on this birth certificate," Jared said.

"Sure it is!" Bud snickered. "Didn't you see where I penciled it in?"

Jared consciously filled his empty lungs. He hadn't believed it an hour ago and he still didn't believe it.

"Bud, are you trying to tell me that Leslie had this kid—my kid—nine years ago, and never said a word to me?"

"Well, you didn't stay in touch," Bud scowled petulantly. "How could she let you know?"

Jared took a step toward the bed without knowing he had left the chair. Bud slid down on the pillows, clutching feebly at the sheet. His wispy hair fell over. Jared's ears pounded. He tasted something metallic in his mouth. Consciously loosening his shoulders, he pried his hands from the bed rail.

"You motherfucker," he hissed. "After all you did to me, I didn't know about this because I didn't stay in touch? This was my fault? You cocksucker."

"I had to bring her back home!" Bud insisted earnestly, still cowering. "You were always getting your sorry butt into trouble, no matter what I said or did for you! You weren't *right* for her."

Jared felt the blood from his temples drain to his chest, clogging everything, including his resolve not to get sucked in again. "Once I left Shady Rock, you asshole, my sorry butt became a Chicago cop, and then a consulting Special Agent for the FBI! I'm getting together my own international business now; I'm worth more than this entire town, and you're still saying I wasn't right for her?"

"Yeah, but back then you were nothing but a drunken, pot-smoking punk! What about when I had to have you picked up for joy-riding in my car?"

"Goddammit, I worked for that car!" Jared heard himself almost pleading for Bud to remember; to agree, or something. "That whole summer, baling your lousy hay, you told me it was mine! Bud, you gave me the keys! The next thing I knew I was in jail for stealing it. Do you know, I thought Neugebauer was actually going to kill me that time!"

"I never could trust you!" Bud snarled. "You were always raisin' hell of some kind. Somebody had to knock you down a peg or two, and it had to be me. Your mother sure as hell didn't have the guts! And you talked Leslie into running away with you—snuck out of town like a pair of thieves! She was my baby and you took her!"

"No, no; it was her idea to run away, not mine!" Jared corrected sharply. "I loved her; I would have done anything for her, and when she asked me to go, of course I went. She wanted to get me away from you—you never let up on me!"

"And that ain't gonna change, boy!" Bud growled warningly. "But I wanna know who killed her. If you find out for me, I'll give you your daughter. I have legal custody of her; I can do that." He suddenly looked hugely pleased with himself.

Jared turned away with a groan he couldn't help. "Pieces, Bud! Bits and pieces, that's all you've ever given me…never a straight answer, never a chance to do anything right! You keep changing the goddamned rules!" Jared battled a debilitating gush of nausea, endured a wash of sweat. "I was fucked the day I met you and every time I talk to you, I get fucked again. How do I know the kid's mine? What makes you think I even care?"

"Oh, she's yours, all right," Bud said, sounding surprised. "I had Leslie write it all out for me, and I stashed it at the bank. Always thought it might come in handy." He smiled nastily. "I guess you're the only one who knows if you care or not. But why are you here whining at me, if you don't?"

It was a damned good question. Why was he here again? Was he so far gone that he had hoped for some kind of reconciliation with the old man? He had loved Bud once. Briefly, in pure, childish, ignorance.

Jared grabbed the chair and thumped it down away from the bed, barely able to keep from spelling out exactly why he could be here, in large deadly letters. "You son of a bitch," he grated. "You can't blackmail me!"

"I sure as hell can, Slick; I'm doin it!"

"All right," Jared said with a shred of control. "I'm here; I'll nibble. Get it out here in complete sentences. Who do you think killed Leslie?"

"Nope." Bud's jeer turned grim. "I have an idea who did it, but I want you to come up with it on your own. Prove it for me." Then he faltered, looking away. "Only, you'll want to maybe hurry a little. For Jordan's sake. I been thinkin'…I mighta got her in a little trouble."

Jared rubbed his face, ending by using both hands to drag his hair back so hard it hurt. "Why don't you explain what kind of trouble, Bud? That way I'll know, too."

"Well, I changed my will—left everything to her." The old man's jaw jutted. He glared at Jared with the glazed bulge of an elderly bulldog. "See?"

"You left the Flying D to a child?" Jared gaped.

"I had to! Those two boys of mine never amounted to a hill of beans! They're vultures, I tell you, flockin' around, waitin' for me to die! Aren't you hearing me?"

Hate-hazed pictures of the pair spooled by in Jared's mind

uninvited. One of them had thrown his beat-up old Schwinn, the only bike he had ever had, into one of the granite quarries outside of town. Then they had beat him up again.

"Why didn't you leave the ranch to Leslie, then," he floundered over the memory, "if your sons are such a disappointment?"

"I didn't like the son of a bitch she'd taken up with, that's why! A real estate weasel by the name of Reynolds. Wouldn't he love to get his grubby hands on the D? But I ain't going to live forever and I can't be with those kids every goddamned minute! You gotta get this all straightened out for me! And soon, you lazy punk!"

"I've given new meaning to the word since we last met," Jared snapped. "Don't ask; you aren't up to hearing it!"

"Ha, I can take care of myself, don't you worry about that! You just tell me what you find out; tell me I'm right, that's all. And you better figure it out if you ever want to see your little girl!"

"Which of your boys do you suspect of killing Leslie?"

Bud abruptly stopped huffing and puffing. "You found out something?" he asked uncertainly. "Already?" Then his face grew red with rage. "Goddamned peacock! Tell me; Leslie wasn't killed by that creep, was she?"

"It's likely Les's man used the other killer to hide behind," Jared allowed harshly. "So jump right in here any time. I'm listening."

Bud dropped what was left of the toast onto his plate and gave the wheeled cart a violent shove. They watched the plastic tray slide off and dump upside down onto the bed where Bud's feet should have been. The coffee-oatmeal mixture made an immediate brown ring on the pristine sheet, spreading rapidly from under the bowl.

"I knew it!" Bud breathed heavily. "I just knew it. I didn't need any dickless wonder to tell me, either! Get out—I know who killed her and I'm going to handle it my way!"

"How?" Jared demanded. "Are you going throw toast at him?"

"You damned rodent! I don't need you!"

Bud grabbed the Kleenex box and heaved it. Jared caught it easily, crushing it in his hand. For a moment the air around them crackled like severed power lines—Jared could nearly hear it. He stepped over to toss the mangled box in the garbage can by the bed.

"Think about it," he said forcefully into the old man's purple face. "If you know who killed her, he can't let you live. And you're telling me that I can't let you die, not if I want the kid. Which one of your sons do you suspect? Spit it out, or I'll walk out of here right now and put them both out of my misery!"

"You wouldn't do that," Bud tried, shriveling into the pillows. "You couldn't! You'd never get away with it!"

Jared gave him a pained look. "I don't know what chemicals you're getting here, old man, but they're making you delusional. I'll unwrap them like goddamned presents and mail their ugly hearts to you!" Tossing his hair back to finish the threat, Jared backed off as far as the chair.

"I can't tell you which one of them did it, because I don't know," Bud mumbled darkly. "Not for sure."

"Besides the fact that they're related to you, what makes you think one of them is guilty?"

Bud ignored the insult; he was suddenly in a hurry to air his familial grievances. "Well, okay, about a month before Leslie died—wait, no; let me back up. See, I didn't get around to calling up Abe Johnson about my will until late January. I was sick to death of handing out money to those bums like it was candy, and I wanted them to know I was serious!" Bud suddenly chuckled. "So I got everybody together and told them I was making a new will while I carved the turkey for Christmas dinner."

"Nice." Jared wilted in disgust.

"Yeah, they didn't like it much, either!" Bud cackled. "Okay,

then I got together with Abe, and everything settled down for
a while, because they knew it was done. I didn't have to bail
Larry out of his bookie debts, or Lyle out of his credit cards,
so I thought my little joke had worked."

"Joke? You're going to take the kid's name off the will?"

"Of course not! She's the only one of them worth a hill
of beans. She's a spunky one," Bud bragged proudly. "She
stands up for herself, gives me sass like none of my own ever
dared!"

"Sounds like she got more than my name."

Jared examined the idea as soon as it popped into his
head, suddenly taken aback. His unruly temperament rein-
carnated into a small girl? Then he frowned. Did he believe
Bud? Worse yet, how real was he going to let this kid become
to him?

"It has nothing to do with you, you skunk! She's sweet
and decent and – "

"Get on with it," Jared said tightly.

"Now I lost my place! You keep interrupting me, making
it so I can't think…oh, yeah; so I was getting to hang on to my
money for once, instead of shelling it out to those boys, when
Leslie comes to me and asks for ten thousand dollars! Well,
damn…I'd bought her a house and a car and that silly little
business uptown already; what the hell else did she need?"

"Let me guess: either Larry or Lyle wanted it, but was
afraid to ask. Which?"

"I never found out because I told her no! She wouldn't say
what she wanted it for, so I said to hell with you—"

Bud stopped, stricken.

As Jared watched, his face went gray and his bony shoulders slumped. "It's just an expression, Bud," he said impatiently.
"Don't get all weepy on me."

"Goddammit, I'm not! You think I don't know that you'd
shoot me in the back if I didn't have a good hold on your
throat? It's the only thing trash like you understands!" Bud
laughed gleefully at the renewed hate he must have seen in

Jared's face. "You keep a rein on that temper, boy," he sneered. "We're an unholy pair, but it's the way it is! Now, shut up and let me finish this; I'm sick of lookin' at you. I turned Leslie down, and she just kind of drifted away, like she was mad at me. When my second grandchild was born a few weeks ago, I didn't even hear about it until the next day! I've only seen him once 'cause I ended up here right after that. But the thing is, both of those boys was pesterin' Les. She took it for a while—all their grand talk about what was best for her and the kids—then she got mad and told them to leave her alone. She told me on the phone not a week before she died that she was kinda afraid."

"But she didn't tell you which one she was afraid of," Jared said distantly.

"No, we weren't exactly speakin' right then. I feel bad about that now. I'd have given her the money if I'd a known it was going to turn out like this!"

The old man's pathetic bid for sympathy turned Jared's stomach. He stood up. "Talk to Howard Griffin," he said coldly. "He'll figure it out."

"I don't want him to make the arrest, damn you! I did at first; I was so mad she was dead, I would have done anything to get some action from Griffin. But him and the rest of those clowns wouldn't take me seriously! And now I've had time to think about it and I can't stand to think of one of mine sitting in jail because I got tight with the purse strings!"

"Well, what the hell am I going to do, chain the chump to my ankle for eternity?" Jared demanded.

"Nah, I figure you can get him into one of those plushy places, where they put politicians, you know? One of those country club jails. At least he'd be comfortable."

"Jesus Christ, Bud! Do I look like a judge? How the hell do I know where he'll end up?"

"It's part of the deal," the old man said stubbornly.

Jared had had more than enough. "No deal until I see the kid," he said.

Call it research. Call it analysis, or investigation, experimentation; whatever. His impulsive desire was a fact.

Bud reacted as if he'd been stuck with a pin.

He hopped up and down on the bed, yelling, "No way! You stay away from her, you hear me? She's mine and she stays mine until you fix this for me! Don't you go near that ranch, McCormick—I'll have Griffin haul your worthless ass in for trespassin'!"

The door flew open and the little nurse from yesterday popped into the room, not looking nearly so sexy now. "What in the world is going on in here?" she scolded, her eyes blazing. "We could hear you all the way—what happened to your tray, Bud? Oh, my gosh, look at this mess!"

Jared set the chair back in its corner and left. He drove fast but carefully, the dark glasses taking the glare off the road. He needed something similar to block the explosions going off inside his head. He was presently engaged in grasping at razor blades and coming up roses; didn't he have enough goddamned troubles? What damned difference did it make if the kid had his genes or not? He wasn't daddy material on his best days; what could he do for her in the little time he hopefully had left? Nothing. But he did have to mend some fences, somehow.

He parked the Porsche in front of the police station on Sadler, with a chirp from the tires. A different uniformed officer was at the front desk today. Gus, the older, beefy man who had chauffeured the Texans to the hospital yesterday, waved Jared through with a definite lack of enthusiasm. Jared contemptuously wondered if the mayor had called him at five in the morning, too. Misery does love company.

Griffin was hunched over the computer. He looked unhappy, and when he saw who was in his doorway, he looked even more unhappy. Jared knew the feeling, so he returned the expression as he put his hands on his side of the desk and leaned rudely into Griffin's space.

"Don't you even think about yelling at me again," he

emphasized. "It's not my fault Bud is ragging on your mayor! I told you last night, right here at this desk, that I am not interested in your froot loop. I do not care what that old fart is telling the town; what you and I did here yesterday evening was for you, not Bud. But other than giving him an enema with a LAWS rocket, which assuredly would give one of us a colossal thrill, I can't think of any way to shut him up!"

Griffin pointed to the chairs. "Sit down," he said.

"Fuck sitting down," Jared seethed. "I said I was going to have nothing to do with Bud—do you believe me or not?"

Griffin stood, his lined face completely empty. "I took this job knowing I wouldn't always like it," he said slowly. "I have the usual problems in juggling political and moral obligations, but I like to think that I balance them with what is good for everybody. Bud Doherty is a crusty, ornery old man with a mind that never came out of the back woods, but he's also a major power in this county. He has money and he has influence. When he asked me to find you, I refused. I downplayed your name as much as possible because I didn't want to bring you and Bud back together again. You had been nothing but an out-of-control delinquent, and the two of you had been a brass band marching up and down these streets for years. I wanted no part of your quarrel, especially now with the town coming down around my ears. I told you this, didn't I?"

"Yes," Jared replied tersely, waiting for the point.

Griffin went on. "Yesterday you dropped in on me. I didn't like it that you were back, but you stopped in to pay your respects. I did like that. You showed me your credentials without being asked, and I liked that even more—both your thoughtfulness and your occupation. Since then, admittedly with some very iffy moves, you've proved over and over to be a man of bravery and distinction." Griffin had been talking in a monotone, but his fist suddenly crashed onto the desk top. "Yes, I was mad about the mayor's phone call! And I wasn't happy that you broke into the house. But based on your ultimate results, I have to believe in the integrity of your procedures. If I didn't, I would have booted you out of town by now!"

Jared wished that for once the moron could get to Point B directly from Point A. "You understand that I'm not trying to override or otherwise show up your department by deliberately getting any further involved in Leslie's death?" he demanded. "Are you saying you believe me, instead of Bud?"

Griffin frowned. "Why wouldn't I believe you?"

Jared returned the frown. What kind of a question was that, coming from Shady Rock? He sank into the nearest chair. He scraped his hair back and let it go, glowering suspiciously up at Griffin. "Fine, go ahead and stab me right in the tantrum," he growled. "It doesn't hurt much."

Griffin sat down too, and reached for the computer mouse. "The only thing I want a stab at," he said to the screen, "is keeping my job. I'm guessing you were just out to see Bud; did he survive?"

"I didn't whack Bud," Jared said, "although the inclination was definitely there. The fucker threw things at me. I solemnly swear I'll never go near him again."

"I'm all for that," Griffin muttered.

"It's still not my fault that the mayor gets up so early," Jared grumbled. "Or that you have rogue bikers, or that convenience stores are flammable. Tell you what, though, I'll buy you a decent lock for your door. I'm on a roll here; what other groveling can I do?"

He had been fishing for a smile, but all he got was another sigh.

"Well," Griffin sighed, "I ran your inability theory past some people this morning. All that did was get my butt chewed for trying to go off on a tangent, but you don't need to apologize for that. As much as I hate it, I happen to think you're right. It sounded right last night, anyway—the way you told it. Maybe you could tell them, too?"

"I never explain," Jared said definitely. "I sail. I agreed to look for you, and I sailed. I don't care to convince. Didn't the mayor thank you for taking down the Texas terrors?"

"Oh, yeah, sure," Griffin nodded. "He loved it. The sheriff loved it, too—he picked them up a while ago, took them over to County. They both think I'm some kind of strung-out, trigger-happy cowboy, but they loved it. And the Rangers were obliging enough to let us keep them for a hearing. Oh, I forgot—Tom McGuire's conscious and he says thanks. Somebody at the hospital told him about you and the fire. He was more worried about his cat than his store, I think."

"I love a man who has his priorities straight," Jared laughed, standing to go. "So dream of me, Chief," he winked, "not your mayor."

CHAPTER

9

AFTER STRAPPING THE GLOCK into his armpit, Jared slid an ancient cutoff sweatshirt over his head, freed his ponytail, and pulled his Reeboks snug. Badly needing to commune with something beside all this rampant, emotional nothing, he closed the door to unit number ten behind him and did a few stretching exercises, using the side of the Porsche for balance. Jogging north, he quickly broke into a sweat in the hot morning sun. Once he reached the city limits, he headed for open country.

He ran easily, finding it a novelty not to have dodge other joggers, in-line skaters, or park-goers, as he would have along Lake Shore Drive or in Lincoln Park, near his townhouse. The closest thing to traffic was a muskrat that scuttled across the gravel road in front of him. It scared him out of stride before burrowing into the verge. He heard it splash into a marshy patch of tall grasses and cattails. A meadowlark in a stand of three ancient, twisted oaks by the road trilled a signal as he passed under its branch. Several red-winged blackbirds fluttered onto barbed wire, their scarlet patches brilliant in the surrounding browns, greens, and yellows of the fields.

Jared did some of his best thinking while on the run. Jogging had always been a poor second, but he made himself focus on the pounding of his feet and the steady rhythm of his heart. It was a welcome exercise in organized application, taking up the slack of his unusual, unwanted inactivity.

As he ran, he replayed recent conversations, and found himself unwillingly examining the hate that had originated inside him during the years he had spent in torment in this town. It was a defense mechanism, he decided, subconsciously built to protect the soft underbelly of his adolescent vulnerability. Beginning with his father's crummy life and dirty death and ending with Bud Doherty's daily betrayals, hatred had shielded him against fearful, irresolute, bewilderment.

But the boy Maggie remembered—the one who had felt bad for laboratory mice—had long been buried under heavy blankets of justified self-confidence. Mama's sunshine boy had grown from a hostile, mixed-up kid into a deeply rational adult, heavy on the pragmatic and even heavier on the immediate moment. It was what he had been taught in the paramilitary surroundings of his first profession. He had loved the bonding closeness of the law enforcement brotherhood, and, equally, the satisfying self-reliance required in later federal work. Transferring the protection of his early hatred to anything dishonorably unfair had made him both impervious and immoral, and therefore useful in an increasingly amoral world. Whatever it took to both survive and do the job—that was his creed.

So why was this insanity happening to him? Especially now, when he had written the book on success?

He didn't dwell on the question anymore—he had seen enough, done enough, and lived enough to finally accept that not every question had an answer.

Sometimes there were only responses.

He was almost back to the edge of town when a rusted red pickup rattled up from behind. Its driver beckoned, so he went over to the open passenger window, eyeing lawnmowers, rakes, and shovels piled in the box of the truck.

"Want a lift, mister?" the driver asked, smiling tentatively. "It's awful hot to be walking."

The Good Samaritan was skinny, hollow-eyed, and leather-skinned from many hours of baking in the sun. His biscuit-colored hair was trying to be stylishly longish, but merely wisped limp. He appeared, at first glance, to be in his fifties, but with a blink Jared realized he couldn't be. This was the youngest of two vultures, not a day over thirty-three.

"Well, well," Jared said, getting an eager nudge from his opportunistic inner predator. "As I live and breathe; it's Lyle Doherty."

Lyle recognized him then. His face registered first shock, then outright fear.

Instantly intrigued by that fear, Jared's inner predator urged him to open the truck door and get in. He held out his hand. "Been a long time, hasn't it, old buddy? How are you?"

Lyle took his hand but let go as fast as he decently could. "Uh, fine. Hi, Jared. I didn't know you were here." He flushed. "No, Dad said you—I just didn't expect to run into you, that's all."

"It was bound to happen though, wasn't it?" Jared asked breezily. He tamed his smile, not wanting to further spook the timid animal behind those faded hazel eyes. Not yet. "Shady Rock's too small to hide in for long, right? Say, I was sorry to hear about Leslie." And by the way, did you kill her?

Lyle self-consciously got the aged truck moving again. It was missing, sending up a blue smoke signal. He glued his eyes to the road ahead. Jared curiously watched a droplet of sweat creep from under the choppy hair and run down the sun-wrinkled jaw.

"Yeah, I still can't believe she's gone," Lyle finally said. For a moment, his worn face twisted with a surprisingly deep show of grief. "Um, Dad said you were some kind of a special cop now, that maybe you'd find out who did it?"

Not knowing how it was possible, Jared was now even more infuriated at the old man than he had been before. The goddamned old cripple was going to talk himself into a early date with an undertaker. "No," he said positively, shaking his head. "No way. I'm just here for a family visit."

"That's not what I heard." Lyle looked surprised. "I thought—Dad said he hired you."

"Now, Lyle, how likely is that?" Jared laughed. "And, can you honestly see me doing anything nice for him?"

"I guess not," Lyle muttered, ducking his head. "I couldn't believe you would even come back here."

Jared couldn't believe it either by now, but he said, "What are you up to these days?"

"Not much." Lyle grabbed at the change of subject. "I do some landscaping for people. That's where I was coming from just now. There's a new addition out north." He shrugged, but on him it looked more like a shiver. "It's a good job."

Oh? Lyle's work clothes consisted of a ragged checked shirt and a pair of thin jeans with holes in the pockets and knees. His hair looked like it had been self-trimmed with hedge clippers. His boots were new, however, the steel-toed kind, expensive.

Jared heard himself volunteer, "I'm going to be around for a day or two, visiting a few friends. Maybe I'll stop by."

The look Lyle shot him was clearly perplexed. "Okay," he said doubtfully. "Sure. Uh, where did you want to go? I'll drop you anywhere."

Jared hurried through his shower, something he despised doing to himself. He brushed out his hair with savage speed, then allowed himself ten minutes of further blazing wrath. He sat on the bed with his foot up, chain smoking when he wasn't grinding his teeth over Bud's idiocy. When he finally got a grip, he picked up the telephone. He had communed with nature and renewed a hateship; now he needed to reconnect with the inner workings of the Porsche—get into a metaphoric driver's seat and stay there a while.

"I'll reconnoiter the area," he murmured at the sound

of Griffin's voice. "Button down the perimeters. Extend the parameters; anything that will put a loving look in your eye. May I borrow your eldest daughter?"

"She's my only daughter," Griffin reminded him cautiously. "What are you going to borrow her for?"

An insight into how a young girl thinks? An experiment in his ability to relate to children? An extension of the obsessive, self-inflicted torture at which he had apparently become so proficient? He really didn't know.

Jared replied with a shrug in his voice, "A guide?"

"Just don't do any reconnoitering or buttoning-down with her," Griffin warned.

"Oh, no, it's much too early. I don't turn pedophilic for at least another couple of hours."

He said it because he was pissed—did he look like a fucking pervert?—but at long last Griffin gave him a weary chuckle.

"Okay, then," Griffin said. "I'll call her."

Ten minutes later little Molly was sitting on the curb outside the motel residence, waiting. She wore new jeans, a tank top, and a touch of makeup. He pulled around. Leaving the car idling, he got out to open the door for her.

"Hi," she said shyly.

"Hi yourself," he said as he got back in and put on his seat belt and dark glasses. What the hell was he doing? Nothing but wasting time… "I thought maybe you could point out the hot spots in town?"

"I don't think there are any," Molly giggled uncertainly. "This car is about the hottest thing around!"

"You like cars?"

"I like horses better, but I love this car!"

Jared checked the traffic and pulled from the motel lot onto Sadler, going south.

"Do you like horses, Uncle Jared?" Molly asked timidly.

"'To turn a fiery Pegasus; And witch the world with noble

horsemanship."' Jared quoted. Molly looked puzzled, so he lied. "Sure. Do you have one?"

"No," she sighed, sounding just like her father. "I have a friend who lets me ride hers once in a while. She has this really gross donkey, too. I usually have to ride that."

He turned left onto Main, with a glance at the still closed convenience store on the corner. They reached the eastern outskirts of Shady Rock—the way he had come into town yesterday—a few minutes later. Instead of continuing straight onto the highway, he turned right, entering a road lined with tractor sales lots, battered trailer homes, and a truck stop. None of it had changed a bit.

"Thanks for saving my dad," Molly said somberly. "I went and saw Tad's truck. It was awful."

"Is Tad a friend of yours?"

"No, he's a creep! And everybody knew he was going to have a wreck. He's in pretty bad shape; I think they flew him to Rapid City or something. At least he didn't hurt anyone else, thanks to you." She ducked her head. "And I heard Dad telling Mom about how you tried to put out the fire last night. I think—I think you're pretty neat!"

"Thank you very much," Jared said.

He wasn't neat, he was nuts—but blinding with bullshit had become a way of life lately. At least it still impressed twelve-year-olds.

"Where are we going?" Molly asked, but when he didn't reply, she settled in and watched the side window, seemingly content in her own thoughts.

The town dropped away to nothing more than a billboard or two and the odd shack alongside the narrow highway. Soon the landscape changed from grassy weeds to weedy bare spots and scrub trees. The Flying D was six miles east of the city limits. Jared knew every foot of the way. After Larry or Lyle had tossed his Goodwill bike into the quarry, he had walked it twice daily. He slowed a little as he passed the gravel road that bisected to the ranch, then sped up to avoid downshifting. Going back toward town, he took a different road, passing fields of shimmering oats and tossing alfalfa, and several head of cattle looking bored to tears.

"Here's the thing," he told her, finally catching up to her question. "I'd like to find some addresses." He felt for his small leather-bound notebook, tore out a sheet, and handed it to Molly. She looked at it, then wrinkled her nose with an uneasy giggle. "We aren't going to stop anywhere," he said. "I'd just like to see where they all lived."

"Okay. Do you want me to start at the top, with Mrs. Madden?"

Molly had a good sense of her town, and Jared remembered it intimately. It took less than thirty minutes to drive by the homes of the five murder victims, including the ones out on the county roads. Bud had bought an angular yellow and white Victorian house in the center of town for Leslie. It was the kind of place burglars had wet dreams over—banks of thick lilac bushes framed it, front, sides and back.

After they had gone through that list, Jared parked in a shady spot on a side street just off the business district and got out the notebook again. With his fountain pen, he wrote another short list of names and handed it to his niece. Might as well do it right, he thought with a mental shrug. In fact, he was incapable of doing it wrong, or half-assed—and what else did he have to do?

"Yeah, okay," she said, frowning interestedly over the paper. "I think I can find all these people, too. Um, turn left at the next corner."

Molly turned out to be a gold mine of information.

Larry Doherty, Jared learned through her giggles, worked at the hardware store on Main during the week, the sale barn on Wednesday nights, and gambled twenty-four hours a day. According to the gossip, Larry had no prejudices; he liked the ponies, dogs, football—anything that offered a buck. He and his wife Arlene lived in a low-rent housing addition set back almost to the foothills east of town. The houses were lined up like dominoes and had the flimsy look that said they would also fall the same way, with a good sneeze. Some of the yards contained a furry rug of crabgrass; Larry's had car parts.

Lyle owned a tiny ranch to the southwest. It was stuck in a low, swampy, pocket of land formed by the sluggish river and the boundaries of a large, state owned wildlife preserve. From the shade of a billboard that urged the passage of a state funded road improvement plan, Jared looked over the cluster of warped, old buildings around the ramshackle farmhouse. The fences were straight and taut, there was fresh paint on one of the barns, and the weeds had been cleared from the barnyard, but the whole thing looked as worn out as its owner. None of this told Jared what Lyle was raising out here, grain, livestock or pot, but he thought he saw a horse stick its head from the barn as they drove away.

Steven Reynolds, Leslie's former lover and father of her second child, had a pricey, brand-new house built on a pleasant patch of ground a mile east of the nursing home. Most of the established trees had stayed on the lot, fitted into a great deal of new landscaping. Jared idly wondered if Lyle had done the creative work on the yard. The three remaining names on his list were simply names he had subconsciously collected since yesterday; Abe Johnson, Bud's lawyer, Butcher the bartender, and Avery Lyons, the fiancé of one of the murdered women. With Molly's help and chatter, he pinpointed them all. For what it was worth.

They returned to the motel in time for lunch. As Maggie trapped and seated the kids one by one, she complained that Howard had gone with the sheriff to look into a report of vandalism. In his place at the head of the table, Jared toyed with a salad with hardboiled eggs, carrots, onions, and vinegar on the side. He picked out the onions and ignored the vinegar.

"Wouldn't it be fun to look up some people, Jared?" Maggie asked perkily. "You could ask them over here; the lobby's a great place to sit and gab."

"Like who?" He was enormously skeptical at the thought of entertaining anyone from here on purpose.

"I don't know…how about Terry Anders, or Mike Butcher? They're both still in town."

"I ran into Mike at Stony Creek last night. He said Terry would be there tonight, so maybe I'll see them."

"Oh, good!" Maggie smiled. "If I was a night owl, I'd go with you! Say, how about taking Marsha Elleson McNally? I mentioned to her that you were in town, and she'd love to see you. She's divorced with three kids, and a terrific cook."

"I'm not making any plans, Maggie," he said with finality. "I'm on vacation."

CHAPTER

10

LESLIE'S PETS WAS ON Main Street, a few doors down from the tobacco and magazine shop that had always stocked the latest comic books. After parking, Jared studied the sign, briefly wondering about this side of Les.

She had been seventeen when they had left Shady Rock, just five years older than his niece Molly. Although Chicago had frightened her, Les had been the first to land a job, in the Chinese restaurant below their first, one room apartment. He could still smell it. They had both worked steadily over the next four years in several places, but none of her jobs had had anything to do with animals. He had brought home a starving alley cat once, but it hadn't stayed around long after receiving a bath and dinner. Les hadn't been heartbroken to see it go. A true farmer's daughter, she had believed that animals belonged outside.

How had she ended up with this kind of business? Not only had he forgotten her, Jared began to wonder if he had ever really known her.

He legally parked on the diagonal, risking the fenders of the Porsche due to lack of spaces. After putting out his cigarette, he went looking for Leslie's sole employee. From the reports, he knew that Abigail Olson had worked for Leslie for almost five years. She was single, ten years younger than him, and lived in an apartment close to downtown. Her parents were dead; her siblings scattered. She had been interviewed extensively since Leslie's death, but Jared was at loose ends, unable to think of anything more constructive to do until Griffin let go of his iron sense of duty.

He had let Bud annoy the hell out of him, collided uselessly with Lyle Doherty, and was living a big so what when it came to those damned burglaries he couldn't talk Griffin out of. He had learned that he wasn't much attuned to giggly little girls, and that he could care less that Larry Doherty liked to gamble. Events were not only not unfolding, they were welded at the joints.

Feeling uncharacteristically incompetent, he opened the film-darkened glass door and was face to surprised face with a scarlet macaw. It bobbed and weaved on an open perch, fixing him with a baleful glare not unlike Bud's. After ruffling its glowing feathers at him, it went back to crumbling a dog biscuit between its huge beak and scaly foot. Jared took a cautious step past the perch and tripped over a large baggy black puppy on its back on the doormat. It didn't move. After suspiciously checking its breathing, he ventured further with a more careful tread.

The store was spotless, but cluttered with racks and bins, shelving and pegboard. Displays of stacked birdcages and aquariums were piled everywhere. He passed the jumbled counter, following a narrow, crooked aisle to the center of the store. A large tank stood there, filled with coffee-colored water and long, spindly plants anchored in dark sand. It took him a moment to locate the inhabitants, they blended in so well. The palm-sized fish seemed to be hanging in a swimming dusk.

Looking at this showpiece, Jared couldn't help but recall the little goldfish he used to get from the dime store. The fish had come in a small plastic bag, two for twenty-nine cents. The bags had been stapled to a cardboard stand by the cash register, where he couldn't steal them. His excitement of buying the little fish was usually dashed fairly quickly with their overnight deaths, but he tried it again each time the store offered them and he had twenty-nine cents.

One had managed to live for a long time, he vaguely remembered. He could see himself dipping it out of the dirty water into fresh with his cupped hand—still feel its slipperiness and cold wiggle. He had tried a painted turtle once, too; a tiny red-eared slider with a garishly colored shell. But after it refused to eat and slowly withered away, he gave up on them.

Every early memory he had caused a distant ache in him somewhere. No wonder he had never come back.

"Those are discus," a female voice informed him. "I just got them in. Three reds, three turquoise, and a blue. They're still pretty scared, so their colors are faded."

He turned, to the present.

"*Symphysodon aequifasciata axelrodi,*" he supplied politely. "Or a variation thereof. I ran into them in the Amazon Basin a few years ago. Those didn't have much color either, once they were cooked."

"Oh, yuck!" The woman made a face at him, as if she couldn't have heard him right. "You mean you ate them?"

"They were much larger than these. Pan-sized."

"You've been to the Amazon Basin?" she asked, tilting her head. "Is it as pretty as it looks on TV?"

"It's green and wet," he said honestly. "I was happy enough to leave." With his life, if not the skin on his back, intact. "As with most things, the reality is never quite as good as what we imagine." She looked disappointed, so he added, "It has its own mystique and grandeur, but I prefer not to wake with scaly or poisonous creatures in bed with me."

"I can't imagine why not," she said, smiling. "What can I help you with today? I'll sell you that nice Lab puppy up front if you promise not to make her your bedtime snack."

Jared didn't know about dogs, but the woman would make someone a very tasty bedtime snack. She was tall enough to look him in the eye, and nicely substantial where substantiality counted. Her straight hair was cut just below her ears, and an intriguing shade of dark red. It was brushed back from a satiny fresh face. Her eyes were storm-gray and, at the moment, sharp with humor and inquisitiveness.

"I met the dog just now," he said, shaking his head. "I could never lunch on an acquaintance. Are you Miss Olson?"

"Call me Abby. Somebody should have introduced you to those poor discus, then. You really ate them?"

"They're a staple in the diets of several peoples in Brazil."

"If you say so." She looked him up and down in open appraisal. "Well, sir, let me see...I can usually guess what a customer is looking for, but you aren't quite my normal, run-of-the-mill shopper, are you? Gerbil food is definitely out, and I don't think bird toys are on your list. Hmm...you look like a wild animal tamer." She shrugged. "Sorry, I don't sell whips and chairs."

"I don't need them," he returned readily.

"I'll bet you don't," she laughed again, folding her arms against the touch of smugness that had slipped out. "So, what can I help you with?"

"I'd like to ask you a few questions about Leslie Doherty."

"Oh, you must be her ex," she guessed, her smile fading. "Bud called yesterday, and said you would be coming by."

Of course he had, the dumb old man. Mentally coming up with several creative and obscene ways to gag the idiot, Jared still heard Abby's odd note of retreat. He had gone from intriguing to untouchable, just like that.

"You're not what I expected at all," Abby frowned. "Should I be asking to see your badge?"

"I'm not a policeman," Jared said, "and I don't have anything on me that would prove I was married to Leslie."

"McCormick, right? She said she changed her name from McCormick back to Doherty."

As he got out his wallet and a business card, he was wondering what had happened to the Frenchman who should have showed up in there somewhere.

Abby slid the card into her smock pocket, while accepting his open wallet. "Jared Jordan?" She looked up from his driver's license, as suddenly erasing her odd distance with a radiant smile. "What a name! Is it for real, or is it part of the image?"

"Image?"

"Well, yeah," she gestured with his wallet. "The gorgeous hair and fancy duds; you know. Do you put on the name when you get dressed, or was it given to you?"

"It was given to me."

"Somebody really had a way with words, then! Great alliteration." She gave his wallet back without snooping further, and took a deep breath. "Okay, Jared Jordan, if you aren't a cop, how come I heard that you're investigating Leslie's death?"

"Rumor," he dismissed. "I'm on vacation. But I can't help being curious—she was my wife, after all."

"Not a very nice way to spend your vacation, is it?" Abby mused. "Anyway, I worked for Leslie, but we weren't buddies. She was older, and had Jordan—" She stopped, looking puzzled. "Well, isn't that interesting. She named her little girl after you, didn't she?" When he made no comment, she shrugged and went on. "I'm just an employee. A good one, mind you; I know my stuff, but Leslie and I didn't go out for drinks or anything. Okay, go ahead and ask your questions."

"What about her second husband?" He couldn't help it; it was just so wrong. "The one in France? Did she ever talk about him?"

"No, not really. Just that he died a few weeks after they got married."

So the little fiction Leslie and Bud had cooked up to cover the paternity of the kid held up. Well, why wouldn't it? Complete indifference was typical of Shady Rock, unless there was something damaging or hurtful to spread along at the speed of light. But he couldn't help but wonder why they had cooked it up at all. Stupid, he realized with some self-disgust; so it could be used against him sometime, somewhere. Like now. Typical Bud, but not so typical Leslie. Not the Leslie he had known.

"The thing is," Abby went on unhappily, "she brought up your name about a week before she died. That's how I knew it was McCormick. We had been saying how scared we were because of the murders, and she mentioned she wished she knew how to get a hold of you. I think she might have tried, if she had been given the chance."

Jared flatly refused to entertain that invitation to guilt. It wasn't his fault Leslie was currently dead; he had literally, tearfully begged her to stay, all those years ago. "She wouldn't have found me," he stated. "I was out of the country – just got back."

"But you were a policeman, right?" Abby asked, as if suddenly doubting everything about him. "Sometime?"

"I was in law enforcement for several years," he replied, "in one capacity or another. Read my card; I'm a businessman now."

"A businessman?" she repeated even more dubiously. "No, that can't be! According to the grapevine, a god has come to earth to save humanity, and he miraculously ended up here in Shady Rock." She grinned. "The impression I got was that you're kind of a cross between Batman, Mad Max, and Dirty Harry."

"That's ridiculous," he snorted his annoyance. "While I might be a miracle, I don't own a single cape."

"Being a miracle, you shouldn't need one," she pointed out, "should you?" Then she wrinkled her nose. "Were you really married to Leslie? It's just that I can't see you two together. What broke it up?"

"She left me," Jared said with deliberate curtness. "And if I sound cross it's because you just asked an impolite question of a total stranger, Miss Olson. If you do it again, I'm going to take my whip, my cape, and my miracles and go home."

"Where's that?" she laughed. "Where you hang your cape, I mean."

"I live in Chicago," he said with cool patience. "I'm single, thirty-four, and mildly addicted to tobacco. I have to run miles each week to keep in some sort of shape. I file my tax returns on time, and give to several worthy charities—does this sound like Mad Max?"

"It sounded like a sales pitch to me." She glanced around as the front door opened and a small boy came into the store. "There's coffee in the office, if you'd like some," she said. "Excuse me; this won't take long."

As she walked away, something gold flashed on her left ankle, below her jeans' hem. Contemplating her snap assessment, Jared located the coffee pot among samples of dog chews and fish food, on the messy office desk. A row of mismatched but clean mugs stood on a shelf that also contained a cracked aquarium and a coil of red leather leashes. He chose a mug that said 'I'm busy, you're ugly; piss off!', and squinted at the label of a small packet of what he hoped was sugar before adding it to the coffee. Without his glasses, it could just as well have been iguana vitamins for all he knew. He was still frowning as he stirred the coffee with a plastic spoon from a box of fifty. Sales-pitch?

There was a tinted observation window above the desk. He used it to observe Abby Olson catch a spotted mouse by the tail and deposit it headfirst into a small box. The little boy solemnly looked on. Then they laughed about something as she led him to the register and rang up the purchase. She came into the tiny office, and without looking at Jared, stepped around him to reach the pot. She smelled of roses. Lush, European cabbage roses—the size of dinner plates. In antique colors.

"What were we saying?" she asked briskly.

He contemplated the snotty slogan on his cup as he obsessed a little on roses. He couldn't avoid the perfume; they were almost shoulder to shoulder in the only space left by the desk, shelves, and filing cabinet. He leaned on the doorframe and she perched on the corner of the desk, giving him a good look at the thin gold chain on her ankle. And a nose full of something to plague him.

"You were interrogating me," he reminded her. "You had established several verifiable things about me, and I had yet to ask one penetrating question about Leslie."

"I'm sorry," Abby laughed, flushing a little. "It's just that I'm sick of talking about it. It doesn't seem to do any good; you know what I mean?"

"Then we won't. What will happen to this store now?"

She looked up at him in surprise. "Just like that? You're going to let me off the hook?"

"Were you on one?"

She blinked, then frowned. "Was that a tricky cop question?"

"But we've established that I'm not a cop."

"Well, I don't care if you're a well-dressed ditch digger." she said. "That sounded like a tricky question to me! How am I supposed to answer it?"

He shrugged, feeling his dimples leap unbidden to medium power at her expression of injured innocence. The doorbell jangled again. She set her mug on the desk and stalked past him, trailing fragrance. He finished his coffee and left the mug beside hers, walking back onto the sales floor.

He paused to look into a dry aquarium draped with sleepy-eyed chameleons. Their cricket dinner was livelier by far, under the heat lamp. After a few minutes, Abby silently joined him as he meandered around the store, his hands in his pockets. He looked at a price or two, raising his eyebrows in sticker shock, and walked on. The puppy was awake now, languidly chewing on its feet as they approached the door. Jared knelt to massage its loose ears.

"I'll give you a good deal on her," Abby offered stiffly. "She's been here two weeks, and that's too long."

Jared looked up from his crouch. "What's a good deal?"

"Three-fifty. She's registered; top bloodlines. We got her from a local breeder, so you can check out her parents."

"Three-fifty and dinner with me tonight, that's my best offer."

It was an impulse; he was getting used to them.

"Dinner with—?" Abby looked at him with surprise that turned to ironic doubt. "Are we going to eat the dog?"

Cute. He didn't smile. "What kind of food does the Stony Creek Bar and Grill serve these days?" he asked.

"Steak and eggs for breakfast, steak sandwiches for lunch and steak for dinner," she shot back. "It's a grill; what do you expect?"

This time, his dimples escaped altogether, and he barely smothered a chuckle. Damn, what was this? He was used to instant attraction, but he was rarely the one attracted. He heard himself getting almost pushy, for him. "How about it?"

She looked at him trying to keep the puppy from shedding on his jacket and shook her head. "You don't want that dog," she said. "She's a great dog, but I don't see you out slopping around in the back yard, throwing a Frisbee for her. You'd have one with its nose in the air—a Saluki or an Afghan hound, something a whole lot more like you."

"What can you possibly know about me?" he actually laughed as he stood, dusting off his hands.

"Are you kidding?" she laughed right back. "You don't exactly hide anything, do you? If you don't have at least one full-length mirror in every room at home, I'd be surprised. You'd be the kind of guy who pouts when you aren't pampered, asks way too much of himself, and never does things just for fun, like buying this dog. You'd also be a perfectionist and a control freak—it goes with the territory."

Hackles bristling, Jared almost fell back a step. He had never been stripped so painfully so quickly by anyone, not even goddamned Emilio. And she was giving him a brazenly knowing smile.

"Did you get all that from the grapevine, too?" he demanded. "If so, I think I'd better change my advance man."

"It wouldn't do you any good," she hooted. "You're your

own advertisement, aren't you? Listen, I grew up with three type A brothers and I know all the signs, believe me!"

"If I promise to leave my mirrors home," he pushed firmly, "how about dinner? I know somebody who would like the dog. Several small somebodies, in fact. I wouldn't buy her if I didn't know she would have a good home."

Her smile heated up and he was staggered once more, this time by a long delinquent tingle. Goose bumps sensuously tickled his chest, too; a definite improvement over the deadness he sometimes experienced there.

"You're not the kind of guy to ask twice," she was saying, "so I won't be ladylike, and play hard to get. It's your vacation, Jared Jordan; if you really want the dog, she's yours. And you have a date. I'm warning you though: I'm a big girl, and I'm hungry by the end of the day."

Jared parked in front of the motel and, somewhat amazed, looked over at the puppy in its brand new carrier. The dog looked very woebegone, huddled in a corner. How well he knew the feeling. But he had obviously fallen for Miss Olson's flirtatious salesmanship. The mutt and its accessories had set him back well over a thousand dollars—his second unplanned major purchase in twenty-four hours. Not like him at all, as Abby Olson had guessed.

And he hadn't learned a damned thing from her, except that he could still rise to the occasion.

After Leslie's abrupt departure from his life ten years ago, he had moped for a while, licking his wounds and building huge plots of revenge around Bud Doherty. Going after the bastard hadn't really been an option, though—Les had left of her own free will and she had filed the divorce papers almost immediately.

But going without sex of some flavor had never been an option, either. He was the horniest son of a bitch he knew. And, as he had told Griffin, he generally preferred feminine appreciation directed toward him, because women had a way of keeping him amiable. For the last year or so, however, amiability hadn't been the problem.

He had been finding it impossible to get it up with *anybody* and consider ways of cashing out, at the same time. Instead of degrading himself by pushing the issue, he had slipped into a bleak box of avoidance. One by one, his lights were going out, and he had hunkered down in the dark—isolated, along with sick and depressed.

But since his plan was in place now, maybe he could poke his head out of the box for a minute while implementing it. It wasn't like he had anything else pressing this evening. And he was still tingling.

He cynically hoped Griffin liked dogs, because he now had one.

Later, he and Maggie stood in the living room, watching the boys and Molly wrestle with the rambunctious puppy. It preferred the cloth diapers the baby wore to any of the expensive chew toys Jared had chosen. It tugged and growled, its tail rotating like a propeller.

"I just don't know what Howard's going to say," Maggie marveled for the tenth time over the excited laughter, "but thank you, she's adorable!"

Jared shrugged. "He hunts, doesn't he? It's a hunting dog; how can he object?"

"Howard has never hunted in his life," Maggie giggled. "He makes me empty the mouse traps!"

The telephone rang, and Molly ran to answer it. She came back on dragging feet, fear etched on her face.

"That was Daddy," she said, gulping tears. "He wants Uncle Jared down at the police station right away! I...I think there's been another one..."

11

HE SHOULDN'T BE DOING this; he wasn't up to it in the least. Shooting the shit over the files was one thing, but attending a scene? He knew better. But maybe Griffin just wanted him there on the sidelines for show, or needed him as a prop. He could do that much, if it meant strengthening the bond he so badly needed in the interim.

As Jared swung the Porsche into the alley parking lot, the big cop came out of the building flanked by two men in dark suits. Seeing the pair ignited a resentful burn in Jared. In another life, they wouldn't be looking over at him now like he was something stuck to their shoes; he would have been one of them. Hell, in another life he would have been in charge of them.

Griffin pointed to the Porsche and said something as they split up. He got into the passenger seat and buckled his seat belt with fumbling hands. "Follow them," he muttered, indicating a black sedan.

"You got it," Jared murmured back, his teeth just as tightly clenched.

But Griffin wasn't pissed. He was on the brink of somewhere unspeakable. As white as anyone could be and still have a pulse, his fists were knotted, his eyes fixed and blank. Jared darkly hoped the man wouldn't hatch a massive coronary here and now—he didn't have time to come up with another plan.

"He did it again," Griffin grated. "Same story. Must have happened this morning. Her kids found her. Her kids!" He choked, had to stop. "How am I going to tell Maggie?" he groaned. "It's her best friend, Marsha."

Jared took a deep breath, suddenly rushing on his fundamental hate. It was just a name – the victim didn't mean a damned thing to him. But an innocent had been caught up in a madman's fantasy script; complete indifference to her death was not possible.

It took only minutes to reach the north edge of town. A mile west of the nursing home, a scattering of houses stood in a park-like setting across the blacktop. Their well-kept lawns were strewn with primary colored toys. Jared parked under a children-crossing sign, the Porsche resembling a coiled snake in the thick of more official looking cars. He had his heavy briefcase in hand and was out the door before Griffin had gotten his open.

This was not the way to a dignified death and a respectful memory. Intellectually, he understood that. But he couldn't stop. Bonding with Griffin had nothing to do with it – he suddenly simply couldn't stop the rage that was like internal iron filings stuck to the magnetism of the crime. Screw the sidelines; he had never been a prop in his life. This murderous prick was going down one way or another.

But he would have to work damned fast.

Squawks from radios and walkie-talkies filled the steamy afternoon air. Strobed by flashing blue lights, knots of uniforms, suits and TV crews stood around the sunny yard, conversing in funereal tones. Neighbors and on-lookers huddled in fearful expectation. Jared ignored them all and entered the house through the open front door.

A sheriff's shield flashed from one of the broad chests in the hall, but the corpse through the wide doorway to the formal living room commanded him; its orders blanked out everything else. Within two steps, Jared found himself surrounded by hostiles. He stood on tiptoe to see beyond matched state trooper shoulders.

"Anyone been in there yet?" he demanded over the general discussion.

He was physically shoved back and told in raised but polite tones that he would have to leave at once.

"But if it's virginal," he explained, "this is the optimal moment. It's clean—useful. Workable."

"Get him out of here," someone growled.

He suddenly frowned at the blank nothing he was getting. Jesus Christ, how many ways could he say it? Seeing red, he turned to the open front door that he was about to be ejected through, furiously surveying faces. "Griffin!" he shouted out over the crowded lawn. "Where the hell is Griffin, goddammit?"

"Mac?"

At an incredulous roar from deep in the house, Jared swung back around. He peered through the hedge of bodies that had grown around him, blocking his way entirely.

"Can it be?" he heard in theatrically exaggerated joy. "My stars and garters—Mac, is that you pitching that zealous fit all over the place? Yo, Mac, over here!"

"Torey?" he called out suspiciously.

Someone with ears? About goddamned time. Griffin appeared at Jared's shoulder from the yard while Special Agent in Charge Andrew Torey parted the hedge around him like a well-oiled chain saw.

"You little bastard!" Torey shouted gleefully. He grabbed Jared's offered hand and pulled him to his Kong-sized chest in a crushing hug. "You silver-tongued, sneaky little devil! It's been what? Six years?"

Jared struggled to extricate himself. "Andy," he wheezed, "let go."

Torey did, but then shook him by the scruff of the neck.

"What the hell are you doing in Ass End, South Dakota, Ace? It's not even close to Pluto, am I right?"

"Watch your language, son," Jared warned, reclaiming his hair. "This is my home town."

"You mean you were born?" Torey gaped. "Not assembled?"

"What are you doing here?" Jared scowled. "Last I heard you were in Boston. Who did you piss off?"

"Everybody, but shh! Rapid City hasn't heard yet." Torey's nod was solemn. "Say," he added cagily, "you aren't killing off your townsfolk one by one, are you? Christ, I hope not! I'd hate to have to give you a prison buzz."

"No, this week I'm on vacation," Jared said. He had to make a fast association here, get things moving. "Have you met my brother-in-law, Chief of Police Howard Griffin?"

Torey's eyes widened as he looked at Griffin. "Whoa!" he said, holding up both hands in self-defense. "I didn't mean to insult your sweet little town, Chief! I call every place I go Ass End, South Dakota. Really!"

Griffin barely found a nod, but Torey pulled the cop to his side and draped a comradely arm across his shoulders. Smiling broadly, he studied Jared, who leaned against the doorframe with his arms folded. He was already claustrophobic as hell, but Torey's comedy act couldn't be rushed.

"Now, Chief," Torey said with loud confidentiality, "I'm sure Mac's told you how lucky you are to be related to him, but let's be honest, okay? Inside that wimpy little body beats the weirdest heart you'll ever come across. This is one extremely odd human being; are you on my page?"

"For Christ's sake, Andy," Jared grumbled with some pained indignity. "I just got him eating out of my hand."

Agent Torey smugly patted Griffin on the back. "Forewarned is forearmed, huh? I just did my good deed for the day."

"Fuck you." Jared pushed off from the doorframe. His

back was sweat-soaked, his belly incandescent. "What about my good deed? You want it or not?"

Andrew Torey rubbed his hands together, his eyes suddenly greedily crawling all over him. "See, what we have here is pure nonsense, Chief Griffin," he explained grandly. "Have you worked with Mac before? No? Well, prepare yourself for the silliest method of investigating you'll ever come across! While he tippy-toes around the deceased, does the spaceman see blood and guts and shit, like us humans would? No, sir! He doesn't see what is; he sees what was. This little screwball has a trick of getting his yummy little ass right inside an incident and becoming an integral part of it." Torey shook his head. "I personally don't believe in voodoo, but he has it bad."

"Yes, I think I've seen that," Griffin conceded somewhat dully.

"Excellent!" Torey guffawed. "Then you won't think I've slipped a cog if I turn him loose in there." He boomed expansively to Jared, "Have at it, son! I hear my next advancement calling already. But listen; there's a meeting of the really great minds going on in the next room, and mine is surely missed. If not before, see you in hell, right?"

He nodded genially at Griffin and melted back into the crowd, which was now looking at Jared with outright, muttering, disbelief. The SAC had just handed the longhaired interloper the keys to the investigation. Although Griffin had to be shriveling inwardly at the serious rupture in procedure, he staunchly turned to Jared.

Jared ignored him, and the poisonous atmosphere. He lost touch with everything around him as he crouched in front of his briefcase. He unlocked it and removed gloves, plastic overalls, and shoe covers. Before putting them on, he stuck a micro-cassette recorder into his jacket pocket and clipped the tiny stalk mike to his lapel. He shook out his hair, then quickly tied it back with a leather thong and stuffed it down his jacket collar. He dressed in plastic, then threaded his way through close-packed bodies to the doorway, tensing further.

Don't do it, he kept hearing from somewhere far away; you know better. But he was shaking in anticipation…it had been so damned long. Griffin was beside him, looking distinctly freaked. Jared elbowed him back to avoid escalating his own anxiety, then stepped into the murder room at the far left. After dating the tape and identifying himself, the time, and his present location—including state, county, city, address and room—he began speaking non-stop into the mike. He paid no attention to the argument that had broken out by the door with some new arrivals; he dove deep into his purpose in life.

Working toward the body by inches, he at first stayed to the outer-most edge of the room. He stooped several times to scrutinize the rug. In the sunlight shafting through the bay window, he spotted a longish pale hair four steps in. He didn't give a shit about evidence just anyone could collect, but he used a plastic evidence bag to cover it anyway, after marking the bag with his initials.

When he reached the corpse, he stood still. His eyes dissected the table, the sofa, the floor, and the body into separate pieces of the whole, and he minutely and obediently logged as many details as were there.

With that very small part of his brain, he told the recorder that the table was polished cherry veneer, no visible finger-prints no matter which way the sun hit it. It was neat with magazines and a clean ashtray. The floral couch had loose cushions on the back. One of them had fallen forward. He located another hair—dark this time—on the arm of the couch, and treated it as he had the first.

The charcoal-colored carpet under and around the body was blood-soaked black, but not as severely as it would have been had she been alive when put through the drill. Yes, indeedy; toasted, then assaulted.

Jared remembered Marsha McNally, nee Elleson, as

a pleasant, serious girl of Maggie's age, president of her senior class and editor of the school paper. The face he was describing now didn't much resemble that memory. The eyes were bloodshot scarlet, her skin mottled and swollen with the force of the strangulation. Her larynx was obviously crushed, as was her trachea.

She lay on her left side, but was twisted flat at the waist. Her jeans, panties, bra, and shirt had been bundled under her buttocks, raising them from the floor. Jared circled her in a slow crouch. Using his gloved fingertips on the rug to balance, he examined the surface of her spattered marble skin. A tiny scrap of something he couldn't identify was under her left elbow. He scribbled on another bag, stretching to place it close by. Her legs were spread, not out-flung, but actually positioned. There were scuff marks in the congealed nap of the carpet where the killer had knelt.

Jared stared at the indistinct impressions in the oozed blood, giving his mouth time to catch up to his eyes. The majority of his brain paid no attention to either. After one last lingering gaze, he began to work his way back exactly the way he had come, still recording for Torey. His hallway audience had grown, by now attending in silence. It made room for him as he stepped from the carpet back onto the hardwood. He didn't give anyone an invitation to speak; he was calculating and concluding: hearing stories being told by other killers on one level, his own stories on another, and this man's on yet another. As items from all over began to collate and drop into categories, he finally looked up.

"Who was first on the scene?" he barked, shedding his plastic skin.

"Um, I was, sir." Young Randy from the control desk palely and self-consciously raised his hand.

Jared bagged each of his gloves, and marked the bags. "Yeah, so?" he said with a preoccupied scowl. "Come on, come on, sometime this millennium!"

"I, um, I was on patrol, sir," Randy fumbled. "The call

came in at three thirty-three. I was told that the ambulance had been dispatched and would meet me here. I found Marsha's—um, the victim's, kids in the front yard with a neighbor; they had come home on the bus after day camp at the school and found her. They ran to the neighbors, and the neighbor called 911."

"Bathroom window was the point of entry," someone else grudgingly volunteered. "It's broken in, and pushed up."

Jared shook his head as he bagged the shoe covers next and scribbled on the bags. "Bullshit," he snorted contemptuously, glaring at Randy. "You didn't walk into the living room at all, right? Did the kids? Anybody?"

"No, sir," Randy replied with more confidence. "The kids saw her from here in the hall, and ran. I was told to secure the scene, which I did—the FBI hasn't even been in there yet."

Jared smiled his infinite pleasure. Bingo – the bastard was leaving a signature.

"No fucking way did anybody come in the bathroom window," he said with absolute confidence. He dragged his hair from his collar and pulled the leather thong from it. He shook it out, focusing on the ceiling. "I don't mean to sound obstructively cynical," he added, considering at warp speed, "but this bastard's trademark is to use a carrot to lead you around like jackasses. He's not breaking into these places. He didn't break in here. Take a look."

With Jared in the center, as many bodies as would fit stuffed the doorway.

"This is a spic-and-span lady, right?" he lectured fast. "No dust, no trash, no wax build-up on the furniture. Probably puts the TV in the dishwasher on a weekly basis. This room is not lived in; it's for special occasions. The carpet is immaculate, even brand new. I'll bet my essentials that she vacuums it on the hour. With me so far? Okay, take a peek at where I walked. You saw me; you can see my tracks—there, and there. You can also see where she walked through from that doorway across there, and then over to there. Look close; her bare feet are a dead giveaway. Toes dig in, leave little humps in the carpet loops behind the joints. Anybody seeing this? Okay, now look over there."

Ten heads swiveled in the direction he was pointing. From the corner of the doorway leading from the hall where they now stood, another set of flattened marks was just visible in the silvery dark pile. The scant impressions led to the coffee table, went around, and were lost in the carnage.

"He came in the front door, and it's a given that she let him in. Right into this little-used room...maybe to impress?" Jared asked himself aloud, staring at the far wall. "Is he that special to her? Yes. Was the timing special for them? Absolutely. Summer school; no kids around." He nodded, again with certainty. "Your take on him being local is dead-bang on, Chief Griffin. She knew him. She let him in, brought him to her special room. Not a salesman, not a Jehovah's Witness. She has the front hall or the family room over there, for conducting that kind of business. Okay...he's nervous, sits where she put him and doesn't move until he holds his own personal Armageddon. Not a smoker, or he'd have had six butts in the tray by the time he was through here. Not a heavy man, or there would be more disturbance on the couch."

Jared turned in sudden irritation. A distinguished-looking older man in a well-cut suit was crowded against him, breathing in his ear.

"Christ, back off, will you?" Jared growled, running his hand through his damp hair in frowning distraction. He was completely unable to relate to anything mundane yet, and he was out of time. "Where's Torey?" He switched off the recorder and swiftly bagged the tape. "Never mind, doesn't matter—when the SOC persons take over, give 'em these; they're all ID'd." He shoved the plastic envelopes into the suit's hands. "While they check under the other bags in there, somebody might want to mention that they should vacuum each of those tracks individually, and to look for something hinky on the backs of her thighs or on her hips."

The florid man backed away from Jared, holding the bags out as if they smelled. He cleared his throat, glancing darkly at Griffin. "Something?" he repeated. "What kind of something?"

Jared got lost for a moment as a demon slithered ominously through him. He was seeing spots. "Yeah…" He fell silent…no, no more time. He abruptly glared at the older man. "What do you need, for Christ's sake, an illustration? You want me to draw you a fucking picture so you can hang it on your refrigerator and study it, asshole?" He didn't pay any attention to Griffin's quiet groan. "He's got her on the floor, but she's a body now, right? Not willing and cooperative anymore, so he's got to help her out. She's up high across his thighs, her legs forked around his waist. See, he had to hang onto her somewhere, she's slippery and dead—don't forget fucking dead—and the most natural place to hang on would be her thighs right here," he grabbed the backs of his own legs, "or here," grabbing Griffin just over the pelvic bones, and jerking him forward. "Get it? If not, wait for the fucking movie."

He snatched up his briefcase while the older man sputtered. Others glared their astonishment or turned away in various degrees of shocked embarrassment.

"I don't care for your attitude, sir!"

"Fuck my attitude instead of your girlfriend, Grandpa," Jared snarled in haste. "Give yourself a real thrill!"

He parted the startled huddle like barroom doors—dashed out the front door and into the front yard. Griffin was one silent, appalled step behind, but Jared couldn't do anything about that. He couldn't do anything, period. The first slice of the unsheathed talons had shredded his lower back at the couch, releasing the noxious vapors and fumes of full-blown blood phobia. Simple breathing fanned the embers the waking demons exhaled. On the lawn, he blindly pushed past a clutch of noisy reporters with microphones for hands. He tossed the briefcase into the back of the Porsche, and lunged inside to escape the watching crowds.

"That was the mayor you were talking to in there," Griffin offered hopelessly as he slumped into the other seat. "I have to answer to him, you know."

"I don't," Jared said through clenched teeth, popping the clutch with a rough lurch.

The incinerator blasted full force now, igniting up his ribs and down his legs with a fury that made him fight a wilting groan. He drove fast and loose along the highway out of town—too loose for the machine's hair trigger steering; a front tire hit the shoulder, spitting gravel. He eased up on the gas, feeling more and more queasy. It was impossible to shift and faint at the same time.

Griffin was still muttering morosely a minute later when Jared slammed on the excellent brakes. He killed the engine in his breathless panic, skidding the Porsche to a careless stop. Stumbled out of it. Staggered blindly across the pavement—landed at the bottom of the deep, overgrown ditch, heaving six cups of coffee, half a salad, and a grape.

Then it got bad.

Griffin slid down into the ditch after him. Doubled over on his knees, hugging himself, sweating from the all-consuming pain, Jared instinctively went for instant annihilation—Griffin's, not his own. He couldn't have a witness to this display; it was the principle signpost of his mental condition.

But Griffin smashed into him, unintentionally knocking the Glock out of his bungling hand. Swiftly regaining control of his feet, Griffin grabbed him by the shoulder. "What is it?" he was shouting, the fear in his voice making everything worse. "What's the matter?"

Jared twisted away and fell into the dusty, razor-sharp grass, gagging and groping. But the Glock was lost, and he was lost too, in the torture. He curled into an agonized ball, unable to move. Griffin panted over him, his hands clamped onto his wrist and twisted in his hair—he had to kill the bastard.

"I'll get an ambulance!" he heard.

"No!" Jared gasped into the gritty grass. "Jesus, no—bottle…glove box…!"

A brand new, unopened, remembered, bottle.

He irrationally tried to crawl away as Griffin rustled off, but lost all strength in the wracking dry heaves he experienced next. They went on forever, leaving him dazed and gutted. He stopped caring about what Griffin was seeing, he stopped caring about his stupidity for attending the crime scene—he stopped caring. He wished himself dead a thousand times over, any way he could get it. His chest and belly felt like a molten lump of magma, about to split wide open.

Griffin came hurtling back down into the ditch. Jared was shaken as violently as the bottle as his head and shoulders were dragged to Griffin's thigh. He choked and retched and swallowed until he couldn't taste anything anymore. He wrestled the bottle and hands aside and rolled facing away into the weeds, hugging his pounding chest in both arms. Eventually, he could at least breathe again; the blessed, foul tasting stuff was on the defense. It wasn't enough—it was never enough—but it helped. Panting, he rolled to his back, blinking sightlessly up at the sky. This had to stop.

And it would, just as soon as he stopped screwing around and got himself dead.

"Goddammit, that sucks," he moaned.

He dizzily forced himself into a sitting position with Griffin's watchful, silent, aid. Griffin let go of his arm—took the clumsy hand out of his weedy hair. Jared saw fewer spots, but stayed hunched, rocking—waited, cursing steadily. The flames died by degrees, the pain by millimeters. Fifteen eternal minutes later, the teeth and claws had pulled back a little. The nausea he lived with.

"Hey, you okay now?"

Jared nodded at the intently quiet question, squinting

off down the ditch. He dropped his head, trying to loosen his shoulder muscles. When he rubbed his tingling face, he encountered tears and was deeply humiliated. He groped for his handkerchief, but used Griffin's instead when it was thrust into his hand. After wiping his face, he twisted the cloth tightly in his fists and took a deeper, ragged, breath. At least he wasn't puking blood. Yet.

"You sure you're okay?" Griffin pressed anxiously. "Let's go to the hospital."

Jared shook his drooping head, studying his limited surroundings and what was going on inside. And mentally yelling at himself. Jesus, he had almost shot the clown in cold blood—wouldn't that have been wonderfully counter productive to his goal of going out with dignity? Raving Lunatic Kills Cop.

"No, I'm fine," he mumbled, tossing his hair aside. "Fucking heartburn."

"Heartburn?"

"Okay, it's an ulcer," Jared admitted after clearing his raw throat several times. He had to downplay, and fast. "No big deal."

"It looked like a big deal to me!" Griffin growled. "This have something to do with your retirement from the Feds?"

"Medical, yeah."

Needing time to get a spine back, Jared fumbled out a cigarette, watching his hands shake. He looked at the cigarette in disgust, then stuck it in his mouth anyway.

Griffin lit it with a red disposable lighter, then took one from his own pocket and lit that too. His hands were shaking as badly as Jared's. "You should have told me," he chided gruffly. "I never would have asked you to…it's the blood, isn't it? I saw you go six shades of white when you got close to the body, back there. But how come it didn't bother you to shoot the Texans? No, wait; you refused to pick up the pieces at the ER. You have to be right on top of it, right?"

"It's much better if I'm not," Jared managed with a smile

he had never felt less like smiling. To shift the subject, he scowled at the cigarette Griffin held and then at the pack of Camels in his pocket. "Are you smoking again for real?" he demanded. "Jesus, I got you hooked again, didn't I? Some brother-in-law I turned out to be!"

"You're a treat all right," Griffin agreed soberly, still studying his face too closely. "From Pluto, like your friend said."

Jared coughed on a harsh scrape of smoke that tasted much better than mint-disguised chalk. "Torey's nobody's friend, but it was worth kissing his ass a little." He rested his forehead on his hand, his elbow on his thigh, and looked over at Griffin from under his fingers. "Don't you think?"

"Well, for me it was," Griffin replied with impotent honesty. "Even if anyone else had seen those tracks the way you did, I'm not sure I would have been told about it." He hesitated. "I'm not sure what you got out of it, though. What it did for you besides make you toss your lunch."

"Are you kidding?" Jared asked, still clammy. "You ought to see the way you're looking at me. At long last, I might add. Just call me phenomenal."

Griffin ducked his head, embarrassed. "You aren't very tactful, but I guess I can live with that," he said. "You are phenomenal. And that silver tongue isn't just bullshit, either. I'm going to listen to it, even if I don't understand everything it says." He stubbed out his smoke in the dirt beside him. It was apparent that he wanted to say something more, but the diversionary ploy had worked; he ended up only asking, "Want me to drive? I have to tell Maggie about Marsha, if she hasn't heard it already."

"No, I can drive." Jared hesitated strategically, then added, "But we'll keep this messy little item in our pocket, Chief. It's such an ugly blotch on my robust superiority."

"Sure," Griffin nodded, standing. "I understand. No problem. Here; you dropped your weapon."

CHAPTER

12

JARED PARKED IN FRONT of number ten, glancing over at the motel office. Griffin had just gone in. Jared was still telling himself how fortunate they both were that the cop wasn't stone cold dead. He would have shot him—no doubt about it. Paranoid didn't begin to describe his present outlook. But Griffin wasn't a gossip, and better yet, he was grateful now. Obligated, even. What he had seen in the ditch would stay there.

Inside, unit number ten had the atmosphere of a malfunctioning pizza oven. Jared turned the window air conditioner on High after he closed and locked the door. Stripping, he tossed the ditch-stained clothes over the chair. At the rate his luck was going, he would have to find a dry cleaners pretty soon. As he took off his watch, he saw that it was just after four—plenty of time for a badly needed lie-down before picking up Abby Olson for the impromptu date he now wished he hadn't made.

The shower's hot water was indecently soothing. He stood under it until it began to cool. His back ached, but it was a relief to scrub the dry taste of antacid from his mouth. He found himself lingering in front of the big mirror above the desk while he brushed his hair. Abby Olson's insulting comment about one in every room hung in the air, but he didn't leave it until the snags were gone.

When he had first begun to splinter like construction-grade plywood, he had earned a BA in Psychology in his secret search for answers—but had finally only worked out that sometimes the sight of blood meant nothing to him, as per usual. But more and more he ended up behaving like a rookie at his first fatality, fainting, puking, and generally unable to cope.

How could such a stupid thing have turned into his death warrant?

He had clutched at the straw of retirement, thinking that it would stop there. To keep from getting bored, he had invested a huge amount of time and money into the corporate challenges of ISC, only to find himself falling into insomnia and hyper activity, as well as buying liquid chalk by the case. ISC represented another weak straw clutched-at and broken.

It had finally come to him that somehow, somewhere, he had picked up a severe case of battle neurosis, something that could only be chipped away with serious rehabilitation and therapy—in short, spending years erasing everything he was and becoming someone else. Which was preposterous. And depressing with a capitol D. He would die first. Somehow.

After putting on clean boxers, he stretched out on the bed and listened to violins over the rattle of the air conditioner.

Abby Olsen ordered the special, barbecued ribs with a tossed salad. Jared closed the menu after a quick, blurred, scan. He could have read it with some effort, but didn't bother. He had downed another dose of chalk before picking her up, but he heard his gastrointestinal man in Chicago telling him nothing would hold him for long, at the self-destructing rate he was going. Stress was out. Smoking and drinking were out. Spices were out, as was grease and salt. A bar and grill in a town drenched in blood was not the ideal place for him to be. He ordered a BLT with a mental shrug, and milk.

Abby wore a white, short-sleeved cotton sweater with a disappointingly high neck and a scattering of pink embroidered rosebuds across one shoulder. She had traded her jeans for a pair of pleated pants not unlike his own, and had on sandals with a small heel. In her earlobes were porcelain rosebuds to match her sweater. He wondered, as he sat across the table from her, if she was still wearing the gold chain on her ankle. He had dreamed about it during his short, useless nap.

She caught him looking and smiled inquiringly. At the downstairs door of her second floor apartment, she had been full of horrified questions about the latest murder. She had heard he was there, but he had put her off by saying only that the investigation was underway.

"Did your small somebodies like the pup?" she now asked.

"More importantly, she liked them."

"Is it a state secret who got her?"

"My sister's kids," Jared said. "She's married to your chief of police."

"Chief Griffin's your brother-in-law?" she asked in surprise. "Well, that's wonderful—he's such a nice man! How many kids do they have?"

"Five, but don't ask me their names."

"I wouldn't dream of it," she said. "What else should we not talk about? I'm sorry," she apologized quickly. "It must have been really bad. You're pretty quiet for a superhero."

He wished he was alone.

"Next time," she suggested gently, "you might want to think about vacationing away from your brother-in-law?" The waitress brought their food, letting him evade comment. Abby looked from her platter to his plate. "I should have brought you a few discus," she observed a little dryly.

"Not at the prices you charge."

He idly performed surgery on the sandwich, lifting the top toast and scraping as much of the mayonnaise from it as he could with his knife. He stacked the four strips of bacon to one side, and covered them with the tomato. He replaced the toast, then ignored the lettuce sandwich, drinking the milk instead. It was too damned cold.

"Somebody told me you haven't been back to Shady Rock since you and Leslie left," she tried again after a few minutes. "It's hard going home under any circumstances, but to come home to find her dead?"

"I didn't come to see her," he objected without expression, "and superheroes don't like to hear about anybody's death. That's what makes us superheroes."

"Uh-huh," she said, skeptical of his aloofness. "By the way, your business card didn't tell me very much."

"I think it's tastefully complete," he disagreed, "without being ostentatious. I worked hard on getting the wording just right."

"Ostentatious?" she laughed, raising her eyebrows. "I don't think I've ever heard that word actually used in a sentence! Anyway, I called the number on it."

"Yes?" he asked with a brief stirring of amusement. "Checking up on me?"

"Of course I was checking up on you. Who's Rachel?"

"She's the only true battle-axe I've ever met; she runs my professional life."

"Well, I asked her what International Security Company, Inc. is," Abby stated. "She took my address and said she would send out some material for me to read. Then I asked her what kind of a person you were, and she asked me why."

"What did you tell her?" he asked, hooked by the glimmer of laughter in her storm-colored eyes.

He suddenly wanted more than anything to be in bed with her. Not for sex—that would be too much to hope for—but for simple warmth and rest; a cocoon of comfort. She had both the sense of humor and the body for it.

"I told her I was having dinner with you tonight, and that I needed to know whether I should wear armor or not. Do you know what she told me?"

"Armor?" he felt himself smile.

"She told me it wouldn't help. She actually said that—it wouldn't help. Am I in trouble?"

He picked up his glass and wrapped both hands around it, hoping to take off the chill. "It's a matter of definitions, isn't it?" he asked, finally feeling a few tight muscles relax. "And points of view. One person's trouble might be another person's good fortune. I imagine it depends on how you personally define trouble."

"I imagine it does," she said, mocking him. "But I think she was just jealous, myself."

He felt himself smile again. She picked up her fork and resumed eating. He drank the icy milk, hoping it wouldn't void the antacid. Absent-mindedly nibbling a corner of the soggy sandwich, he looked up toward the door, where he saw some familiar faces. He grimly referenced a tutorial for Social Intercourse 101, and stood. If he didn't go to them, they would just come to him.

"Excuse me, please," he said. "I won't be a minute."

He made his way through the tables to the front door. Four men had gathered there, blocking traffic. He broke it up by walking up to one of them and holding out his hand. "Mike said you would be here tonight, Terry. It's good to see you."

"Jared!" Terry Anders whooped in unbridled astonishment, causing heads to turn. "Jesus Christ! Yeah, Mikey called last night and told me you were in town, but I just couldn't believe it!"

Anders had aged fairly well in fifteen years. Always large, his boyhood pudginess had turned to muscle and strength, which he used in his enthusiastic handshake and the slap on the back that threatened to rattle Jared's teeth. His blond hair was thinning, but he kept it short and neat, so it was hard to fault.

"Let me introduce you!" Anders beamed. "Guys, this is Jared McCormick, a buddy from way, way back! Wouldja just look at what he turned into? You look like a damned movie star! Huh? Oh, yeah; this is Andy Malone, Jared. He has a car dealership in town, and Jeff Warner here runs the biggest auto parts place in the area. And you remember Lyle Doherty, Leslie's little brother."

Jared shook Lyle's hand for the second time that day. Lyle sported a new shirt, but that was the only self-improvement he had accomplished in the last ten hours. His handshake was flaccidly damp and he looked like he was waiting for someone to tell him to leave. After borrowing an ashtray from a nearby table, Jared smoked while he shook his head over just how hard it was to believe he was back, and how good he looked. Ho hum. Leslie, the Texans and the tackle comprised most of the conversation after he discouraged questions about the McNally murder. Jared finally glanced over his shoulder.

Anders noticed. "Oh, no—no, no, where do you think you're going?" he demanded. "We're going to toss down a few; come on, I gotta to hear what you were doing before you finally remembered your way home!"

"I'm with someone," Jared said. "I'll see what she wants to do."

Anders looked around the Grill and spotted Abby looking their way. He punched Jared on the arm with a hard fist. "Well, looky there!" he laughed. "Forget how you saved Griffin; I want to know how you got that gorgeous gal this far! From what I hear, she has prudish streak a mile wide!"

Jared took the juvenile teasing for a little longer, then went back to the table.

As he sat, Abby used her napkin and put it back on her lap. "Old friends?" she asked sweetly.

"Terry was the only..." Jared sensed her thin cloak of defiance before he saw it. He interrupted himself to ask warily, "What?"

"I ordered you something different," she said with her chin up. "You were kind not to call off our date after your afternoon with the police, but your heart isn't in it. So I'm going to be kind, too, and pamper you until you get your dash back, okay? And don't worry—if you don't like what I ordered, I'll eat it. It won't go to waste."

Just then the waitress plunked another plate in front of him. It contained a broiled chicken breast, baby carrots, plain pasta, and thin slices of dry wheat toast. Not a spice in sight. Had it been on the menu? He looked at it a little numbly, wondering what she would do if he crawled across the table and curled up in her lap. He was so goddamned tired.

"If you don't keep up your strength," he heard her tease, "we'll never know how much trouble I could be in, will we?"

Suddenly, he was famished.

She casually took his hand when they walked into the crowded bar. He had eaten every scrap of dinner and, whether it was that or the uncomplicated way she had flipped the male/female cliché, he felt better than he had in days. No, not better, but at least less stressed.

When Terry Anders saw them in the doorway, he leaped to his feet at a far table, whistling and waving. Mike Butcher behind the bar saw him too, hollered, and reached for a bottle.

"Do you mind if we sit with Terry for a while?" Jared asked, maybe a little more humbly than normal.

"Not at all," Abby replied, leading the way.

Chairs were found, and they crowded six at a table for four. Jared didn't mind; he deliberately placed himself next to Lyle in case the sorry bastard found a need to confess to being a murderous vulture, and he tucked Abby under his other arm. Mike punched him in the back, and set a full fifth and a glass firmly on the table in front of him. He took Abby's order over the general din. For the first fifteen minutes, the saga of the Texans and the truck was thoroughly rehashed. Somebody brought up the fire, too, and when Mike came back with Abby's beer, he eagerly added bikers to the conversation. Abby smiled Jared into an accepting mood.

Eventually, he learned without surprise that Terry had

taken over his father's grocery store. He had married a girl
from the next town and had a couple of kids.

"Not nearly as glamorous as you, James Bond!" Terry
laughed. "You deal with bad guys, and I deal with bad potatoes, but it's a living."

On Jared's left, Lyle was an avid listener, only needing a
tail to tuck between his legs to match his built-in slink.

"Where's Larry?" Jared asked him. "What's he up to?"

"Screwing around, as usual." Lyle had had a few beers, and
it showed. Jared could almost see his tail raising to half-mast
at the unexpected attention. "Pissing Dad off, mostly," Lyle
added bravely. "He's married, works at the hardware store.
You know, Jared, he was mad as hell when Dad told us you
were here. You might want to be careful around him. Larry
always hated you more than I did."

He blushed even darker and collapsed in the small silence
his comment had created at the table. Then Terry laughed
like he thought Lyle was funny, and turned to yell a greeting
to somebody.

Abby's glass was nearly empty. Jared picked it up and told
her he'd be right back. As he worked his way through the
milling bodies, he was hindered by handshakes from total
strangers and received several comments that contained
fire, truck, or Griffin in their garbled, juke-box-smothered,
content. Waiting at the crowded bar, he saw a familiar green
Mohawk. The biker under it saw him at the same time, and
shoved his way closer. They eyed each other, with Jared
wondering where the rest of the clan was.

"Fuckin' tough mother," Mohawk told him miserly. Jared
waited to see where the weighty monologue was going. The
kid grunted, "Need anything, ask for me. Slade."

Jared ordered Abby's beer without taking his eyes from
the pitted young face. "And get my friend here whatever he
wants."

Abby welcomed him back with a smile, but resumed her
conversation with Lyle. To make herself heard, she had to

lean across Jared. Bummer; he studied her ear and throat, and obsessed on roses.

After one drink, intelligence kicked in and he pushed the bottle away. He was bored, though, listening to the good old days with one ear and a discussion on flowering bushes with the other. He was about to suggest departure to Abby when Randy came into the bar. The infant cop was oh-so-aware of his uniform and just as self-consciously looking for someone. He spotted Jared at the table, and made a beeline.

He leaned to speak close to Jared's ear, in the table-hush he had brought. "Hello, sir!" he whispered excitedly. "I'm sorry to bother you, but Chief Griffin asked me to tell you that there was stuff on Mrs. McNally!" *Stuff?* Jared thought blankly. "The Chief said to tell you to talk to him tonight if you can; he'll be at home. Okay?"

Jared nodded. He could do that, on his way to number ten with Abby where he hoped he wouldn't make a fool of himself. Apparently, he'd have to talk to Griffin, if he wanted to find out what stuff had been found.

As Randy importantly left, Jared smiled at Abby. "Ready to go? I have to make a stop."

"Sure." She picked up her purse.

He glanced at the rest of the table, seeing only normal curiosity over the huddled conversation, and Lyle's habitual cringe. "See you later, Terry. You guys split the bottle."

Terry was still shouting friendly obscenities about secret agents at him as they left the bar. In the cooler dark outside, Jared checked his watch. Ten on the nose; plenty of time to see Griffin before finding out if Abby was still wearing the tiny golden chain. Thinking about that chain gave him a pleasant quiver—weird, but he wasn't going to question providence, whatever form it came in. He opened the passenger door of the Porsche for her. After starting the car, he asked if she minded if he smoked.

"It's your health. Where are we going?"

"Griffin asked me to stop by," Jared replied. "It won't take long."

The motel office was lit up like a mall, as were most of the windows of the adjoining house. All the watts gave the low building a festive air. In the lobby, the two smallest boys, uninhibited, romped with the puppy on the plastic-covered couches. Faintly wary at the sight, Jared nodded to them and escorted Abby on back through the door to the living room. The other two boys had littered it with toys and games, and were now inexplicably hitting each other with pillowcases stuffed with crumpled newspaper. Griffin, Maggie, and Molly were nowhere to be seen.

"Wait here, please," Jared told Abby.

Picking up on his frame of mind, she nodded gravely. Following the lights, he walked through the dining room, into the kitchen. Griffin was slumped head-down at the table among the leavings from a supremely messy meal that seemed to have consisted mostly of potato chips. Jared stepped on a few as he crossed to the table.

Griffin rolled his head to one side at the crunch. He looked worse than the kitchen. "Hi, McCormick. I guess Randy found you."

"I'm hard to miss," Jared grunted, personally affronted by the mess, the noise from the other room, and the man's endless fatigue. "What's going on here?"

"Going on?" Griffin blinked, slowly sitting up. "Oh, the kids. Well, I had the doctor here earlier for Maggie. He gave her a sedative and she's sleeping now. We just finished supper and I haven't gotten around to getting the crew to bed."

"Where's Molly?"

"Babysitting. She'll be home by eleven."

"Chief," Jared said with an amount of exasperation, "you aren't going to last that long. You look like the ultimate in leftover, unrecycled shit."

"Thanks." Griffin sighed. "I don't feel that good." He brightened a bit. "Randy told you we got evidence off the body?

Traces of powdered calcium. The lab in Rapid is working on what kind. It was right where you said it would be—might be a real break. Good work."

"It would have showed up in the autopsy, but thanks." Jared flinched at shrill peals of muffled, childish, laughter. They felt like chalk on a blackboard, but he said. "Go to bed; I'll watch the litter until Molly gets back."

"I'd like to see that," Griffin snorted weakly. "They'll have you tied to a chair in five minutes flat."

Jared didn't doubt it for a moment, but Griffin was totally trashed. He had to keep him going even if it meant taking guard duty.

"Another ignorant leap?" he said disdainfully. "Just because I didn't put myself out to stud like you doesn't mean I can't get a handle on a few rug-rats. Besides, Abby Olson is here too; she'll protect me."

Griffin slowly nodded, his eyes deep pits of misery. "Well, I wouldn't have asked, but since you offered, thanks. But you aren't going to get me out of bed in the middle of the night again, are you? I gave you the cabin to sleep in, so you'll do that tonight, right?"

Jared tersely summarized the situation to Abby. It didn't help his disappointment any when she cheerfully took charge.

"Of course we'll stay, but these kids should be in bed. Do you want to take them, or start cleaning?"

Jared frowned down at the baby who grinned up at him, catsup-smeared and droopy-diapered. "I vote we wait for Molly."

"Okay," Abby agreed in a honeyed tone. "What do you want to do for an hour, roll on the floor in the dog hair, or hit each other with pillowcases?"

He frowned at her. "I'll do the dishes."

He went back to the kitchen, took off his jacket and rolled up his sleeves.

Thirty minutes later, Abby stopped in the doorway. "Well,

this would be a heartwarming, domestic little sight," she said faintly, "if it wasn't for the gun."

He was up to his elbows in sudsy water with a dishtowel tied around his waist. "No, now, get your terminology straight," he advised, unsmiling. "It's either an automatic or a weapon; not a gun. Get a towel or I'll shoot."

She did as she was told, and they worked in silence for some minutes.

"Nothing wrong with lending a hand," she finally prompted.

"I'm on vacation."

"It's your good deed for the day."

How many fucking good deeds did he have to do in twenty-four hours? "I'd rather put out another fire."

"You are. Is your sister okay, do you think?"

"I'm sure she is," Jared said, reaching for a pan.

"Somebody better get that guy, huh?" Abby said a little heatedly. "And soon! He's wrecked enough lives, and it seems to me like Chief Griffin's might be next."

"Without a doubt, but don't look at me," he returned. "This isn't my party, Abby. I wasn't invited and I have no credentials."

"And you're on vacation."

"That's right; I am."

He had had enough of being wrongfully poked in the conscience. What had started out as an impetuous notion in a pet store had turned into a prolonged chore. Bodies, buddies, and babies had gotten in the way.

He let the water out of the sink, rinsed his hands and dried them on the towel he took from his waist. While she found the right cupboards for the dried dishes, he put his watch and jacket back on. Then he corralled her by placing a hand on the counter on either side of her.

"Forget it," he said close to her ear. "I don't do floors."

"No? What are you going to do?"

"I'm doing it."

"Here?"

"Saves time."

"Um," she said, smiling negatively. "Your niece should be here in a few minutes. How about a drive in the country, then? I'd love to look at the stars."

CHAPTER

13

TURNING OFF ONTO THE first gravel road he came to—and then another and another—he worked his way toward the first of the abandoned quarries that were beyond the southeast edge of town. He parked on the granite flats, as close to the water as he dared go with the low-slung car. The moon spun a cool web of light over the gray and pink rocks, and the water beyond and below was blacker than the sky.

The three old quarries were two miles from the Dairy Queen, five from the Flying D. All three were deep, and dangerous because of submerged rock ledges. This one had been a popular place while he was growing up, regardless. His bicycle was at the bottom of this quarry.

"You aren't going to tell me that we're out of gas, are you?" Abby asked dryly as he switched off the car. "I'm not nearly as naive as I look."

"I sincerely hope not. But weren't you the one who wanted stars? Come on; I'll give you stars."

He led her by the hand over the smooth stone surfaces. Close to the edge of the final drop-off, he found a natural bench of quarried rock with a back to lean against. He dusted it off as best he could with his handkerchief and they sat, she already pointing out various constellations. Stretching out his legs, he put his hands in his pockets, obediently looking up. He didn't necessarily want it fast and anonymous, as he might have taken it with the skinny cowgirl, but this was becoming ridiculous.

The bright, warm night had a backdrop of muted sounds. Nighthawks, sharper than any high-tech fighter plane, shrieked and whistled overhead, snagging mosquitoes. The water made little kissing noises a few feet below their bench, and he could hear the breeze combing the grove of trees a hundred yards across the way. Frogs and insects chirped all around them. The shadowy air smelled of wet earth.

"Sorry?" he said, when he realized he had let his disinterest wander too far afield.

"I was telling you that Zuben Elgenubi is only visible when—oh, never mind," she laughed. "Where were you?"

"Listening."

"Not to me and my stars, you weren't. What do you hear?"

"Kids screaming as they hit the water," he said, looking down at the black shimmer. "It's damned cold. Mothers yelling at them to be careful. Dogs barking. Robins in those trees over there."

She turned to face him on the ledge. "You came here a lot."

"I did," he admitted reluctantly. "We all did. Shady Rock didn't have a pool back then. Before I started working for Bud, I made fifty cents a week cleaning the motel rooms. I blew that on the movies every Saturday. I came out here on Sunday."

Abby asked curiously, "Did Leslie come here too?"

"Everybody came out here," he repeated. Then he answered her real question. "I knew Les from grade school, and then from working at the Flying D. We started hanging around when we hit puberty."

"You were together for a long time, then," Abby observed. "Why did she leave you?"

He suddenly felt stupid—no, even worse, silly—sitting out here on these old rocks with this young girl. Silly, and irate; was he really going to try to justify his failed marriage to her? No matter what he said, she would just have another question. But if he didn't say anything, she would assume one of the worsts—had he been screwing around? Was he impossible to live with? He hated personal questions, because people couldn't possibly understand the short answers.

Looking at her, a light bulb went off in his head, giving him a clue to something he hadn't even been consciously questioning. His mother and sister had shut him out by making him supreme male in their female domain. They had really and truly isolated him from them. He had needed a net for loneliness—a guide to life—and at the first sign of attention from Bud Doherty, he had run as fast as he could to keep it. And had paid dearly for that need.

But without beginning at the beginning and explaining the whole thing to Abby—his barren home life, his early devotion to Bud, his rivalry with Larry and Lyle, the long, hot work in the fields and barns, the responsibilities, discoveries, and later, the complete bewilderment at how Bud treated him—there was no way she could ever understand why Leslie had left him. How could he relate with any meaning the incredible hold Bud had had on all of them?

Eventually, he realized that Abby was examining him closely in the silver light. He shook his head a little, dragging his hair back. He had no idea how long he had been lost in her last question, but evidently it had been long enough to make her uncomfortable.

"It was a decade ago," he said. "It really doesn't matter."

"It does to you," she said meekly. "Sorry." She asked, "Do you dream in color?"

He felt his senses fade, losing him in the reoccurring nightmare he had had as a small boy. He saw again a blind dog wrapped in coils of rusted barbed wire, its drying and dusty hide peeling off in hanging rags. It walked beside him down an endless dirt road. The dog talked to him, telling him significant, ponderous things in a deep voice. Although he could never bring those conversations back in his waking hours, they were every bit as terrifying as the image of the dead or dying dog.

He had had the dream many times throughout his prepubescent years—long before he had been forced to kill the old dog with the shovel—but had stopped calling out in fear for his mother or sister after the third or fourth time. They couldn't help him; they couldn't keep him from having the dream. Nobody could.

"You know," Abby said confidentially, "what you say is interesting, but what you don't say is driving me crazy. I feel like somebody gave me a book, a really nice, unusual book—but when I open it, lots of the pages are blank."

He decided to light a cigarette instead of attempting to take on that absurd parallelism.

She saw his on-going refusal and mimicked his off-handed shrug. She turned her back to him, putting her feet up on the ledge and lacing her fingers around her knees. But she leaned against his shoulder, looking up at the sky.

He found himself being careful not to disturb her as he smoked the cigarette. Her back had become a boundary, and a mood was sneaking over him. In an attempt to forestall it, he made himself say, "Yes, I dream in color—and you ask the damnedest questions."

"Thank you. You smell really nice, by the way. I like your cologne."

"I don't even need a mirror to put it on." This wasn't working. He had to get up, do something. "Do you want to go swimming?"

She turned to look wide-eyed at him and then blinked down at the moon-glinted blackness. "You aren't serious. In the dark?"

"Why not?"

She laughed a little fearfully. "I don't know how to swim; I sink like a rock. Did you want to?"

"No, forget it."

The water looked like cooling oil, and some fast hard laps might un-kink the worst of the knots in his shoulders. But if he couldn't get her naked with him that way, he'd just have to find another.

She looked at him for a moment longer, then was warm against his shoulder again. "Do you ever wonder if there's life up there?"

"Mathematically, philosophically, or chemically?" he asked, field stripping his cigarette butt and tucking the remnants into a pocket.

"Good grief," she burst out laughing. "All that called for was a simple answer! Either you believe in other life forms, or you don't. Yes, or no."

"You're talking about accepting an answer on faith, not data," he disagreed. "Believing and knowing are two entirely different things. If you don't know something as fact, how can you believe in it?"

"Uh-oh," she said good-humoredly. "I have a feeling I'm getting in over my head, but okay; what do you believe in?"

"Myself." He smiled at her quick look of astonishment. "There's your simple answer."

"That's it? Just yourself?"

"What else is there?"

"Well, start with the obvious: God."

"Which one?" he snorted. "There have been hundreds—no, thousands—of gods throughout pre-recorded and recorded history. Which is more omnipotent than the rest? Which one should I choose to trust the way I trust myself? I know I'm real; I see myself every day in my full-length mirrors, don't I? Introduce me to one proven god."

"Okay, how about love and hope and—"

"Justice and the American Way?" he interrupted rudely. "Aren't those things only what I make of them? Use them in a sentence: I hope I win the lottery, I love apples, I have faith in the Stars and Stripes: I, I, I. I make those things real, not the other way around. As soon as I learned that, I realized that I have complete power over me; it's up to me to live the life I want." He was over-reacting; he could see it in her face, but suddenly it was of the utmost importance that someone hear him. "I know me," he tried again, more slowly. "I know what I need. Nobody can look at me and say, oh, poor thing; you have a headache. Only I can know that. They can't tell me how I feel, how I think, what I want, or who I am."

He stopped, shaken to the center of his soul.

He was perspiring, talking himself too close to the core of the matter. Who he had been, was this instant, was becoming, and worst of all, might have to be... He sat forward and lit another cigarette with a quick snap of his lighter. Then, needing to be free of her inquisitive eyes, he got up and walked to the edge of the quarry. A minute later, he heard her come up beside him. He took a last drag off his cigarette before carelessly spinning it over the black water.

"I'm being nosy again, aren't I?" she said doubtfully. "I'd call it getting acquainted, but you wouldn't. Anyway, stop pouting." She smiled, touching his chin. "I got us through dinner and babysitting—do you have your dash back?"

"And then some," he clipped, pulling her close.

A tiny red light appeared on the side of her head, zigzagged, and reappeared on her neck.

Jared lunged sideways, taking them both away from the precipice. He landed on top of her—heard the breath whoosh from her lungs as they hit the hard ground. She squirmed violently, trying to get away from what must have appeared as an attack. The report from a high-powered rifle thundered across the water and echoed from the granite around them. She froze then, but he scrambled to his feet, roughly dragging her with him.

The rifle was in the trees across the quarry—there was no cover on this side, but they didn't have to be sitting ducks. He half-carried her at a run toward the Porsche as something snapped past his head. Under the rolling echoes, he shoved Abby to the right, sending her sprawling into a shallow, weedy, gully. Chased by the third report, he dove around the Porsche. He wriggled his way to the front and from the ground, yanked the door open.

He eeled into the front seat, reaching for the ignition. The next slug thwacked somewhere into the car body as he released the brake. He crept the Porsche across the rocks—his foot itched to floor it, his mind sternly told it no. The car dragged on a lip of rock anyway, with a metallic screech that set his teeth on edge. At the gully where Abby huddled with her arms around her head, he applied the brakes and leaned to open the passenger door. She beat him to it, slithering across the seats until her upper body was in his lap. She clung to his neck, whimpering into his hair.

He couldn't tell where the next rounds went, but now the echoes rolled non-stop. He tapped the gas pedal, the lurch closing the door as he babied the suspension to the gravel track. As the wheels dug into it, rpm's climbing, he managed to shift with her weight on his arm. Moaning, she tried to crawl into the front of his jacket.

The Porsche vaulted forward, hitting the straight doing seventy. The county road was perpendicular ahead. He braked just enough to get across the built-up pavement without going into orbit. The car landed the other side without a wobble and he gave it more gas to glue it to the gravel. He ordered Abby to move to her own seat; he wanted both hands on the wheel. As she clumsily obeyed, he pushed it to 90. He kept the speed up until he'd gone six more miles, then let up, downshifting smoothly. The Porsche coasted into a tree-lined lane leading to an abandoned farmhouse. Letting the car idle, he turned on the interior lights to inspect Abby for damage.

She was chalky in the bad light, her eyes black with terror as they fastened unseeing upon his. Her hair straggled even in it shortness. She had a streak of dirt along her jaw, and the front of her sweater was snagged and filthy. There was a small cut on her forearm. He got out his handkerchief and tied it around that, looking further. He saw no more of her blood on her, but her entire right sleeve was dark-stained where it had been in contact with him. He looked down. He had met something sharp next to the car, sustaining a three-inch gash across his sternum. He yanked his tie aside and his outer shirt free, wadding the material over the source of the blood.

Abby openly sobbed. He switched his left hand to the pressure bandage. After getting his hair out of the way, he hauled her back onto the console and onto his lap. He hugged her hard, forcing her to acknowledge his muscles while he rushed on the pound of his heart. Her arm crept under his hair, around his neck. Weeping with child-like abandon, she buried her face in the hollow between his jaw and collarbone. Although he kept an eye on the rearview mirror for head-lights, he felt safe enough in the leafy dark tunnel.

The sharp sting from the cut on his chest was actually welcome; it counteracted some of the bitterness that was a bad taste in his mouth. Another lost opportunity, goddammit. That laser had been looking for him. But he couldn't have let Abby Olson get shot any more than he could have let Howard Griffin get run down. He was suicidal, not negligent.

When she finally began to shiver more than cry, he loosened his arm and looked at her face in the bright moonlight. "Okay?" he asked. "Anything you can't move, or feels numb?"

She shook her head, avoiding his eyes. Her trembling hands wiped at her wet and smudged face. She didn't seem to want to move away, so he tightened his arm again and put his head back on the seat. He closed his eyes to the emptiness of coming down from the adrenaline high.

"Was that him?" she finally whispered.

Him? He thought about it. Which killer had it been in the bright moonlight across the black water, the haywire wingnut who could only reach orgasm in a pool of blood, or the vulture who felt he had the most to lose under his daddy's new will? No way of guessing, really. Bud had tossed him to both, by flapping his big mouth. And if he had been alone, he would be dead by now.

He sat bolt upright, scaring her, and threw a nervous glance into the shadowy shrubbery. "You mean that wasn't your boyfriend?" he demanded. "Christ, then it must have been Rachel!"

Abby blinked at him in confusion, then she got mad. He laughed at her, deliberately feeding the sparks in her eye. She pushed off him, snagging his hair, and sat stiffly in her own seat.

He started the car. "How the hell do I know who it was?" he chuckled disdainfully. "I'm hunky, not omniscient."

"You saved us!" she gritted with tears still in her voice. "How did you know he was there? You must have seen him!"

No, the real question was how did the asshole—whichever asshole it was—know they were there? Jared didn't point it out, but that was the interesting part.

"Are you sure you're in one piece?" he asked again, more matter-of-factly. "If I have to start pulling up trees for splints, I'll have to get a better bandage on this."

She gasped, her anger gone. "Did he hit you?" she squealed, grabbing at his stained hand. "Are you shot? My God, let me see!"

"No," he said sadly, looking down while she unbuttoned his shirt. Evidently, thank whatever god Abby wanted to mention, his own blood didn't rile his demons. "Nothing so romantic. I think it was a busted beer bottle. I remember seeing the label."

"Oh, Jared, this is awful," she gulped, shaking her head while she peered closely in the dim light. "We'd better get you to the hospital! You need stitches; Dr. Lightner can—"

He frowned at her, effectively shutting her up. What was it with everybody and their urge to give him to that damned witchdoctor? "My shots are current, and it just needs to be cleaned up," he said. "It's almost stopped bleeding; no big deal. I'll take care of it."

She sat up farther, looking around. "Where are we?" she asked. "We need to get back to town and tell Chief Griffin!"

"Oh, yeah," he scoffed. "Tell him what, Abby? Half of this underdeveloped, uneducated, county is armed with one kind of weapon or another, and half of those get stupid drunk on a weekly basis. You want me to wake him up to tell him something he already knows? I don't think so."

He kept an eye on the mirror all the way back to town, although knowing the shooter, whichever it was, had never left the quarry. Their midnight drive had been spur of the moment, which meant they had run into an opportunistic over-achiever with an agenda of his own. Very, very, interesting. When Jared reached one of the two stoplights on deserted Main, he saw that Abby was still pale, but more composed.

"All right," she said, as if he had asked. "I'll do whatever you say. But, Jared, if you won't see a doctor, let me fix that cut for you."

"Now you're talking," he purred, revving the engine playfully. "My place or yours?"

But it still didn't work out the way he had envisioned it, even after they got to her place and she had put him back together with little bits of tape and a gauze bandage. While he sat on her kitchen table to be fussed over, they argued about shaving his chest. They argued about him needing stitches and they argued about what kind of a treat he would get, if he sat still for her first aid. She mentioned a beer; he pushed for a shower and her.

"I can't think when you look at me like that!" she complained, once he had trapped her in his arms and knees. Ducking her head, she held him off by putting her hands on his bare sides, just above his belt. "And after what we just went through, I don't see how you can be serious about—wait a minute; what's this?"

He was so serious about it that it took him a second to catch up. She had felt the knife scar under her fingers. She grabbed his arm and lifted it. Unbelieving, she moved from between his knees and went around the corner of the table, where she pulled his hair aside. He jumped down.

"Ain't that pretty," he said coldly.

"Oh, my God, what happened?" she breathed in horror.

"Nothing that concerns you."

He had been angry with himself for letting Maggie see the scars without warning her first, but for some reason, he was disappointed in Abby for having the same natural reaction Maggie had.

"That's it," Abby announced, surprising him for the last time that night. "I can't take any more; this date's officially over." She was handing him his bloody shirt and wrinkled jacket, the second one he had dirtied that day—that made all four since yesterday—and pushing him toward the door. "I didn't need armor for a date with you," she sniffled ferociously, "I needed a bodyguard! Go away; I'm exhausted, scared, mad, and upset."

She kissed him soundly, then shoved him out.

Slamming his car door, he felt like seventeen kinds of jackass for letting himself get so preoccupied with so many non-essentials. He had to get back on track. No, he had to find, build or invent the goddamned track, first—while doing his damnedest to keep himself together.

CHAPTER

14

THE NEXT MORNING, JARED was up by six. He showered and dressed in his last clean shirt, staring at himself in the mirror. He still looked normal enough, wasn't foaming at the mouth or gnashing his teeth. Just before seven, he bought a quart of coffee from the truck stop, brought it back to number ten, and drank some of it while contemplating the sunrise. After creeping away from Abby's like a scolded two-year-old last night, he had slept fitfully and woke up horny and hemmed in. This wasn't good.

The thing was, he was here. He wasn't leaving—not alive, anyway. That was a given. And now he wanted that woman. Maybe finagling an hour or two in bed with her wasn't essential to dying with dignity, but the whole dismal production was turning into a patchwork of chafing irritations that she could conceivably soothe. He needed soothing. Evidently, she needed romance—a midnight drive in the country, for Christ's sake? Whatever. But she also expected him to be selfless, daring, and responsible. In short, being as advertised.

If she had met him earlier, her expectations would have been met. But if she had, he wouldn't have looked at her twice—he would have been too busy taking responsibility to bother with such a high-maintenance woman. It was paradoxical that the very thing that she found desirable was the thing that would eventually kill him. He was taking responsibility, wasn't he? For destroying the threat he had become.

But maybe she would settle for just a nice guy. He could put on a show of being one of those as well as the next man. If last night at the quarries was any criteria, it would be a show with a short run, anyway. Something was starting; all he had to do was add a little fuel and close his eyes. He idly wondered which he would achieve first, her willing surrender, or a bullet in the back.

Griffin emerged from the motel residence as the sun topped the trees. Jared had just started searching the body of the Porsche. He straightened at the sound of the door, still holding his Styrofoam coffee.

"Morning," Griffin greeted him almost cheerfully as he came up. "Thanks for taking over last night, McCormick. Looks like you survived it."

"Survive—oh, you mean the kids? Not a problem, Chief." Time to put Operation Ingratiate into place. "Did you get some sleep, sir?"

"I sure did; thank you very much."

"You're welcome." Then Jared dutifully asked, "How's Maggie?"

"She's better," Griffin nodded in relief. "She got some sleep, too."

"I'm thinking about taking her shopping," Jared ventured, hoping he didn't sound too contrived. "I'm going through clothes like grain goes through a reaper; I was thinking maybe she'd find something she'd like, too." He shrugged. "Cheer her up, maybe."

"Oh, yeah," Griffin said. "I forgot to thank you for the puppy, didn't I? The kids love it, but none of this is necessary, you know."

Jared didn't want to adopt the Griffins; he just wanted to show Abby what a selfless, charming person he could be. "I've missed out on a lot of things with your family, Chief," he logically pointed out. "I'd like to make up for it a little, somehow."

"Well, sure then, go ahead. Maggie'd love to spend some time with you."

"And when do you like your daily revelation served?" Jared asked more smugly. "Before or after roll-call?" He started looking again along the side panels and front fender, running his hand over the gleaming paint.

Griffin began looking, too. "What revelation?" he asked. "Revelation of what?"

"Don't have a clue, really, but there it is." Jared crouched, inspecting the right back panel. He pointed with satisfaction at the smashed slug embedded there. "Interesting, huh?"

"What's that?" Griffin asked, a flush creeping up his neck. "Is that a—when and where did this happen?"

"Last night, at the quarry."

"The quar—I thought I told you to spend a quiet night in number ten!" Griffin scowled, all trace of friendliness gone. "What were you doing out at the quarries?"

"Well, Jeez, Dad, don't have a cow," Jared chuckled lewdly. "I didn't get anywhere with her."

"Somebody shot at you out there?" Griffin was still struggling with disbelief. "Why didn't you come and get me?"

Jared put his smile away. He equated the shooting with positive action, of course—but he had to remember that everybody else would tend to see it as a negative thing.

"My car was hit," he corrected. "I don't know what was the actual situation. Could have been anything from poaching to a high school six-pack party. Tell you what, Abby made me keep my shorts on, so you do the same, okay?"

Griffin stayed pissed. "You didn't see anything?"

"Nope."

"Is Abby Olson okay?"

"I got nowhere," Jared repeated. "Damn my luck."

Griffin glared down at the smashed slug. "Look, we both

know that Bud and you are making somebody nervous. Which one do you think it was; the killer or the copycat?"

"Doesn't matter," Jared smiled without meaning to. "He missed."

"So far!" Griffin huffed. "You will let me know if it happens again, understand? I'm going to be tied up in meetings all morning, but I'll send somebody over to dig that slug out. Any idea what he used?"

"It doesn't matter," Jared repeated for the moron. "He missed."

Griffin shook his head, frustrated. "How's your ulcer?"

"What ulcer?" Jared asked.

Griffin wisely returned to glowering at the car as he walked off. "I'm giving you a lot of rope, McCormick. I sure hope you don't hang us both with it!"

Thinking a dark fuck you, Jared wiggled his fingers in goodbye as Griffin drove away. Then he walked to the motel office. Little Molly was doodling horse heads on a piece of paper at the desk. She looked crushed and tossed aside, but brightened at his entrance. With an inward smirk at her adoring expression, he began to roll down his carefully arranged shirt cuffs. Operation Ingratiate plus small town grapevine equaled, hopefully, similar stars in Abby's eyes.

"I wonder if you would fix these for me?" he asked his niece. "I can't ever get them right."

"Sure!" Molly said fervently, jumping down from the tall stool. She meticulously tugged and straightened everything, including his collar and tie.

When she started fussing with his hair, he handed her his comb. "How's your mother?" he asked as she walked around him, running the teeth slowly through the ends.

"Awful," Molly replied, heartless in her concentration. "She just sits and cries." She stepped away while she critically looked him over. "There, that's better."

He located his dimples and agreed. "Much better, no

doubt about it. Thank you. I'm going to kidnap your mom for an hour. Would you mind watching the kids?"

"No, I don't mind, Uncle Jared," she said, surprised. "But I don't think she'll go anywhere. She's a mess!"

Maggie moped at the kitchen table in a faded cotton housecoat. Her eyes were swollen and her dyed hair stood on end. After he had given her a stiff, one-armed hug, Jared got himself a cup from the cupboard—one he had washed last night—and filled it with coffee from the pot on the stove. He re-filled hers before sitting across from her. Maggie continued to dab at her eyes.

He cleared his throat. "Say, Mags?" he said hesitantly. "I have a little problem."

He almost laughed at himself. How many times had he sat here and said those words to her in the dim and dirty past? He even remembered the exact inflections he had used. Pity poor me. Back then, his problem could have been anything from needing a five to take Leslie to the movies, to preparing the household for yet another visit by Neugebauer's gorillas at Bud's instigation. Now it was digging up some useful smiles.

"What's that, honey?" Maggie said obscurely.

He played with his cup, turning it around and around, then sighed. "I met someone yesterday..." He let his voice trail off and deliberately smiled a little into the cup.

"Really?" Maggie asked around a wad of Kleenex. "You mean a girl?"

"Well, a woman actually." He couldn't help the tone. Had she really once looked at him since he got here? "Anyway, I need some advice."

"Who is she?"

"Somebody who has a temper a mile wide," he said with studied wryness. "I pissed her off last night, and that's the problem. I'd like to get her something to make up for it. What do you think?"

"How about flowers?" Maggie blew her reddened nose, getting interested. "I love flowers."

"I'm not a flower kind of person, Mags."

Maggie was visibly thinking now. "You must have only met her yesterday—oh, Abby Olson! That's who she is! Howard told me she was here last night, helping you with the kids. My God; I couldn't even take care of my own—"

"You were understandably upset, Maggie," Jared interrupted before the waterworks could start again, "and yes; Abby is who I pissed off. I want to get her an apology present." A sweater, of course, to replace the one that had been ruined. "What about jewelry?"

"Oh, dear; I don't know, Jared! I can't think."

He nodded sympathetically, and sipped his coffee. "I don't suppose—no, this isn't a good time to ask. Forget it."

"What?"

"Well, I don't suppose you'd go with me to look? I don't know where to start. I'd ask Molly, but I think she's too young to understand."

"But I'm a mess!" Horrified, Maggie grabbed at her hair. "I can't go out looking like this. I have to get ready!"

"You sure you feel up to it? I could get flowers."

"No, no. I need to get out, don't I? Get a little fresh air? Wait for me; I won't be long!"

"I'm sure you won't," he said dryly to the empty room.

He asked to take the station wagon, saying his car was low on gas. Maggie didn't bat an eyelash at the ridiculous excuse; she was too busy questioning him about Abby.

"I don't know her, but I know who she is. What's she like, Jared? She has a temper? Well, what did you do to find that out, I'd like to know!"

He didn't bother. Even an un-illustrated version of last night's shooting would have negated his current effort to cheer her up and reduce some of Griffin's strain. Let her think he had been all over Abby, as he surely would have been before he had come down with the human equivalent of rabies.

After stopping at the dry cleaners to drop off three

jackets—the one from the hold-up, the one from the ditch, and the one from the quarry—the one from the fire had been a total loss—Maggie happily directed him to a clothiers down the block from the theater. In between being introduced to everyone she saw, he found slim pickings there—in fact no pickings at all when it came to what he had been wearing for the last five years as chief executive of ISC. But his tailor was 800 miles away.

He settled for a knock-off jacket, a couple of cotton shirts and a three-pack each of sleeveless undershirts, socks, and silk boxers. He also found himself considering a pair of stone washed jeans and a short-sleeved, V-neck sweater. How suburban. Finally, shrugging, he added them to his pile on the counter. Emilio, who existed for blue jeans, would have laughed himself sick at the thought of Jared owning a pair.

While nodding pleasantly to each new face Maggie dragged over, Jared held up women's sweaters until he found one that made him grin. He also bought a pair of Black Hills Gold earrings. To Maggie's ultimate delight, with his subliminal suggestions, she ended up with more bags and boxes than he did. He stowed their purchases in the back of the wagon, and listened to her animated chatter all the way back to the motel.

Molly's mouth fell open when her mother came in laughing and talking. Jared set a small jewelry box in front of the girl as he went past, carrying the brunt of the shopping. While he kept an eye on the kids and the puppy, all of which seemed to have grown since yesterday, Maggie wrapped Abby's presents for him.

"I'm going to borrow Molly," he told her. "I'll have her back by lunch."

Molly had crept away to admire her gift. He found her out on the step, the gold ring shaped like a horse head on her finger. "It's beautiful, Uncle Jared," she squeaked. "Thank you!"

"I'm a frog in a prince's body," he warned. "Don't kiss me. Let's go for a drive."

"But Mom—"

"Already cleared it," he smiled.

He looked to be sure that the slug was gone from the Porsche, opened the passenger door for Molly, and got in himself, reaching for the dark glasses. He parked in front of Leslie's Pets, and went in with the tissue-wrapped box. Abby was nowhere in sight, so he set the box on the floor behind the counter and left.

"Where are we going next?" Molly asked excitedly.

She reached over to brush away something non-existent from his new jacket sleeve with a proprietary air. He didn't tell her he was out to seriously ruffle some vulture feathers. Her role belonged in another scenario altogether.

"I thought we might see if Lyle Doherty's home."

Lyle was just coming out of the ramshackle barn when Jared parked in his yard. He looked absolutely unstuck at the sight of them, but sidled around the car to shake Jared's hand. He was back in his ragged clothes, and unshaven; the scared animal cringe fit right in.

Jared understood perfectly why Lyle's attitude irritated him so much. Lyle had had all the breaks, growing up. The son of a bitch literally could have become anything he wanted in the county—maybe even the state—with Bud's money and influence. Yet here he was, scratching out a living on a Green Acres farm and mowing lawns for others. He was pathetic. Jared found it difficult to picture him uttering a harsh word, much less killing his own sister or taking potshots in the middle of the night. But if he had, he could be provoked.

After Molly was introduced to him, Lyle irresolutely asked what Jared wanted.

"Just hanging out, Lyle," Jared said innocently.

"Oh. Okay." Lyle nervously jingled a pocketful of keys, an annoying habit Jared had noticed at the Grill last night. "You want to look around?"

"Let's start with the barn. We have a special attachment to barns; don't we?" Jared smiled broadly.

Lyle reddened. "Yeah, Larry and I chased you around Dad's lots of times, didn't we?" he gagged out as a terrified giggle.

Lyle went in first, almost scuttling. Winking at Molly, Jared waited for her to go in next, then followed. She stopped dead at the sight of the two horses that swung their heads over the stall doors.

"Well, well, what do we have here?" Jared asked breezily. He went closer, but not too close, to the first animal; a bright bay with a white blaze.

"Yeah, they're my vice!" Lyle giggled again, deeply flustered. "I've always loved horses, but Dad never let me have one at the D. That was the idea when I bought the place, that I could keep a few. Can't afford it really, but what the hell." He slapped the bay's iron neck with the first real assurance he'd displayed to date. "This is Ringo. The mare is Sally. She's an old lady, but still a great horse. I bought her for Jordan, my niece." The rapt look on Molly's face was hard to miss, Jared was pleased to see. "Do you like horses?" Lyle asked her tentatively. "Would you like to go for a ride?"

She swung around to Jared with mute but frantic appeal.

"It's okay!" Lyle said quickly, also looking to him for permission. "She's as gentle as a baby, really."

"Fine with me," Jared said as if it was out of his hands.

The two saddled and bridled the mare without asking his advice, which was good, because he had never saddled a horse in his life. As far as he was concerned, they were nothing more than a thousand pounds of teeth and kick. He smiled at Molly high up on the animal's back, hoping like hell she knew what she was doing. She nudged the horse with her heels, and Lyle went to open the gate to the pasture.

Then he fell all over himself to lead Jared into the relative coolness of the small, two-story frame house. The floors were out of square enough that Jared felt he was walking with a list, but the narrow oak boards had recently been stripped and re-finished, glowing as richly as Ringo's hide. The living room was an uneasy mix of Victorian gingerbread and Goodwill furniture. In one corner stood a gun cabinet with a glass door exposing a full compliment of rifles and shotguns. Most showed some wear, but one rifle was brand new. Jared didn't see a targeting scope lying around in the clutter of newspapers and beer cans.

They moved into the kitchen, with Jared murmuring inane comments as he was shown the new sink and plumbing, still thinking about rifles. Upstairs, Lyle carefully pointed out the new paint in each of the two bedrooms. He explained how he was going to tear out the entire bathroom layout and start over, when he had the time.

"Sounds expensive, Lyle. Landscaping must pay well."

"Pretty well." Lyle hung his head. "I take care of a lot of yards in the spring and summer, and driveways in the winter, too. People are good about paying me."

"Great," Jared said, thinking ho hum, let's keep it moving, please.

"It's nothing fancy, but it's my own business. I even have a helper, a great kid named Kenny that I pay to do some of the hauling and raking."

"Bud must be proud of you," Jared said with a straight face.

Wincing, Lyle looked away. "Well, you know Dad." He escaped back down the winding stairs.

Jared stopped him in the front hall. "Let's talk about Leslie."

"Huh? What about her?"

"She's dead, Lyle," Jared poked. "I don't like that."

"Well, I don't either!" Lyle stuck his hands in his pockets and the jingling started again.

"I heard that you and Larry were giving her a bad time. Which one of you needed ten grand?"

Lyle flinched. "You've been talking to Dad!"

"Bud and I have had occasion to yell at each other, yes," Jared snapped, "but let's leave the old cockroach out of it. I'm the one with the grudge! Answer the question."

Growing petulant, Lyle said, "We both did, all right? We were going to split it, if she could talk him out of it. I'm going to lose this place, but Dad won't lift a finger to help! He started out making half the payment for me, but for some reason he stopped a couple of months ago. I never would have bought it if I'da known he was going to do that! And do you know what else he did? He signed a new will, leaving everything to that kid of Leslie's! We couldn't believe it; it all goes to a kid! Me and Larry can't even go out to the D anymore. He kicked us out!"

"Why?"

"To keep us away from her, that's why! The old man's jealous or something!"

"Yeah, he's something, all right. How close are you to foreclosure?"

"In money, or time?" Lyle asked hopelessly. "I guess I can stick it out for another few months, but the bank's getting pretty mad." He lowered his voice, letting it lose steam. "Why are you asking me all this?"

"I was a cop, Lyle," Jared reminded him. "When cops hear things, they like to substantiate them. I heard you and Larry were on the outs with Bud, and I wondered why."

"Okay, I guess that's all right, then. Yeah, we're mad at him; I admit it. But listen, Jared, I want to help you; I really do! Leslie was more than a sister to me; she was a pal—I could talk to her. Back when you started hanging around her, she didn't have time for me anymore, and I didn't like you. But when I got older, I knew she had done the right thing by leaving. I should have left, too. I wish she would have stayed away!"

Jared shrugged, finding himself treading carefully for them both. "It's hard to break ties, Lyle. Especially like the ones you guys have. Leslie came back because she wanted to."

Lyle looked sharply at him, then away, nodding.

Excuse me? Jared asked himself as a double take. He could have sworn Lyle had just exposed equal parts of fear, guilt—and what? What else had been in that look? Defeat? Acceptance? It couldn't have been pity; could it?

"You mean the great Doherty name, I guess," Lyle was saying with a brave roll of his eyes. "I always envied you, you know," he announced with a stinging blush. "You were always so damned cocky! Larry and I could never break you. You'd just lay there in the dirt laughing at us. God, you were a fearless little brat!"

"You thought I was fearless?" Jared laughed in genuine surprise. "Lyle, I shit my pants every time you guys looked my way. I was not without fear, I assure you."

"But you wouldn't back down! We beat you stupid, and you just kept coming back for more!"

This conversation was lapsing into nothing he wanted to get into. "And here I am again, Lyle," Jared said with some heat. "So Larry needed cash, too? What for?"

"How do I know?" Lyle muttered uneasily. "Since when did he ever tell me anything? Listen, Jared, you don't want to get him all riled up. He really hates you! There was always this thing between you and him and Dad. Remember?" Lyle was almost assertive in his insistence. "Well, this makes things worse!" he went on emphatically. "Knowing Dad's talking to you, instead of him? Larry's taking that very personally. He's—he's said some things, and he's not kidding!"

This wasn't news; Larry had always taken Jared personally, and had always been quick to prove it. And Bud had always avidly listened to Larry's lies and had been swift with the punishment, the goddamned sadist.

The bare-ass whippings in the barn had stopped by the time Jared had reached twelve or so, but the hatred between Jared and Larry had just been getting started. When Leslie had begun to smile shyly at Jared, Bud had yelled at him until he was purple, beat the hell out of him a couple of times, and eventually set the cops on him; Larry had merely gotten perennially uglier.

"Well, thanks for the warning, Lyle," Jared said politely. "I'll be sure and keep it in mind."

As well as the rifles, the billboard on the edge of your property, and your eagerness to suck up to me after all these years.

CHAPTER
15

JARED DROPPED MOLLY OFF at the motel an hour later, her excited thanks music to his nice-guy ears. The Porsche had him in front of Larry's prefab house within minutes. Time for another poke with a sharp stick, but he instinctively didn't want Molly anywhere near this vulture. He sat in the car for a moment, looking over the ruin that was the yard. He wasn't seeing the rusty car bodies, inexplicable twists of iron, or the broken bricks that had once been a short retaining wall; he was still hearing that odd note of Lyle's. Fear, guilt, and what? Had that subtle look been defiance? Jared had missed it, and it was driving him to distraction.

He hung the Ray Bans on the wheel and got out. The air temperature was already well over eighty, and he felt a sticky dampness at the back of his neck as he picked his way through the junkyard to Larry's front door. The window air conditioner poking from a side window rattled rhythmically as it fought the heat. He didn't see a doorbell, so knocked loudly on the splitting veneer. He was in the process of lifting his hair with both hands to cool his neck and shoulders when the door opened.

Arlene Doherty turned out to be Lena Jacobson, another old classmate. He recalled her best working behind the counter of the Dairy Queen, slipping him freebie sundaes when business was slow. Jared smiled his blank astonishment; her, with Larry? Time or the marriage had not been her friend. She was going gray, and didn't give a damn. Her cotton housecoat was snapped over a body that had spread in all directions, and her bare feet were splayed under it.

"Yes?" she asked suspiciously.

"Lena?"

"Yeah?"

"Jared McCormick. We went to school together?"

"Jared?" she gawked. "My God, you shouldn't be here!"

"Good, Larry's home? I'd like to talk to him."

She hastily shook her head. "No, he's at work, but he'd kill you, if he caught you here!"

Jared smiled harder. "Just here? From what Lyle says, Larry would like to kill me anywhere I am. Some things never change, I guess. Mind if I get out of the sun?" He stepped into a stuffy, messy front room. "Bud's taking Leslie's death hard, isn't he?" he asked conversationally.

"I just don't understand that old coot!" Lena huffed, leaving the door open. "Larry would be more than happy to help him with whatever he's doing about Les. Why did he ask you?"

"Bud didn't ask me, Lena," Jared lied sharply. "I'm butting in all on my own, so if Larry's mad, tell him to be mad at me. What I want to know is why Bud's so down on Larry and Lyle."

"It's that goddamned ranch!" she burst out, her chins wobbling. "I am so sick of hearing about it, I could just scream! Bud dangled it over Larry's head for all these years, and then he just snatched it away—gave it to that snippy little granddaughter of his! Well, Larry told Leslie that it wasn't right, but she didn't care, oh, no! She was glad about it, in fact. Said it was only right that the kid got something back from the old man. The idea!"

Jared shook his head in feigned empathy, but he was actually confused. Did Leslie think the little girl should get the ranch in place of the father Bud had deprived her of?

Sounded weird to him, but just barely plausible. Except then why had Leslie left him in the first place? He would have been a father if she had bothered to let him. And she couldn't have known Bud would eventually disinherit the boys. Maybe she hadn't known she was pregnant when she left? He was confused.

"It's not like Larry didn't want the kid to have anything!" Lena back-pedaled at his frown. "He's a generous guy—he even offered to adopt the kids so they could live a normal life with both a father and a mother! And he told Leslie that she'd look better to that boyfriend of hers, too, because Stevie Reynolds doesn't want anything to do with kids. But Leslie wouldn't hear of it. She and Larry had a big fight about that, let me tell you! I guess if that crazy killer hadn't got her, Larry might have; he was that mad!"

"Is that right," Jared said without expression. "Was Lyle mad at her, too?"

"Lyle?" Lena hooted, making his skin crawl. "Get mad? Lyle's got the balls of a scarecrow." Suddenly she was jabbing his bandaged chest with a thick forefinger. "You get out of here, Jared McCormick! I don't need the neighbors spreading a lot of talk about you and me!"

"Neither of us need that," he agreed wholeheartedly.

He drove back uptown, his flesh still crawling. But on his way into the hardware store, a yellow poster taped to the window caught his eye. He stopped and read about a carnival, his mind clicking through the wide array of possibilities the large black letters offered. Then, he pushed the door open and went to look for generous old Larry.

A few overalled duffers stood around in the musty, wood-floored store, retired ranchers gossiping with an old man behind the counter. After nodding genially, Jared asked for Larry. He got bemused looks and a thumb gesture to the back in reply. Six pairs of eyes followed him all the way out of sight.

Larry hunched under a long fluorescent light at a workbench. He was threading bolts into a heavy metal pipe, lining up the dirty, blackened nuts with dirtier, blacker fingers.

"Yo, Larry, my man!" Jared swept into the cavernous room and planted himself on a second four-legged stool at the bench. "I was in the neighborhood, and thought I'd stop in and see how it's hanging."

Larry glared at him with a look so like Bud's, Jared felt his blood pressure shoot up. He had a time of it, keeping his grin airy.

Bud's older son had turned into a pig, not a vulture. He was a hundred pounds overweight, and greasy—greasy hair, greasy face, and greasy clothes that fit him badly. "What are you doing back here?" he snarled with a distinctive wheeze. "Customers aren't allowed!"

"By no stretch of the imagination can anyone call me a customer, old son," Jared said with an insulted laugh. "Bud's been telling everybody that I'm working for him, but I'm not. I wanted to set the record straight."

"Why are you in town, then?"

"I'm on vacation. Why Leslie was afraid of you just before she died? And where were you yesterday when the last woman bought it? Was she afraid of you, too?"

"What are you sayin'? That I killed those broads? You're fuckin' nuts! I was right here yesterday morning when Marsha got it!"

"How do you know when Marsha got it, Larry?"

"Everybody said it was yesterday morning, and I was here—ask anybody!"

"Who's saying it?"

Larry re-hunkered over the bolt he was holding, wheezing like an asthmatic. "I don't know—I heard it more than once. From Lyle, maybe, and at the cafe. Everybody was talking about it there."

"And what about Leslie? What did you do to frighten her?"

The big man scowled so hard that Jared expected droplets

of grease to come wringing from the wrinkles in his face. "I didn't mean to scare her," he grumbled. "I was just trying to let her know that me and Arlene should have the kids. We have a good home—not like her, the trampy little bitch. And not like Lyle, out there with his fuckin' horses. He probably does fuck those horses, he loves 'em so much. Why don't you go fuck them, too, and leave me alone!"

"Did you miss me last night with a high-powered rifle, using a targeting scope?" Jared asked curiously. "I figure it was you—you never could hit the broad side of a barn."

Larry came up swinging. He stood on the rungs of his stool and gripped the iron pipe like a baseball bat, aiming for Jared's head. Jared ducked, then drove a right uppercut from the soles of his Italian shoes into the man's massive midsection. He immediately followed it with a quick snap with the heel of his other hand to Larry's flabby chins. He used his open hand to save his knuckles, but his fist had nicked the corner of Larry's buried belt buckle. At the flash of pain, he stuck his knuckle in his mouth as Larry hit the floor.

Jared was satisfied. He had found a killer, yes indeedy—and had righteously provoked him.

He got off the stool and checked Larry's breathing. Wouldn't that be the ultimate in sucks-to-be-me, to finally have found a mechanism for his death, only to break it before it could be used? But it had been like slugging a side of raw beef; Jared knew he hadn't done much damage from the shaky stool. He righted the other stool, set the iron bar on the bench and left. He was still sucking his knuckle when he walked out from under the six bemused stares, into the sunshine.

Over a cup of truly good coffee in the tiny cafe next door, he came up with several possible plots that might work to get both him dead and Larry caught. He had to be careful to get those two things in the right order, however. He shook his head over the complexities involved.

"You could at least let me ask if I can sit before you turn me down."

He looked up. Abby stood with her hand on the back of the chair opposite his. She was wearing her work smock, but it was unbuttoned, showing the new sweater. The low-cut neckline in turn showed her. She also wore the earrings and a softened air of uncertainty. He sat back, feasting on the view while she blushed around a well? smile. Then he got up to hold her chair. As she sat, he leaned to kiss her, letting his hair spill down her exposed front.

"You really have to work on that shyness!" she gritted, pushing him away with a nervous glance at the next table. "It's a terrible affliction."

"I spend an hour on it every day, right after my push-ups," he dimpled a nice-guy smile at her. "Thanks for wearing it; I half-expected you to throw it away—or at me—after last night."

"This?" She put her hand over the deep, delightful hollow he openly appreciated. "Why would I do that? Mostly you were wonderful last night." She blushed all the way down at how that sounded, but smiled sweetly at the people at the next table before continuing. "You have good taste, too, but you need to stretch your imagination a little when it comes to sizes. I told you I was a big girl; you bought a Small."

"But now I don't need to stretch my imagination, do I?"

"Sit down," she said with a pained giggle. "People are staring!"

The waitress came to take her order and refill Jared's cup. Jared lit a cigarette.

"How's your chest?" Abby asked when the waitress had gone.

"Not nearly as pretty as yours," he said gallantly, "but thanks for asking."

"Oh, no! What did you do to your hand?" Alarmed, she reached for it across the table, pulling it toward her.

"Is the answer to that question fundamental to the bridge I'm trying to build here?" he asked, semi-seriously. "Is it part of getting acquainted?"

She looked at him for a moment, her fingers warm in his. "No," she relented gently. "It's none of my business. But expressing concern for another human being is. My question should have been, does your hand hurt? Is there anything I can do for it? That's bridge material."

"It hurts like hell, but it's just a bruise."

She accepted his non-answer, but her gaze was impish. "Must have gotten it while you were reaching for your credit cards," she teased. "I hear they got another work-out this morning. How's your poor sister?"

"She's better," Jared said with satisfaction. The gossip mill was working just fine. "And the Chief finally got an opportunity to vent. You were right; I should have reported to him last night. But look at it this way," he smiled virtuously. "My negligence saved his men from bearing the brunt of his foul temper, didn't it? And, I introduced my niece to a new four-footed friend."

"Let me guess," she smiled back. "Another dog? A cat?"

"Hmm, bigger."

"A cow? A horse? A horse!" Abby laughed. "Did you buy it?"

"No, I was pretty sure Maggie would draw the line at a horse on the furniture with the kids. Do you want to go to a carnival tonight?"

"A carn—" she began, puzzled. "Oh, the one in the park?"

"I'll buy the cotton candy."

"It's for kids, Jared," Abby laughed again. "Little munchkins. Why on earth do you want to go to that?"

"I dig the music."

"Sure," she helplessly gave in. "If that's your idea of a good time."

After her lunch break he walked her across the street. He kept her laughing on the sidewalk until an elderly lady tottered between them, into the pet store. Then he got in his car. What he was thinking right then meant nothing to his ultimate goal, but Abby would never agree to having it off in the aisles.

Tangled in some mental loose ends, he found the court-house and the tiny library. Cursing his forgotten reading glasses, he spent an hour at each place, taking notes. Then he stopped at the police station, only to find that Griffin was still in his meetings. Resenting that he wasn't a part of them, he asked Randy if he knew a green-haired biker named Slade.

"Yes, sir," Randy said promptly. "His real name is Frank Dotter. He lives in a trailer house on the east edge of town, with a woman named Patty. Sometimes he rides with a gang out of Rapid City, but mostly he just hangs around here. No wants or warrants, and no job. He lives on his father's social security."

"I'm impressed," Jared said, making sure he sounded it. "You know your citizens."

Randy reddened gratefully with a laugh. "Actually, I graduated from high school with him and Patty, sir."

Jared went back out into the hot sun. He made one more stop at the optometrist's next door to drop off his prescrip-tion card, then drove to the motel to shower the first half of the day away. Remembering almost too late to tape a plastic evidence bag over the slightly stained bandage on his chest, he stepped into the spray.

Afterwards, with a towel around his waist, he removed tags and laid out the gray short-sleeved sweater and the pre-washed jeans. They were perfect for a romantic stroll through a small town park on a hot summer night. Camouflage. He sneered at Emilio for sneering at him in his thoughts when he had bought them. He turned the TV on low, but unchar-acteristically fell asleep as soon as he hit the bed.

His watch told him terrible things about his self-discipline as he stumbled to the door. A knock had dragged him from a viciously pornographic dream that left his mouth dry, his expectations hanging. Abby stood on the step. She blinked at his pale blue silk boxers, but stepped into the cooler room and pulled the door shut against the late afternoon heat.

Residual degradation and prickling edginess clung to Jared like cobwebs, causing his already uneasy stomach to roll. Wordlessly, he took the jeans into the dark bathroom. He threw water on his face. A number of cold showers was what was really needed. He pulled on the jeans, immediately feeling strangled in their heavyweight snugness. Unable to shake the enticing repulsiveness and obscenity of the place he had just been, he went looking for his cigarettes. Abby had her back to him, hanging up his new clothes.

"I'm not late," he growled from a far corner. "I wasn't supposed to pick you up for another hour."

"I know," Abby said. "I called your sister to invite your niece and nephews along for the carnival, and she asked me to come to supper. You missed out. But I brought you a new bandage—when you wake up."

He scratched his temples, then massaged them, but the sleazy headache persisted, along with something else he didn't need right now. She opened her purse and took out gauze, a roll of tape and a spray can of disinfectant. She set them on the desk, turned on the lamp, and looked at him. He unwillingly abandoned the corner, bringing the ashtray. He dragged his hair back while she tried an edge of the surgical tape with her fingernail.

Unsmiling, he said, "Ouch," as he memorized cleavage.

"You should have let me shave the spot," she chided, her wrist caught in his hand. "Now how am I going to get that off?"

Already overheated from the dreams, the expanse of naked skin so close to his and its scent of roses brought him to exquisite, raging lust.

"That's the very least of your worries," he promised, backing her two steps to the bed.

He didn't sympathize, recognize, or even acknowledge

her angry protests – it was much too late for sensitivity or moral braking. As if he ever used either.

"We'll be late," she said flatly, later.

He hoisted up to an elbow, surfacing in an ocean of stupefied relief. "Christ," he groaned through the dwindling flash-burn.

"I guess there's a place for selfishness, after all," she observed coldly. She held up the stained gauze. He blinked at the wiry black hairs adhered to the tape.

"Didn't even feel it; did you?" she seethed. Then she said, "Get off me."

16

THE CITY FOREFATHERS HAD laid out the park to include a bend of the river. It also contained groves of old oaks and elms, a ball diamond with rickety stands but no dugouts, sun-blistered playground equipment, a stone shelter with a massive fireplace, and scattered green picnic tables and benches. The small carnival had sprouted up just across the wooden entrance bridge, but the canned organ music boomed halfway through town. Abby had driven; she had an older four-door Dodge with room for them all.

Griffin's kids lined up at the gate while Jared paid their way in. Then three of them scattered like shot into the considerable crowd. Young Molly trailed after her brothers more sedately, joined by two giggling girls her own age. They chirped over her new ring, and gave Jared shyly thrilled looks over their shoulders. He solemnly winked at them. Somehow, he had found himself in the tenacious grip of the fifth child—the smallest boy—who patently did not trust the noise and lights and crowds. In his baby shoes and shorts, he took three stiff-legged staggers to each of Jared's steps.

Jared hadn't apologized to Abby for assaulting her; he wasn't sorry. In fact, he had considered locking the door against kids and carnivals, and seeing how many encores he could manage—maybe he could stupefy himself into a fatal heart attack. Before he made the move, however, she had gotten away from him. Then she had guilted him into their date.

"Since I took it upon myself to invite the kids," she said coolly while fixing her hair in the bathroom, "I can't disappoint them." Propped on the headboard, he stabbed out his cigarette. "The carnival was your idea," she reminded him as she opened the outer door. "Are you still going?"

There wasn't any reason to stay in bed, now was there. And the carnival *had* been his idea, no matter how much he resented her jab. Never content to let things lie, his earlier strategy had been to tempt fate a little—to see what was happening to his goal in the light of a birth certificate and a small girl.

He had gotten up and gotten dressed.

Abby kept up a stinging commentary of her opinion of carnivals and circuses as they toddled along at baby-speed. She hadn't fought him off in bed, but her on-going hostility worked like car wax, tough and repelling. He still didn't apologize; he bought the baby cotton candy. They sat at a table just outside of the dilapidated little midway. Abby shredded the baby's candy, feeding it to him in small bites while she carried the strictly impersonal conversation.

Jared eventually spotted what he had come to see; two middle-aged men in working jeans and checked shirts stumping along through the masses of kids, mothers, and fathers. The pair was as out of place as pants on a skunk. Three steps ahead of them danced a little girl.

Jordan Elaine Doherty had gotten two of her names from her father and her father's mother, but her size and demeanor was pure Leslie. Elfin tiny, she skipped excitedly before the bookend cowhands who were doubling as security. She also had Leslie's coloring, but her coppery golden hair was nearly as long as Jared's. She pointed toward the rides, obviously asking permission. Jared watched her vanish in the crowds.

When the baby was done drooling over the spun sugar, Abby washed him up at the drinking fountain, using Jared's handkerchief. Jared carried him on his arm after that. Abby stayed with them, but she wasn't inclined to hold hands. The nice guy had fucked up, and she wasn't going to let him forget it.

They drifted through the noisy confusion, pausing occasionally to replenish dwindling funds for the other four. Once, at the merry-go-round, they accidentally came face to face with the bookends. The weather-beaten ranch hands squared off with instant recognition. Jared nodded briefly and walked away, shifting the baby to his other arm.

He caught one more look at the little girl after that. He saw her run her fingers through her hair and smile his own sunshine smile at someone else, before she ran off. Her dimples were like a stab in the back; it took him several minutes to iron the knots out of his jaw.

An hour later, he stood with Abby under the lights in the motel parking lot.

"Say something," he ordered, his arms folded resentfully. She had her car keys in hand, but he leaned against the car door. "Call me names and get over it."

"I already did," she said defiantly. "I called you selfish, you jerk. What are you going to do about it?"

"And you accused me of asking tricky questions," he snorted, squinting up at the bug-infested light. "Are you asking if I'm going to stamp my foot at being called names, or do you mean what am I going to do to make up for being a jerk? Clarify, please."

She looked at him for a long moment. "The thing I hated most about living with my brothers was that I had to put up with their insufferable arrogance," she said. "No, more than that, I had to find a place for me, in it. I did a pretty good job of that. I even learned how to get over it. But I shouldn't have to do that with every man I meet! Why don't you get over it, instead?"

"Being humble tops my to-do list," he shrugged. "It's right up there with getting over my shyness."

"Bullshit," she spat. "You and all the other arrogant men in the world are destined to be class act liars—it's how you balance the arrogance!"

"Terrific," he returned furiously. "You've now joined the club. Jesus, what do I have to do before somebody – anybody—in this fucking town realizes that I'm more than just a trouble-making prick?"

"Maybe that's all you let anybody see!"

"Oh, don't give me that crap about blank pages again! If they're so goddamned blank, why did you bother picking up the book?"

"Because the cover's so damned interesting!" she blazed back.

He snorted bitterly, "Yeah, and everybody wants a piece of me—you, Griffin, Bud, Maggie—I don't think it's too unreasonable that I get something in exchange!" She looked away, her jaw set, and he sneered, "Did you ever think that maybe those pages only appear blank to you? Just because you can't see or don't recognize a thing doesn't mean it's not there. Talk to any goddamned astronomer!"

"Shit," she slumped, her eyes glittering with tears. "But you didn't ask, you just went for it! You didn't even use a condom!"

"You aren't as naïve as you look," he sternly repeated her words from the night before. "You knew what was coming – and you'd never leave something that important to you, to a mere man."

"I sure wouldn't!" she vowed. "No matter how much I like him!"

He pushed off the car and held her by the shoulders. "I'm stuck," he said tightly. "All I can give you here is the Grill and a sleazy motel room. Neither of us like it, so make me an offer we can both live with."

The little girl was his. The birth certificate was blank where his name should have been, but he had seen her now and was convinced. The other child, the one born two months ago, also had a blank space instead of a father. Jared had stared for a long time at that birth certificate at the courthouse. Leslie had named him Thomas Jeremiah, after Jared's father.

Deeper and deeper.

If he hadn't come home, he never would have known. Not one aspect of this would matter; not the child with his smile, not the fatherless baby with the painful name—none of it.

But he had come home, and for a reason. The stomach thing could be controlled as long as he behaved like a CEO instead of a foot soldier, but the nightmares and lack of sleep were evolving him into a full-blown schizophrenic, and that was the real worry. One of these days he wouldn't know what he was doing.

He was tired of worrying. He was tired, period. He was dead tired, and that's why he was back in Shady Rock. He had to remember that.

She undressed him beside her bed—clumsily, because the nasty edge was back and his mouth and hands kept her off guard.

"I *was* wrong about the pages being blank," she later whispered in his ear. "I know wistful when I see it."

He stopped everything with an incredulous, savage laugh. He had been waiting for her brand of hurtful revenge, but this was unbelievable. "Me? Wistful?"

"It's very sexy, you know," she breathed. "Wistful Beauty and rampant Beast. Very unfair."

Sometime later still, he got up and went in search of an ashtray. When he came back, he looked at her in the light from the street lamp outside. It streamed through sheer lace at the two tall windows, putting a delicate pattern over her lush, languid nudity. Her gold ankle chain flashed.

"Wistful," he repeated, his ego still stinging.

"When you aren't wonderful," she murmured, patting the bed beside her.

He waited until she was sound asleep before he left the bed again, and gathered his jeans and sweater. Feeling good—loose and light—he went looking for his shoes. Multiple indulgences hadn't given him a heart attack, but they had focused his mind in a way that was as satisfying as the physical activity had been for his body. A few of his lights had come on again—for a while, anyway. But he didn't dare stay in bed with her. Between the insomnia and the nightmares, he didn't make a very snuggly sleeping companion.

He dressed, then drifted noiselessly down the stairs and out into the mild night. The Porsche woke with a snarl. He flicked on its headlights, freezing a dark-striped cat. The cat crouched, but Jared waited until it melted away before he pulled out.

He parked a block away from the yellow Victorian. Not that the car wouldn't immediately be identified as his where ever it was, but it was the only spot open in the sleeping neighborhood. He walked up the sidewalk to the brooding house. Insect noises chorused all around him, and he heard the rustle of some small animal in the shaggy hedge. All of the houses on the block were dark, but Leslie's looked even darker behind its dense parade of lilac. The porch was deep and black, so he went right up to the front door. He wore a pair of micro-thin latex gloves and carried a tiny, powerful penlight as he broke and entered a vestibule. The inner door wasn't even locked.

Someone had obviously cleaned up after the investigation, but Bud hadn't gotten around to emptying the house. Mechanically, Jared first looked in the dining room, where his ex-wife had been murdered. The oriental carpet he remembered from the black-and-whites was gone.

Moving like a wraith in the shadows, he began a dirty search of the front parlor. He tossed aside knickknacks and things that didn't interest him. He pulled drawers from a desk, dumping the contents to the floor and spreading them with a foot. Riffling through books from shelves and tables, he left them in heaps. When he had reduced the parlor to chaos, he went on to the next room, and the next.

He finished the downstairs, checking even the garbage disposal, the freezer, and the toilet tank, pulling aside carpets, and feeling along the tops of doors and windows. He had no idea what he was looking for, but it didn't matter. He was pissed at Bud, pissed at Leslie, and pissed at life, and raping the house was a safe way to work off the excesses Abby couldn't. He checked his watch. Almost five.

Running lightly up the walnut stairs, he found four bedrooms and a large bath. He ignored the nursery at the top of the steps, and went to the next door. Master bedroom. Ferociously, he yanked drawers, leaving them and their fragrant contents strewn. He ripped aside the bedding and felt under and along the mattresses. The bedside stands were bare except for lamps, a tube of KY jelly, and a telephone book. A lamp shattered when he up-ended its stand with a frustrated kick.

On a top closet shelf he found a locked metal box among shoes, sheets, and sweaters. He was allergic to locks—they made him itch. He broke the box open on a corner of the dressing table. Papers and photographs showered to the floor, and he crouched to shine the penlight. His shoulders slumped in dismay.

The divorce papers he had signed so long ago were on top. Underneath were snapshots, trinkets, ticket stubs—it looked like she had saved every note, every scrawl, every scrap he had ever given her. Why? He ducked his head and closed his eyes, his hatred of Bud Doherty growing by sparks and explosions.

Goddammit, he had loved her.

What had started out as an exercise in contempt turned ugly. A metallic taste seeped into his mouth and his bowels churned. He quickly shoved everything into a pile and scooped it back into the box, which he set in the hall. He tore through the closet, finding only an old receipt in one jacket pocket, some book matches from the Grill in another. The receipt was from the hardware store for a set of house keys. She had changed her locks, but it hadn't done her a damned bit of good.

The first room on the other side of the hall was for guests, empty and boring. Then he came to the little girl's room. He stood in the doorway for a while, suddenly uneasy instead of incensed.

It was a large room that overlooked the street. The colors here were pink and white, frilly and feminine even in the poor light. There was a row of storybooks on a shelf above the full size canopied bed, and stuffed animals lined up on the floor below the windows. The only pictures on the walls were of horses and dogs. There was a small desk by the door. He gingerly opened the top drawer to expose color crayons, pencils, and paper, then inched closed it again. His eye fell on a five by seven photo in a frame. He picked it up, and feeling a little panicky, shined his pen light on it.

Leslie had curled the child's hair for the school picture. It hung in waves over her shoulders. His own navy blue eyes looked back at him. With a quick breath to clear the staleness from his lungs, he tucked the photograph under his arm. After glancing around the dim room once more, he crossed to the ruffled bed. On the pillows was a tattered stuffed cat looking back at him with only one green plastic eye. Without thinking about it, he stuck that under his arm, too.

His gut was flexing viciously by the time he left the room and reached the broken metal box by the stairway. Claws advanced. He laid the photo on top of the divorce papers, and the cat fit on top of that, with a bit of shoving. Carrying the box, he ran down the stairs, out the two doors, and down the steps, into the predawn coolness. He forced himself to stroll back to the car, in case Leslie had early-rising neighbors.

Once in the Porsche, he took the half-empty bottle of

antacid from the glove box and shook it, mentally fortifying himself against the taste. He swallowed several times, gagged in distaste, and then waited for it to work. By the time he got back to Abby's, darkness had changed to dawn. Birds sleepily chirped, scaring insects into silence.

He locked the metal box in the car with his briefcase. Then, he changed his mind and brought both, along with the Vivaldi CD, as he sneaked back up the inner stairs. He drank two glasses of milk as he stripped in the kitchen. Carrying the third glass to the bedroom, he dropped his clothes into a chair, put the glass on the table, and got into bed. He lit a cigarette, wondering what the hell he had just done.

Abby stretched as she woke, then moved to cuddle under his arm. "…'morning," she mumbled as he smoothed his hand down her spine.

He closed his eyes, haunted by roses and hate and one-eyed cats. She sat up, pulling the sheet with her and shoving the fringe of hair from her face. He tugged the sheet back down and wouldn't let go.

"What time is it?" she yawned, giving up modesty to cover her mouth.

"Around five-thirty."

"Good," she smiled sleepily. "I don't have to get up until six."

He smiled back, saying, "Even better, I'm already up."

CHAPTER

17

Somehow, he slept until mid-morning.

When he woke—alone and dreamless—he burrowed under the scented pillows and blankets on his stomach and luxuriously dozed for a little while longer. *Then* he dreamed—of chains and horses and locked doors, and more chains. Their links grew from tiny sparkly gold to bloody unforgiving steel. He opened his eyes fast, feeling his wrists burn. There were no scars on them because he hadn't been given time to try to work his way loose. The chains hadn't cut him to the bone like the bullwhip had. Remembering Emilio's long-ago creative distraction, and his own revenge, calmed him down.

He hadn't ruminated on the disgusting incident of his maiming for a long time, but for some reason the chain on Abby's ankle had just stuck it front and center. He had dreamed chains—was now helplessly, obsessively seeing them running from him to Bud and back again, with Leslie, Lyle, and Larry dangling somewhere in between. Weird.

Fixations and preoccupations, nightmares, depression, jumpiness, and insomnia. Shell shock, combat fatigue, post-traumatic stress syndrome; whatever the condition was labeled, in the last five years he had become familiar with the basic concept to the point of over-saturation. And he had run out of both time and options.

The fact that Lightner had recognized it too was just another kick in the face.

He showered in the old fashioned claw-footed tub. The scent of Abby's soap lingered on him, and he thought of her as he dried his hair with one of her fluffy towels. He was a self-diagnosed sensualist, and she had put him in a state of fulfillment he hadn't remotely experienced lately. He would never get enough of her, even in the little time he had left. But he was damned well going to try. Pulling on the jeans while thinking these cozy little thoughts, he felt the floor abruptly rock. Then he heard the explosion.

A heartbeat later, a wavery scream floated from outside, down on the street. He ran barefoot out of the bathroom, snatched up the Glock on his way through the bedroom, and flew down the stairs. The shriek had stopped by the time he burst through the front door, but the fire had just gotten started. Appalled, he skidded to a stop. His wicked, liberating Porsche was engulfed in flames. Pieces of it were strewn smoking on the street, on top of other parked cars, and in several yards.

Decidedly lightheaded, he slowly went down the steps and stumbled a little closer, across the dew-wet grass. Several people who had also come running stood in knots of their own disbelief. He could actually feel the glossy black paint blister and scorch with sickening sounds. The hisses and pops from the intense heat mirrored the vile condition of his belly. He realized he could taste blood, and stopped biting the inside of his cheek.

The goddamned fool could have waited—ten more minutes, and he would have been in it. He could have been dead and lamented over, instead of standing here looking stupid. Ten fucking minutes. Staring at what was left of the car, he numbly scratched at the tape on his chest with the Glock's barrel. He finally looked at a nearby old couple, who were huddled together.

"See anything?" he asked expressionlessly. "Anyone?" At

their negative twin headshakes, he shrugged. "Has someone called the fire department?"

The old man nodded; the old lady gawked at either the Glock or his naked chest—Jared couldn't tell which. He turned his back on her. He didn't need any more fuel for his rage. He sank into the grass in Abby's yard to watch his new car—his sneaky present to himself—go up in dense smoke. Without him. A teasing breeze led some of the thick haze his way, but he sat still, the automatic welded to his hand.

The old couple inched closer, coming around the back end of the inferno on the street. Unlike the rest of the fascinated crowd, these two weren't watching the fire. He turned his head as the old woman took the last timid step to his side and carefully draped a gaudy red and white crocheted afghan around his bare shoulders. His back was protected by his damp hair, but he started at the feel of the scratchy yarn on his arms.

She hastily drew back. "You're shivering," she squeaked apologetically from behind her yellowing bifocals.

"I am?" he demanded up at her. She nodded. He reached up with his free hand to pull the afghan closer around him. "Thanks," he said faintly.

She hobbled back to the old man. A maroon Saturn came slowly down the street, and parked a half a block away. Jared didn't give it much thought until he saw a slim figure get out of it—then he shrank farther into the afghan.

Lightner removed his white lab coat and left it in the Saturn. He carried his bag, studying the burning car on his way to Jared. Once there, he looked down at the automatic, then sat beside him.

Jared unclamped his jaw enough to ask, "What?"

"I heard it on the emergency band," Lightner replied. "The trucks are on their way, but they were at a grass fire so I beat them here. I heard Porsche and thought it was probably yours. Are you all right?"

Jared peevishly twitched in the afghan. Its heavy wool

suddenly made him feel claustrophobic, so he shrugged it off. "I wasn't in the goddamned thing, if that's what you're asking. And I didn't blow it up."

Lightner reached into his bag and produced an open pack of Salem cigarettes, which he held out.

Jared snatched one, glaring at him. "What the hell is this?" he snapped, stabbing it toward the little beggar's nose. "Don't you know it stunts growth, causes low birth weight, and lung cancer? Jesus Christ, what kind of a doctor are you?"

"One who smokes," Lightner replied mildly, flicking a silver metal lighter. He lit Jared's cigarette before his own, but his eyes strayed over Jared's bare torso. They darkened impossibly with concern. "What happened to your back, Mr. McCormick? Those are some bad scars."

Jared wiped all expression from his face. He fought the urge to crawl back into the afghan; it was way too late for that. He grunted, squinting toward the fire. "Yeah, I keep meaning to talk to a plastic surgeon. It's no big deal."

"How long hasn't it been a big deal?"

"Long enough for me to forget they're there," Jared said curtly.

"What kind of a big deal wasn't it?"

Jared had had enough of Lightner's foxy attempts to tuck him into confessions he wasn't about to give. He exhaled smoke into the punk's vicinity with a quick, lecherous smile.

Leaning to rub shoulders, he murmured, "Admit it; you're just following me around because you want to strip me down and tie another bow on my belly button. Don't you, cutie?"

Lightner's ear turned a bright red. "What do you normally weigh?" he persisted gently, not looking at Jared.

"Enough to hold you down and tie you into bows you've never imagined!" Jared promised on a low chuckle.

Flustered, Lightner said, "That kind of talk isn't relative, is it? I'm pretty sure you have a problem that I can help with, and I'm also pretty sure you know it."

"Since you don't know what you're talking about, we're never going to agree on that."

"You're a time bomb."

Jared managed a laugh dipped in rank intimacy. "And you keep trying to trip my fuse, don't you, darlin'? Be careful what you wish for—they don't call me Superman for nothing."

Lightner reached to stub out his cigarette in the grass, with an agitated swallow. "As interesting as the notion might be, Mr. McCormick, I'm not offering sex."

"Then you aren't offering anything remotely interesting," Jared shot back.

"You don't want to talk about those scars?"

"Now we're communicating."

Jared sat back, feeling much better. What the hell he was so damned afraid of? Not this pliable boy.

An old man ventured near, his suspenders hanging down to his knees, suspending nothing. Chewing on a green apple, he fished another out of a voluminous pocket. He held it down to Jared, who took it with the hand that held the cigarette.

Lightner weakly smiled up at the old man and shook his head when he was offered one. Still blushing, he stood. "I have to get back," he said to the inferno, "but I'll be in my office all day. I hope you'll stop by."

Jared didn't watch him leave; he crawled back into the afghan and communed with the dying car, starkly claustrophobic even in the open.

"That's a damned shame," the old man commented toward the Porsche.

"That it is."

Jared heard more sirens and flipped his cigarette butt toward the flames. He bit into the apple. At least, he was thinking, he had had the presence of mind to put the CD in his briefcase; he hadn't lost that, too.

Other people had inched closer now, despite the automatic, him, and the overall situation. By the time Griffin appeared, Jared had a choir of people lined up in whispering formation at his wool-irritated back. The fire crew had sprayed the car into a bizarre foam sculpture. Early on, the fire chief had started toward him, but the Glock on Jared's thigh and his negative expression had turned him around.

"Oh, no!" Griffin gasped as he came running up. He stopped beside Jared and the old man, staring in dismay at the wreck. "Just look at this! What happened?"

"What the hell does it look like?" Jared snarled without looking up at him.

He violently crunched the apple to keep from suddenly opening fire on an indiscriminate basis; he was still seesawing dangerously between disappointment and fury. There were excited murmurs from the choir, which had taken a collective step forward to hear better.

"Talk to me, McCormick!" Griffin begged. "It was your brand new car! They don't just spontaneously combust!"

"Forget it, Chief," Jared clipped. "It had a hole in it, remember? Just wasn't the same."

Griffin finally, finally, lost the tattered remnants of his cool. But he didn't collapse, as Jared had thought he would; he erupted. "Put that piece away and get on your feet!" he shouted down at Jared. "Now!"

The choir stepped back in surprise.

Beet-red and blazing, Griffin continued, "I want to know what's going on here! I want to know every damned thing about it, understand? Get on your feet!"

Jared rose fluidly, losing the afghan. He jammed the automatic into his jeans at the small of his back, and stretched his cramped and sweating fingers. After pitching the apple core hard and with deliberation into the nearest bush, he wiped both sweaty hands on his thighs. Facing Griffin with restraint was the hardest thing he had ever done.

But before he could report anything, Griffin blew up again. "What the hell is this?" he howled, glaring at the bandage on Jared's chest. He poked it with an enraged forefinger. "Is this from the other night? You got shot and you didn't tell me?"

"Hey, ow!" Jared took a fast step back, slapping his hand over the bandage. He suddenly struggled with a laugh that might have come out as pure hysteria. Everything was just getting more and more ridiculous. "Sweet Jesus Christ, you idiot," he returned with clenched teeth. "If I'da got shot square in the fucking chest, do you think I'd fucking be standing here with you now? What the fuck do you use for brains? I cut myself!"

"Well, certainly not shaving!" Griffin raved. "Where were you last night? No—I want to know who you've been talking to and what you've been doing! Every last detail of every second!" He spun on his heel and stomped away, shouting over his shoulder. "You get your butt to my office double quick, or I'll be damned if I won't have it arrested!"

"For what?" Jared yelled, but Griffin kept going, his astonished townsfolk scattering before him like marbles.

Jared scrubbed at his jaw, which was decidedly bristly, yes. He always needed a shave—since when was that an indictable offense? Then he rubbed his bandage and scratched at his tickly back. He glared at the old man with the apples, who was watching him along with the rest of the block. After running both hands through his hair, he turned to the Porsche, still fighting an insane laugh.

"I don't have a car anymore," he peevishly explained to no one. "How quick can I be?"

"Oh, don't worry about that, son," the old man spoke up. "I'll run you downtown."

Jared ground his teeth. Between his insane sense of hilarity, the afghan, the apple, and Griffin's out of control fear for—or of—him, this latest anomaly almost knocked him to his knees. "Whatever." He added grudgingly, "Thanks."

The old man glanced after Griffin, who squealed his tires pulling away from the curb. "He sure is mad." He looked back. "But not as mad as you, I guess."

Jared stalked back upstairs to finish dressing, his rate of

thinking multiplying to the tenth power. Now that death was on its way, what did he have to do first? Suddenly, instead of dragging in it, he didn't seem to have nearly enough time. But he wasted some by mentally debating about the metal box and his briefcase. He needed to deal with the box; it would have to go with him. The briefcase was part of him and everybody knew it—with Lightner jumping out from behind every goddamned rock, he had to act as normally as he could, no matter what. It had to go, too. He ran Abby's brush through his hair and locked her door behind him.

The old man was in the driver's seat of a mammoth old Lincoln, parked down the block. He tooted the horn when Jared came out. There was still a social gathering around the Porsche's remains. Jared stiffly nodded to it as he stooped to retrieve the afghan in the grass. He scanned the faces, then took it to the old lady. She smiled uncertainly at him, and he wasn't sure his smile was much better. He picked up the box and briefcase and went to the Lincoln. After putting them on the front floorboard, he got in.

"My name's Earl Williams," his chauffeur announced, holding out a gnarled, spotted hand. His suspenders were still loose around his legs and his faded shirt gapped at the buttons across his belly, allowing little sprays of gray hair to escape. "Call me Earl."

"I'm McCormick," Jared returned unwillingly.

"Oh, we've met before, Jared McCormick."

Earl crept the Lincoln out onto the street, and gave it a nickel's worth of gas to get it rolling. He drove with his hands precisely at twelve and five. His slippered foot hovered over the brake pedal.

"We have?" Jared gritted, thinking this is quick? "When was that?"

"Well, I knew your daddy, of course. Good man, until the booze got him. I guess you and I weren't exactly ever introduced, but you stole from me all the time when you were a kid. I own the Shady Leaf."

"Oh," Jared said. "Well, shit. Sorry about that."

"Yessir," Earl grinned hugely. "I'd see you coming up the street, and I'd lock up the valuables and set out the comic books. Like clockwork you were…it got so Ed Whitman and I had a running bet going—just between the two of us, of course—on whether you'd hit both places, or just mine." He looked over. "You remember Ed? He's gone now, but he had the dime store?"

"I—um, no, I don't."

Earl gave the heavy car another tablespoonful of gas.

Jared watched the speedometer needle hover just over ten on the gauge, trying to understand. "You had a bet on me?"

"Sure were a cute little shit," Earl chuckled. "I never had any of my own, you know. Kids, I mean. Yessir, I'd watch to see if you went to Ed's first—I didn't trust him to tell me the truth—and then go have a smoke in the alley. Martha didn't let me smoke at home, so I had me a chair and an ashtray out there. I'd set out the comics and go light up. It usually took you about three minutes to decide which ones you wanted, and another three to make sure you were alone. Then you'd be out the door, quick as scat. Five, six minutes—just enough time for a smoke. Worked out fine." He grinned again. "I averaged a dollar a month or so on our bet, so I guess you could say that old Ed bought you all those comic books." He paused, then added thoughtfully, "'Course, I bought you Ed's candy."

Jared heard himself laugh, sort of. "Why didn't you bust me?"

Earl rolled the Lincoln into a diagonal slot in front of the police station. It was going so slowly he didn't need to brake; it bounced to a stop against the curb. He put it in Park, and half-turned away from the wheel to give Jared an enormously guilty look. Jared frowned at it with some alarm.

"Well, sir," Earl reluctantly admitted, "we figured a few comic books and some candy was little enough compensation for what Bud Doherty was taking from you. Poor little tyke. If I could have thought of a way to do something more,

I surely would have. I mean that." He brightened. "Anyway, our generosity paid off, didn't it? Now you're a policeman, I hear, and you saved the bar and Howard Griffin." He nodded toward the front door of the police station. "He sure was mad at you."

"Why did you think I was a poor little tyke?" Jared demanded, completely lost.

"Oh, Ed and I weren't the only ones!" Earl said earnestly. "But what could anybody do? Things like that just weren't talked about in those days, no sir! Sure were a cute little shit," he reiterated with a remembering nod. Then he let his old eyes wander down Jared's hair. "You don't look much like the law, I guess, but nothing looks like it should, anymore. I believe I have lived too long," he chuckled, "but I'm having too much fun to lay down and die." He stuck out his hand, and Jared automatically took it. "Now you catch the son of a bitch who did that to your nice car, hear?"

Jared frowned from the sidewalk as the old Lincoln crept away. Things like what? Poor little tyke? "What the hell does that mean?" he said aloud to himself as he went into the police station.

"What was that, sir?" Randy at the desk asked. He looked worried, like he had missed something vital.

Jared strongly identified. "I'm going to leave these with you for a minute," he said, setting the box and his briefcase on the counter.

"Yes, sir; I'll put them back here. Um, I was sorry to hear about your car, Mr. McCormick."

"Car? Oh, yeah, thanks." Jared started away, then swung around. "Do you think I'm pitiful?" he asked suspiciously.

He refused to use the word "tyke", or worse yet, "wistful".

"Pitiful, sir?"

"Never mind. Don't answer that; I don't want to know, okay? No, no; just forget it."

Shaking his head at his own question, he went back to Griffin's office. Despite the shower, he felt very grubby besides righteously, uncommonly wired. He was wearing yesterday's clothes and really did need to shave. His Porsche was soap-suds and trash, and he hadn't been quite the thief he'd always thought. And Earl Williams and Ed somebody had felt sorry for him. Jared tugged at the sweater, feeling ridiculous in it, and opened the door.

Griffin was behind his desk looking determined to do the worst without delay. He took a badly bitten pencil from his mouth and used it to point to a chair. Jared sat, dragging his hair back. He crossed his legs but hated the way the jeans tended to bind, so he uncrossed them again.

"Now, talk!"

Jared considered the command with only half his facul-ties—the other half was still stealing comic books. "Name your subject."

"Larry Doherty."

"Say, that's good, Chief!" Jared broke into an involuntarily dumbfounded grin. "How did you do that so fast?"

"What?" Griffin scowled at his dimples. "What did I do?"

"Knew that Larry dropped a bomb on my car?"

They stared at each other. Finally Griffin blinked.

"Larry?" he asked. His worn features turned red. "You think Larry Doherty put a—are you crazy?"

"Not so you'd notice," Jared said, still struggling with Earl's infuriatingly oblique words. "Why did you want to talk about Larry then?"

"Because somebody laid him out in the back room of the hardware store yesterday!" Griffin barked.

Jared stuck his bruised knuckle in his mouth, searching for answers on the wall over Griffin's head. But for once he didn't even know the questions.

Griffin sighed, drooping. "Was it you?"

"Was I accused?"

"No," Griffin said with heavy patience. "I'm guessing. There hasn't been a complaint...I heard it from Maggie who heard it from Alice Hutchins who heard it from Arlene Doherty who, presumably, heard it from Larry."

"If no accusations were made, you don't have a problem."

"You don't really—are you actually going to ask me to file a charge that says Larry Doherty stuck a bomb in your car?"

"Did I say that?"

"Where were you last night?"

"What time?" Jared asked with scant interest.

"I don't know what time, dammit!" Griffin shouted. "Somebody got into Leslie's house and tore it up! Was it you? There wasn't any sign of a break-in—did you crawl under the door like you did at the motel?"

"Can you think of a single good reason why I'd do that?"

"Then where were you? You weren't in number ten where you were supposed to be!" Jared finally looked at Griffin. He raised his eyebrows encouragingly, and Griffin caught on. He collapsed face down on the desk with a dismal sigh. "Okay, what do I use for brains?" he muttered.

"I wonder what Bud took from me besides my wife?" Jared pondered uneasily. "I don't remember anything else, but I'm beginning to wonder what I do remember."

"What are you talking about?"

"Well, that's just it; I don't have a goddamned clue. Where's Andy Malone's dealership?"

"Dealer—" Griffin sat up. "You're going to buy another brand new car?"

"I can't see myself riding Molly's bike, can you?"

"Go away," Griffin mumbled, rubbing his face hard.

Jared used Randy's phone to call Maggie at the motel. He didn't have time for her compulsion for self-pity; he laid the bare facts on her so she wouldn't go off on an emotional tangent. His car was out of commission and he wanted a ride, period. Somehow, between the motel and the police station, however, she got the rest of the story. After picking him up, she tearfully insisted on driving past the bombed-out wreck.

"It wasn't meant to hurt anyone, Mags," he lied as she whined and shook her head over it. The damned incompetent. "Somebody just got upset with me, that's all. We're used to that, aren't we?" he added dryly.

She drove him to Malone Motors on the east side of town, where they walked up and down the rows of cars. Terry Anders' friend Andy Malone came out. They shook hands all around.

"Do you have this in black?" Jared asked him, pointing at a white Lincoln Continental.

"No, but I can get it, Jared," Malone said cautiously. "Have it here Monday, if you're really interested."

"Is this the only one you have right here?"

"There's one inside, on the floor."

It was bronze with gold flecks. The interior was pale gold leather.

"Too blonde," Jared said with a shudder. He spotted something through the showroom window and went closer to the tinted glass. "What's that out there?" he asked, and Malone and Maggie came to look, too. "That black one, third from the left. Is that a Concours?"

"Yes; Cadillac. Wonderful automobile. Very solid and plush."

"Does it handle like a Porsche?"

"Well, no—say; was that your 911 that burned this morning, Jared? Sure it was; I should have known! What the heck happened?"

"Give me eight percent for cash, Andy, and I'll take it," Jared said.

Feeling a strong sense of been there, done that, he handed the dealer his wallet, his checkbook, and his bank numbers in Chicago. He then walked out to look at the car. Maggie followed.

"You enjoyed that, didn't you?" she said with a grin he finally recognized as hers. "You always were such a show-off, Jared McCormick!"

"At least I bought American this time," he said. "Think they'll put me in a commercial?"

The smiling car dealer came out with a clipboard. He promised to have the car delivered to the motel in an hour. Jared signed the papers and asked him to arrange plates and insurance. They shook hands all around once more, then Jared and Maggie got back into the station wagon. As they drove off the lot Jared asked Maggie to take him back to number ten.

"I didn't change the sheets in there this morning," Maggie said with a sidelong look, "because the bed hadn't been slept in."

"Just think of the time that saved you."

Maggie laughed and reached over to pat his knee.

"She's a nice girl, Jared, but awfully young, don't you think? And nothing like Leslie, which sort of surprises me."

He abandoned other thoughts to think about that, and found that Maggie was right. Leslie had been bright, tough as nails, but not clever nor remotely empathetic. Leslie had been blonde.

"How are you doing today?" he asked, neatly putting her back on her favorite subject, herself.

A shadow passed over her face, dimming her smile. "I'm all right. I'm trying to keep busy, but I keep reaching for the phone to call Marsha. It hurts." She turned into the motel drive and parked. Then she hugged him. "But at least I have you again!"

18

HE CLOSED AND LOCKED the door to the unit behind him, leaning weakly against it. The metal box had to be gone through, but he still felt supremely cheated and unwilling to conform to shoulds, even his own. He hoped another shower would improve his mood. There were other things to do too, and since talking with Earl he was beginning to wonder if he didn't have even more. But he was exhausted.

He dawdled selfishly over shaving and spent far too much time dressing in front of the big mirror. He eventually slung on the knock-off but not-bad jacket, then walked over to the house to see if he could locate some caffeine. Maggie fussily filled a thermos for him, and stole another hug. He went back into the hot sunshine in time to meet a kid in a jean vest and no hair to speak of, from the dealership.

"What a beauty, sir," the kid said reverently, wiping the door handle with a soft cloth after he closed it. "That's a real nice car."

Jared tipped him and asked if he needed a ride anywhere. The youngster cheerfully turned him down and took off at a lope up the street. Jared went into the room, leaving the door open in the hopes of snaring an unsuspecting breeze. When the phone rang, he was sitting on the desk chair in the doorway, contemplating his latest purchase with a smoke.

This time, he hadn't even flinched as he had signed the check. This impetuosity was getting serious.

The call was from the optometrist office located next to the police station, telling him that his prescription was ready. Not only had he forgotten that he had been there, he couldn't for the life of him figure out why he had bothered. Mystified at yet another mental gap, he locked up the room and drove uptown. The big V-8 was super-quiet and as smooth as oiled glass. While he waited his turn inside, he asked to see sunglasses; his Ray Bans had gone up with the Porsche. The new reading glasses with thin black frames apparently looked good on him; the woman who fitted them said so several times. He gave the girl out front a credit card, signed the receipt, and left.

After picking up his dry-cleaning, he propped the unit door open once more, hoping the fresh air would stimulate his few loyal brain cells. He poured some coffee and set the metal box on the desk. After putting on the new glasses, he flipped back the shattered lid. The patchy, one-eyed pink cat startled him. He held it a moment, wondering what had ever possessed him. And what was he going to do with it now, for Christ's sake? He had to hide it—no way did he want anyone to see this. Feeling utterly nuts, he sneaked it outside and locked it in the spacious trunk of the Cadillac.

The school picture of the little girl was different; he didn't feel odd about taking that. In the first place, who was left to miss it? Leslie was dead. Bud was possessive, not sentimental. The little girl might notice it was gone, but she wasn't living at home right now. Jared eventually stuck the picture in a compartment in his briefcase.

Leslie had taken most of the old snapshots. He studied one picture of himself diving from the rocks at the quarry. Typically, he was flipping off the camera. Leslie must have been laughing because the photo was blurred. He had been about fifteen, thin and intense and to his eyes now, alien. He had been there, but it had been someone else.

There was a picture of Leslie sitting on top of a picnic table in the city park. He was on the seat below her, almost cut out of the shot. She had her arms around his neck and her chin on top of his head. He briefly wondered who had taken it.

They had been so fucking young; younger than his niece Molly when they had first discovered each other. So ridiculously innocent.

With a sigh, he sorted the snaps chronologically and put them back in the box. He didn't delve too deeply into the scraps and notes; he knew what he had given her, and in the end none of it had meant a damned thing, had it? He would burn the works, put the last vestiges of those times to rest. Then he thought of the little girl bouncing around the carnival. He uneasily decided that no matter how he felt about it, it wasn't up to him. Leslie had kept the things for their daughter; he couldn't step in and change her future like that. He wasn't the selfish prick his father had been.

He put it all back, including the divorce papers, and set the box on the floor. Thoroughly, blackly depressed, he knew he couldn't go on much longer. Go on with what? Pretense and denial? And for what? More diluted days and endless nights? The prospect was unbearable, and it had to stop. Now.

The Glock in his hand became weightless as he helplessly shifted into the gray, foggy area in his head that seemed to have no doors, or too many of them; he couldn't remember which one he had come in. He couldn't find his way out. Fretfully, he blinked…

…and found himself in the driver's seat of the new car. He held the Glock in his left hand now, the barrel resting negligently on his collarbone. But its magazine was on his thigh, its cartridges scattered on the floor mat. The Adagio from the Concerto in G minor played quietly on the sound system. His arm was leaden; he let it, and the ineffectual weapon, drop to his lap.

He squeezed his eyes shut, hating the increasingly futile

feeling of been here, done that. His last cognizant thought had been wiped from his mind again, leaving him groping. He was shirtless; he knew that much, although he felt like he had been injected with a gallon of Novocain. What the hell had he been up to in the shifting blackness, that required partial nudity?

The quiet music invited him to look—to open his eyes and reconnect—so he raised his head and dimly watched the backs of a middle-aged couple as they went through the front door of the nursing home. Somehow he had neatly parked in a distant corner of the small hospital lot.

And worse yet, Lightner was beside him—a huddled, still figure trapped under his right arm. He had parked, maybe called the scary bastard on the car phone, and…what?

"I learned a long time ago," Jared heard himself saying almost conversationally, "that you'd better be prepared to accept the consequences of asking difficult questions. And whether you succeed in getting the answers or not, whatever experience you gain is yours alone."

"Can't the experience be shared?" Lightner asked very softly.

"Not if it's classified," Jared said through lips that tingled, wondering how long he had been babbling like this.

"The questions and answers might be classified," Lightner ventured. "But surely the experience isn't."

"They're inseparable," Jared pronounced sternly on an exhale of cigarette smoke. "You can't gain one without the other."

He had undressed to explain the incident of his scars? To give Lightner a view of the old event and get him off his back about his back? But how dumb was that?

He blinked stupidly at the cigarette burning in his left hand. Where had it come from? Hadn't he just been holding that fucking useless gun? It wasn't his brand. Struggling to catch up with what he couldn't follow, Jared knew he had to be very, very, careful; gratitude was a dangerous weakness.

So was familiarity—but he couldn't seem to let go of the other man. Literally. His arm was locked around Lightner's shoulders.

A stray sting emerged from the enormous numbness. He looked down, distracted from the jumbled uproar in his head. The bandage Abby had put on his chest was missing; the edges of the cut gaped wetly through the hair.

"They can be separated, Mr. McCormick," Lightner murmured. "With a little careful work. All we need to do is break down the order. Rearrange the priority—put your wellbeing before your professional conscience. How or why you got the scars doesn't matter, but what you—"

"Pay attention!" Jared interrupted furiously, evidently continuing a conversation he must have begun. Lightner didn't quite gasp as Jared's arm tightened. "The scars don't mean a fucking thing, goddammit! Even with the meat hanging off my bones, I got what I needed from the cocksucker and then I killed him!" He stuck the cigarette between his teeth and groped for the other scar, between their tightly pressed sides. "This one's even older," he laughed harshly. "I was set up, then knifed in a waterfront bar. But I drowned that fucker in an alley garbage barrel! Get it? They *aren't* a problem."

"Then maybe it's something else," he heard said with a dubious note, "but you can't do what you've done and not suffer some kind of—"

"Stop it," Jared commanded on a raw surge of rage. "I don't fail; I learn!"

"Your entire physiology is failing—what are you learning from this?"

"There's nothing wrong," Jared said flatly.

"But, Mr. McCormick, you—"

"Stay out of what you don't know," Jared seethed. His arm had yanked Lighter around, into his chest. Jared stared into the terrified eyes, only inches from his. "There's *nothing* wrong with me, understand?"

"May I get out, then?" Lightner asked a heartbeat later.

"And do what?" Jared snarled.

"Um, attend a prenatal exam? Please, I'm late."

CHAPTER
19

By TEN TO TWELVE, his hallucinatory encounter with Lightner had been dismissed from his mind. He was dressed again, but still wholly numb. He didn't mind; he needed to think, not feel, and it was rapidly getting so that he couldn't do both at the same time. He also had to act on one thing at a time for fear of forgetting something—or of getting lost in the growing insanity altogether. He had to concentrate.

He drove to the bank his father had failed to rob. There, he rented and filled a large safety deposit box. He disposed of the broken metal file box, then went on to the cafe to find Abby already there. She was sitting at the lunch counter, her purse on the stool next to her. He picked it up and sat, putting it on his lap. She was very pale.

"Hi, gorgeous," he joked. "What's your sign?"

"Oh, your poor car, Jared!" She gripped his arm, fear simmering in her eyes. "I didn't hear about it until just a little while ago! I went right home, but you had already gone."

"It made a mess on your doorstep," he conceded with a shrug, "and gave everyone in town something to discuss for a month, but it's being looked into."

"You don't want to talk about it," she guessed. "Or you can't. I'm so glad you're all right." She took his hand, still needing to cling, but changed the subject. "Did you get any sleep at all?"

Raising his eyebrows, he asked, "Is this really the place to discuss what a voracious woman you are?"

She blushed scarlet, only then realizing that they were being watched by the waitress at the soft drink dispenser, the cook through the window, and most of the other patrons. She let go of his hand and ducked behind her menu. The waitress brought him one. He put on his new glasses.

"Nice." Abby emerged far enough to study them, still pink. "You look like a with-it professor. Literature, maybe?"

"Coffee and a tuna sandwich," he emoted to the rapt waitress. "Wheat, no butter or mayo."

Abby looked at him with a new warm light in her eye. It was humiliating, the need he abruptly felt for her—even this numb. He took her hand this time, and held it on his thigh under the counter.

"Magic, that's what you are," she leaned to whisper seriously. "It's remarkable. Everybody sees it."

"Nothing up my sleeve and rabbits out of my hat?" he smiled.

"No. Spells and hexes and sorcery. More like that."

Oh, well, it sounded better than wistful.

He left the cafe with her. She spotted the new Cadillac immediately. It was hard to miss, wrongly parallel parked beside a hydrant.

"What's this?" she asked, walking around it. "You bought another car already?"

"I've misplaced the spell to make me fly," he replied, "so I drive. This is the Taj Mahal of the automotive world, baby. It has a monster V-8 with cast aluminum block and heads, rack and pinion steering, disc brakes all around, and a spacious back seat."

He winked obscenely at her. She regarded him for a moment with a silent expectation that changed his joke into pure want. It was nice. Then, she gave him a quick kiss and went back to work. With primal urges ticking over agreeably, he started walking toward the bank once again. He went past that, however, and turned into a door at the beginning of the next block.

He was glad to see that he wasn't the only one with obsessions. Realtor Steve Reynolds had a definite hard-on for the color red. He wore a red shirt, had a red cordless telephone, red upholstered chairs, red drapes, and a red carpet. Even the file cabinets along the back wall were red. Reynolds was a trim man in his late thirties with ginger hair and a ruddy complexion. He wore a red shirt. His white tie sent a screech down Jared's spine like chalk on a blackboard.

Reynolds looked up from his desk. His interest shifted straight into defensive when he recognized Jared.

Jared took the chair across from him, the notes he had jotted down at the library yesterday in hand. "Good afternoon," he said politely. "I'm looking at a property, and heard that you were the man to talk to."

"What property?" Reynolds asked suspiciously.

"Lyle Doherty's ranch."

"I don't think it's for sale."

"Well, of course it isn't. Bud has the option when Lyle defaults. That's why I'm interested."

"Talk to Bud, then."

"Not again in this lifetime," Jared promised mildly. "I'm curious: not only did you sell the place to Lyle, you worked out the financing for him, and even fronted him the down payment. Why did you do that?"

"He's a friend."

"No, sir," Jared said, still gentle. "By no stretch of the imagination can we call you a friend of Lyle's. You charged him an inflated price for a lemon. The buildings are falling down, where they aren't rotting away. The land floods in the spring without fail and the topsoil blew into Kansas looking for Dorothy about a decade ago. I don't care how much sugar Lyle puts on it, it's still going to come out sour."

"He wanted it."

"Or you and Bud wanted him to want it?" Jared suggested. "Lyle signed away his life for a place to keep a horse. When he defaults, he'll lose everything—the horse, the land, his truck, his lawnmowers, and rakes. It's amazing how many similar foreclosures there have been around here in the last few years. I'm guessing Bud's money; your office. Tidy little scheme you two cooked up together, but how did Leslie get mixed up in it?"

"I don't know what you're talking about."

Reynolds was reacting to Jared's friendly tone—wasn't nearly as worried as he needed to be.

"She was just a price-per-fuck thing, wasn't she?" Jared asked candidly. "A side deal?" He closed the small notebook and folded his hands loosely in his lap. "Bud Doherty bought your dick, and told you where you to put it, right? Substantial cash up front so you could build your pretty new house, and final installment when? After you knocked her up? After the kid was born?" He nodded, coolly staring the asshole down. "Yes, that sounds more like Bud; he'd want guarantee of live delivery. Like royalty, he wanted an heir and a spare."

Reynolds' face turned the same violent shade as his shirt. He stood and placed his hands on the desk. "That's ridiculous! I cared for Leslie very much—we just couldn't agree on the baby. And Bud wouldn't do anything like that!"

Jared snorted. "No, Bud wouldn't do anything else. In fact, this is all he does every day of his miserable life, in one form or another. What I don't get is why nobody ever sees it but me."

"Listen, I'm going to have to ask you to leave!"

Jared shook his head in profound pity. "Okay, if you want to get pissy, Stevie, we'll get pissy. Talk to me about Project 1634, or I'll have to ask someone else. Maybe somebody at the state level?"

Reynolds sank back into his chair, suddenly a clashing green. "It's a proposal," he replied, almost without gagging on the fright that had knocked him down. "An exchange that would swing the Interstate closer to Shady Rock. It's only proposed, though!" he emphasized quickly. "It's been tried before."

"Oh, it's more than proposed," Jared smiled serenely. "It's going through. Maybe not this week or this month, but it will go through. Big changes are coming up for this small town; aren't they, Stevie-boy? You know how I know that? Because Bud never, ever does anything unless it means sticking somebody—and Lyle comes up as a principal stickee in this particular case.

"Here's how I see it: Bud doesn't want anybody to get the jump on him by tipping his hand, so he entices Lyle to take on a loan he can't possibly afford without help. Lyle gets stuck but good when Bud collects his option. Then Bud sells the option as right-of-way to the Interstate project, or busts up the land into prime lots for the new Wal-Mart, or whatever." Jared stood and waved a hand. "I sincerely don't care how many friends and neighbors you two fuck over this project, but your son is in Bud Doherty's hands now that Leslie is dead. What you are going to do about it?"

"I'm not going to do anything about it!"

Jared dropped to his hands on the desk this time, claiming not only Reynolds' personal space but the entire office. "If you," he said very softly, "ever attempt to go back on that statement, you will be exposed as the sniveling little crook you are, and then you'll be dead. Is that clear?"

After leaving the phantasm in red, Jared next stopped at the first law office he came to—one thing at a time. The office happened to belong to Abe Johnson, Bud's attorney, but Jared decided that it wouldn't matter in the long run. Now that Reynolds had been buttoned down, Jared could proceed with the plan that had occurred to him right after trashing Leslie's house. He needed to draw up a new will.

He explained his business to the receptionist, who spent several flirtatious minutes telling him how lucky he was;

apparently an appointment had just canceled. After using her phone, she told him that he could go right in.

Abe Johnson was a severe man in his early fifties who wore suspenders with his black suit. Jared heard from him that his business would be a bit complicated, and would take some time. Jared told him he didn't have either time or explanations, and offered triple rates. They spent about an hour drawing up the document together. Yes, he could come back in the morning to pick it up. He hoped.

He stopped at the police station after that. Randy was reading at the desk. Jared glanced at the book upside down, recognizing a textbook on procedure well advanced for the kid. Not small town stuff at all. Well, well. He might be losing it, but he could still appreciate ambition. Randy tried to hide the book under some papers.

"A little light reading?" Jared asked.

"Yes, sir. I mean, no, sir. Um, it's just interesting, that's all."

"That it is." Jared took one of the business cards from his leather holder and dropped it face up on the desk. "Call my office when you start shaving. Is Griffin in?"

"Yes, sir, he's with the mayor. Thank you, sir!"

"The mayor, huh?" Jared frowned. "I'll wait outside."

The mayor wasn't a happy man when he left the police station. Everybody seemed to be in a mood but Jared—he was still absolutely, indifferently emotionally paralyzed, and glad of it. He watched the angry man stalk down the street, then went back in. Griffin was on the phone, asking for coffee.

Griffin contemplated him, then folded his hands on the desk. "It was ammonium nitrate and fuel oil," he said tiredly. "ANFO. Fused, not timed. No witnesses. Tell me about Larry."

"I pissed him off," Jared shrugged as he moved into his usual chair. "Hell, I've always pissed him off."

"You still think he blew up the car? How about the shots fired, the other night?"

"Something's happening. It'll come to me."

"I'd say it already has!"

"Amateurs," Jared sneered, "sticking out tongues."

"But I want you to be careful of what you say," Griffin warned. "It looks to me like you're sinking deeper into your feud with Bud by bringing his boys into it."

Jared dressed himself in hurt. "What feud?" he asked. "I haven't seen Bud for a full day and a half! And when did I actually accuse anybody of anything? You brought up Larry's name, and I simply agreed. Did I once dramatically say, 'He did it!'? I did not."

"Okay, okay." Griffin rubbed his eyes, then blinked up at the ceiling. "Larry and Lyle. I've had some trouble with Larry. Nothing much; he drinks and gets into fights once in a while, but he isn't the gangster you're making him out to be. Lyle's okay." He bit his bottom lip, pondering. "They're a pair all right—but either get off them, McCormick, or give me some evidence that Larry is actually guilty of the bombing so I can get involved." He paused with a faint scowl. "Um, speaking of involved, things are moving pretty fast with you and Miss Olson, aren't they?"

"Let's see," Jared mused. "So far today you've accused me of redecorating Leslie's house, knocking Larry on his ugly fat ass, and not shaving before going public. Are you adding corruption to the charges?"

Griffin sighed. "You didn't sleep at the motel last night, and that was you, wasn't it, sitting half-naked on her lawn this morning, exposing your hardware to the neighbors?"

"You don't miss a thing, do you, Chief? Has she filed a complaint?"

"Not with me," Griffin said wryly.

Randy came in with two cups of coffee, and shyly handed Jared three extra sugar packets before leaving. Jared set his mug on the corner of the desk and ripped the corners off the packets, dumping them all at once. He used the plastic spoon he had been given, too aware of Griffin's now-silent scrutiny. He didn't like it. All of the sudden, Griffin had a paternal grimness around his mouth—as in *This is going to hurt me more than it hurts you*. Jared sipped the coffee—a fresh, awful batch—nearly retching on the bitterness. He made a face.

"Sugar just makes it worse," Griffin determined, still eyeing him. "Cream makes it undrinkable. Maybe Randy needs a new coffee pot."

"I think you should just get a new Randy," Jared said shortly. "What is it, Chief? You have that look."

"You shouldn't be drinking coffee, right?"

"Well, it's not the best—" Jared began, but Griffin interrupted him.

"How bad is that ulcer? Are you really seeing a doctor?"

Jared sat back. "Of course I've seen a doctor. Several times, in fact. I only turn stupid on alternate—"

Griffin shook his head, looking both wary and more insecure than usual. "No bullshit, understand? This isn't just an ulcer, is it? What is the ulcer a symptom of?"

"Bad habits," Jared stated, feeling a chill run down his spine. *Symptom* was not a cop word. "It's stress-related, and you had a front row seat to what kind of stress it won't take. Not only am I allergic to blood, I'm moronic because I still smoke. You should see what a few drinks do to me. It's a symptom of bad habits and a sorry lack of self-discipline."

Griffin sat on Jared's answer for a moment. Then, with a small furrow between his eyes, he picked up his coffee and swiveled the chair around to contemplate the fax machine. "I told you we were lucky to have Rick Lightner as our—" he began.

"I'm not in the mood for fairy tales," Jared interrupted brusquely. "Not before bedtime."

"It's interesting, though." Griffin frowned at the blatant insult, but didn't slap his hand for it. "Rick's a lot like you, McCormick—small town boy makes good, you know? He was the only child of an older couple who died in a car accident when he was sixteen. He graduated from high school that year; a real genius. When his folks were killed, Shady Rock got together to pay his way through medical school with the understanding that he would practice here for five years after he graduated. We only have the right to him for another two, and the whole town is already campaigning to do whatever it takes to keep him here."

Griffin paused to sip his coffee and Jared did the same, knowing it was a mistake. His gut was corroded enough without it, and the protective numbness was suddenly ebbing.

"There's no comparison between Lightner and me," he said civilly enough, "either in who we are, or in how we were treated here. But I'll bite—are you looking for a donation, or what?"

Griffin went on without either answering or looking at him, telling Jared he hadn't yet heard the worst. "The Doc planned his intern and resident schedule to take him into as many types of medicine as he could. He didn't want to specialize. He wants to be just what he is, a general practitioner. He's worked with the elderly, the very young, burn victims, accidents; you name it, he's had a taste of it. He hates suffering of any kind." Griffin looked at down at his cup. "He's very interested in the connection between mind and body."

"Oh?" Jared put in with just the right amount of apathy.

"Yeah, he spent a year of his residency at a veterans hospital in Maryland, studying soldiers with mental problems." Griffin added slowly, "He called about you, McCormick. He's worried."

Had it been his imagination, or had he not sat in that fucking parking lot and warned Lightner to leave him alone?

"He's worried?" Jared questioned levelly. "Catch me up here—what's he worried about?"

Griffin faced the desk, sat forward and spoke to the computer monitor next. He obviously wanted to say these things as much as Jared wanted to hear them. "He was talking a little about the men he had worked with. He mentioned some things—" Griffin stopped with a grimace. "You aren't suicidal, are you?" he demanded, embarrassed. "You really did jump in front of that truck and all the rest because you knew what you were doing, right? Not because you have a death wish, or because you're getting orders from Beyond?"

Jared sagged in his chair, nearly losing the cup from his hand. How about that – despite express orders, the treacherous little faggot had rabbited to the nearest phone and dumped the works into Griffin's ear.

Some of Jared's indignation must have shown, because Griffin tried his best to disperse it. "That's why I asked about your stomach just now!" he rushed in. "You said the ulcer was why you quit the FBI. There isn't more to it, is there?"

"I don't believe I'm hearing this," Jared said. He honestly didn't; why hadn't he killed him while he had the chance? Both of them.

"Do you have trouble sleeping?" Griffin pressed uncertainly. "Is that why you roam the streets at all hours, looking for trouble?"

"Let me see if I have the gist of this," Jared said, guessing the source of Griffin's guilt. "Your wonder boy thinks I'm a burnout? What on earth have you been telling him?"

Griffin ducked his head, then guiltily cleared his throat. "I didn't tell him anything," he denied, red-faced. "I just asked him a few questions about what happened yesterday, when you got sick. Okay! I broke my promise, but he's a doctor, McCormick! He isn't going to tell anybody what we talked about!"

"He's certainly told you something that's got you reeling," Jared murmured furiously.

"I'm sorry. I shouldn't have asked him behind your back, but you scared me!"

And that was the problem.

"I've done that all along, haven't I?" Jared reached into his breast pocket for his notebook and fountain pen, and began writing. "It's an occupational hazard," he said with stinging arrogance, "but I live with it. Here; eat this when you're done, but call these people—do us both a goddamned favor, will you, and investigate me once and for all?" Jared tore out the page and stood to drop it beside the telephone. "In the meantime, I want you to think about this: either the little cupcake is absolutely right about me—I'm afraid of him locking me in a padded cell with no access to suicide—or else he's crapping on my reputation because he can't fuck me any other way."

"What?" Griffin said blankly. Then he scowled. "He hit on you?"

"Call those numbers," Jared said coldly. "Then decide what you choose to believe."

He sat in the new car out front for a moment with the air conditioner on high, hoping to dry or freeze the flood of perspiration that was suddenly pouring down his face. He was more than jittery now. Fuck jittery; he felt like he was about to shatter into a million sharp pieces. He should have done more to muzzle Lightner after conducting his stupid little confessional—he was slipping; no doubt about it. But it wouldn't get any farther; not now. Lightner had sent out a feeler, but Griffin would make some phone calls and then step on him.

But on top of his negligence, other things were chipping away at Jared in places that were getting painful, and that wasn't good. This weird nervousness, plus a growing suspicion from elsewhere could easily yield a huge crop of deadly paranoia. Instead of dwelling on the niggling stimuli, he told himself to go bully Lyle into a heart-to-heart over things that hadn't been said yesterday.

Anything to replace the numbness he had lost.

But Lyle wasn't home. In the shade of the big state-bought billboard on the blacktop, Jared briefly thought about tossing the dump for the targeting scope he was somehow sure was there. But then he couldn't be bothered. He had a pretty good handle on Lyle's main problem, and its name was Bud.

Bud had suckered Reynolds into suckering Lyle into buying the property that had the potential to be worth a fortune. And the state project had to be more than a developer's wet dream or Bud would still be bailing Lyle out.

Jared was sure that Bud had his anvil thumb on Larry too, somehow. It was a familiar feeling, and the idea of going out to the nursing home to harass the old man for a while greatly appealed—which was exactly why he didn't do it. Now was not the time to draw attention, especially not on Lightner's turf.

Hampered to the point of gray jeopardy, Jared turned the Caddy loose on miles of empty back roads. It wasn't the evil Porsche, but it handled well and had an attitude that would be hard to contain, without concentration. But he concentrated; he didn't want to do it that way. He had to calm down—find a den to hide in. Larry's issue would grow up in its own inadequate, inefficient time; he just had to make himself wait for it.

It was nearly four o'clock when he returned to town. He prowled a grocery store for twenty minutes, coming out with two full bags. Then he went to the motel to pick up some clothes and his shaving tackle. His last stop was the pet store, to make sure of his welcome—he really was pitifully paranoid.

The parrot was screeching, and there was a litter of three Pomeranian puppies yipping at each other in a wire kennel below its perch.

A few customers were browsing, but Abby was at the counter, paging through a catalogue. "Hi," she said with a smile that could start dead hearts at twenty yards.

"Hi, yourself," he replied coolly, hiding his debilitating sense of relief. "What are you doing?"

"Daydreaming."

He looked at the catalogue. It seemed to be a dealer's list. "But I'm not in there," he pointed out.

"I don't buy dirty magazines."

"I'm not in those, either," he said contemptuously. "They would never be able to capture the real me."

"And the center-fold wouldn't be large enough," she ended the witticism. Then she ruined it with a chuckle. "For your ego, that is! I have to go catch some fish for that customer. If you can get your head through the door, there's coffee in the office."

He didn't need any more stimulants. Jittery had just metamorphosed into heated arousal—which was much better, but equally as hard to live with. He stuck his hands in his pockets and went to walk it off around the small store.

A tiny dark-headed girl in miniature jeans attached herself to him in the first aisle, keeping precisely one step behind. They stopped to look at the discus, now glowing neon in the darkened water. They dawdled beside the little fluffs of orange electric fur with snapping black eyes. When he moved on to look at the glass room filled with birds in their cages, she followed, stepping where he had, stretching her stride to match. Even on tiptoe she couldn't see anything but the ceiling of the bird room. Her glare was as accusing as any Bud had ever used on him.

She tugged on his sleeve and held up her arms. He gingerly picked her up, smelling candy and fabric softener. They stood there for a long time, watching conures, cockatiels, finches, parakeets, and canaries leap and flutter from perch to perch. She took a handful of his hair and stuck her thumb into her mouth.

He didn't try to talk to her—he didn't know the language—but she seemed happy enough without his input. Her mother eventually reclaimed her with thanks. Abby's smile championed him as he handed the child over, and he decided that her desire to take custody of him was a damned good thing. He needed a caretaker. He smoothed out his jacket sleeve where the child had sat, shook the hand-print out of his hair and followed Abby to the counter as if he was on a leash.

"I bought a few groceries," he mentioned, waving vaguely

toward the car on the street. "Want me to cook, have it ready when you get off?"

"Sure, but what did you want to do after that? There aren't any more carnivals in town."

"I'd give my shot at a being centerfold," he said, "to sit down and take my shoes off. There are some reports that I was supposed to have done before I went on vacation."

"Perfect," she smiled, starting his heart. "I should clean my bathroom."

20

JARED PARKED THE CADDY at the end of the block, as far away from any other cars as he could. Goddamned Larry had a hardware store full of pipe bomb-makings; it just seemed like a neighborly thing to do. He juggled the groceries, his briefcase, and his clothes bag up the block, passing the scorch marks on the street where his Porsche had met its destiny. He didn't dwell on it, though—he didn't dare. He went up the steps to the white two-story and set the bags and briefcase down to use the key Abby had given him.

The door at the other end of the porch swung open. A short, very stout woman in her sixties stepped out, holding the screen door between them like a shield. She peered around it, fixing him with a glower, then looked at the clothes bag and briefcase. The groceries at his feet got a thorough inspection as well.

"Are you the young man whose car burned up?" the woman called out. "I was at work and missed it. I saw them haul it off, though."

"Yes, ma'am," Jared replied. "It was my car."

She stared at him belligerently for a moment longer. He wondered how he would react if she told him to leave.

"Well, come here then," she said. "Hurry up, the bugs are getting in!"

Jared hung the suit bag over the railing. He put the

briefcase inside the door and walked the length of the porch. Maybe she had seen Larry light the fuse on her way to work. If so, he would pretend to care. Or maybe the old hen was in cahoots with Larry, and he was walking into an ambush. He could only hope. He followed her strenuous waddle into a wide front hallway. A broad staircase rose on one side, and a spacious living room opened up on the other. He trailed her through a formal dining room, into a large, aromatic kitchen.

"I own this house," the old lady informed him in no uncertain terms. "I've been renting the upstairs for the past five years. Abby is my first and only tenant. Never had a bit of trouble either, until now. Come over here."

Hating, he wordlessly followed her again. In an old-fashioned pantry, she opened an older-fashioned pie safe with a punched tin front. Three pies to a shelf, five shelves.

"Now," she directed, "you pick one of those out and take it on upstairs for your supper. There's apple, blueberry, peach, cherry, and on the bottom is mincemeat, but those didn't turn out very good. A pie won't get you a new car, honey, but it's the best I can do."

He looked at the broad, unsmiling, face. It was like cutting open an onion and finding Mozart.

"That's kind of you, Miss—?" he faltered when he could speak.

"That's missus," she corrected sharply. "Mrs. Frank Holbert, And you're the McCormick boy—the little scamp who made everybody so miserable in my Sunday school class!"

Jared ran his hand through his hair under her eagle eye. His thoughts stuttered, trying to place her—but Christ, the last time he had been to Sunday school, he had been about eight. "Well, yes, I imagine I am."

"You were a naughty little boy," she told him firmly, "but the Lord works in mysterious ways. There's a nasty man out there hurting women, and I'm glad you're here now to look after Abby. I feel better with a man in the house, too. I suggest the peach, the crust is best on those."

He was forced to make two trips to carry everything up the stairs to the apartment. He took the grocery bags and the pie to the kitchen and left the briefcase on the couch. He put the suit bag on a hook in the bathroom; the scented bedroom closet was too intimate for him. He left the shaving kit zipped in the bottom of the bag, and as many non-essential topics from his over-loading brain as he could in an equally dark place. Why should he remember the old woman?

He shed his jacket and set to work in the kitchen, but things kept shaking loose…

Earl Williams, proprietor of the Shady Leaf, not only remembered him, but also had brought up things about cute little Jared that his elderly conscience would only hint at…and what the hell had that odd expression from Lyle been? Superiority? Close. But superiority implied advantage, which in turn implied knowledge. What did Lyle know that Jared didn't? They had been talking about Leslie—the young Leslie, not the dead one…and why did little old ladies keep trouncing his expectations?

After turning the oven to Warm, he scouted the cabinets for a casserole dish for the chicken Diane, his specialty. He sliced French bread, and was tossing a salad with avocado and canned crab when Abby came into the kitchen. He looked over his shoulder at her.

"I might have mentioned this already," she laughed dubiously as she put her purse down, "but there's something really obscene about an armed man looking so at home in the kitchen." Then she kissed him on the cheek. "Has anyone told you today that you are incredibly handsome?"

"Not today," he said, wiping his hands. "Can I still be handsome if I'm armed?"

"Armed with those dimples?" Abby tossed right back as he put his arms around her. "You'd be handsome without them, but with them, you're downright gorgeous!"

He kissed her, feeling her fingers threading eagerly into the hair draping his back. "You," he said semi-seriously, "are gorgeously close to changing my schedule. Shall we forget dinner, and—"

Abby laughed, putting fingers to his lips. "Can't you take a teeny little compliment?" she teased. "I never said anything about skipping dinner, did I? I said you are the most beautiful man I have ever met, but that doesn't mean I don't want to sit down and eat."

"You left out noble, gallant, and dauntless," he frowned. "Are you going to let go of me?"

"As soon as you let go of me," she giggled.

They stayed at the table for quite a while, with her rendering him blessedly mindless by describing her day. He cut the pie.

"Oops, I recognize that crust," Abby cringed. "You met Mrs. Holbert, didn't you? Is she going to kick me out for having no morals?"

"She called me a scamp. I would have been insulted, but she said she was glad I was here. She was very nice to me, in fact."

"Well, what's so surprising about that? You're a nice person, Jared Jordan. Polite, refined, funny, and a damned good cook."

"Not to mention noble and dauntless," Jared repeated, "but I don't remember her as being nice. I don't remember her at all. She said I was in her Sunday school class." He shook his head. "Maybe I was. And somebody else said some things I don't remember, either. But I wasn't a particularly unobservant kid."

"I think kids have an awful time knowing what's really going on," Abby said. "What they're told and what they see is so different, usually."

"Points of view," he agreed. "But I go with what I collect. Trust what I know."

"What happens when you're given something else?" she asked. "Or learn that you're just flat wrong?"

"I adapt," he said.

"Then you'll have to adapt to the fact that your memory might have a few holes in it," she smiled. "Just like a normal person."

What constituted normal was a slippery road he wasn't going to go down with her, or anybody else. But too many questions did lead to self-doubt and indecision. Did the growing list of answers he didn't have, have anything to do with successfully accomplishing his goal? It did not. He had to exploit the present, not let himself get bogged down in the past.

He took his second glass of wine into the living room. There, he turned on a lamp and located an outlet by cleverly following the cord. From his briefcase he took his laptop and plugged it in. He set the laptop on the coffee table and took his shoes off. Abby wandered by carrying a mop. She took one of his cigarettes.

He sat on the couch, cracked his knuckles and went to work. For the next two hours, he gave himself completely to the screen and his imagination. Designing abstract strategies was his favorite pastime, one that he had turned into a solid, full time job. He finished one proposal and got a handle on another before he finally sat back. Emilio could finish it. His wineglass was full again, and a small plate of cheese and apple slices sat beside it. He drank and nibbled while reviewing what it would take and what it would cost, bottom line. Clients from all over the world scratched their heads over spreading global crime; ISC provided soothing rhetoric. Fear, risk, and experience over dollar signs, an exponentially growing equation.

He finally lit a cigarette, and shut down the PC. Picking up his glass, he sat back. Only then did he see Abby across the room from him. She was tucked up in a chair, wearing a demure, rose pink robe that covered all of her. Her hair was

damp from the shower, her nose shiny in his lamplight. She
was watching him; he had no idea how long she had been
there.

He smiled. "I just earned my next paycheck."

"The boss has to wait for a paycheck like the peons?" she
asked lightly.

"I'm the last to get paid," he shrugged. "That's what
happens when you go into business for yourself."

"You don't seem to be worried about it."

"Yes indeed, I'm your basic worrywart—I save or invest
about half of what I earn. Well, that's not correct. I don't save
it; I have a bad-tempered man take it away from me for my
own good. And I pay him for this. I also have a battalion of
accountants lined up like a firing squad to keep me honest."

"How many employees do you have?"

"Enough to keep me scrambling to keep them all busy."

"I'd like to sit by you if you're done working."

He slipped the PC into his briefcase and locked it. As he
was setting it aside, she sat close, smoothing his hair out of
the way. He lifted her robe to uncover just the chain on her
ankle. She smiled at him.

"Maybe we should just go to bed, huh?"

"Who needs a bed?" he asked.

It was two-thirty a.m. by his watch as he left the apartment,
resolutely staying tuned to the moment. The Caddy turned
over with a muted roar that settled into a docile growl. Respect
was prerequisite of his goal, but just when he thought he had
it, it kept getting away—wistful and naughty didn't come
close.

He had been in crisis for months, but he couldn't let that
get in his way now. If it did, he would be talked about with the
same note of condescending pity as his father. Or worse yet,
the town's golden boy would pump him full of Thorazine so
fast he wouldn't have time to say ouch, and have him hauled

off in a jacket with no arms. He would become a case study—a guinea pig in an imperfect science; a sideshow.

He had failed to find a cure, and was spiraling out of control.

His plan to outwit the crisis for this night was to discover how the sniper had known he would be at the old quarry the other night, so he could be shot at. It was one of several things currently chewing at him in tender places. Whether or not it mattered didn't matter; he had to keep busy.

The simple answer to the meaningless question was that the asshole couldn't have known. Even if the Porsche had been followed from the bar to the motel, Jared was sure that it had not been followed later, on its subsequent ramblings down dark and empty gravel roads. His inner sentry would have noticed.

Before coming to hate and fight it, Jared had relied a great deal on that part of his intellect. It was a creative, intuitive creature that leaped to visualize conditions and develop educated guesses that more often than not turned out to be fact—Torey's "silly method of investigation". By combining the creature's stratospheric fancies with his total lack of inner censor, Jared had grown such a strong sense of self-preservation over the years that even thinking of dying by his own hand blacked him out. An odd pair of headlights would certainly have set off every alarm he owned.

That meant that the rifleman had been at the quarry for reasons of his own, and that Jared had stumbled onto him by accident that night—a supremely messy way of doing things. But, whatever the method of detection, Jared suddenly needed to know why the sniper had been out there ahead of him and Abby. The answer might end up being something he could use.

The shooter hadn't been Griffin's sexually hinky froot loop; Jared was convinced of that. Thanks to Bud's boasting, the serial killer might find him a threat and want him dead, but the son of a bitch wouldn't have been sitting at a quarry in the middle of the night on the off chance a woman might show up. But Larry frequented bars and bookies, not the great outdoors. Lyle had the means locked away in a gun cabinet, but Jared didn't like him for it, not really. Lyle's lack of backbone was too pronounced. So, who the hell else wanted him dead, that he could possibly aid in killing him?

This night was soft and muggy, the sky punched with stars as brilliant as diamond chips on dark velvet. Once he left the sleeping town behind, Jared took a gravel road a mile farther east from the one that led to the three quarries. He had worn the crotch-hugging jeans because denim was less likely to snag noisily on bushes or rocks than his sweatpants. His old sweatshirt was too hot, but he left it on when he got out of the car because of its protective coloration. Knee deep in clinging weeds, he tied his hair back while looking over the eerie nightscape—thickets of silvery tall grass, soldierly fence posts iced with moonbeams, and scrub trees etched black against a sky that was the exact color of his eyes. He ended his meticulous survey by looking back west, the direction of tonight's exercise.

He slid down into the ditch and climbed up the other side. After stretching two strands of barbed wire apart with his hand and his foot, he twisted through the fence. Then he started off at a jog, wary of prairie dog holes and rocks in the pasture. The sweatshirt was soaked within a few minutes, but he didn't fret that. He was looking for the next fence, not wanting to end up skewered on the clutching barbs in the dark. When he came to the shining strands, he followed them to the grove of trees he had been watching all along—the trees that stood in a wild tangle between the first and second of the quarries. At the heavy underbrush, he went through the fence once more and carefully worked his way into the center of the grove.

Pausing often to listen, he eeled through wild raspberries and stunted cottonwoods, angling toward the first quarry. He eventually saw black water in the distant clearing. The rock bench where he had sat with Abby was plain in the muted light. They had made an easy enough target—he should be dead. He turned and melted further into the brush. The second quarry had never been used by the town kids for swimming, as far as he knew. Anyway, there were no trails to it. He had to fight for every step.

After about a hundred yards he reached the beginnings of the next rock flats, where the scrub thinned out and treacherous holes underfoot began. He was negotiating a particularly wide crevice when he heard the sound of metal on rock from somewhere just ahead. Dropping into a crouch, he strained his eyes and ears. The grating sound came again. He crept forward, testing every surface before putting his weight on it. Soon, a green Dodge pickup truck loomed in the moonlight. It was directly in front of him, backed up to the edge of the quarry. He left the trees, edging toward the truck. He paused at the rear wheel, reaching for the Glock.

In the silence, he stole along the side of the truck until the drop-off to the quarry was only a few feet away. The sound came again, from below. He inched across the bare rock on his stomach, feeling like a bug under a microscope in the moonlight. More than anything, he didn't want to die here and now—being left for vermin fodder would hardly be dignified. He hitched an eye over the edge.

The black water in this quarry rippled twenty feet down from where he was, but directly underneath him was a series of step-like ledges long ago hacked from the granite. Scattered along the ledges were burlap bags, bulging like rustic Santa's packs. All were tied shut with twine. He couldn't for the moment imagine what was in them, but whatever it was, there was a lot of it. He counted seven bags without moving.

Distracted by the temptation to poke his knife into the one closest, he almost missed seeing the figure coming up from below. He shinnied back a foot, flattening himself like a threatened badger. Heart pounding, he listened to the sound of burlap being dragged over stone, and a grunt. When he looked again, there was a space where a bag had been removed.

Pondering cluelessly, Jared wormed his way back to the trees, and holed up in a patch of deep shadow to wait. He waved away mosquitoes for a full twenty minutes before he heard footsteps on the rock in the clearing. Then he heard the truck door open. He was moving before he heard the truck start. Slithering lightly over the tailgate, he stretched out on the box floor as it began to move.

The truck bounced and swayed over the uneven flats. Jared clung to whatever was at hand to keep from rattling around like a pinball. He eventually got himself into a tight corner in the front of the box, wedged between a lone bale of straw and several bags of dry fertilizer. The truck picked up speed on a gravel road. Drying sweat cooled Jared's face as he closed his eyes and went along for the ride. He didn't raise his head to see where they were going; he concentrated on being tiny and invisible.

The ride wasn't a long one. He could tell they had come to a farmhouse by the sudden appearance of tree branches arched uniformly overhead. He got into a crouch as the truck slowed under a yard light, and was over the side and moving low in the shadows on the ground before the truck stopped. Scuttling for the first cover he saw, which was a tiny, dilapidated shed, he hugged the ground and peeked out. The driver closed the door to the truck and walked up the steps to Lyle's crooked little farmhouse.

Jared glowered at it in disappointment—been here, done this—but the driver of the truck gave him a slight tingle. His was a new face, anyway…and he evidently had free access to Lyle's rifles. The front door was unlocked—the man casually spit into the bushes before he walked in like he owned the place. The screen slapped shut behind him.

Jared darted from behind the sorry shed and around the still ticking truck. He went for the lighted side of the house, burrowing into ragged honeysuckle bushes. From a corner of the nearest window, he saw that the man was only eighteen or nineteen, muscular and dark-haired. He wore a sweat-blotched dark tee shirt and cowboy boots with heels that did not bode well for Lyle's newly refinished flooring. There was a tattoo of something black and red on his upper right arm. It looked decorative, not military.

Jared followed along outside without speculating – observe, then theorize; his hard and fast rule. The next window he came to was open. He was still trying to find decent footing in the bushes below the higher kitchen window when he heard Lyle greet the cowboy with a terse whine, "What took you so long?" Jared paused, blinking at the unmistakable sound of an open-handed slap. A chair scraped on floorboards, and there was a grunt of effort as someone apparently fell or was forced into it.

"Get off my case!" The kid's voice was deep and unrelenting. "You don't pay me enough to break my fucking back over it, Lyle. Maybe you just want to do it all by yourself, huh? Yeah, I didn't think so. Keep your fucking hair on."

"I'm sorry!" Lyle's familiar grovel came out in his voice. "I *worry* about you, that's all. Especially now, Kenny! I wish you hadn't shot at McCormick. He wasn't out there again tonight, was he?"

"You shoulda seen 'em!" the kid laughed derisively, leaving Jared highly insulted. "Scampering like bunnies—I was laughing so hard I couldn't shoot straight. Damn, that was funny! Nah, I busted up his little party, and the chicken-shit hasn't been back. I don't know what you and Larry are so scared of—longhaired creep!"

"You didn't grow up with him," Lyle moaned tearfully. "He's trouble, Kenny; I'm not kidding! No matter what we did to him, he'd never back down. He's *dangerous!*"

"Yeah, yeah, that's what you keep telling me, but I sure as hell don't see it. And I don't get why Bud's all hot that he's here, either. I thought your old man hated him. Get off your lazy ass and get me a beer."

"No, you've got it all wrong," Lyle sighed. "The old man hates everybody *but* Jared! Dad always loved him more than he did us." Over the sound of aluminum can tops being popped, he miserably mused, "I keep thinking that Dad's using him to keep Larry in line like he used to, but that doesn't make any sense! The old bastard's pushing *eighty*, and he's dying! I can't believe he's still fooling around with Larry!"

Jared felt a chilly blanket of speculation settle around his hearing. Was this old Ed's source of bottomless guilt?

"Kinky old fart," the kid drawled, obviously bored.

"Dad's using Jared, somehow!" Lyle charged resentfully. "It must have to do with the ranch. But Jared wasn't the one that made Dad have a fit and change his will—Larry did that all on his own! If he'da just left things alone, we would have been fine, but those damned loan sharks were after him again. You shouldn't have shot at McCormick!" Lyle suddenly snapped. "Larry's gonna take care of him; I told you that!"

"Yeah, and talk about stupid!" Kenny's jeer was scathing. "The stupid slob! We could have boosted that fancy-ass car and sold it, but no, Fatso blew it to hell! I feel like shooting *him*."

"Don't say that, Ken," Lyle begged. "And don't stir Larry up! He's figuring out what to do about everything—we just have to give him some time."

Jared heard the sound of water running from the tap, but he couldn't see anything because the ground under the window was void of stepladders. He was mangling flowers of some kind, but he was three feet too short.

"Larry's dumber than a box of rocks," the kid growled.

"He came up with this deal, didn't he? He's got the connections and everything!"

"Yeah, yeah, whatever; I don't care. I'm going home."

The sound of boot heels was loud on linoleum, then stopped.

"You don't really want to go, do you?" Lyle pleaded.

"You want me to beat the shit out of you again?" Kenny's

chuckle was cruel. "Is that what you want, huh? But what are you going to do for me?"

Jared finally just jumped up, catching the sill with his fingertips. He hung there, not wanting to bounce off the siding. Kenny muttered something more as Jared chinned himself high enough to peek through the screen. He made it brief, trusting his eyes to make it count, and dropped lightly back to the dirt below. He crouched there, frowning at the shadows. The snapshot in his head showed him Lyle sitting in a chair, his arms around Kenny's waist, his thin, leathery face pressed fearfully against the kid's stomach.

Well, well. Lyle wasn't intimate with his horses after all, as Larry had suggested. He apparently preferred young bulls, instead. Jared listened some more, still frowning, but when steam started oozing through the screen along with furtive noises, he inched away. He kept to as many moon shadows as he could until he came to the road, then struck off to the right at a trot.

What the hell had he just heard?

No, what he had heard didn't matter, he crankily reminded himself. What was of much more importance was that Kenny-the-cruel was the shooter. Now he just had to figure out how to piss him off again, and get himself caught at it.

If box-of-rocks Larry didn't get him first.

CHAPTER
21

EARLY IN THE MORNING, he washed her back with a sponge. Then he pulled her against him, stretching his arms around to wash whatever he could reach. The more slick suds, the better he liked it.

She dragged some of his hair forward over her soapy shoulder, smoothing its glistening blackness against her skin. "I'm going to wake up one morning and find you gone," she said out of nowhere. "Aren't I? I can't decide which would be worse, having to say good-by or not getting the chance." He didn't comment or reply, and she turned her head to eye him fondly. "You should know about this weird effect you have on people, Jared Jordan. You say we make you rip out pages for us, but you invite it. Most people pull away from others, but you volunteer yourself—wherever you go, whatever you're doing. Nobody can keep their hands off you; not even kids…it's your saving grace, you know."

"Excuse me?" he said with a wary smile as he ran the bar of soap over her breasts, watching the bubbles shine. "Saving—are you—you aren't going to call me wistful again, are you?"

Resettling her head beside his jaw, she shook it with a sigh. "No, I'm the one feeling wistful right now. I hate time."

"I have great timing."

"Yes, you do, but that's not what I meant. Time," she

repeated dreamily. "What's your interpretation of it? I'll bet it's good."

He toed the hot water tap off and held her more tightly to his chest. The wet bandage pulled his chest hair, under her spine.

"McCormick's Law of Continuity," he lectured, mocking her. "Each day is a new lifetime—I wake up; I'm born. Things begin to happen and I live with them. Eventually I lay down and die for a while. It starts over." He shrugged modestly. "All I can do is my damnedest to survive each successive life. Whatever happens, happens. I adjust."

Abby twisted her head around to kiss him. She probably meant it as a reward for sharing, but he took it as a trophy. He helped her turn and get on top of him by sliding down.

"Each day is a lifetime?" she asked huskily as he soaped her bottom with his chin submerged. "I like that." She hesitated. "Are you going to answer my first question?"

"I just did," he replied without any particular inflection.

After getting out of the rinsing shower, he stuck a towel around his waist and used the bathroom mirror to work the wide-toothed comb through his wet hair. Abby dressed for work in the bedroom, but came back to hang up her towel. She stopped, watching him for a moment. Then, looking for permission in his eyes in the mirror, she took the comb from his hand and led him to the vanity bench.

When she was certain the tangles were out, she continued combing the length slowly. He sat with his head bowed, looking down at his hands on the towel. When he felt her lay her fingers on his jaw and smooth the bristles there, he closed his eyes, fully absorbing the new sensation. Her fingers ran down his neck and over his shoulders. Then she parted the hair that lay smooth over his back and gently traced the long scars underneath. He didn't move or tell her to stop. He owed her; he could momentarily surrender.

She openly watched him dress—it was better than using

the mirror. When he holstered the automatic, she asked if she could look at it. Without a word he reached behind, pulled it back out. He thumbed the button to release the magazine, and held out the unloaded weapon butt first. She examined it thoroughly, even peering down the barrel. She memorized his hands as he reloaded and put it away. He helped her make the bed before they left the apartment.

They parted on the sidewalk in front of the house. He didn't offer her a ride, but she set off in the sunshine with a self-assured stride. He watched her go, suddenly feeling incapable…hollowly defenseless. Cursing his unforeseen and ridiculous dependence, he carried his things to the car. By his watch it was nearly eight. By ten after, he hadn't blown up, so he drove to the truck stop at the edge of town and sat in a booth by a window. He drank a glass of milk, then promptly ruined it by drinking three cups of coffee in rapid succession.

This was Friday. He had been here since Tuesday. The mere fact that he was still alive introduced vile things into his thoughts. In fact, there were ugly things all over the place, but nothing concrete enough—nothing he could get his teeth into, chew up, and digest.

Pot shots and pipe bombs were beginning to seem tame after what he had heard last night, and couldn't seem to forget. Something genuinely corrupt was hanging over Shady Rock like an acid rain cloud, and he had this suspicious feeling that he was somehow part of it. As was, of course, Bud.

…Bud Doherty had detained him on the street one hot summer day. Jared clearly remembered this because he had just pocketed a box of rolled exploding caps. The adult hand on his shoulder had scared the hell out of him—he thought he had been caught. Instead, he had been offered a job. A real job, working for a real wages on the Flying D. He had been gape-mouthed at the amounts that were mentioned. Compared to the pittance his mother gave him each week, it had seemed like millions. Within a month, eleven-year-old Jared's first paycheck went toward paying the motel mortgage.

Initially, he had been shy of the tall, broad man with the rugged face and gruff manner. Then he stood in awe of him, privately vowing to grow up to be just as successful and powerful. It had been sometime later—when Bud had caught him reading a comic book in the loft—that his admiration had been tainted with the first of his guilty confusion. The comic had been snatched away, and he had been dragged to the loft ladder. Jared clearly recalled his irrational kid's terror, thinking Bud was going to toss him through the hole to the concrete floor below. He had been shirking on the job, after all. But Bud had tucked him under his arm and carried him down, shouting for Larry and Lyle.

Bud had assembled all three in a corner of the barn and explained Jared's misdeed to the boys while getting a leather harness strap from a nail. Before Jared understood what was happening—he had never been spanked in his life—Bud had yanked his too-large jeans down and pushed him over a viciously prickly hay bale.

The punishment had been swift and shocking. Five agonizing slashes on the butt with hard leather, and harder muscle behind it. When it was done, Bud had left him bawling on the bale with orders to get back to work. At the end of the day, however, instead of making him walk the six miles back to town, Bud had dropped him off at the motel. He had also asked him if he would come earlier tomorrow. Jared had gratefully agreed. While stacking bales, he had been doubly miserable, believing he had lost his job as well as Bud's trust.

The belt in the barn was soon taken for granted; it was used on all three of them, although Larry had escaped it after the first year or so. Five years older than Jared and Lyle, Larry had been a man-sized boy. One day he had flatly refused to submit. He was always there to witness the others' punishment, however; Bud had insisted on that.

Bud and Larry had fought constantly; shouting matches

that threatened to erupt into physical violence, but never did. Bud and Lyle, as far as Jared could remember, got along all right. Lyle, being the youngest of the Doherty kids, was treated differently, anyway.

Bud and Jared, however, had eventually moved well beyond the realm of father/son clashes.

Once puberty and Leslie entered the picture, his and Bud's dealings went from five across the cheeks to total war. With a paycheck. An extra fifty at Christmas. A new shirt for his birthday. Ma had taken his money to save the motel, and inadvertently built his ego. Bud had hated Jared's interest in his only daughter, but also had made sure of his continuing willingness to work at the ranch.

Bud had caught them naked together in the loft one rainy summer afternoon, just after Jared had turned fourteen. He stood over them wrathfully while they scrambled into their clothes. Then he had sent Leslie weeping to the house and had beaten the bejesus out of Jared. As soon as Jared could breathe again, Bud had helped him to the truck and taken him home.

Thankful that his face was unmarked, Jared had avoided his mother and crawled into bed. Stiff and sick, he had reported for work again the next day as usual because he didn't know what else to do. He hated Bud more than he had ever hated anyone, but he loved Leslie, and had to see her. Bud had greeted him with the day's list and a stern lecture on original sin, hellfire, and condoms. He had caught them a couple of more times after that, but he had never used his fists to that extent again—he started using Neugebauer instead…

Jared rubbed his tingling face before drinking the last of the coffee. There had been nothing sexual in his relationship with Bud. It had been twisted and abusive but not carnal, as old Earl Williams must have mistakenly assumed.

But where had Earl gotten that weird assumption? Was there fire where there was smoke? Jared had never seen anything to suggest Larry as Bud's victim, but that had been

Lyle's implication last night, hadn't it? Larry and Lyle as a repulsive combination actually made more sense than Bud and Larry. Lyle had always been his older brother's drudge, a victim of absolute tyranny. But surely Leslie would have said something about that kind of family breakdown, sometime during their years together? If she had known about it. She had been Bud's little princess, so he concluded she probably hadn't known anything.

Jared was suddenly swamped in emotion, both past and present. Need, desire, jealousy, fear, doubt, hate, love…they were everywhere, but whose were they, and what had they led to?

Last night's eavesdropping had put a whole new spin on his already convoluted situation, and he was becoming increasingly apprehensive about where the spin was taking him. As his mind struggled to categorize and decipher, he tried to keep calm. Somebody was going to end up dead all right, but the more he thought about it, the more he was cynically worried that it wasn't going to be him. There were much more vulnerable victims hovering in the wings. But what could he do about them? Not a hell of a lot, that he could see. There just wasn't time.

He paid for the coffee and drove uptown for his appointment with the attorney. Ten minutes later he was back on the street. Finally operating on pure instinct, he went looking for a trailer on the edge of town.

Green-haired Frank Dotter/Slade was not overjoyed about being hauled from his lair so early in the morning. He yelled obscenities at Jared's ruthless knocking and finally opened the door wielding a machete. He paused, mouth hanging open, when he saw who was on his wobbly concrete-block step.

"Good morning," Jared said pleasantly. "May I come in?"

The young biker had trouble focusing. The reek of beer and pot wafted from the doorway in nearly visible clouds. Slade stumbled backwards a step.

It had been a mobile home, at one time. Traces of wall-paper still showed through the grime on the walls. There was a built-in china cabinet on the right wall, but the glass was long gone from the drooping doors. The shelves were stacked with beer cans, dirty dishes, dirty clothes, and dirty things Jared didn't want to recognize. The carpet was a mottled mauve, nearly obscured by heaps of clothing, tattered maga-zines, and curling pizza boxes. The furniture was a nightmare in crummy, and he didn't go near it.

"Hell of a party," he observed.

Slade grunted and fell onto the sagging sofa, rubbing his face and striped head vigorously.

The kitchen had been on the left. Jared's shoes stuck to the scarred and torn linoleum while he located a jar of instant Folgers in the depths of a cupboard with no door. He scrubbed a small pan, wishing he had some bleach. Then he filled it with water. He had to light the stove burner with his gold lighter; grease and garbage blocked the pilot light. There was an unopened package of Styrofoam cups under the table. He lit a cigarette, waiting.

Patty—he assumed it was Patty—came down the hall wearing nothing but a filthy lace teddy. Underneath the neglect, she had a decent body, but her bare feet were dirty and he stopped looking at her.

"Who are you?" she demanded, shoving matted hair out of her face.

"Avon calling," he said, studying the stained ceiling.

"Slade, who is this?" she whined.

"Shut up, Patty—get the fuck outta here! It's business."

She turned and went mumbling back down the hall, slamming a door. The whole trailer shook. The water boiled, but Jared gave it an extra minute to be sure all the crawlies were dead. Then he shook coffee from the jar into a cup. He used his fountain pen to stir it, then dried the pen on his handkerchief.

Back in the living room, Slade was sitting up—always

a good sign. He looked blearily at Jared, who held out the coffee. He groped for it.

"You mentioned assistance the other night," Jared reminded him.

"Whaddaya need?"

"I want Larry and Lyle Doherty tailed," Jared replied. "I need to know at regular intervals what each is doing. What kind of activity they are up to." He pulled a cellular phone from his jacket pocket and tossed it on to the couch beside Slade. "The number to call is on it. Bud Doherty is in the nursing home. He won't be going anywhere without help, but I need to know if either of his boys go to see him. Pay attention—if they do, I need to know immediately."

Kenny was another issue entirely, but if he was Griffin's serial killer, Special Agent Torey would just have to deal with him. Right now, an old cripple and a little girl were locked into Jared's muddy focus.

Slade guzzled the scalding coffee in one long swallow.

"I also need to know if either goes toward the Flying D," Jared went on. "I understand that you can't be in several places at once, so this means moving around. Here's gas money." He dropped a hundred-dollar bill on the couch next to the phone. "If you lose one of them, ride around until you find him again. If you lose either of them completely, call me. Call me often, understand? Keep me updated."

"Sure, man, I can do that."

"What do you charge?"

Slade thought about it. "'Nother one of those?" He indicated the bill on the couch.

Jared took out his wallet and dropped four more, one at a time. "I pay well for work done well," he said coldly. "I expect value for my dollar. And I need yours and Patty's signatures as witnesses to mine, on a document. Get her in here."

On the way back into town, Jared stopped at a drug store to use the telephone book. He wrote down a number from it, but went back to the Caddy to use the phone in the visor.

He smoked heavily while he talked to Earl Williams—the man with the apples, comic books, and guilty conscience—at great length. Then, he wrote down more phone numbers as he was given them. After several hang-ups, he reached an elderly woman who told him what he needed to hear. She knew everyone and everything in town, but it took most of his charm and all of his patience to get anything out of her.

He made two more phone calls in an attempt to confirm her information, but got nowhere. Bud's name meant too much to these people to be flinging it around like confetti. He went to the bank to deposit his will, and back to the attorney's with the vault key and written instructions.

His stomach was beginning to argue with either the coffee or the despicable summaries he was quickly reaching. He had probably gotten interested way too late to stop the inevitable. But he welcomed the understanding his creature was now feeding him, almost non-stop.

It was coming, and his last wishes were covered; fuck the rest.

He pulled into the slot in front of number ten. The telephone on the visor chirped at him. Slade's first check-in.

"Yes?"

"Uh, I got Bud alone at the Home. Larry is on the streets and Lyle is mowing a yard."

"Do you have a destination for Larry?"

"Huh? Oh, no, uptown, I guess. I can be there in three, four minutes."

"Do it. Keep on him, no matter what. Do not lose him!"

The back of his neck shrieking with tension, Jared got out of the car. He dimly wondered if he should take his briefcase from the locked trunk. Couldn't concentrate on the question. He suddenly couldn't concentrate on anything but the smothering of red flags flapping in his head. He carried his garment bag to the door and took his time reaching into his pocket for the key. Any minute now. What would it be? An iron pipe to the head? A bullet? A baling wire garrote? It didn't matter;

hopefully, Slade would be a crafty, elusive witness. He had paid the ugly asshole enough.

22

H E MATERIALIZED INTO CONSCIOUSNESS on the floor of the back seat of a car. New leather smell—he subliminally recognized it as the Caddy. It jolted at high speed over a gravel road—the noise of spitting rock under his ear compounded the awesome pain lodged in his skull. He was wrapped in rope. Not tied; he could feel it wound around his entire body… A wad of cloth was stuffed so far back in his throat he was afraid he might swallow it. Something was tied around his mouth to keep it there. Blindfolded, he tried to move, but the gnawing in his head sent him spinning into darkness again.

An eternity later, he groaned behind the gag when his feet were seized and he was dragged from the car. His back hit the ground hard. Pebbles gouged and weeds slapped his face while catching in his hair. Dimly, he heard panting and grunting from above. His head bounced off a rock. Somebody laughed, puffing, at his muffled gasp. He was pulled and yanked across …a driveway? No, not smooth enough for concrete. Odd steps and small ridges…loose gravel…and occasional weeds. Wide and smooth, but not too smooth. Sun-blasted and pungent.

The quarries.

His feet were eventually dropped. He dizzily listened. Where was everybody? It was hot and dry; he should be hearing excited voices and splashing under the summer sun beating down on him. His confusion was immense, an awful thing that threatened to overwhelm what faculties remained. His head pounded. If he retched, he would choke on the gag.

He heard the clinking of glass in the silence, and the hard breathing of his assailant coming closer. Suddenly, the gag was yanked down and the suffocating wad jerked from his throat. His nose was cruelly pinched off—a bottle neck was forced into his mouth. Gallons of whisky rushed in. He struggled violently against the vise on his nose, grinding the bruised back of his head and inhaling more than he swallowed. The bottle bounced off his teeth and whisky poured down his face and neck. A hand grabbed his hair, wrenching his head around. At the same time, he was viciously kicked in the ribs. Something gave there, with a red-hot explosion—he could only keep choking.

"Don't you want to drink with me, old buddy?" Larry's wheezy, too happy voice drilled into his head. "But we're celebrating, Jared!" He panted a grim laugh. "I got your gun and car, and now I'm going to go kill the old man for us. About time the old fart croaked, ain't it? Here, have another shot. On me, old pal."

Fingers grabbed his nose. The glass ground against his teeth. This time Larry stood on his hair, giving him nowhere to go. Raw alcohol poured down his throat. He gagged on it as fast as it came up. A holocaust in his lungs sucked the ability to breathe right out of them. Larry kicked him again and moved away, muttering. Jared rolled to his glowing side, spitting, but he couldn't bring anything up. He knew it would happen eventually, but he needed it now, before he got totally bombed.

No – no, that wasn't right. What was he thinking? Death was here and he couldn't do a damned thing to stop it. Finally.

"Shoot me!" he gagged into baked dirt. "Hurry!"

"Can't," Larry growled, several feet away. "That would ruin my plan. See, they'd know you weren't out here alone if you showed up with holes or rope marks." He wheezed. "I wouldn't do it like that anyway—I'd rip you to pieces with my bare hands!"

"Please!" Jared gasped. "*Please* shoot me." Quick, heavy footsteps, then his hair was grabbed again, pulling him to his back. He blindly shouted, "Kill me, you fat fuck!"

"Oh, I'm gonna!" Larry spat in his face. "You don't have to ask me twice, no way. But keep begging—I've waited years to hear it!"

Larry knelt. Jared heard the seams of his clothing making popping noises. The Glock dug into his ear, and Larry's hand dove into the ropes at his belt.

"I usta dream of castrating you," Larry puffed maliciously. "Remember how we used to castrate the yearlings, Jared? Knock 'em down and whack 'em off? I always wanted to do that to you...turn you soft and weak, and then make you cry!"

Jared heaved away from the promise of the Glock, away from the grasping, pinching, disgusting hand in his pants. Drenched in alcohol, sweating in agony—he threw up, wrenching his shattered side. Larry chucked excitedly in the distance.

"God, you used to get the old man going! He'd say to me, 'Say, Larry, I think Jared's been bad again, hasn't he?' and I'd say, 'Oh, yeah, Dad, he's been a real bad boy; you better whip his pretty li'l ass!' Nothin' I did ever got him so excited, and I *hated* you for that. But now that he took the ranch away from me, I hate him, too! Here, have another drink before we get rid of those ropes..."

...sounds were loud and mostly meaningless; a vindictive whirl left him without direction. He opened his eyes, but everything was a shocking white blur...nothing worked—brain, mouth, eyes, or muscles. His face prickled. He tried to rub it—his arms flopped uselessly...his side was caved in and he breathed wet concrete. He wanted to turn to his side, to curl up and weep, but he didn't know where his side was…he blindly battled the torment in his body and the weight on his chest and the scum in his mouth. He didn't want to be laying here helpless and hurt, but he would endure whatever he got. He had to. No one could do it for him…

A threatening voice made the splintered shards of his mind hiss, and he struggled to focus on it.

"…rather not have to restrain him. Just guide his hands away until I can—no! Do not sit on his legs…do not hold him down in any way. He isn't going anywhere, and restriction only agitates him further. Yes, that's better…Marie, are you standing by with—"

"McCormick! Can you hear me? Can he hear me, Rick?"

"Howard, please! I can't suture this if you keep getting in the way. I've almost…there; everybody back. He should settle down now that I've stopped picking at him. Get the sides of the bed up. Yes, increase the drip, and let's keep the heart monitor on for another hour, just to be safe. It's hard to know what he's hearing, Howard, but shouting doesn't work; I tried it. I doubt that he's hearing much of anything right now. His vitals are fairly good though, considering."

Griffin grumbled urgently, "Jesus, he looks—can't you clean him up?"

"I'm well aware of how he looks, but how he feels is what drives Mr. McCormick. Give the drugs a chance; when he feels better, we'll all breathe easier."

But he wasn't breathing easier; nothing about living was fucking easy, not even dying.

"Okay, let me get this straight," Griffin said tersely. "You brought him in—is that right, Frank? How did you happen to be riding by the quarries just then?"

"I was out cruisin', that's all. It's a nice day. I saw him out there floppin' like a fish and jumped in after him."

Griffin growled, "I'm hearing so much crap here I need to put on my hip boots! You don't get your butt out of bed before dark any day of the week, Frank, not even a nice one!

Try again—where did you get that five hundred dollars? He paid you for something! What was it?"

"I don't have to talk to you!" Slade insisted, hostile. "I did him a favor, all right? But if you're going to yell at me, I won't do you one—like tell you what he said after I hauled his ass out of the water!"

"He said something? You mean he was conscious?"

"I don't know what he was, man. He was mumbling somethin', that's all. After I emptied half the fuckin' quarry out of him."

"All right, Frank; you're a hero. You happened by, and being the fine citizen you are, you saved his life. Now tell me what he said before I knock it out of you!"

"He said not to tell anybody." Sullen.

"Not tell anybody what?"

"That he was still breathin', man! What do you think? He kept sayin' 'I'm *dead*. Don't tell anybody different'. So I said okay, man, I won't, and slung him over the bike. Tough mother—but he's in bad shape."

"That he is," Lightner interjected precisely. "On top of alcohol poisoning, liquid asphyxiation, two cracked ribs, and the head injury, I'd say he is about half a minute away from a full-blown bleeding ulcer, and even closer than that to a complete mental breakdown. I want—"

"Stop!" Griffin barked, outraged. "Not another word! Frank, go home; do you hear me? I'll be out to your trailer in half an hour, so go home and stay there. What is the matter with you, Rick?" he snapped when the biker had angrily clumped out. "You can't say something like that in front of Frank! Or anybody!"

When Lightner replied, he sounded surprised. "Howard, I was simply stating a diagnosis based on close observation. I warned you—this man is in serious psychological trouble."

"He is not!" Griffin snapped back. "I checked him out—I was on the phone for an hour talking to people who know him better than anybody! Rick, I was laughed at in every case for even suggesting your cockeyed theory. McCormick took a medical retirement from the FBI, yeah, but for his stomach, not because he's nuts! He was on his way to writing his own ticket anywhere! Every one of those people I talked to would take him now, in a heartbeat. How can you stand there and tell me he's crazy?"

"Not crazy, Howard—psychologically out of balance. And while the condition itself isn't a crime, he did kill that helpless old man!"

"He did *not* kill Bud Doherty," Griffin said in deep disgust.

"That was his gun beside the body; you told me that! And his car was seen here this morning. Howard, he shot Bud, drove out to the quarries, got drunk, and dived in. It's as simple as that. You told me that he never sleeps, and I personally saw him in a psychotic episode that was a textbook indication of that! He's got the background and the symptoms. What more do you need?"

"Rick, you're the other smartest man I know, but I just don't believe it! Tell me why he would leave his weapon at the scene? Not only was it evidence, but it's part of him—he couldn't do it! I don't doubt that he's used it with deadly force, but I guarantee that when he did, he didn't just lay it down and walk away from it!"

"If he knew he was going to die, Howard," Lightner said more reasonably, "he probably didn't even miss it. Stop thinking of him as rational. He's over the edge; he doesn't know what he's doing. And what about his blood alcohol? Whiskey is a potent anesthetic; it helps a lot of suicides take the last step."

"If he wanted to kill himself he wouldn't screw around with an anesthetic! He'd eat a bullet, wouldn't he? Wouldn't he?"

"It wouldn't surprise me," Lightner hedged cautiously, "but that doesn't mean—"

"No, Rick, whoever threw him in the quarry wanted it to

look like he got drunk and jumped in." Griffin hesitated, then said, "Look, you don't have the whole story here. Besides the bomb, McCormick was shot at the other night. Somebody's out to kill him, and almost damned well succeeded this time."

"Howard, you said he had been helping your investigation, but if this hypothetical somebody is the serial killer, why did he kill Bud?"

"I don't know why Bud is dead. I won't know anything until McCormick can tell me!"

"I'm sorry, Howard, but things are probably just the way they look. And furthermore, McCormick doubtlessly survived this suicide attempt because he saw the motorcycle coming and knew he would be saved. He doesn't want to die; he wants help. I told you he came to me yesterday morning without even knowing he had!"

"He wants somebody to think he's dead," Griffin said adamantly, "so he can nail him. Besides Frank, who knows he's here?"

"Myself and Nurse Oswald. We put him back here, away from the medical wing, because I don't want him near anyone. If he killed Bud, and it stands to reason he did, he's your problem as much as he is mine."

"We're going to keep this quiet, understand? We're going to play it how he wants it."

"Howard—"

"Rick, unless or until Bud's death is connected to the other murders, it's my investigation. So, until McCormick can tell us what happened, nobody says a thing about him being here, about him being alive—about anything! Is that clear?"

"What's clear," Lightner said evenly, "is how easy it is to let your faith rule your logic. You don't want Mr. McCormick to be anything less than his reputation, do you?"

"Are you thinking of his welfare while you trash that reputation, Doctor, or are you hurt enough to do it because he rejected you?"

"I don't know what you're talking about, Howard, but I suggest you stop right there because it's obvious that you don't either."

"You didn't make sexual advances toward him?"

"Chief Griffin, will you just *listen* to yourself? You've known me for my entire life!"

"You're gay!"

"But I'm not stupid! Mr. McCormick scares the heck out of me! And the fact that you don't feel the same leads me to wonder how badly job stress is affecting *you!*"

Griffin was quiet, then he apologized. "You're right; I'm desperate, Rick. I'm sorry. But I think McCormick is onto something. Please help him."

"I am helping him! Oh, all right. I'll keep his presence here quiet for tonight, but only on one condition: I want an officer with him at all time. For the hospital's protection, not his!"

...eventually bumping into silence, he gave up his struggle with even a pretense of consciousness.

An incredible desiccation of body and soul eventually dragged Jared fully awake. He pried gluey eyes open to a darkened, functional hospital room...flashed back to a lush jungle hideout that had harbored a small Guatemalan man with a very large bull whip. He sat up with a groaned curse, thinking he had somehow rolled to his back in the night, ruining all the time and work that the medics had put into repairing it. But a razor sharp spear in the side nearly toppled him over. He grabbed his ribs. Somebody resembling Randy caught him and lowered him back down. Through the ringing in his ears he wondered how the hell had Randy gotten to the jungle.

Then he was sick.

He had never been so sick, and it wasn't just the smell of the leftover booze and quarry water coming up, or the demons slashing up his back and mutilating his insides. It was the caustic memory of what had happened at the quarry that turned him inside out. The wheezing voice. The fat, eager hands on his genitals, the booze spilling down his face, the ropes that gave him nothing. He didn't remember being untied or going into the water, but he did remember dying, the wonderful stillness…

Why was he here then, moaning and puking? Why wasn't he at the bottom of the quarry with his old bike, drifting with the nibbling bluegills instead of praying for his head to just explode and get it over with? Crushing headache, deadly hangover, lava in his stomach, napalm in his side—and had he been raped before going in? He was so damaged in so many places that he didn't know.

He passed out again. But when he couldn't stand the swamp in his mouth any longer, he willed himself to wake up and try once more. Fighting his ribs – everything—he dragged himself up using the bed rail. His watch was gone; he thought it must be late. Much too late.

Randy was at his side in a moment, looking pitying, and very disillusioned. Jared woozily plucked at the tube that ran from the stand above the bed to his inner forearm. The tape pulled his hairs, reminding him of Abby's bandage. Her sense of fairness clashed with Randy's disappointment, hanging so close to his malfunctioning eyes. Something had definitely happened to turn Randy against him, but he couldn't remember…

"Water?" he whispered.

Randy mutely put the tall Styrofoam glass into his shaking hand, moving the straw closer. Jared choked, making Randy jump. He cleared his sore throat several times and drank again. It was too late; it had to be. He squinted at Randy who watched him with a profoundly uneasy look on his face. He wasn't going to get anything from the little shit, but he had to try.

"Thanks," he said, his voice a little stronger. He applied himself to making his words clear. "That's better. Time is it?"

"A little after one in the morning."

No respectful sir, and sixteen hours too late.

"How'd I get here?"

"I don't know. I was just told to sit with you. Uh, I don't think you should talk."

"Okay," Jared whispered, closing his eyes to the whirl. "Are you supposed to call Griffin now?"

"No, you were pretty sick again a while ago. I heard the doctor tell Chief Griffin that he's giving you something to help you sleep."

Jared blinked stupidly up at the clear plastic bag on the frame. Well, that would have to stop, wouldn't it. He very much wanted to just lay back, to feel the cool sheets against the burning and to let the dope carry him away. He wanted to sleep, oh, yes. He was too late, and he was so fucking wasted.

The ice water seemed to be making his overall dizziness worse, but he was so thirsty he drank about half of it anyway. Then, he tried on a smile for the twitchy infant cop. Echoes of a ghostly conversation rumbled through his mind, but it was frustratingly distorted and patchy.

"Bud's dead, isn't he?" he rasped. "Who has my weapon? Has it been found?"

"I really can't talk about it," the little brat said with finality. "Will you please lay down? Maybe I'd better call the nurse."

Jared remained as upright as he could, shaking his head. He tried to run his fingers through his hair, but met with only lifeless tangles. So far, he had only been feebly testing hand or toeholds in the sides of his black well of ignorance, injury, and drugs. Bud was dead, and Larry had used his automatic. But so what? That didn't tell him a damned thing. He absolutely had to do better.

"Gotta get up and pee, Randy," he whispered wistfully. "Give me a hand?"

Randy wisely hesitated, but then foolishly leaned to undo the catch of the bed rails. Jared grabbed him just under the jawbone with a pained grunt and a determined squeeze. He let go a scant second later, when Randy dropped. The weight of the rookie's body clattered the bed rail to its lowest position.

Jared slid to the floor. Hunched and faint and nauseated, he yanked the IV needle from his arm, ignoring the spurt of blood. Staggering, he made it to the closet and found his damp, reeking clothes in a plastic garbage bag on the floor. His fingers weren't cooperative, but they finally got his pants up and zipped. That was all he needed. His shoes were missing anyway. He jerked the flimsy cotton gown off and tottered back to Randy's still form hanging over the bed rail. After unsnapping the kid's .38 from the leather holster, he slid it into the waistband of the clammy pants.

He somehow managed to heave Randy the rest of the way onto the bed without falling on his hung-over, doped, ass. After wasting precious seconds and leaving bloody fingers on the boy's uniform while rummaging through its pockets, he finally spotted car keys on the bed side stand. He covered Randy to the nose with the sheet.

He got the sliding window open somehow, and punched the screen with a loose fist. He fell more than climbed out, landing heavily on the lawn just below. Struggled with the powerful urge to simply succumb to Lightner's drugs. He lurched to his feet and trudged around the building, looking for the patrol car that had to be there. Glancing over his shoulder once in the dark, he saw that the open window was still as dim as his vision.

23

THE OFFICIAL WHITE CROWN Victoria waited for him at the front door of the hospital. He scarcely felt bits of sharp gravel scattered over the blacktop cutting into his feet as he approached it.

No way a half-naked, barefoot man with wild long hair could look anything but suspicious under the circumstances, but he couldn't help it. He walked up to the car, unlocked the door, and got in. Griffin, the conscientious cop, saw to it that the town's patrol cars were taken care of; this one started right up. Jared didn't wait to see if anyone took notice of the noise in the hush of the night. He reversed and stepped on the gas. He didn't think to turn off the radio or to even grope for the headlights until he had reached the very dark road into town.

The two stop signals blinked yellow as he drove through; his was the only moving car on Main at this hour. His soggy mind kept playing tricks on him and his eyes blurred occasionally, but he made it to Larry's house without hitting anything. He killed the lights and engine, and picked his way through the mini-junk yard. He went through the flimsy front door as if it wasn't there.

Larry Doherty was on the couch. Even running on only one rail, Jared could tell that the lump was Larry because of its massive size and from the constant wheezing. A closer look in the dark told Jared that Larry saved time in the morning by sleeping in his clothes. Larry had stirred slightly at the sound of the door, but it would take more than a burglar to interrupt his sleep. A quick if bleary look in the back of the house told Jared that Lena was dead to the world, too, her pitch-black room reeking of gin. He re-closed her door and trailed his hand along the wall to keep his bearings back to the living room. He and Larry were going to have a little chat, but he knew without a doubt that he was too late.

When he heard an unexpected noise, his up-till-now steady heart gave a perverse lurch. He reeled, then heard the noise again. He faced a dark doorway, fumbling for a light switch just inside. The sudden glare of the un-shaded bulb nearly knocked him down. He grabbed the doorframe and hung on until his indignant vision returned. When it had, he hung his head for a moment, taking several shallow breaths. Not too lat, after all.

Maybe.

Thomas Jeremiah wriggled fretfully in the middle of an unmade bed. Jordan Elaine was a small ball at the foot, dressed in jeans and a tee shirt and tennis shoes. She hadn't moved when the light came on. Not good.

She had been sick before falling into unconsciousness or death, and had crept away from the mess. Her left thumb was in her mouth, but her mouth was slack, and she was marble white.

"Shit," Jared swore, a truckload of hate hitting him squarely and violently.

The hate put a measure of strength into his backbone, allowing him to take a step forward and press a shaking finger to her jugular. The tiny vein throbbed. The little girl had tossed up some of whatever drug she had been given—enough, hopefully. He couldn't stand here wringing his hands about it. What were Larry's plans for them? The sham adoption that Leslie had died trying to forestall? The quarries? Black market? Deep burial in the junkyard out front?

He staggered to set the .38 on top of the squirming baby, then picked up the little girl under her arms. When he hoisted her slight weight to a shoulder, her head fell limply onto his matted hair. Overbalancing for a moment, he steadied himself against the mattress. Then he scooped up the bundle of blankets and weapon in his other arm. Bouncing off walls, he made his way toward the living room. The open front door afforded him some light from a pole outside.

Larry snored on asthmatically, so Jared kept going—down the steps and then the broken sidewalk, to the car. He put the baby on the trunk in order to open the back door and lay the little girl on the seat. The baby was making real noises now, but they seemed tiny and weak to his inexperienced ear. He tucked the bundle on the floor behind the driver's seat. Safer than beside the little girl, he dully reasoned. Convulsions weren't out of the question. He retrieved the .38 from the moving folds of the baby blanket.

Back in the house, he braced his knee against the couch and jammed the barrel of the .38 into Larry's nearest ear. He cocked it emphatically. Larry opened his eyes and squawked.

"Oh my, Larry," Jared rasped with enormous, gentle pity. "You're in some shit now." Larry rumbled something disbelieving deep in his barrel chest. "You should have shot me like I asked," Jared said into the shine of panic in Larry's eyes. "You really should have. Oh, well; too late now, huh? Let's go for a spin, shall we?"

He kept the .38 snug under Larry's chins as the big man struggled to his feet. With the pistol as his guide, Larry stumbled out of the house and down the sidewalk. Jared opened the car door for him.

"You get to drive. Climb over."

"Listen, I—"

"Shut up, you inept piece of shit!"

Jared was beginning, at last, to feel the welling rage that rendered every other emotion nil in its dominance. His aches were falling before it; his fears and doubts shriveling away. It felt so good he suddenly wanted to stretch widely, giving it more room in every nerve ending and muscle fiber. Instead, he pressed full-length against Larry. He stabbed the .38 into a belly-buried crotch and draped his other arm intimately around the heavy shoulders. He whispered their destination into the hairy ear that was only inches away.

Larry's eyes kept darting toward Jared. Perspiration poured down his round face, and his thick fingers left wet marks on the wheel. They rode through the night, wordless until Jared was satisfied that Larry had brought the Vic as close to the third, most disused, quarry as he could. When Larry had jerked the car into Park and shakily turned off the ignition, Jared moved away, inviting him to get out. Larry did, and predictably tried to run. Smiling from the passenger seat, Jared squeezed the trigger.

With a screech that further shattered the night's tranquillity, Larry landed on his side. He clawed at his leg, heaving in the moonlight.

The report of the gun inside the confines of the car had driven the baby to screams. Jared frowned over the back of the seat at it, under the dome light. He obscurely wondered what to do. He hadn't meant to frighten it. In fact, he had completely forgotten the kids were there. He hesitated, but the little girl dropped her hand to the floor, feeling around with her fingers. Never opening her eyes, she hitched herself forward on the seat and felt again, this time finding the squalling baby. She clumsily patted it. The baby hiccuped loudly.

Jared got out of the car and closed the door. He took his time picking his way across the rocks in his bare feet. Sobbing loudly, Larry had been trying to crawl away, but when he looked up and saw Jared standing over him he collapsed face-first into a patch of weeds. Jared crouched. What blood he saw was black in the silver light—not a problem. So far.

"Don't kill me!" Larry howled into his arms. "Please don't

kill me! I didn't mean it. I was just fooling with you—you didn't die!"

"Stupid bastard," Jared hissed. "You loser, you would have done me a favor! I wanted to die!"

But now he couldn't; there were babies in his way. Larry would kill them, too, if Jared gave him the .38. But, he could—no, he would have to…he teetered, suddenly overwhelmed both physically and mentally.

Then, a certain higher ascendancy flowed through him like a smooth bourbon—a rise in composure lifted his chin and allowed him to wring twice as much good from each breath he took with lungs that were lungs again. His thoughts and actions quickly re-stabilized at this new height. He had a job to do. One thing at a time—and past was just going to have to catch up to present whether he liked it or not.

He said from the heights, "Connect some dots for me, Larry."

"Don't shoot me!"

"Why was I hired at the Flying D?"

"Wha—? D-Dad saw you in town one day—couldn't stop talking about you! He—he wanted you at the ranch."

"To spank? To admire my dimples, what? Come on, Larry!"

"Jesus, Jesus!" Larry wept noisily. "Don't shoot me—he wanted – M-Ma left him because he couldn't do it. He said looking at you could help him get it up again!" Larry labored to sit up, clutching his thigh, in his earnestness to explain. "He said – "

Without thought, Jared slashed the short barrel of the .38 across his face, driving him back to the ground. "Don't, Larry," he warned remotely. "Blatant brutality bores me, but I'll risk being bored if you move again. Tell me why you killed Leslie."

Sobbing on the ground on his back, Larry used his sleeves to mop his bloody face. "She—I didn't mean to!" he gasped. "I was only trying to talk to her! I just wanted her to see that it wasn't fair that her kid got the ranch!"

"So you choked her when she wouldn't listen."

"I—I didn't know she was dead! I didn't mean to!"

"But Larry," Jared said with aloof irritation, "you aren't seriously trying to make me believe that your dick just accidentally fell out of your pants and scummed her up, are you? That she fell out of her clothes on the way to the rug? Try again."

"I was scared!" Larry shrieked hysterically. "I killed her—I had to do something! I made it look like that other guy had done it. Everybody believed he had!"

"Not everybody," Jared mentioned. "Bud didn't. He knew it was one of you."

"Yeah, I couldn't believe it! How did he know? I was so careful!" Larry stopped to swallow his dumb amazement. "I had to kill him then, don't you see?" he finished lamely, with the wheezy whimper sneaking back into his voice. "He said he was going to turn me in!"

Big mouth Bud. He must not have had any toast handy.

"You used my gun on Bud. My car."

"Yeah, it should have worked! Everybody knows how much you hate him..." Larry added plaintively, "My leg hurts!"

"Oh, does it?" Jared asked. "Shall I shoot you in the arm to take your mind from it? No? Then tell me about keys. Tell me about the pocketful of keys Lyle jingles. May I assume that they fit most of the business doors in town? And that you cut them at the hardware store?"

"How'd you find out about that?" Larry gaped.

One of the niggling, jittery things had finally, finally become clear. The receipt in Leslie's jacket pocket had made him fixate on keys. Lyle jingled keys and Griffin had yelled at him for not needing keys. Lyle and Kenny had talked about an arrangement, and there had been no signs of forced entry in the burglarized businesses. It had taken its sweet fucking time, but comprehension had finally come to him.

"You made a deal with Lyle, right?" he encouraged. "I'm chock-full of anticipation, Larry. Why don't you tell me what that deal was?"

Larry had stopped bawling, but his huffing and puffing was alarming. It made his mountainous belly jiggle. "I just made 'em—he and his kid stud used 'em!" he insisted sullenly, "My leg hurts – I'm gonna bleed to death! Did Lyle tell you about the keys and everything? He said you came sniffing around, but that you didn't know anything. Who told you? It had to be Lyle!"

"What don't I know?" Jared asked. He was trying to draw his fingers through hair that had the texture of picture wire, from all it had been through. "I've learned that Bud used my dimples as a jack, and you were jealous. You screwed Lyle as often as Bud screwed you; am I right? But what don't I know?" Jared could hear nighthawks whistling, see them dipping athletically to brush the water below for mosquitoes. The white stripes on their wings flashed in the moonlight. A cricket peeped at his bare, bleeding feet. He suddenly didn't want to go on. "I have five bullets left, Larry," he intoned, "and I will serve them to you one by one until I get what I want. Is this clear? What don't I know? Are you going to tell me that you were abusing Leslie, as well?"

Larry suddenly wheezed a different wheeze through his renewed tears—he was laughing. "It ain't abuse when it's asked for, stupid!" he jeered sloppily, momentarily sounding like the old Larry. "We loved each other, all of us! And you helped – it started with your bare ass, in the barn. But, later you stole Leslie. You weren't supposed to do that! Dad blew a gasket that night, when you and her ran away…he couldn't watch you screw her anymore. You weren't supposed to leave like that!"

The belly demons stirred. Jared wiped his forehead,

feeling their bared claws testing Lightner's deadening drugs. "Did she know he was watching us?" he asked emptily.

"Sure she knew, stupid! Once you got smart enough to figure out what your dick was for, Dad put her with you. You two really got him going!"

"Why did she leave me?" he heard himself unwillingly ask the question he had asked countless times. "She talked me into running away. She married me and she put me through night school. She loved me. Why did she leave?"

Larry's next laugh was uproarious and gleeful. "Stupid, McCormick!" he shouted. "You were always so goddamned stupid! I used to love the look on your stupid face when Dad grabbed you to beat you! You always looked so surprised, like how can this be? I'm too good for this! And you convinced Leslie you were just too damned good to live with. She called Dad to tell him she was knocked up, the bragging bitch, and Dad went to Chicago to tell her if she didn't come back to Shady Rock with his grandbaby, he would tell you all about her loving us. She couldn't stand the thought of you knowing that, oh, no! So, do you get it now, dummy? Dad screwed us, using you, and he screwed you, using her! But I screwed him good!" Larry gasped his manic pleasure of finally getting to brag about what he had done. "With your gun!"

Jared got to his feet, his matted hair blowing across his face, momentarily obscuring his view. Larry's expression turned to stark terror in the moonlight. He covered his head with both arms, his entire form shaking with hysteria. As quickly as he could, Jared pressed the barrel of the .38 into his own temple. It was cold and hard.

…and came back to find himself on the lip of the quarry.

One slug, or one more long step would have killed him, but he hadn't given himself either. Of course fucking not. He stared at the jagged rocks and black, black water far below. Feeling the gray lead-in chaotically beginning yet again, he spun around, putting his back to the forbidden idea. He dropped to a comforting crouch, still gripping the weapon.

He had failed to shoot himself, and he had failed to jump, but he couldn't fail at everything.

He was trained. Talented, intelligent, remorseless, immoral—and unstoppable.

He stood, a fountain of ice. Already calculating his next move, he knew he would finish this job correctly, because he was incapable of doing it any other way.

But first...he went back to the sagging dark mound on the rocks that had been Larry. It took only a moment to roll it over the cliff.

CHAPTER
24

THE WARM NIGHT GROUND on, taking him with it. By the time he reached town, resolve was an actual taste in his dry mouth, and it was sweet. The headache from the booze and the concussion was so encompassing as to be forgettable; it had become a part of him. His scorched throat and the spikes in his ribs were in deadlock, but he had passed beyond tired, was able to stand aside from it all. The ice he had grown was an unyielding stalagmite up his spine.

He parked the patrol car next to the Cadillac in front of unit number ten. He eyed the Caddy blankly for a minute, then decided that Griffin must have put it there for some unknown reason. Maybe Slade had actually passed along the message to keep him dead? Didn't matter; it was over.

In the orangey haze of the outside lights, he kicked in the flimsy unit door. After slapping on a light, he checked the interior, then went back to the car to get the kids. He didn't know if they were sleeping or dead, only that they had been quiet all the way into town.

The little girl was still breathing, but she was limp in his arms as he carried her in and laid her on the bed. He covered her with the spare blanket. He went back out and picked up the blue bundle from the car floor. His filthy hands left smudges. After laying the bundle in the middle of the bed, he tried to brush the smudges off. That only made things worse.

He stood back, looking down at them. The baby made a small noise, but didn't wake either.

He found he wanted to get the one-eyed cat out of the trunk of the Caddy.

Things worked for him this way sometimes; he would do something for the hell of it—like stealing the toy—only to see later that there had been a reason. The intuitive, impish creature in him kept him alert to many future possibilities.

The cat was balding and worn, obviously a favorite at sometime in the girl's life, and he thought she ought to have it now. But the car was locked and the spare keys were in his briefcase—which was in the trunk, too. He didn't have the time or inclination to break into the car. Maybe Griffin had the other set.

More keys.

He had two phone calls to make, but couldn't possibly conduct business in the condition he was in. Trembling only slightly, he went to shower—blistering hot to sterilize everything, and then straight cold to keep the core solid. He washed his hair twice.

He left the heavy tape binding his lower chest, but ripped the dirty hospital gauze from the pathetic little cut and threw it on the floor of the shower. Eight tiny, stiff stitches held him together now, instead of Abby's tape crosses. For a moment he stood with his mouth open in the frigid stream of the shower, drinking it in as fast as he could. He heard the magical violin over the spray and realized he had turned the CD player on…sometime.

Humming along, he dialed the number he had to obtain from Information. When Lightner answered, Jared looked at the teddy bear clock on the wall and registered that it was four-twenty a.m.

"Good morning, darlin'," he purred. "I'd very much appreciate you making a house call. Griffin's motel, as soon as possible."

There were some fumbling noises with the phone, and Jared assumed Lightner was looking for the time, too.

"*Where* are you?" Lightner croaked. He cleared his throat. "You said the motel?"

"On the end," Jared said, bemused by the enormity of what he was doing. "Number ten."

He replaced the receiver and took the towel from his waist to use on his hair. As he dressed in new silk boxers, cream pleated pants, and a white tank tee shirt, he drank two more glasses of water in quick succession, desperate to re-hydrate. His hair and the tape around his ribs wet the snugly fitted tee shirt, but he concentrated instead on impassivity as he dialed the number for the motel residence. He was hearing the entire orchestra now, the brilliance of the violin blending and intertwining, guiding his speeding thoughts.

Griffin answered. He sounded remarkably awake, more so than Lightner.

"As Emilio would say," Jared murmured, "deny everything, and bring lawyers, guns, and money. I'm in number ten."

He dropped the receiver to its cradle and propped open the unit door. Then he picked up his comb. Standing in front of the mirror with every light in the room on, he dealt patiently with the mats and snarls in his clean hair. A few minutes later, he heard the office door bang shut in the distance.

Griffin, dressed only in jeans and a flapping shirt, skidded to a stop just outside. Jared watched out of the corner of his eye as the cop gave the patrol car a double take, and then scowled at the splintered doorframe of the unit.

Griffin ran into the room as Lightner's Saturn pulled up outside. "What's going on?" he gasped. His face was a gray mask of confusion and fright at what the official car out there could/might/did imply. "What are you doing here? Where's Randy? What's happened to Randy?"

"He's all right, Howard," Lightner said as he came in. "I spoke to the hospital—they found him in Mr. McCormick's bed. He has a stiff neck, but he'll be fine."

Griffin attached his gape to Lightner. "What are you doing here, Rick? What the hell is going on?"

"I was asked to come." Lightner had put on jeans, tennis shoes, and a polo shirt. His face registered only mild curiosity as he studied Griffin's. "Take three deep breaths, Howard," he advised.

Jared hadn't paused in the monumental task of getting through the tangles, but he kept Lightner under close surveillance in the mirror. When both men looked at him, Lightner didn't meet his gaze. Jared found some hope in his submissiveness. As long as the son of a bitch hadn't packed a tranquilizer gun, they could do this.

"Those are Leslie's children on the bed," Jared said to the mirror. "The girl has been drugged."

Lightner was already bent over at the bedside, but Griffin was slower, just turning to look.

Jared watched Lightner as he ran the comb down the full length of one handful of hair without a snag. "No questions yet, Chief," he warned as Griffin swung back with his mouth open. "I'm not finished with your doctor. At the risk of being called psychopathic and delusional, I would like to suggest to him that there is a possibility that the girl has also been sexually molested."

Griffin's jaw finished dropping. "What?" he shouted. "By who?"

Jared locked gazes with Lightner in the glass, but Lightner quickly looked down.

"Who - what—? All right!" Griffin snapped at Jared, taking a step. "McCormick, I've had about enough—"

Jared dropped the comb to the desk top with a warning clatter. He put his back to the mirror, feeling charges of fury strengthen and swell at this deliberate attempt to push him. "You're in serious trouble then," he observed frigidly, "because I'm merely beginning. I strongly suggest that you take yourself to that corner over there and rethink your position on the subject of what's enough!"

Griffin closed his mouth, startled.

"I would like to know," Jared prodded Lightner, who was just pulling the blanket back over the little girl.

"I don't see any physical signs of interference," Lightner reported gravely. "I would say not, but she needs to be examined—"

Griffin jumped between Lightner and Jared.

"You start talking," he snapped, "and you start talking now! What are you—"

"Definitions," Jared snapped back, moving a step sideways. He was glad to see Lightner resolutely staring at the carpet. "I'm saying, Griffin, but you're not understanding. Until you do, get out of my way. And do not shout at me again!"

Before Griffin could explode, Lightner sidled around the bed and put his hand on his arm. "Howard, calm down," he urged quietly. "Remember that Mr. McCormick is a professional, goal-oriented person. If there was something that you needed to know this instant, don't you think he would have said so immediately? Right now his concern is for the children. Mr. McCormick, do you know what kind of drug was used?"

"I haven't a clue," Jared said with a cold smile. "Are you saying that you can't tell just by looking at them? I'm so disappointed."

Lightner blushed. "You called me," he said to the floor. "I'm trying to understand."

Jared turned to Griffin. "In the trunk of my car is a stuffed toy that belongs to the girl," he gritted. "Will you please get it?"

Apparently chastened by confusion, Griffin nodded silently and left the cabin.

"Would you agree that you are becoming dangerous?" Lightner asked the carpet.

"I'm extremely dangerous," Jared said with silky smugness. "But I foresee no problems. Especially not with Griffin.

You're the one who keeps sticking out your foot, darlin'. If I trip over it, you're falling with me."

"May I take the children?"

"Of course. That's why I called you."

Lightner, although pale, looked at him much too directly then, and didn't back down. "Mr. McCormick, you called because you want to trust me."

"In your dreams, son," Jared denied loftily. "I simply don't know another doctor."

Griffin came back into the cabin with the one-eyed cat. He set it in the crook of the little girl's arm before carrying her out. Just as wordlessly, Lightner went past Jared with the baby, his bag in hand.

He and Griffin exchanged a few mumbled words outside, then Griffin came back into the unit. "I'm sorry I yelled at you," he said wearily, slumping into the desk chair. "Talk about stressed-out? Um, can we start over?" He lit two cigarettes from his shirt pocket and held one out—a peace offering.

Jared accepted it, willingly taking more management time. He wandered the small room smoking, finally ending up propped against the pillows that were still warm from the kids. He put one bare, bruised foot on the bed. He looked at Griffin, who had returned to the epitome of restraint and patience.

"Listen closely," Jared ordered, "because this is going to get a little complicated." Griffin nodded expectantly. "There's currently a three-act tragedy showing in Shady Rock," Jared expounded toward the ceiling. "With the program I'm going to give you, you're about to bring the curtain down. Act One is your burglaries; the theme is keys. Larry Doherty works in a hardware store where he can and did make keys that could get into places with no sign of forcible entry."

"Larry's the burglar?" Griffin blurted with a confused frown. "But how—"

The sunshine boy never had any problem getting people

to listen. If charm and dimples didn't work, stark terrorism did. Jared turned his head and gagged Griffin with the searing hate that currently sizzled through his every cell. For the first time since they had met, Jared made sure that Griffin saw reality, and it wasn't a delinquent, aggravating troublemaker who didn't keep in touch with his sister.

Griffin, staring back, grew very still.

"Larry is many things," Jared stated coldly, "but not, as you say, a burglar. In order, goddammit, or we're not going to get through this, Griffin. Larry made extra sets of keys at every opportunity, in the back room of the hardware store. For remuneration, he gave them to his brother Lyle, who is your burglar. Lyle has a partner named Kenny. The two of them have been fixing up Lyle's place with some of the stolen goods and, I'm guessing under Larry's guidance, shipping the rest out on some black market pipeline. What's not moving is stored at the second quarry. A cave or something; I didn't get a good look, but you won't have any trouble finding it."

Griffin kept his mouth closed, obviously trying to tie a few things together in his mind. Jared ran fingers slowly through his drying, tangle free hair.

The violins soared as he took a moment to process and render. "Next, Bud and his new will; Act Two. I don't know if you're aware of how much Bud's empire is worth, but it must be millions by now. He had a new will drawn up and wrote his three kids out of it. He left everything to Leslie's little girl."

"Your little girl," Griffin blurted again.

Jared nodded, momentarily impressed. "Very good, Chief; that's correct. My little girl. Is this a recent discovery for you?"

"No," Griffin shook his head. "As soon as I saw your name on your business card, I saw the resemblance. I kept waiting for you to tell me," he added in a slightly hurt tone. "She was the only thing I could think of that Bud could use to force you into coming back to Shady Rock. I didn't know why he wanted you to, or anything about his will, though. Are you saying that one of the Doherty boys had Jordan tonight because he isn't in the will anymore? If you knew her life was in danger, why didn't you tell me?"

Jared tilted his head to squint through the cigarette smoke. "'Get off those boys, McCormick,'" he scathingly mocked right back at him. "'You're dragging them in on your feud with Bud, McCormick.'" Griffin shriveled as much as a six-foot veteran cop could, upon hearing his own words. "You wouldn't have believed me, huh?" Jared snarled at him next. "But I worked for my facts, goddammit; I earned them, which is more than I can say for you!" Jared stubbed out the unfiltered cigarette and lit a Marlboro. "So shut up and listen for once," he growled. "Bud realized after Leslie was dead that he had set off one of the boys. He had it figured that because of his meanness, they had decided that either getting custody, or getting rid, of the little girl was the only way to his millions. Fact: he had figured right.

"Larry had a wife, so Larry decided he most resembled a family. He tried to talk Leslie into giving him her kids. He tried several times, and became nastier with each try. Leslie finally got pissed, so Larry got pissed and he killed her. Fact. He tried to make it look like your other man had done it, but he had no idea what was happening there, so he didn't do a sterling job of it." Jared stopped, furious. "Ask your question, Chief," he said impatiently. "It's distracting, watching you wiggle."

"Are you sure Larry killed Leslie?" Griffin asked in a terrible voice. "Absolutely sure? Have you talked to him?"

A muscle knotted in Jared's jaw; he felt it jerk. "Larry and I had two significant encounters. The first was when he tossed me into the quarry, took my car to the nursing home, and shot Bud with my weapon."

"I knew it!" Griffin grimly crowed, leaning to reach for the phone. "I knew you didn't do it—I'd better arrange some backup and go get him. Did he have the kids, too?"

"I found them at his house, yes. But you don't need backup. He's left town."

Griffin slowly replaced the receiver and sank back. "What do you mean he left town? You let him go? Why?"

Jared shrugged. "You forgot our second encounter. I didn't say I let him go, did I? He's not home. He's gone. He left town. How many ways can I say it? The thing is, Randy's .38 left town, too. Don't bother looking for either."

"Oh," Griffin breathed, turning grayer. "Shit."

Jared got off the bed and went to the desk where he opened a new box of Marlboros from his briefcase. He lit the fresh cigarette from the butt of the last. He leaned against the desk, studying the floor without seeing it.

"So far, we have Larry, Lyle, and Kenny as your burglars and assorted accomplices. You won't have any problem proving that, once you locate the cave. We also have Larry killing Leslie and his father over the will, kidnapping the kids, and incidentally responsible for my attempted murder. Since he's no longer available, I doubt very much that I will file a complaint. Are you with me so far?"

Griffin nodded, ashen.

"Good. This brings us to Act Three: the grand finale. Your serial thing started in February. Before that, Bud started boasting to everyone who had to listen that he was making the new will. In the time between the two events—Bud at his spiteful best in December and then through February when the will was actually signed—the boys realized that they had to get control of the little girl. Each went about achieving his goal in his own way. We've already discussed Larry's methods and their results. But Lyle figured that Larry might have a better shot getting Leslie's girl than him, because Larry did have the vestiges of a marriage. This is a crucial point, Chief—Lyle equating a wife with success.

"Lyle wants to look like a real man, but he has several strikes against him. He portrays some heavy-duty masochistic qualities, almost certainly as the result of being indoctrinated to sex by his father, brother, and sister, as a child. Indications are that he is sexually confused, besides."

"Sex – what, you mean Bud molested his kids?" Griffin barked in shock. "Are you sure?"

"Without a doubt," Jared said.

He saw Griffin's dismay turn to startled pity, clearly telegraphing his next question.

"Oh, my God, McCormick. Back when you were—did he…?"

Holding his side, Jared stretched carefully and saw that the sky outside the open door was showing the very first traces of light. A mere glow, not the streaks that would follow. "I mentioned once that it would take a fleet of shrinks an eternity to pick Bud and me apart," he murmured. "I spoke more intelligently than I knew. But I was nothing more than a catalyst of sorts. No, I am not going to share, so don't ask."

"But—" Griffin breathed, still stunned. "I can't believe— Bud? Are you absolutely sure he abused them? All of them?"

"Would it make it less icky if it had only been one?" Jared asked with an irritable glower. "In any case, you'll want to talk to a Mrs. May Schneider, the old grade school nurse. She knew about it." Jared had promised to keep Earl's name out of it, if it came to light. He owed the old coot that much for the comic books, offered in true if ignorant concern all those years ago. Jared said, "She's willing to give you details that will fill in the blanks as well as put a kink in your hair. But, we're not finished with Lyle. He knew if he wanted the means to keep his ranch, he had to try to be quote normal. Several times he tried." Jared smiled tightly. "He's one fucked-up, frantic human being, Chief, just like we agreed the other night in your office."

Griffin hunched forward abruptly, as if he'd been kicked in the gut. "Lyle's the serial killer? How can that—?" He was suddenly sweating. But he straightened his shoulders and took a breath, bracing himself. "Okay, tell me about it."

Jared cleared his raw throat and said, "The calcium we

found on the last body will probably turn out to be bone meal, used in gardening. I saw some bags of it in Lyle's truck. You won't have any problem linking Lyle to the serial killings; you've already got all the physical evidence required. Since Larry is gone, tie Lyle to Leslie's death, too, if you feel a need to clear it, too. Just get creative with the hair and semen evidence you already have."

"Lyle," Griffin gagged. He didn't seem to be scandalized by the offhand, illegal-as-hell-suggestion; his mind was apparently floundering elsewhere. "And Larry." He swallowed hard, rubbing his face. "It was them all along…and you tried to tell me. I'm – I'm sorry."

Jared folded his arms with a disdainful shrug. "Coming from Shady Rock, I expected nothing more than what I've always gotten."

Griffin stood, looking like he didn't know which way to go first. "I'd better get on this," he said. But he still paused. "What about you? Are you all right?"

"I'm good, thanks. A little tired," Jared admitted.

"Then can I talk you into going back to the hospital? Getting some rest and deluxe care? You've been through hell. McCormick—come on; I'll give you a ride."

"No, I'm going to crash right here," Jared lied with a smile. "For once."

Griffin nodded, then nodded again—years were dropping from his face by the second. He was gearing up to take charge. "You do that; you deserve it. Oh," he stopped himself, digging in his pockets. "Here, I've been keeping these for you." He fished out the fountain pen, gold lighter, and Swiss watch. "They're worth thousands, aren't they? I didn't want them to get lost at the hospital."

"Thanks," Jared said, but reluctantly. He wanted to tell him just to keep them, but didn't know how. "I appreciate it."

"And this," Griffin said with a trace of an actual smile, reaching behind and under his shirt. He withdrew a Glock 19. "It's not yours, of course. I'll have to keep that for a while, but consider this a loaner. I don't want you to be without while I get this mess all wrapped up."

Jared reluctantly and gingerly took the lesser automatic. "I'm touched, Chief. Really. Thanks."

"Sure, and here's your car keys. I'll get back to you when you wake up."

CHAPTER

27

JARED STOOD MOTIONLESS AGAINST the desk long after Griffin had left, eyeing the loaded weapon in his hand. The violins and orchestra had deserted him. The performance was over; the audience gone. There was nobody left to provoke and no more time. He had solved everyone's problems but his own—and he was in free-fall.

Wide open with hopelessness and barely cognizant. And deadly.

He set the automatic on the desk. After wiping his sweating palms on his pants, he began to pack.

One thing at a time.

He had to get away from town before he slid all the way off the deep end, but habit made him to cover his tracks. Fifteen minutes later, the tiny room was neat. The bed was made, the bathroom clean. He had even washed the ashtrays. He had also finished dressing the dead-eyed stranger in the mirror, and stowed his briefcase and suit bag in the trunk of the Cadillac.

The little girl would inherit the Flying D through Bud. She and the baby would share Jared's personal assets. And, they would eventually see what he and Leslie had once been—at least on the surface—together. Attorney Johnson held the key and instructions that would unlock the safety deposit box at the bank, in five years.

What more could he do for them?

Nothing.

Emilio would get the company…

Okay, he had failed to die with dignity; now he had to accept the consequences.

He put the Caddy in gear and guided it onto the deserted dawn street. As he drove into the spreading sunrise, he fumbled at the CD player. When the sweet, sad violin began to play, he cranked it loud and rode the strains of the Allegro in E through the still-sleeping town. He turned onto the first dirt road he came to and boosted the Caddy to eighty, the music swelling in his head and chest. His face was going numb, but he ignored it and drove with skill.

He flew past golden wheat fields and deep green bottom-lands, watching wheels of crows in the mid-foreground and a hawk high in the distance. The hawk floated down rays of the rising sun. He slid around corners every chance he got, not letting up enough on the gas, not keeping track of anything but the music and the road in front of him.

He reached the first quarry by the Adagio in G minor—not intentionally, but by simple gravitation. He impulsively crept the car close, beyond where he had parked the Porsche the other night. Except…this time he pointed it directly toward the wide green-black water. It would be bumpy, but he took solace in the fact that the higher suspension on the Caddy would have an easier time of it than the Porsche would have. As long as he didn't think about it.

From the passenger seat, he picked up the automatic Griffin had given him. He held it sideways on his palm, caressing its lines as if he'd never held one before. It was so comfortable, so right in his hand. They had had him in mind when they had designed it, and his relationship with it had been far more intimate than with any human being he had ever known.

He was ashamed of the tears he felt on his face—didn't know what to do with them. Only a few fell, and then he felt the claustrophobic trembling begin, first in his belly, then moving through him like an asphyxiating tide. He opened the door and got out, looking for air. He leaned against the car, hugging himself to make it stop. The early morning was cool, but he was sweating like a pig. He pulled his hair back.

The imaginative imp running endlessly in its mental wheel had seen this possible moment long ago—had fantasized means such as the Porsche as a last resort; max the beast out at 180 and beyond, and then give the light steering a thoughtless yank. He had paid over a hundred thousand dollars for that chickenshit but spectacular way out. Larry had taken it from him with fertilizer and a spark.

Jared got back into the Cadillac. He pulled the seat belt tight and reached for the ignition. A drowning death would be peaceful. It had been peaceful, come to think of it. It even pleased his sense of order, and humor, to think that his first and last forms of transportation would be down there in the oily-looking water together. He shook his head, trying to clear it of the annoying gray fog…

…and found himself sitting on a high, wide ledge directly over the rock-studded water. Down below, to his right, all four car doors were open. Vivaldi spilled gloriously into the sunny morning at full volume. No, of course not. Drowning would never work—not twice. He knew better; he had to hit the gravel roads pretending. Why was he up here then, tapping the gun barrel against his leg in time to the resonating symphony? Because he didn't want to die like his father had, cowed and chased. But he had run out of both options and time; he was a hazard. He didn't even remember shooting Larry.

Simply put, he had finally gone postal.

"Spring" began to play again, and he realized he must have hit the repeat button before doing a bit of rock-climbing. He put his head back and let the sun have its way with him. He barely felt the nose of the weapon snuggling into his jugular…then he felt tears drying on his face—again. This just wasn't going to work. His head was still tilted back, the sun warm, but the music had changed to the Largo in E. He lowered his chin, wincing at the stiffness in his neck—how long had he been fucking sitting here, for Christ's sake?

Abby was on a boulder about five feet from him, her hands resting quietly in her lap. She was so still as to be part of the rock; he had to squint to make sure she was real. He couldn't see her breathe, but the gold chain flashed in the noonday sun.

Noon?

"Shit," he said.

He wiped his tears with the back of the hand full of automatic. She didn't say anything. Her eyes were on him, but not taking anything. Her expression was one of serenity, perfectly matching the surroundings and present concerto.

"Go away," he growled in self-disgust. "I don't require mirrors for this."

"I wondered which would be worse," she said thoughtfully, "saying good-bye or not saying good-bye, and now I know. I'm staying to say good-bye."

"How did you find me?"

"Chief Griffin called me and said he had followed you here. He said—"

"He *followed* me?" Jared gagged in disbelief. Hadn't he given the asshole enough to do?

"He said," she went on bravely, "that Dr. Lightner told him you were going to kill yourself."

"That son of a bitch!" For a minute, Jared wasn't sure which one of them he meant. "They can't stop me!" He fought to make the words less than a snarl. "None of you can. I have surfed the Pandemonium channels quite long enough, thank you, and have opted to stop. That's all it is, and I have that right!"

"You haven't been doing anything nearly so fun as surfing," she frowned. "You've been working up to this, haven't you?

All along. And yes, you do have that right. Who am I to tell you to stop?"

"Nobody!" he snapped. He couldn't seem to let go of the wad of hair he gripped. "Get out of here! I don't love you. I never could, or would!"

After a moment she mimicked his disdainful snort, gently. "'Just because you don't see a thing doesn't mean it's not there,'" she quoted quietly. "'Because you don't recognize it doesn't make it any less real.' I've seen it, Jared Jordan. You love me, and it's damned real."

He dropped his head to his knees and squeezed his streaming eyes shut. Goddammit, that hurt—using his own words against him like that. "Please—just go away!"

"No!" she said with a spit of real anger. "I'm not trying to talk you out of anything, am I? When you're ready, just go ahead and do it. But until then, this is what I get of you. It's all I get, and I'm not leaving until it's gone!" She stopped on a choke, and then said more calmly. "I'm staying because I love you too, and you shouldn't be alone. No one should die alone."

He tilted his head back against the rock, searching for breath. Opened his eyes and stared down his nose at her for a long time, inspecting every line and curve of her. His hands and face were numb, and he had to swallow twice because of the continuing dryness in his mouth. "You have to leave," he said dully. "There's so much wrong with me, I can't guarantee I won't—"

"Jared, you caught him!" she interrupted, the surprise in her voice arresting and holding him for a moment. "You single handedly caught the animal who killed all those women. And you saved your daughter and her brother, too—you stopped *two* killers!"

"I'm coming apart!" he shouted, hating her misplaced idolatry.

But saying it aloud pushed a panic button. He found himself on his feet - desperately propped against the rock for support. She slowly stood up, too. His head wouldn't stop shaking negatively; this was all bad. Without meaning to, he would shoot her trying to flee the threat he couldn't get away from—and he would still fail to shoot himself. He had to get down to the damned car.

"Get away from me!" he yelled.

"But it's a new day, Jared," he dimly heard her shout back. "Isn't it? It's time to start over, and get through as best you can. It's time to adjust! Isn't that what you believe? Or was it all lies? Was every damned thing you said to us a lie?"

The loaner Glock skittered and rattled away down the ledge as he grabbed his head with both hands. Ripping sparks crackled through his mind and the bottom dropped away. He felt Abby plaster herself to him. He was on the ground. He couldn't move; was temporarily incapacitated by bald incoherence.

"I have a syringe, baby," he barely heard her say. "Doctor Lightner asked me to bring it to you."

Keeping his head tight against her with the hand caught in his hair, she let go with the other arm. She opened her fingers to let the syringe lay in her palm in plain sight. He was beyond verbal reaction; merely stared at it in helpless abhorrence. It was such a little thing on her hand—slender and opaque and inert. He stared at it for a long moment, overloading on what it symbolized—the very thing he had been fighting for so long, the total loss of identity.

A fate worse than death.

"I can't," he gagged.

"I can," she soothed. Her fingers closed around the syringe. Her thumb flicked off the plastic cover. "If you don't tell me no, I'm going to do it, Jared. It's your life; you decide."

He had already decided—more than a year ago.

She positioned the syringe like a dagger above his leg.

"No! Help me down to the car first, Abby," he gritted into the front of her shirt. He would just have to hope he would let her go. "Not here; I'll end up falling off this damned cliff."

A big, tanned hand moved into his narrowed field of vision. It enclosed Abby's fist and quickly forced it downward. Jared felt the nip of the needle in his thigh while violently twisting off Abby's lap. He crouched, staring up at Griffin who stood like a wall between him and the cliff edge.

"Bite that silver tongue, McCormick," Griffin grunted, watchful. "You aren't going to fall off of anything. We won't let you."

Jared fought the drug, but it ate into him fast and hard—not giving his sense of vengeance a chance. He sprawled into a space that was neither up nor down. A silent, smooth spin made breathing elementary again. He found only a tenuous, sliding grip on perception, however—was barely aware of Abby whispering over him, around him, smoothing his face and hair with her hands. The smell of roses, her touch, and the violin that had been speaking to him for months, all removed him to a vacant place built by the dope. He felt his arm being lifted and fought to open his eyes.

Griffin knelt beside him. While taking Jared's pulse, he smiled his fatherly smile. "Okay?" he asked quietly. "I've had the ambulance waiting. Just be a few minutes."

A few minutes to fucking what? Jared wanted to scream... but he couldn't even talk. He couldn't do anything—he wasn't dead, but this was hell.

Still loosely holding his hand, Griffin lowered himself to the ground and carefully laid a rifle nearby. Jared eyed it, hating. Abby had never been in any danger.

"...fuckin' tricked me," he finally managed through a glowing haze.

Griffin sadly shook his head. "According to the other genius I know, you've been tricking yourself, McCormick—I just followed along, reaping the benefits. I didn't believe Rick, but he insisted that one of us follow you, if you left the motel. So...here we are. Um, you won't be surprised to hear that Lyle was taken to County a couple of hours ago, charged with five counts of murder. Kenny's in my jail for burglary, and

Arlene Doherty too, on charges of kidnapping. Too bad Larry skipped out on her, huh?"

EPILOGUE

THE BARN'S SMALL DOOR objected with a rusty screech as he pushed it open. Before he went through it, he glanced back at Griffin's dusty black Tempo with some contempt. What good was a suicide watch without the watch? Jared had agreed to it in exchange for his release from the hospital. It was a trade entirely to his benefit, especially now that he saw how easy it was going to be. Lightner wasn't even here yet. He stepped from hot sunshine into deep shadow.

Standing still for a moment to let his eyes adjust, the must of dried hay filled his nose. The smell slapped him with memories that he absolutely didn't want to recall, and wasn't about to attempt to deal with. He had worked, dreamed, and lost his virginity in this barn, but those normal character-building activities had been contaminated from the start—and had eventually turned into demons.

His belly was quiet now, though, the demons chemically caged.

When he could make out the enormity of the space he was in, Jared strolled forward, his jaw set. He did his best to at least pretend to be detached. Lightner had set up this meeting, and he hadn't argued. He was beyond arguing. After being hauled off the rocks like a roll of carpeting, he had spent the last four days flat on his back in the hospital, surrounded by pitying, vigilant faces…

Abby had held his hand for the first eleven unconscious hours. Several nurses had commented on her loving perseverance to him.

Ignorant, traitorous woman.

Rookie Randy had stopped in when he had been allowed to wake up, on the second day. The little puke didn't mention the bruise under his collar; he quivered with puppyish excitement over Lyle's unspectacular arrest and Larry's mysterious departure.

Jared had covetously eyed the new .38 in his holster.

Abby's landlady had sent a pie, and Slade stopped in to return the cellular phone. The biker also tried to return the five one hundred-dollar bills, suggesting gruffly and obscenely that he hadn't done a very good job of keeping track of Larry. Slade was the only one of the bunch who understood the part about fuck off.

His sister Maggie had gloried in running through the full range of her selfish emotions all over him, and Griffin stood around looking capable, protective, and fully revived. The son of a bitch had helped hold him down when Jared had refused to let Agent Torey see him. He had been knocked out again, in the middle of that noisy little discussion. Ever since, he had behaved—he was caught, but he wasn't stupid.

Old Earl Williams had brought a dusty box of Marvel Comics last night, reducing him to a sniveling idiot. Nobody had asked for explanations, which was good because he sure as hell wasn't sharing.

Handsome young Emilio had blown through the hospital room like an ethnic tornado at noon yesterday. From the foot of the bed, he had spit a total of six highly offended words that nobody, including Jared, understood, and then he had proceeded to take charming charge of both the hospital and the town. Jared hadn't seen him since and was glad somebody understood his hatred of being stared at…

The idea was that tomorrow he would be flown to Maryland. Emilio and a representative from the private hospital were on hand to make damned sure he got on the plane, didn't highjack it, and was safely kenneled at the other end. Lightner had consulted, and had already begun a maintenance dose to keep him muzzled until then.

However, the cute little bastard was clueless as to what kind of a favor he had done Jared, by giving him that muzzle. Jared almost wished he could discuss the discovery with him—one intellect to another, comparing notes. But of course, he hadn't.

He went to the sturdy open ladder on the left wall and started to climb. There were fifteen rungs, but he found himself counting them again out of old habit as he went up. When his head went through the hole in the floor, he stopped and looked over his shoulder.

The large double doors at one end of the loft were open, the first of the years' bales tossed in, ready for stacking. One of his hardest early jobs. In the opposite direction were the last of the bales from the year before. They were in scattered building-block disarray. The tallest stood at the far end, then the stacks stepped down in front of the hole in the floor, where the bales were dropped down as needed. There were narrow aisles wandering the uneven walls of bales, and through one he thought saw something white.

He unwillingly climbed the last few rungs and rigidly walked toward it, his shoes crunching on the mat of straw and dried stems. When he was about halfway across the floor he heard crying. Cursing, he broke into a run. He had been thinking about reels of baling twine and/or pitchforks all morning; a working barn was not a good place for either suicides or children. When he got close, though, he realized that the weeping wasn't urgent. The little sobs were merely devastated.

He stopped dead, a thousand tons of alien guilt landing squarely on his chemically challenged nasty disposition. He didn't need this, goddammit. He hadn't caused this sadness.

He made himself duck through the tunnel-like opening,

and found himself sharing a small, cozy space with the little girl. Sunshine flared vertically through the cracks of the closed doors, back-lighting her. She was crouched on her feet with her forehead pressed to her knees. Wisps of hay sprouted in her loose golden hair, on her white tee shirt, and her jeans.

She huddled tightly, lost in grief.

Jared glanced at his watch. Thirty minutes. Everybody had agreed on thirty minutes, and he hadn't argued. Plenty of time.

He took a few steps closer, then noticed the cat. It was a dirty white and orange calico, laying on the hay in front of the little girl. It panted; its devil eyes were half orbs of black barely rimmed with yellow. As he watched, it moaned and sat up, licking itself avidly. In some blossoming comprehension, he took the last few steps and gingerly lowered himself to the dusty floor beside the little girl. He leaned on a bale to accommodate his torturously taped ribs. To save the crease in his pants, he extended his legs and crossed them at the ankle. The little girl paused in her weeping but didn't raise her face from her knees.

"What's the problem?" he asked, slapping hopelessly at the dust.

He made his tone neutral in case he was wrong and would have to defend himself against hysterical accusations. He didn't know what she knew.

He got a prompt if muffled answer to his obviously dumb question. "Kitty's dying!"

Her innocent mistake did something to galvanize his tarnished self-possession. "No, she's not," he said curtly. "She's not even sick."

"Is too!"

"That might be what it looks like, but I assure you she has other plans."

The cat squalled and the little girl broke down all over again, muffling her sobs with her hands.

"Stop that," he said uncomfortably. "You're wasting tears

without even knowing what you're crying about. The cat isn't sick; she's pregnant. She's in labor." He frowned at the miserable little shape. How many ways could he say it? "Look, do you know about babies? She's having them."

He saw her peek through her dirty fingers at the animal. "Babies?"

"Yes. Baby cats. Kittens."

"How d-do—you know?" the little girl choked.

"Because I've seen it before, and that's what's she's doing. She isn't dying."

There was a flurry of activity in the straw.

Jared watched the streaked little face go from woebegone to frankly amazed. Wet round eyes grew rounder. Smudged sulk turned to wonder. Wonder turned to a fearful, hesitant delight.

"Oh! Oh, look!" the little girl exclaimed, pointing. "It's a *kitten!*"

"Excellent observation," he murmured wryly.

Something in the handful of pills and capsules handed to him twice a day had made smiling moot. Right now, he even hated the absence of nausea that Lightner had given him. He was pharmaceutically flattened. But, along with his smile and his senses, the dope had also killed the eyes in the back of his head—Lightner's unforeseeable and accidental favor. His defense system was gone, and the mad dog was free to bite itself and die.

None of the last hideous, debilitating five years had anything to do with the scars on his back, just as he'd thought. The combination of his ineffective mother, his loser absent father, and Bud, had turned him into a casualty long before he had known what the word meant. It had just taken a lifetime for the effects to come to light. Things he couldn't possibly have known or understood—much less remembered—were killing him.

Lightner, too, had come up with it, all on his own. Jared found Lightner's confirmation welcome...in a purely academic way, of course. And the spooky little witchdoctor had had the balls to admit his mistake in diagnosis. He had stopped asking Jared about his scarred back.

Late last night, Jared had opened his eyes in the dimly lit hospital room to find Lightner lounging in the chair beside the bed. His crisp white coat was unbuttoned, his ankle on his other knee, his eyes mildly inquisitorial.

After more than an hour of being locked into serene versus resolute silence, Lightner had finally given in. He ran a finger over the last of the IV tubes, then had matter-of-factly retied the drawstring at Jared's waist with a playfully quirky bow.

"You were right, Mr. McCormick," he had said with an air of shy acceptance. "It wasn't your professional past after all, was it? Somehow, you tracked it back to Shady Rock, and once again came to our rescue. Amazing. Anyway, sleep well—I'll see you in the morning."

Confirmation was nice, but so what? He was caught and exposed. This was still a bad thing.

He had drifted. There were three damp kittens struggling in the straw now, and the little girl was looking at him with open curiosity.

She sniffled loudly at his tardy notice. He automatically handed her the handkerchief from his breast pocket. After making inefficient use of it, she reached to stuff it back into the pocket. Then she stood, the cat completely forgotten. Brazenly dropping onto his lap, she faced him with a foot planted on the floor on either side of him. She gravely studied him with replicas of his own dark eyes—exact right down to the lurking bewildered hurt that he had seen in the mirrors he tended to avoid now. Ruins, he thought bitterly, staring back at her. That's all they both were, helpless, hopeless, wreckage.

Fifteen more minutes.

She cautiously touched his trailing hair with a small grimy hand. When he didn't tell her not to, she pulled one long handful forward, smoothing it all the way down his jacket lapel. Then she left dust on his tie and hay wisps in his shirt pocket, where she had discovered his fountain pen. He kept his eyes on her face while she fiddled with the pen. She frowned. Not at him, at the ink that had dribbled onto her fingers.

She quickly wiped large black smears onto her shirt, then put the leaking pen back. "Sorry," she muttered with an expectant little flinch. "I made a mess."

"It doesn't matter."

She looked at him again, the mess as easily forgotten as the cat. "I know who you are," she taunted sternly. "You're my daddy. Dr. Lightner said so." She picked at the small diamond on his tie tack with bitten, inky, fingernails. Without waiting for him to agree or disagree, she abruptly bragged with a dimpled grin, "I found a frog!" Then she made a tear-smudged face. "So I put him in the bathtub, but he jumped out and got all hard and dried-up."

"I had a frog once, too," he remembered neutrally. "I let him go."

"Then you didn't have one," she pointed out like he was dumb.

"Yes, I did," he heard himself argue. "Before I let him go, I put a dab of barn paint on his back. Then I could catch him again any time I wanted, because I knew it was him. He lived under that rock beside the pump handle in the stock tank."

"That big pink one?" she asked with a frown, evidently dubious of both the rock and the story. "Okay, let's go find him," she ordered, bouncing to her feet. She straddled his lap and tugged at his jacket shoulder. "Show me!"

"He's not there now," he said, looking up at her. What the hell was he doing? "That was a long time ago—when I was just a kid."

"But he might be!" she insisted brightly. "Or we could catch another one. Yeah, you could show me how to paint it!"

"No," he said, thinking dispassionately – and freely—about the large beams overhead, twine, and time.

The little girl sank back onto his lap, disappointed with his lack of enthusiasm. She peeked under his lapel, grimaced at the inky blotch on his white shirt, then looked him in the eye. She demanded, "What do you mean no? Don't you wanna have fun? What kind of a daddy are you, anyway?"

His side throbbed, and he felt a little uneasy under her unwavering gaze. "I don't know what kind of a daddy I am," he heard himself growl back. "I've never been one before. Christ, I wouldn't know how to begin."

The little girl traded him scowl for scowl. "Well, do you want to go ask somebody?" she asked with patient impatience. "*Then* we could catch a frog!"

A strand of copper-blonde hair fell over her cheek, and he saw his hand go up to smooth it back. He was doped to the toenails—not numb, but…empty. He wasn't a risk to anybody but himself now, and that was by choice, not essentiality. He could send her out on a frog hunt with a promise of being right behind; he could die now—finally. Not with respect, maybe, but certainly with relief.

"Do you?" she prodded.

"Do I what?" he asked.

"Do you want to go ask Dr. Lightner how to be a daddy?" she said. "He's outside; I saw him drive up." She bounced off his lap again, and dashed away. "Come on," she giggled, peeking from around a bale. "Catch me!"

He grabbed her at the ladder, his heart in his mouth at her dangerous, headlong haste. She let him carry her down, but wriggled off his arm as soon as his feet reached the concrete floor. Then she grabbed him in turn—leaving inky smears on his cuff and hand. As he was determinedly tugged through the door, he grew more and more lightheaded with the enormity of what he was—or more accurately, wasn't—doing. How many more chances would he get?

Lightner loitered in the sunny barnyard, casual in jeans

and sneakers. He gave the little girl a quick smile, but Jared got arched eyebrows over the sight of the dust that had settled on his jacket and pants, the hay wisps stuck to his hair, and the ink stain that had spread over to ruin his tie.

"We're going to paint a frog!" the little girl crowed up at Lightner, her dimples blinding.

Lightner looked blankly back down at her. "Are you?" he asked.

"Yes, then we can let it go so it won't get all dried out, and then catch the same one again tomorrow! He said he did it when he was a little boy!"

"Oh, I see," Lightner said with a more assured smile. "What a great idea! He must have been a smart boy to have thought of that; don't you think?"

"He *is* smart," she bragged, swinging Jared's hand. "He knows all about kittens, too! But he doesn't know how to be a daddy. Can you tell him?"

"I'll bet he can figure that out all by himself," Lightner said warmly.

Jared stared back at him while he held the child against his side to stop her fidgets. Griffin was still in his car, but he was armed—this eternal farce could end quickly enough. All he had to do was run. He shook his head.

"Mr. McCormick," Lightner said practically, "you've eliminated the last of her elders; what she has left is a drooling baby brother, and you. If you die, she won't have you."

"If you put me away," Jared said, "she won't have me."

"But not for long. They can help you."

"If you send me to Maryland, I'll do what I've always done."

It was an embarrassingly incoherent statement, but he didn't know how else to say it. He hadn't meant to say it at all—the dope was making him chatty.

Lightner studied him, and Jared sweated every second of scrutiny.

"You mean you'll expend all your energy reacting to

enforced confinement," Lightner interpreted. "Instead of working on the real problem."

"I don't have a problem that I can't solve."

"We're still not agreeing on that, are we?" Lightner nodded. "Look, you told me once that you live for success, Mr. McCormick. But you believe you've failed at something, don't you? And because you can't accept failure, you are disabling yourself. Like a chain reaction, the disabilities are forcing you into thinking you must give up. But as one who never gives up, you can't quite accept that, either. You're the most purposeful man I've ever met—if you wanted to be dead, you'd surely be dead by now."

"Give me ten minutes alone in the barn," Jared murmured, his lungs frozen. "No, make it five."

"But I'm seeing a man who's asking himself for time to decompress, and reconstruct," Lightner explained earnestly.

Jared wished he could wipe the sweat from his face without drawing attention to it. "I can't be anything different," he said.

"Let's say you have a natural reluctance to abandon a heretofore winning strategy," Lightner countered. "But couldn't you be different, and maybe even more? Listen, being uncooperative will only negate whatever help you'll be offered in Maryland. And by the time you've dealt with those perceived threats in your indomitable way, you'll either have succeeded in committing suicide by proxy, or you'll still be pathologically depressed because nothing has changed. Is that what you really want?"

"I don't need help," Jared gritted.

"No, we *all* need help," Lightner corrected matter-of-factly, leaving Jared feeling scolded. "We just have different issues, different interpretations of the word help, and different ways of asking for it. Can we agree on that, at least? Look, you seem to be at a level in your neurosis that doesn't allow for anything but rationalization. You don't know what you need, therefore you're operating on the presumption of intelligence without the control of thought."

Jared, hyper-aware of Lightner's every word, looked down at his fingers, which were obsessive in the little girl's silky hair. He was torn between a sick fascination and a smothering dread.

"Mr. McCormick," he heard over the pound of his heart, "I take my responsibilities seriously. I wouldn't be much of a doctor, if I didn't. You," Lightner softly chuckled, "on the other hand—well, you have turned responsibility into an art form. How many times have you risked everything this week alone, helping out total strangers? Why can't you apply that helpful single-mindedness to yourself?"

"You have no idea," Jared said numbly, "what I've done for myself."

"But you could tell someone qualified to hear it, couldn't you? They could take that input, work on understanding the hang-up, and help you attack it from the other side."

Jared looked up, bristling.

Lightner guessed what was behind his expression. "You wouldn't be confined for long, Mr. McCormick," he repeated quickly. "I realized what it does to you from the moment we met—you paced my ER like a lion in a cage. I understand, really. You aren't locked up now, are you? What's stopping you from using the child as a hostage to get away from this rather strained situation? Why didn't you bushwhack Howard on the way out here? You *aren't* locked up because I understand that your instincts tell you to react when provoked. You are probably feeling extremely provoked right now, but Howard and Jordan don't provoke you—on the contrary, you found them both worthy of your expert efforts. That's why I could allow this time-out. I can't trust you with yourself, but I most sincerely trust your unwillingness to harm the innocent. I'll definitely pass that along to Maryland. So, couldn't you trust someone there enough to help you redescribe your perceived failure?"

Jared heard himself blurt, "I've fucking *failed* to stop what's happening to me—is that what you wanted to hear?"

Lightner was silent for a minute, then he said sadly, "Considering your formative years, it's probably what you've always wanted to say."

"Don't make me go," Jared said harshly, ready to break and run. "It won't help."

"How can I avoid it?" Lightner asked curiously. "What can we do for you? Be specific."

"Jesus, you can specifically drop dead!" Lightner kept looking at him without leniency, and Jared had to swallow. "All right, put me on house arrest," he seethed off the top of his head. "Out here on the D. You or Griffin can move in to keep an eye on me, if you have to."

"And then what?" Lightner persisted.

"I don't know!" Jared shouted on a new burst of panicked frustration. "If I fucking *knew*, I wouldn't need you, would I?"

Appalled by the full retreat he found himself in, he watched for any hint of triumph in Lightner's eyes. He didn't see it. He didn't see pity, either – did he? He looked very closely and saw a clean, impartial concern. And a guileless, candid respect. He saw…compassion.

Fighting a groan of utter bewilderment, he wondered if he really was seeing a guide capable of leading him out of this hideous morass of insanity.

Did he, or was this pathetic hope just *more* insanity?

Lightner lowered his eyes, not giving him anything to judge by. He hesitated, glancing over his own shoulder.

Somehow, Abby was there, sitting in the porch swing holding Leslie's baby. But she was nothing more than a blur in Jared's blinding ache for simple answers.

"It makes more sense to talk Abby into being your watch dog," Lightner laughed gently a heartbeat later. "Doesn't it? She's prettier than I am and not nearly as annoying as Howard. And she won't put up with any nonsense." He reached to touch the little girl's cheek. Then he walked away, cheerfully warning, "I'm *definitely* going to need your help in sorting you out, Mr. McCormick. So, be ready to work hard. My office twice a day for your meds, starting tonight—I'll provide the tea, you bring the topics. Oh, and happy frogging!"

Dumbfounded by the unexpected acquittal, Jared managed to hold himself up by placing both hands on the little girl's sturdy shoulders. He mutely watched Lightner drive away. Griffin beeped his horn, as his Tempo followed Lightner's car out of the yard.

The little girl happily waved goodbye to them while Jared fought to regroup.

One thing at a time, he ordered himself rigidly, over and over. Maintain.

A frog, then a cup of tea and the muzzling drugs…

He'd give it a week and see what happened.

He probably could do that.

ISBN 141206550-X

9 781412 065504